R J ADAMS

THE TIME PROJECT

WHEN YOU TRAVEL THROUGH TIME,
YOU CAN CHANGE YOUR OWN HISTORY...

K S ADAMS

THE TIME PROJECT

WHEN YOU TRAVEL THROUGH TIME,
YOU CAN CHANGE YOUR OWN HISTORY...

MEREO
Cirencester

Published by Mereo

Mereo is an imprint of Memoirs Publishing

25 Market Place, Cirencester, Gloucestershire, GL7 2NX
info@memoirsbooks.co.uk www.memoirspublishing.com

The Time Project

ISBN: 978-1-86151-033-4

Dedicated to my grandparents, Barbara and Gordon, for nurturing my imagination as a child.

A special thank you to Amanda for all her support.

CHAPTER 1

"This has to be the coldest place in all of Denmark" the man said, holding up his scarf closer to his face and pulling his beanie hat down.

"Come on" the other man said. "It's not that bad."

"Goddamn it!" the first man said, picking up his trowel and started working on trench two.

"I haven't seen the boss man today at all yet. Bet he's nice and warm back at the hotel."

"Actually mate, he's over in trench four, the other side of the dig site. Apparently they've found something over there."

This was the third week on the archaeology dig, and the first time they had found anything of significance. Everybody was cold and getting very fed up with it all. But Dr Thomas Long had worked for years to get here, and he wasn't going to be put off by a few people with no ambition.

"Dr Long, it's amazing!" said Gracie Stevenson, his young assistant, looking at him with a big smile on her face.

"Do we know if it's male or female yet?" replied Long, crouching down beside her.

"It's male, I would say. Look at the pelvis and the brow bone. Definitely male." she brushed the dirt and snow off the skull.

"By the findings around the body, I'd date it to around the late 790s" he said, holding up one of the items. It appeared to be a small knife, but until it could be cleaned up, it was hard to tell.

"Are there any more, do we know yet?" he said, standing back up straight again and surveying his dig site.

"No. Not yet anyway. Dr Long - this is unique."

"I know" he said. "People in this time tended to burn their dead."

"Exactly."

He took out his notebook from his rucksack and started writing frantically. Gracie stooped back over the skeleton and carried on brushing the fragile bones with her brush. After about five minutes, Dr Long stopped his scribbling and put his tattered notebook away.

"OK." he said. "We need to get the bones out and shipped to the lab in England."

She looked up. "And what about the Danish authorities? I'm sure they'll have something to say about that."

"Leave them to me" he replied with a smile. He walked away to go back to the tent that was set up as a HQ and somewhere to put the finds. He kept his laptop in there. He pulled aside the tent opening, just a simple bit of fabric, and walked in.

It was surprisingly warm in there. A small portable

heater was sitting in the corner giving off some much-needed heat. He opened up his computer and started typing. within minutes his contact in the Danish government had emailed him back with all the necessary documentation he would need to transport any items he found to his lab in England, including the long-dead skeleton.

Long stood up smiling, very pleased with himself. Having a father who was an ex-MI5 agent came in very handy sometimes. As he was about to walk out, Gracie walked in and almost bumped into him.

"I'm so sorry, doctor" she said with embarrassment. He gave her a slap to the arm as if she was an old friend. "Don't worry about it Gracie. More importantly, I've sorted the little problem out with the Danes." there was a big smile across his face. She looked at him, confused. "What do mean?" she asked, taking a seat near one of the fold-up desks.

"Well, we can ship the finds out whenever we wish, including our dead friend."

"That's fantastic. How did you manage to persuade them to let us take it back to England?"

"Don't ask!" he replied, still smiling. He took a plastic cup from one of the boxes and a flask of hot coffee and started to pour.

"Would you like a cup?" he asked her, holding the flask up. "It's good. Made it myself."

"OK, thanks. That would be great." she handed him a cup from the desk just behind her. As they started to drink, the cellphone near to him started to ring and vibrate. It startled him and he dropped the hot liquid down his front.

"Shit!" he said, attempting to wipe it off himself. He picked up the phone, pressed the red 'decline call' button and slammed the phone down again on to the desk. Almost straight away it started to ring again.

"I'm thinking maybe you should answer that, it must be important" Gracie said, putting her cup down and getting back to her feet.

"I really am too busy to take calls at the moment, Grace" he said, still dabbing his jacket with a cloth.

"Like I said, it must be important" she said, opening the tent flap and walking out.

"Please, call me Thomas!" he shouted after her over the loud ringing of that damn phone.

He took the jacket off and put it over the chair where Gracie had been sitting. Turning round, he sighed and walked over to pick up the ringing cellphone.

"Hello?" he said abruptly.

"Hello? Thomas, are you there, can you hear me?" the voice on the other end said, almost too loudly.

"Jon, why are you shouting?" replied Thomas, recognizing his friend's American accent.

"Oh, sorry Tom. Thought the signal wasn't very good. I got cut off the first time I called."

Thomas sat down and poured himself another coffee.

"Jon, for one thing, the signal is fine. This is 2026, we can get signals anywhere these days. And another thing, I cut you off."

"Really?" Jon said, more shocked than annoyed.

"Yes, I'm very busy here Jon. It's turning out to be a great dig. I've found a complete skeleton from the late eighth century." he stopped talking sharply as Jon began to interrupt him.

"Tom, listen to me. I've had a breakthrough with my project and I need you to come here straight away."

"Are you joking Jon? I can't just leave here now, I'm about to start shipping my finds and the skeleton back home, I'm far too busy for this." Thomas was almost getting angry.

"Tom, please, I wouldn't be calling you now if it wasn't important."

Now Thomas was starting to get angry.

"Jon, if this is about that stupid idea you had when we were at uni..."

"I've done it Tom. It's worked" Jon interrupted again. The look on Thomas' face was one of pure shock. He replied "Jon, I hope you're not messing with me?"

"No Tom, I'm not messing." he paused. "So, will you join me in Washington?"

"Well, Jon" he said trying to regain his composure. "This is all very interesting, but what do you need me for?"

Jon gave a little chuckle on the other end of the phone. "As an adviser, of course. Thomas, listen, I'll pay for everything, your flight here, even to ship your finds back to England. And you can carry on with your work after you're done here." there was a pause which seemed to last for ages. "Well Tom, seem fair to you?"

"OK Jon. I'll do it. When do you want me there?" Another little chuckle came down the phone.

"I've already booked the flight for you. And there will be a chopper to come pick you up from your dig site and take you to the airport. It'll be there in about thirty minutes."

Thomas was shocked. He rubbed his head. "That soon? OK, but it had better be worth it Jon."

"It will my friend, it will. You have my word." Thomas cancelled the call and rushed out of the tent.

"Gracie, Gracie!" he shouted. He saw her sitting down in the trench which had been hiding the skeleton for so long. "Gracie!" he shouted again. He started to run over to her but slipped in the snow.

"Shit" he said aloud. Scrambling back to his feet, he began to run again. As he reached her, she got to her feet.

"Dr Long, what is it, are you OK?"

"Thomas, call me Thomas." he replied slightly out of breath. After a moment he regained his composure and his breath.

"Gracie, I have to leave, something important has come up. And I'm going to need you to come with me" he said. The look of shock on her face said it all.

"Doctor…" she began.

"Thomas!" he interrupted.

"Sorry - Thomas. What on earth are you talking about? We can't just leave now, there are things we still need to do and the shipping to organize."

"I know, but we really need to do this. There's a

helicopter on its way now, so I'm going to leave Billy in charge to sort all that out."

"But Thomas..." she began again.

"No buts, Gracie. Believe me, you're going to want to see this." He gave her a faint smile.

Twenty minutes later they were almost packed. Thomas, making sure he had his precious notebook, turned to Billy, one of the site supervisors.

"So Bill, are you sure you can sort all that out for us?"

"Of course Thomas, but I don't see what the rush is all about" he replied, handing Thomas his laptop to put in his bag.

"Believe me mate, it is the opportunity of a lifetime" Thomas said, pushing his computer into his huge rucksack.

"OK buddy, consider it done. The finds and the skeleton will be at the lab by the time you get home."

"Cheers Bill" Thomas said, patting Billy on the back.

"I'm ready" Gracie said. Thomas turned round to her. She looked so small, standing there with a gigantic rucksack on her back. Thomas gave her a smile.

"So you are. Me too." she smiled back at him. "Gracie, this will be something remarkable. We'll go down in history for what we're going to do."

"Well, you still haven't even told me that, or even where we're going."

"Well, at first we're going to Washington DC. But after, well - who knows?" he replied, still smiling from ear to ear. They stopped as the sound of the helicopter came roaring over the snow-filled valley. They walked out of the tent to see the helicopter getting closer, the black metal standing out against the white. As it got closer they could make out that it was a military helicopter.

"You didn't say the army was coming for us" she said, turning to Thomas. There was no reply. The helicopter began to hover near them and finally descended. Snow and dirt were blown everywhere as the rotors spun round with a roaring sound. The pair shielded their eyes from the debris as slowly the sound and the wind dropped. The rotor blades finally stopped. Thomas took his hand away from his face and started to walk over to the helicopter. The side door slid open and a man stepped out. He was huge, and dressed in military uniform with a pistol strapped to his leg. He walked over to greet Thomas with a firm handshake.

"Dr Long, I presume?" he asked.

"Thomas Long, how do you do" came his reply.

"My name is Lieutenant Karl Mackenzie. I've been sent by Dr Jonathan Walker. I'm to escort you to the airport."

"Yes, I know" replied Thomas, rubbing his hand from the handshake. "I wasn't aware that the army was involved in Dr Walker's project."

The tall man looked down at him. "Well, I'm sure Dr Walker will explain everything to you himself" he said. As they got to the helicopter Lt Mackenzie looked back at Gracie. Billy had already scuttled away at the sight of the big man with the gun.

"And who is this?" he asked, looking at Gracie.

"Oh, I'm sorry. This is Gracie Stevenson, my assistant" Thomas replied. The Lieutenant looked her up and down.

"And what's she here for?"

"I've been asked to accompany Dr Long to Washington" Gracie interrupted, holding her head up defiantly. She could tell that he didn't like women, or didn't respect them, and she wasn't about to let him bully her, or for that matter Thomas.

The lieutenant looked down at Thomas. "On whose authority?"

Thomas looked straight back up at him. He was thinking that if Gracie could stand up to this man, so could he.

"I'm Miss Stevenson's boss, so it's under my authority. I need her with me. And that's final." Thomas was feeling a little out of his depth. The lieutenant curled his lip.

"Very well. Get in." He turned around and got into the helicopter. Thomas and Gracie looked at each other with a sense of pride mixed with relief and followed the man through the metal door and into the helicopter. The lieutenant slammed the door behind them and handed them a pair of ear protectors each. They put them on and fastened their seat belts. The engines started up with a roar and the rotor blades started spinning. They could see through the small window that the snow was blowing all over the dig site again. They could see their colleagues looking up at the helicopter as it began to get higher and higher until the site was a small dot in the middle of the snowy valley.

All the way to the airport the lieutenant said nothing. He just stared out of his window. Thomas and Gracie talked quietly together. Thomas knew why his old friend was calling them to Washington, but he did not tell Gracie; he wanted it to be a surprise, one that she wouldn't believe even if he did tell her.

Gracie looked out of the window and could see the airport getting closer. there was less snow here than in the valleys, and she could see the runways clearly. The helicopter landed on a helipad the other side of the airport and the engines slowly began to stop as the helicopter started to power down. Lt Mackenzie opened the door and got out, followed by Thomas and then Gracie.

"Well, here is your ticket Dr Long" he said. "If you make your way to the terminals I'll sort out another for Miss Stevenson. It'll be waiting at the desk for you when you get there." He handed the ticket to Thomas and then shook his hand again. The same bone-crushing hand shake as before.

"Thank you" replied Thomas, the pain visible in his face. "I appreciate it."

"You're welcome" Mackenzie said, turning to walk away. He was met by another soldier, and they both disappeared through a door. Thomas looked down at the ticket in his hand.

"Wow!" he said. "First class. And the flight leaves in

forty minutes. Grace, we have to hurry." he picked up his rucksack and threw it over his shoulder. Gracie did the same and they both ran across the car park and into the terminal building. They stopped and looked around. People were dashing in every direction. Then Thomas noticed a man walking very calmly towards them. He was wearing a dark suit and had a wire running up to his ear. More military, thought Thomas.

"Dr Long, nice to meet you. I am Agent Summers. I'm assigned to Dr Walker's project, and I'll be accompanying you on your flight to the States." He shook Thomas' hand. Thomas was relieved that it was a normal handshake.

"Hi, this is Miss Stevenson, my assistant."

"Ah" the agent replied, looking at her. "So this ticket must be yours then?" she took the ticket from him and shook his hand. "Thank you" she said with a smile.

"We should board now, please follow me" the agent said, leading them to the departures area. They walked through the doors and started walking straight past the security checkpoint. Thomas looked round at Gracie, who was following behind with a questioning look on her face.

"Don't worry doctor" the agent said, briefly glancing at him, "I've already cleared it with security." He smiled.

Soon enough they were taking their seats in the spacious first class area. Gracie looked over at Thomas, who was sitting on the other side of the wide aisle. He looked back at her, and she gave him a smile. After putting his bag in the overhead compartments Thomas sat down and fastened his seat belt tightly. He wasn't a very good flyer.

"Are you OK?" the agent said to him.

"Yeah, I'm fine" Thomas replied, getting himself comfortable. The agent took his seat next to Thomas and clicked his seat belt together. This will be a long flight, Thomas thought.

Two hours later he was just finishing his in-flight meal.

"Well, the food in first class is much better" he said to the agent.

"Indeed" the agent replied, putting down his knife and fork.

"So then" Thomas began, turning round in his seat to face the agent, "what interest does the military have in Jon's work?"

The agent looked at Thomas, confused. "Surely you are aware of what Dr Walker's work is all about?"

"Yes, of course" Thomas replied. "He's been talking about it for years."

"Well then" the agent said. "The significance of such work would be very useful to the government and the military. Surely you can understand this?"

"I'm beginning to understand, I think. And I'm not sure that I like it."

The agent turned to him. "Do you realize what could be accomplished by using this kind of technology, Dr Long?" he turned back round and faced forward.

"The possibilities are endless." Thomas shook his head in disapproval.

"Maybe. But at what cost?" he said, in a low voice.

Nothing more was said on the matter and both men started to relax in their seats. Thomas closed his eyes, hoping to get some much-needed sleep. Gracie was already fast asleep.

"So what has Jon decided to call this little venture of his?" Thomas asked the agent, still with his eyes closed.

The agent closed his eyes. "The time project" he said.

CHAPTER 2

Thomas opened his eyes and looked round the hotel room. He still felt jet-lagged from the flight the day before, and he had a pounding headache as well. He sat up and moved to the side of the bed. Opening the drawer of the bedside cabinet, he took out some of the painkillers which he took everywhere with him. He wasn't going to let one of his migraines get in his way today. He took two of the small round pills and got straight into the shower.

Thirty minutes later he was dressed and in fresh clean clothes, provided by his friend Jon, who had paid for everything. He picked up his small satchel and opened the zipper. He grabbed his notebook and pen from the table and his electronic tablet from the bed and shoved them into the satchel. Fastening up the zipper, he threw the strap over his shoulder, picked up the room keycard and walked out. Stepping out of the elevator, he heard Gracie's voice.

"Hey, Thomas."

"Morning, Gracie."

"Are you OK? You look ill."

"I'll be fine" he said. "Just a headache. It'll go soon."

"Well, if you're sure?"

"Yeah, no worries. I'll be fine" he said, forcing a smile and patting her on the arm. Agent Summers appeared from nowhere and walked over to them.

"Have you eaten yet?" he asked abruptly.

"Not yet" Thomas answered. "Have you, Grace?"

"No."

"Well, you won't have time now" the agent said impatiently. "We'll grab you something on the way. We're already running late." He started to walk towards the main entrance of the hotel. Thomas and Gracie followed quickly behind him; they didn't want to irritate him any more than they already had.

As they stepped out into the busy street, a long black car pulled up in front of them. The agent opened the rear door and gestured for them to get in.

"Shall we?" he said. Thomas got in, followed by Gracie, and the door slammed shut behind them. The agent walked round the car and got into the passenger side.

The vehicle began to move off into the Washington streets. They were quiet for the whole journey, staring out of the windows at the huge, busy city. The new ATV air buses were passing over their heads just above the skyscrapers. Gracie watched them in awe. They hadn't come to England yet and even in the US only Washington DC, New York and Los Angeles had them.

Finally the car stopped and the agent got out. Thomas strained to see where he was going, but he quickly returned with a bag and plastic coffee cups in a holder. He opened the door and handed the food over to Thomas.

"Here" he said, and smiled. Thomas, a little shocked at this unexpected act of friendship, handed Gracie one of the coffees and a bagel and started eating.

After a short while the buildings began to get smaller and fewer. A long straight road was before them, and the car began to gain speed. An hour later, with not much to look at through the windows, the car turned left down a narrow side road. The road opened up towards the end and a huge building stood in front of them. It was a massive facility, with smaller side buildings dotted around the larger one.

The car slowly came to a stop in front of a security gate and one of the guards stepped out of the little hut. He was wearing black, with thick body armour and a large pistol on his belt. The agent got out and walked over to him. They seemed to speak for a minute or two, and then the guard gestured for the driver to go through. The gates opened automatically and the agent got back in. The car drove in slowly and went forward towards the large building. As it came to a halt Thomas could see through the window that his old friend was standing outside waiting for them to arrive. Thomas opened the door and got out. Jon walked over to him and gave him a hug.

"My friend!" he said. "I'm so glad you could come."

"Well, you didn't really give me a choice did you

Jon?" Thomas replied, smiling at his friend and gripping his arms.

"So, what have you done, Jon?" he asked. Jon was about to answer when he looked over Thomas' shoulder and saw Gracie standing next to the car.

"And who is this, Tom?" he walked away from Thomas and over to Gracie.

"My name is Gracie Stevenson" she said, before Thomas could reply. "I'm here to help Thomas with whatever work you have in store for him." Jon smiled.

"The work I have in store for him, he's gonna need that help!" he laughed.

"Please, come inside" Jon said. He started walking over to the huge metal door of the building. Thomas and Gracie followed him, their eyes adjusting to the dimmer light. They could see vast amounts of equipment and computers dotted around the room. There were security guards walking around with assault weapons and men and women scurrying around going about their work. The three of them walked into an elevator and Jon pressed one of the buttons. The elevator carried them up several floors and they walked out.

"So, did you both have a good trip here?" he asked, as they made their way down a long corridor.

"Yes, it was fine. Bit of a rush though" Thomas replied. Jon turned to him and laughed.

"Yes, well I'm sorry about the haste, but you're the best historian I know. We couldn't do this without you." he gave Thomas a pat on his back.

"Jon, I'm the only historian you know!" Thomas said jokingly. Jon gave another laugh. They finally got to the end of the corridor, where before them was a door with a keycode lock. Jon punched in a code and the door opened. Walking in, Thomas could see that it was an office. it was quite large, with a single window looking down on a huge darkened room. Jon sat down at what was quite obviously his desk and gestured for Thomas and Gracie to sit on the sofa next to it.

"Well Thomas" Jon said. "You know why you're here?"

Thomas rubbed the stubble on his face. "Of course I do, Jon. "So, have you done it?" Gracie looked at both of them in turn and said "Done what? Will someone please tell me what the hell we're doing here?"

Jon looked over at Thomas. "You didn't tell her?"

"No" replied Thomas. "I wanted it to be a surprise."

Jon leaned forward and looked at Gracie. Straight into her eyes.

"I've asked Thomas to come here as a field agent and advisor" he said, his friendly face becoming quite stern. She swallowed and took in a breath. "What sort of field agent?" he sat back in his large leather seat.

"I have done something no one has ever done before" he said. "I have made it possible to move and travel through time."

Gracie looked at him with a blank expression on her face. "Are you joking with me or something?" she turned to face Thomas. "Is this some kind of joke

Thomas? Because if it is it's certainly not at all funny." she got to her feet and picked up her bag.

"Gracie, sit down" Thomas said to her calmly.

"We've travelled around the world, left our dig site and for what... a joke?"

"Sit down, Gracie!" Thomas repeated, more loudly. She stopped her ranting and sat back down. Jon was back in his seat with one leg crossed over the other.

"It is very true, my dear. I have made it possible" he said to her. "And what's more, I've really done it. I've sent a living human being back in time."

At this point Thomas leaned forward. "Who did you send?"

"He was a test subject, nothing more, supplied by the military."

Thomas gave Jon a disgusted look. "A test subject? A *test* subject? This was a human being Jon, what the fuck were you thinking?"

"He was a criminal, Tom, sentenced to death. He gave away his rights when he took the lives of others."

"But Jon, you've sent a murderer back in time. Do you realize what could happen?"

Thomas stood up, not believing what he was hearing. "Jon, if this man starts killing people in whatever time he's in, it could alter the future. It could change history forever. The implications of what could happen are devastating!"

Jon stood up and walked over to Thomas to try and calm him.

"I know, Thomas" he said. "I know. That's why we're going to go after him to bring him back here, to this time." Thomas stopped and looked at him. "You're right Tom, I made a mistake but with your help I can right this wrong."

Thomas took a breath and began to calm down. "How do you know he's still alive anyway, that he even survived the time jump?" he asked.

"We surgically implanted a device that will let us know if any of the jumpers die" Jon answered. "Tom, he's still alive. But we need to get after him."

"OK, when?" Thomas said picking up his satchel."

"We can leave this evening, but before we go you'll have to have a briefing regarding the equipment and procedures. And you'll both have to have an implant put in."

"Yeah, whatever" Thomas said. Gracie hadn't said another word. She just sat there in disbelief.

"OK, well let's get started." Jon said, opening the office door. Thomas looked round at Gracie and held out his hand. "Come on Grace. It'll be fine. I promise."

She looked up at him and took his hand. "How's your headache?"

He smiled at her. "It's a lot better now, thanks. Come on, I'll go first to have this device put in."

"Oh, it's a simple procedure. Nothing to worry about" Jon said, holding the door for them both. They walked out of the office and back towards the elevator. On the floor below them, they got out. They were standing in a huge darkened room. Then the lights suddenly came flickering on. Thomas looked round and saw Jon standing near a panel on the wall.

"There" Jon said, "a bit of light." he picked up a small handset from a nearby station and said "We're ready for you now".

Within minutes the room seemed to be filled with scientists and other workers. One man walked over to Jon. He was scruffy with a long beard and wore a long white lab coat. They seemed to speak for a minute or two and Jon gestured over towards Thomas and Gracie. The scruffy scientist then walked over to them, smiling.

"So then, who's first?" he said. Thomas presumed he was talking about the device which they were to have surgically implanted. He looked at Gracie and then back at the man.

"I am" he said.

"Excellent" the man replied. "Please follow me, would you?" Thomas and Gracie quickly followed after the scientist, who was walking very fast towards one of the side rooms. He pressed his keycard against the flashing red device on the door frame, which quickly turned green for them to enter. The man pushed open the door and the three of them walked in.

"Lights!" the man said quite loudly, and the lights flickered on automatically. There was a single seat in the centre of the room with computers and devices all round. Surgical equipment was set up next to the seat and an oversized light was fixed over it. It reminded Gracie of a dentist's chair. Thomas was equally apprehensive. Was this crazy-looking man going to be cutting him open?

"And what happens now?" Gracie asked the man, stepping in front of Thomas. The scientist stopped fiddling with the computers next to the chair and looked at her.

"Dr Long will sit down and we can begin" he said. He gestured to Thomas to sit down. "That is, if you still wish to go first?"

Thomas looked at Gracie, and she looked back at him with soft hopeful eyes. He looked back at the man.

"Yes yes, of course I'll go first" he said. He walked over and sat down in the chair. The man immediately leaned over him and turned the huge light on. Thomas was blinded for a second, until his eyes adjusted to the bright light. The man started messing with something to Thomas' right and he felt his sleeve being rolled up his arm.

"This isn't going to hurt, Dr Long. Please relax." Thomas could now smell the scientist's breath. He felt a needle go in and within seconds he couldn't feel his arm at all. He looked down, feeling more confident now that his arm was numb. The man's hand was holding a scalpel, which he put against Thomas' forearm and drew across. Blood seeped out of a small cut, which the man gently mopped up. He was holding a pair of tweezers with something small and black gripped in them, and he now pushed the black object into the cut. Thomas could feel it lock into place. The tweezers were pulled out, and the man picked up another little tool, which he ran across the wound. A small curl of smoke came off the cut as the tool was dragged along; the smell of burning flesh made Thomas feel sick. The wound was now closed up and hardly visible. The man took of his latex gloves off and stepped back.

"There" he said. "All done." Thomas got up out of the seat, looking at his arm with suspicion.

"My turn" Gracie said, pushing Thomas aside and jumping into the chair.

Ten minutes later the two of them walked out the room. Jon walked over to them.

"Told you it wouldn't hurt" he said with a smile, holding up his own arm. There was a small, hardly visible scar.

"Great" Thomas said sarcastically. "Guess we're in the same club now. So, now what?"

"Over here" replied Jon, smiling. He was not letting the fact that Thomas was annoyed get to him. They walked over to a monitor which had a green line waving up and down along it, and what appeared to be a heart rate indicator in the left-hand corner.

"So, this must be your test subject's cardiac monitor" Thomas said, looking intensely at the big screen.

"Sure is" replied Jon, walking over to the touch panel below the monitor. He touched a few buttons and more of the same lines appeared on screen, followed by three more heart rates.

"And here" Jon began, "are ours." Jon looked back at his friend and gave a hopeful smile, one that suggested he hoped Thomas would smile back. Thomas did manage to force a smile, which pleased Jon, and he rushed over to his friend and gripped his arm.

"I'm so glad you're with me now, old buddy" Jon said.

"There's nowhere else I would be" said Thomas.

"Well, I'll show you the equipment we'll be taking with us shortly" Jon said. "But first, how about a coffee?"

"I'd love one" answered Gracie.

"Yeah, me too" said Thomas.

"Excellent" Jon said, and he walked over to a table near one of the computer monitors. The table had all sorts of refreshments on it, including a coffee machine. Jon took three cups and started to pour.

"Thank you" Gracie said, taking one of the cups of coffee from Jon. The other was handed to Thomas, who took it and started drinking straight away.

"So, then" said Jon after taking a sip of coffee. "You found a complete skeleton, did you?"

"That's right. From about the late 790s. I'm hoping it's a Viking warrior."

"Wow, that's remarkable" Jon said.

"Not as remarkable as what you've done, Jon. The idea that we can go back in time and see exactly how people lived is amazing. You have accomplished something unbelievable."

"Thanks Tom" Jon said with a warm smile. Gracie looked on as the friends became engrossed in deep conversation.

"So tell me Jon, how does it work?" Thomas asked.

"It's all to do with dark matter." Jon put down his coffee cup and started explaining, using hand gestures. "You see, we can manipulate the atoms in our machine and fire them at the beam array plate, and it can open a wormhole at any point in the past, from a few minutes ago to thousands of years back."

"Wow" Thomas said. "You make it sound so easy."

"Well, it is, really. Once we figured out how to manipulate the dark atoms of course."

"So, is the time random when the wormhole opens, or can you control where and when to open it?"

"Not random. We have complete control over what time period and where on the planet we can jump to. The first jump was random of course, but after that we managed to lock in precise dates and locations. We just punch the date and the coordinates into the matter beam and there you have it. Bang, you're there."

"And the test subject?" Gracie said.

"Like I said, it was random. The first jump. He's ended up in England in the late 19th century."

"Then that's where we're going" Thomas said, squeezing his empty cup and throwing it into the trash can next to him.

"Well, the sooner the better Tom" Jon said, doing the same. "Come. I'll show you the equipment. It's over here." he started walking away. Thomas and Gracie followed eagerly behind him. With a beep, the door slid open and they walked in. The lights came on, activated by Jon's verbal command. Along one wall hung black all-in-one suits with various gadgets lying next to them. Jon walked over to them and pressed a button on one of the display cases. The glass covering the suits slid smoothly away.

"This, my friend, is a conduit suit" Jon said, holding up his hand to one of the black suits. "It protects the body from the dark matter beam and makes the jump back in time more smooth and less painful. It's also lightly armoured, just in case we run into any trouble." he looked pleased with himself. "It also has a touch panel and display on the left forearm. Gives you the stats on the suit you're wearing, and also a mini map of the area you're in along with a communication device, so you can keep in touch with your team if you're separated from one another."

"You've thought of everything" Gracie said, trying not to sound too excited.

"That's not all." Jon began again. "We'll also need protection." he reached into the cabinet and took out a large pistol. "This is a 9mm pulse burst pistol. Can be switched from semi automatic to full automatic. The clip carries 30 explosive tracer rounds."

Thomas interrupted. "Wait a minute Jon." he said. "We can't just go around killing people in other times. It could have a devastating effect. I've said this already.

That's why we're going after your little test subject."

"Yes Tom. I know. The weapons are just a precaution. We'll have to defend ourselves if we're attacked by someone, or something." Jon was trying to reason with Thomas. Thomas began to calm himself.

"Very well Jon. I'll carry one, but I won't use it."

"Well, as long as you've got one, just in case." Jon said, then turned round and placed the weapon back on its stand below the suits. One of the workers came in and whispered something to Jon. He turned back round to face Thomas and Gracie.

"We'll be ready to suit up in one hour. The machine will be ready then."

They walked out and Jon gestured for them to go to the centre of the huge room. As they walked past all the machinery and computers, the scientists and engineers, they saw the machine at the centre. At one end was a platform, almost like a stage, and at the other end, along what seemed like a runway, there seemed to be an enormous gun, like some futuristic ray gun pointing right at the platform.

"Well" said Jon, "this is it." He stepped in front of them.

"It's... it's big" Thomas said, in awe of the machine.

Jon laughed. "Yes, it is. You see, once we're ready to go, we'll stand there on the platform and the date and coordinates are entered into the dark matter array on the other end. Within minutes the beam will be fired and we'll be jumped to those exact coordinates."

Thomas looked shocked. "Fired at us, you said?"

Jon gave another laugh. "It's perfectly safe, Tom. That's what the suits are for. You'll be fine." Gracie had no worries at all, just pure excitement.

Within thirty minutes they were suited up. They walked back to the centre of the room. The machine was making a whooshing sound now, with lights blinking around it. The sound of power filled the room.

"Are you OK Thomas?" Gracie said, giving his arm a reassuring rub.

"Yeah, I'm fine" he replied, fiddling with the tight suit around his wrists. "Just a bit nervous."

Jon walked over to them. He also had his suit on and like the others a pistol was strapped to his leg.

"So then" he began. "We're ready to leave." he held his hand out towards the platform. Gracie looked up at Thomas.

"Come on" she said. "It's going to be cool."

"Let's do this" he replied, gathering courage. The three of them walked up the steps and stood in the centre of the platform as instructed by Jon. A loud voice came over the tannoy system. "Ten seconds to launch." It started to countdown - 9, 8, 7... Thomas started to sweat and he began to feel so scared that he almost vomited. 6, 5, 4... the machine became louder and the barrel was spinning fast now, with a bright intense light coming from the centre. 3, 2... "Here we go!" shouted Jon. 1... with a blinding flash, they were gone.

★ ★ ★ ★ ★

Thomas looked down at his legs, which were shaking uncontrollably. There was smoke all around them. He noticed that the ground under their feet was broken and cracked. As the smoke began to clear, Thomas could see they were near a river. It was dark, late at night Thomas thought, and he was thankful that there had been nobody around to see them arrive.

"Well, we're here" Jon said, putting his hand on Thomas' shoulder. Thomas looked at him and then turned round suddenly and vomited.

"Are you OK?" Gracie asked, rubbing his back.

"He's fine" Jon said. "It's perfectly normal on the first jump." Thomas wiped his mouth and stood back up straight.

"So, where are we?" he asked. Jon took a step over the broken and scorched ground and turned to Thomas.

"This my friend, is 04:30 on the morning of the 2nd of September in the year 1888. And it appears that we're near the river Thames."

Gracie walked up the bank and on to what appeared to be a muddy footpath. The view before her was amazing. They were in Victorian London.

"We've done it" she said, laughing. "We're actually here, in another time."

Jon walked up the slope to her. "Of course we're here." he looked at her and smiled. Gracie looked back down to Thomas to try and get his opinion on it all, but he had his bag open, which of course he had brought with him, and was frantically flicking through the pages of his notebook.

"Thomas, come and see this" she said to him.

Thomas carried on scanning through the pages of the book. "Jon, the test subject. He was a murderer, right? How did he kill his victims?"

"It was quite brutal. He cut their throats and then mutilated them. Why?"

Thomas looked into his notebook. "Because I think he's doing it here, in this time."

Gracie walked back down to him. "Thomas, what do you mean, how do you know this?" he looked up at her, fixed on her eyes. "Because he shares the characteristics of Jack the Ripper. And, this is the Ripper's time. The first victim associated with the Ripper was found two days before today, in Bucks Row in Whitechapel." he pointed to lines in his notebook. "You see, there were eleven victims in all, but only five were associated with Jack the Ripper, due to the brutality. They were known as the canonical five."

"Tom, are you really saying that by sending him to this time I have created Jack the Ripper?" asked Jon. He began to get flustered.

"It's quite logical Jon. In fact, it makes perfect sense." Thomas said.

"Yes but, in a way that's a good thing" Gracie said.

Jon turned to her and yelled. "How on earth is that a good thing?" he said, waving his hands in the air. "I'm being told that the most brutal murderer in history is down to me!"

"Jon, calm down" Thomas said, holding on to his friend's arm. Gracie tried to reason with him.

"What I mean is, we can stop him" she said. "We know when and where the Ripper kills his victims. All we have to do is wait for him at the place where the second body was found and we'll be able to save her."

"We can't!" said Thomas. Gracie and Jon looked at him.

"Thomas, I can right this wrong!" Jon said, almost pleading with his friend.

"If we stop him before he's killed the five women, then it'll alter history" explained Thomas.

Gracie looked at him in disbelief. "Thomas, are you saying that we just have to let this monster kill these women?"

"We have no choice, Grace, believe me. We have to let him. The last victim was Mary Jane Kelly. She was found at her one-bed flat in Millers Court, number thirteen, just off Dorset Street, on the ninth of November 1888. That's when we'll strike and not before."

Jon looked at Gracie with sad eyes. "He's right Gracie. Thomas is right." Gracie looked between them both, and then down to the ground. "I know" she muttered under her breath. "I know."

Thomas picked up his bag and placed his notebook back inside. Throwing the bag over his shoulder he said,

"Jon, what does he look like, the murderer?"

"As I remember, he's quite tall, about six foot. He's got dark hair, and he's of slim build." he sat down on a large piece of wood.

"We're going to need to know how to identify him as the Ripper. I think we should go to one of the other places where he killed so we can get a look at him."

"We might not be able to stop him killing anyone, but I'm damn sure I'm not going to watch him do it!" Gracie said angrily.

"I know Grace, and we won't. But we need to identify him. just a glimpse of him is all we need" Thomas said softly to her. "We'll sort this, Grace. I promise you." For a moment she held his hand. To him it seemed forever.

"Its going to start getting light soon" Thomas said. "We have to find somewhere to stay." Jon pressed a small button on the inside of his left forearm, and the touch screen panel lit up, bright neon blue, bringing up a mini map of the area.

"There's a warehouse nearby. An old one, not used any more. We could stay there" he said to the others. Thomas nodded. "Good. We'll go there." he walked up the slope and viewed the old city.

"Wow, it's amazing!" It was the first proper glimpse he had had of 1888 London. Jon and Gracie followed him along the muddy path. The smell of damp wood and coal smoke mixed with horse dung filled the air. They passed a row of small houses on their left, and as they got to the end of the row, one of the back gates creaked open. The three of them ran behind a wall and pressed themselves against it.

Thomas peeped round the corner to see a man walk out with a leather bag over his shoulder. He lit a cigarette with a match, pulled his cap down and walked away from them, towards the river. They all took a deep breath.

"That was close" Jon said, resting his head on the wall. Thomas moved away from the wall.

"We can't afford to be seen at all. It's too dangerous" he said.

"I agree" Jon replied.

"Well, I thought that was quite exciting" Gracie said, smiling at Thomas. He smiled back.

"You're really loving this, aren't you?" he said. She laughed, but then she was interrupted by another noise behind them, coming from one of the backyards. "Who's there?" A voice shouted out. A woman's voice, but sounding quite gruff.

"Quickly, this way!" Jon hissed, and they ran towards what looked like an industrial estate. They stopped near a side entrance, and Jon looked round the corner, through the metal bars of the gate.

"This is the place" he said. "One or two of the buildings are still used, so we'll have to be careful." he tried to push the metal bars of the gate open, but it wouldn't budge. Looking down, he noticed that a chain was wrapped round the bars on to a post and fastened by a lock.

"Now what?" Thomas whispered to him, almost panicking. "The wall is too high to climb."

"I've got just the thing" Jon said, taking a small device from his belt. He pressed a button and it opened up with a bright red light in the centre. He pointed it towards the chain and clicked a second button. A thin red beam came shooting out of the device and began to cut through the thick chain with ease. After a second or two the chain fell to the ground, the two ends glowing bright orange with smoke coming from them.

"There we go" Jon said, and opened the gate.

"That's so cool!" Gracie said, and followed Jon into the yard. Thomas came through after checking there was no one following them. The yard was quite big, with decrepit buildings dotted around. Jon ran towards one of the smaller buildings to the right of them and Gracie and Thomas followed quickly behind. Jon took one final look around before opening a large and rotting wooden door. It wasn't locked and opened easily. With a loud creak he pushed it open and peered round. It was dark inside and he couldn't see anything in the shadows. Thomas was getting impatient, not wanting to be out in the yard for too long.

"Come on Jon. Is it clear?" he whispered.

"Wait" Jon replied, and took from his belt a small object.

"What's that going to do?" Gracie asked eagerly. Jon looked at her and said.

"It's a torch." He clicked it on. Thomas laughed

from behind them. Jon pointed the beam into the dark.

All they could see was a few boxes stacked up. There seemed to be a table in the one corner with oil lanterns dotted around. A few chains hung from the ceiling, clanking together as the wind through the old building moved them slightly. They walked in and Thomas closed the door behind them. Jon walked over to the table. There were a few pieces of old paper dotted around and a chalk board just behind the table. Jon picked up one of the bits of paper and shone the torch on to it.

"Looks like it was a storage warehouse" he said, scanning the piece of paper. Thomas walked over to him. There were a couple of wooden chairs next to the table and he pushed down on one to check the stability of it before sitting down.

"Be careful" he said to Gracie as she continued to look around. Jon took the other seat next to Thomas and threw the tattered piece of paper back on to the table.

"So, what do we do now?" he said, looking in Thomas' direction. Thomas was looking through his notebook once more. He had found the page he was looking for.

"The next victim was Annie Chapman. She was found in the backyard of 29 Hanbury Street, Spitalfields, at about half past five on the morning of the 8th of September 1888. We'll try and get a look at him there." He sat back in the chair.

"OK Tom, but we've got to wait six days now" Jon replied.

"I know" Thomas said putting down his book. "So I guess we'll do some research while we wait."

Jon nodded. "OK, sounds good" he said, and both of them looked over to Gracie. There was no sign of her. Thomas stood up.

"Gracie!" he called. "Gracie!" he said again, louder this time. Jon got to his feet and drew his pistol. With a click the safety was off and a blue light on the side of the weapon lit up. Thomas walked over to where he had last seen her. Jon was just behind him with the pistol pointing forward.

"Hello" came Gracie's voice, and she suddenly popped up from a small hole in the floor. Thomas and Jon jumped back.

"Good god Grace!" Thomas said, trying to calm himself. Jon just laughed.

"I'm sorry" she said. "You've got to see this." she disappeared again. The two men walked over to the hole, which appeared to be the opening to what looked like a cellar.

"You first" Jon said, patting Thomas on the back.

"Thanks" Thomas replied and started to climb down the steep narrow steps that led down, followed by Jon.

CHAPTER 3

It was dark and dusty down in the basement of the old building and smelled of damp wood and rotting food.

"It's a passageway" Gracie said, pointing her torch down the narrow corridor.

"But where does it lead?" Thomas said, peering down.

"Let's find out" replied Jon. They had to go in single file, so Gracie went first, followed by Jon and then Thomas. The passage wasn't very long and soon all three of them were standing in a large room.

Thomas shone his torch around. There were old wooden barrels stacked in one corner and crates of rotting fruit in the other. Gracie, shining the beam of her torch along the back wall, noticed a wooden door. Jon tapped away on the panel on his arm again.

"There's nothing on the database about these tunnels at all" he said, looking over at Thomas. "That door could lead anywhere. Or nowhere."

"There's only one way to find out then" Thomas said, and walked over to Gracie. They both approached the door, and Thomas tried the handle. It was locked and rusted over. It was obvious that the passage hadn't been used for a long time.

"Use the laser" Jon said, still tapping away on his arm panel. Gracie took the device from her belt and flicked the small switch on the side. The front of the device opened up with a click. The inside was glowing bright red.

"Stand back!" she said, pointing the device at the lock. With a tearing sound, and smoke streaking from the lock, it popped open with a bright orange flash.

"I love this" she said, pressing the switch again to close the laser. She attached it to her belt again and Thomas moved forward. He gripped the old door and pulled it open. It creaked and cracked aside, the rust on the hinges popping and clanking. It was dark down the other passage and Thomas shone his torch down it, anxious to see what was in the shadows. As he stepped inside he noticed some small marks on the doorframe. Shining his torch on them, he could make out what they were.

"What have you found?" Gracie asked, trying to peer over his shoulder.

"Masonic markings" he said and took out his notebook. He started copying down the symbols.

"These tunnels must have been used by masons to move around the city undetected" he said. "They could lead all over the city." he put his book back in the bag around his shoulder and pointed the beam down the passage.

"That's good. That means we can use them to move about the city too. And no one will ever see us" Gracie said, moving past Thomas and going further into the darkness.

"What have you found?" Jon said, walking up to them.

"Masonic symbols" Thomas said, glancing at him.

"Cool! And where are we going now then?"

Thomas turned around and pointed his torch down the dark corridor

"Down there, by the look of it" he said.

Gracie, already half way down, called up to them.

"It opens up down here" she said. Thomas and Jon followed her down into the dark, and sure enough, as they approached her, the narrow passage started to open up and become wider.

They had found another room. It was smaller than the first, but this time three doors led off it. Each had a destination written on a small plaque hung just above the door. The door on the left said 'Trafalgar Square'. The door in the centre said 'Ten Bells'. The last door said 'Saint Botolph's Church'.

Thomas reached into his bag and pulled out his book again.

"There, I knew it" he said.

"Knew what, Tom?" Jon asked.

"The Ten Bells was a tavern visited by prostitutes in this time, and most of the Ripper victims would have gone there to find customers" he said.

"So if this tunnel goes all the way to the Ten Bells, we might get a glimpse of the murderer there?" Gracie said.

"Exactly" Thomas replied, putting his book away.

"But I thought the next victim was on the 8th of this month?" Jon asked.

"It is, yes. But he still may be there, looking for his next target" Thomas said, walking over to the door.

"Then what are we waiting for?" Jon said. He stepped past Thomas and pulled on the door. It opened with a loud creak which echoed through the passageways. He shone his torch down into the dark and walked though. Thomas and Gracie followed close behind.

The passage seemed to go on forever. The wooden beams above their heads were damp and smelled fusty. They ducked to avoid spiders' webs and had to step over sewerage that had gathered over time. The smell was horrific and Thomas almost choked several times. Along some of the walls, more Masonic symbols could be seen, etched into the stone.

Finally they came to some steps which led up to a small doorway. On the door a sign hung: THE TEN BELLS.

"Here we are" Jon said. Thomas walked past him and up the four steps. He tried to peer through the gap in the planks of the door. He could see nothing, but he could smell stale beer.

"OK, what's our play?" Jon asked him.

"We're going to have to go in there" Thomas replied. "But I really don't know how, without being seen."

Jon activated the touch panel again. "I can scan the

whole building, see the layout" he said. "We might be able to get in there without being seen." And within seconds a mini map appeared on the screen.

"Look, out of this door, if we turn left there is a staircase that goes up to a small room. The room has a window that looks down on the bar area."

"Good" Thomas said. "We'll be able to see if the murderer is here from up there." He started to open the unlocked door. Jon gripped Thomas' arm and pulled him back.

"We can't all go" he whispered. "We're less likely to be seen if only one of us goes."

"OK, wait here" Thomas said and started opening the door again.

"I'm the only one here that has seen the killer before. I should go" Jon said, pulling Thomas back again. Thomas looked at him and then to Gracie. "He's right" she said.

"OK, but stay in contact at all times" Thomas said.

Jon creaked open the door very slowly and stepped out of the passage. He now stood in the basement of the Ten Bells. Looking around, he saw beer barrels stacked up along with crates. There seemed to be hundreds of them. The sound of laughter and merriment could be heard coming from the floor above. There was an old long jacket lying on top of one of the barrels and Jon picked it up. Searching the pockets, he found a tobacco pouch, some matches a penknife and a few coins. Two shillings and ten pence, Jon counted, and a small piece of chalk. He put the items back in the pockets and then threw the jacket on. It might act as a disguise, he thought.

He looked around. It was quite dark, but he did not want to use his torch in case it was seen. The only light came from two oil lamps. He could just about make out some stairs in front of him which must lead to the bar area, but he could also make out narrow steps on his left; the stairs that must lead to the small room.

He walked over to them and peered up. A light could be seen at the very top of the staircase. He crept up very slowly. One or two of the steps made a noise, and he stopped for a second to see if he had been heard. He carried on, and soon he was at the top. There was a door in front of him, and he put his ear to it to see if anything could be heard from the other side. Feeling confident that no one was inside, he pushed open the door. It was clear.

He looked around the small room. A single bed stood in the corner and there was a desk in the other corner with a small oil lamp flickering away on it. There was a narrow window on the wall in front of him and he made his way to it. Sitting on the edge of the bed, he peered through into the bar below. It was very Smokey and the smell of beer and cooking made Jon feel hungry. The place seemed packed with men and women drinking, flirting and having fun. There were a few men sat over in the corner singing away and the sound of very loud laughter just below him.

Then the main door from outside opened and in

strolled a chubby woman. She wore dark clothing and a red scarf. She walked straight up to one of the men stood at the bar and started touching him and playing with him. He looked at her and pushed her away. She fell against another man, a taller man with dark hair, who helped her up. Turning to face him, she started doing the same to him. He stroked her face and gave her what appeared to be a small bunch of grapes. Taking one final glance at her, he walked out of the pub.

It had to be the Ripper. He was wearing a deerstalker hat, pulled right down, but it was definitely him, he thought. He ran back out and down the staircase, a little louder than he hoped. When he came out into the basement again, to his shock a man was standing in front of him; a large fat man with an apron on. The man looked him up and down.

"Who the hell are you?" the man said. "And whatcher doing with my coat on?" he walked towards Jon with his fists clenched. Jon stood there and raised his hands. The man threw a punch at Jon, aiming straight for his face. Jon stepped to the side and simply tapped the man's fist away. As he did, Jon countered the attack with an own open-palmed strike to the man's throat, followed by a punch to his jaw. The man dropped to the floor, out cold.

Jon stepped over him and Thomas pushed open the door to greet him.

"How did you do that?" Thomas said, mouth agape.

"I had some combat training" he answered, and

walked back into the passageway. Thomas followed him through and closed the door behind them.

"That was awesome" Gracie said, smiling at Jon.

"He was there, at the bar" said Jon. "I saw him."

"OK, that's great." Thomas answered. "At least we know for sure that he is coming to the same places that the victims did."

They made their way back to the old warehouse. It was now getting on for late afternoon, and they were all starting to get hungry.

"I suggest we jump back to our time and then come back on the day of the next murder" Jon said, sitting on one of the chairs next to the table. He was still wearing the coat from the Ten Bells.

"But can we go home and jump straight back, or do we have to wait?" Gracie asked.

"No no, we can jump almost straight back. We just put the relevant time into the computer" Jon answered.

"OK" Gracie said. "I think we should go back. Get something to eat, freshen up and come back on the 8th of September." she got to her feet.

"I agree" Thomas said. "So Jon, how do we get back?"

Jon opened up the display again on his arm and pointed.

"There" he said. "We just press the recall button and we're gone."

Thomas walked over to them.

"OK. We should go now" he said. "The sooner we

go the sooner we can come back." he activated the panel on his arm and Gracie did the same.

"OK, after three." Jon said. "One, two, three…" they all activated the devices. Sparks and electricity shot from them to the floor, from the floor to the walls. With a flash and a crackling sound they were gone.

★ ★ ★ ★ ★

"Nice to see you back in one piece" Agent Summers said, walking over to them. They were standing in the centre of the platform with smoke coming from them. The platform was glowing orange from the energy.

"Thanks" Jon replied. He walked down the steps, unfastening his suit. Thomas and Gracie followed.

"And how was it for you?" the agent asked them.

"It was wonderful!" Gracie answered, smiling.

"Yeah, great" replied Thomas. "Your little test subject became Jack the Ripper."

"Really?" Summers said in shock. "We weren't to know what would happen, Dr Long. So what will you do?"

Thomas started walking away, taking his suit off.

"We have to monitor him" he said. "And after he's killed the fifth, we'll take him out and bring him back here."

"Why not do that now?" the agent said.

"Because it would alter history if we did that before the fifth victim died" he said with a sad look on his face.

"I would spare those women if I could, believe me!"

He walked into a side room. Gracie was already in there, her suit off and hung up, being checked by the scientists. She was sitting at a table with a drink in front of her. A worker came over and placed a burger with fries in front of her.

"Would you like anything, Dr Long?" the man asked him.

"The same please" he replied, and sat down in front of Gracie. For a time they just looked at each other, until Thomas said, "Are you OK?"

Gracie put down the burger. "Yeah, I'm cool. Bit weird though, isn't it? I mean the idea that one of history's most brutal killers was in fact created here, in this time." she took another bite of her burger. "We've been reading about what happened in Whitechapel in 1888 for almost two hundred years now. But, it really started here, with us and Jon. It's mind blowing, Thomas."

She looked down. The worker came back and placed another burger and fries in front of Thomas.

"Thank you" said Thomas. He took a bite, not really feeling hungry any more. "I know Grace, it is strange isn't it? But this is now history. This is how this happened and all we can do is make sure that it stops with the fifth murder. If we don't stop him there then that in itself will change history."

"We'll stop him!" she said, and looked straight into Thomas' eyes.

"Its down to us now Grace. We'll stop that bastard and bring him to justice!" Thomas said and gave her a big smile. At that Jon walked in.

"Hey guys, the suits and the machine are ready to go when we are" he said, taking a seat next to Thomas. He picked up one of Thomas' fries and put it in his mouth.

"OK" Thomas said. "So, how do you feel about all this now Jon?" Jon looked away.

"I'm deeply ashamed of what I've done. Regarding the Ripper I mean. But we can sort this."

Thomas nodded. "Sure we can Jon" he said and tapped his friend on his arm. They finished the food and suited up again. The three of them walked back into the large room and the sound of humming could be heard coming from the dark beam array. The machine was ready. Jon walked up the steps on to the platform followed by Gracie and then Thomas.

"We're ready" Jon called to the scientist standing by the control station.

"Wait!" Came a voice from the crowd of workers. It was Agent Summers, wearing one of the suits. He walked over to the platform.

"I'm coming with you" he said.

"We don't need anyone else" Thomas replied.

"Unfortunately Dr Long, there is no choice" Summers answered. "The military have to monitor what you're doing there, and I've been chosen to go with you." He walked up the steps and stood next to Thomas.

"OK Summers" Jon said. "Hold on to your ass!"

After the ten second countdown they were gone again, with a blinding flash.

"Are you OK, Agent Summers?" Jon said. The agent was bent double and vomiting.

"I'm fine." he answered and stood straight. Thomas looked over at Gracie and they smiled to each other with amusement. They were all standing in the warehouse this time. The jump had left a small crater below their feet. Jon looked down at the panel on his arm.

"It's the right time" he said. "The 8th of September 1888, ten o'clock at night."

"Good, we need to get to Whitechapel." Thomas walked over to the passage entrance and they all stepped down into the darkness. The agent checked his pistol. He slammed the clip into the handle and pulled back the slide. Then he put the pistol back in its holster and followed the rest down the tunnel.

"Here" Thomas said as they approached the three doors. "We'll go to Saint Botolph's church." he pulled open the unlocked door. There were more Masonic markings on the wall as they walked down the dark narrow passageway.

Within half an hour they had reached a door above a few steps. Jon walked up the steps and pushed open the old door with a creak. They were now in the cellar of the church. There was no light and they kept the torches on. A mouse squeaked as the agent almost stood on it.

"OK, we're not far from the site of the second murder" Thomas said.

"So we're going to catch the subject tonight?" the agent asked.

"No, god no" Thomas replied with haste. "We can't stop him until the fifth murder."

"So why are we here?"

"We need to monitor him, make sure he doesn't do anything to change history. Haven't you listened to what we've been saying?"

The agent grimaced at Thomas and walked past him towards the cellar door that led to the church.

"We need to get to Hanbury Street, Spitalfields" Thomas said. As they walked up the staircase and into the church, the sound of talking could be heard outside. Women were laughing and chatting to one another. Jon checked his mini map.

"There's a side entrance over here" he said, and ran over to it. He decided to put on the coat he took before - it might come in handy, he thought. The others followed him to the door. He opened it slightly and peered out. There was an alleyway straight ahead of them. It seemed quiet enough - they could make it if they ran.

"OK, on my count" Jon said. "One, two, three." And with that they ran out of the church and into the alley. Just as they made it a woman walked past them and glanced at them. She must have seen them, but now they were in shadow.

"Evening" Thomas said.

"Good evening sir" the woman answered, and carried on her way.

"That was close." Gracie said. "Nice one, Thomas." Jon peered round and watched the woman walk away from them towards a group of other women. She stopped and started chatting to them.

"It's clear" he said. "But there's a lot of them around. I don't think we'll be able to get past them." Jon finished. Thomas switched on the panel on his arm. The mini map came up and he scanned it.

"OK, there's a way at the end of this alleyway. It leads to a side street. It should be pretty quiet down that way" he said, looking up. Jon smiled at him.

"Glad you're liking the suits' functions" he said, heading towards the other end of the alley. The smell of sewerage was almost unbearable and they quickly made there way to the end. Hearing a group of rowdy men walking past they stayed close to the brick wall. Thomas looked round and watch the five men stagger past, clearly drunk and worse for wear.

"OK, they're gone" Thomas said and stepped out. Jon was just behind him, scanning through the mini map on his arm.

"It's not far" Jon said.

"Let's go" replied Thomas, and they ran out and headed down to the bottom of the small street. There were little houses along one side and what looked like lodging houses on the other. At the end they crouched down behind a fence. The sound of a woman talking got closer and closer. Jon peered out and saw the same chubby woman he had seen at the Ten Bells. A man was walking beside her, calmly, not drunk like the other men around the area. The woman had her arm looped through his and she was chatting away while eating some more grapes, clearly given to her by the man.

It was the killer. Jon recognized him straight away.

"That's the guy" Jon whispered. Thomas looked round and stared at the monster.

"So that's the Ripper!" he whispered back to Jon. They ducked down as the woman and the killer approached. He was wearing a long black coat and a deerstalker hat.

"We need to follow him!" Thomas said. They waited for them to gain a safe distance and the four of them cautiously left their hiding place.

"Come on" Thomas said. They ran across the street and down into another alleyway, where they saw the killer and the woman turn left at the bottom of the alley. They walked down quickly to try and catch up with them. Staying close to the wall, Thomas looked out. He couldn't see them anywhere. A policeman strolled past them in the street swinging his truncheon around on its little leather strap. They quickly moved back into the shadows.

A man and a woman came out of one of the side streets, laughing and unsteady on their feet. They stopped suddenly at the sight of the policeman. "On yer way!" he snapped at them and they scuttled off down the street.

"What time is it?" Thomas asked. Gracie looked at her panel.

"It's 05:20" she said.

"We need to hurry" Thomas said, peering out once more. The street was now empty.

"Come on" he said and ran out. The others followed him quickly. Within ten minutes they were at the edge of yet another alleyway. Right across from them, the killer and the woman were in conversation outside number 29 Hanbury Street. A man walked past and seemed to acknowledge the woman, then carried on walking. The woman turned around, followed by the man. He put his arm around her and they walked into an alley which seemed to lead around the back of the building.

"This is it" Thomas said. Gracie leaned against the wall and closed her eyes. Jon was leaning against the other wall. "God forgive me" he muttered under his breath. They stayed where they were, and ten minutes later the killer reappeared from the alley. He fastened his coat and looked around in all directions. When he was sure it was safe, he walked down the smoggy street and disappeared.

"Shall we go and check?" Agent Summers asked quietly.

"No" replied Thomas. "History tells what happened." They walked back up the alley and turned into a back yard. Thomas leaned against the outhouse, looking deeply saddened.

"We should go back to our time" he said. "Come back at the next murder." He walked back towards the group.

"When is that?" Jon asked him.

"The 30th of September. The double event, as it was called."

"He killed two in one night?" Gracie asked in shock.

"I'm afraid so" Thomas said. Jon tapped on his arm device. "OK, are we ready?" he said. They all activated their devices and with a loud crack of electricity and a flash, they were gone, leaving the murderous streets of Whitechapel behind.

* * * * *

Three weeks later Thomas, Gracie and Jon had not left the facility at all. Jon, having undergone combat training, put Thomas and Gracie through a course run by Lt Karl Mackenzie. Agent Summers' right hook came in fast. Gracie shielded it with both arms, then straightening out her arms, she pushed him away. He staggered back and a kick came rushing in and struck his knee. He dropped to the floor and a punch hit him straight on the cheek, which knocked him over.

"How was that?" Gracie said, turning to Mackenzie. He nodded and said.

"Much better. Well done."

Gracie held out her hand to help Agent Summers to his feet.

"Thanks" he said, not knowing whether to hold his face or his knee. She walked off the training mat and over towards where Thomas was watching.

"That was awesome, Grace" he said.

"Thanks." She undid the straps that held the sparring mitts in place. She picked up a bottle of water and began to knock it back.

"Your turn" the Lieutenant called to Thomas. He handed Gracie a towel to wipe her face, and walked over to the mat.

"Please be careful, I'm not really a fighting kind of guy" said Thomas to the agent, who was already bouncing on his toes ready for action. Thomas stepped on to the mat and the first punch came straight in, hitting him in the stomach. He crouched over, the air leaving his lungs and pain shooting to his chest. The agent was still bouncing around him. Thomas managed to stand straight again, but almost as soon as he did the second attack came in. A straight punch to the face, it came in fast, but Thomas managed to step to one side and the agent's fist went right past Thomas' head. Thomas clenched his own fists and hit the agent in the chest with a right. The agent went over and Thomas followed it with a left hook, which knocked the agent down.

Shaking his hand, Thomas walked off the mat and back towards Gracie, who was smiling at him.

"Nice work, Thomas" she said, and stood to greet him. She reached down and held his hands, taking off the mitts for him.

"Thanks Grace." he said. The Lieutenant walked over to them.

"That was good, both of you" he said. "No more today." He walked away from them and out of the door.

An hour later and they were both showered and Thomas met Gracie in the mess hall. As she walked in he was sitting in the centre of the room, with no one else around. She walked up and sat in front of him.

"Big thing, all of this" he began. "I never thought in a million years that Jon would, or even could, do this." he picked up a cup of coffee.

"I know" she replied smiling. "And I never thought that I would be in Victorian London chasing after Jack the Ripper. What he's done is amazing, and there's so much that can be learnt from it. If we're careful!"

He smiled back. "Always the optimist" he said. "You're right though Grace, and we can do so much with this gift that Jon has given to us." she reached forward and held his hand. His eyes moved up to look at her.

"Hey guys!" Jon's voice came from the entrance of the mess hall. "Oh, sorry. Have I disturbed something?" He froze in the doorway.

"No Jon, come in" Gracie said, and released Thomas' hand. She gave him a smile, which he returned with interest.

"Cool" Jon said and walked in. He took a seat next to Gracie. "So, Lt Big Bastard has told me you're doing very well in the combat classes" he said jokingly.

"Apparently so" Thomas said, leaning back.

"Excellent" Jon replied. "Because we're jumping

back to 1888 tonight." Gracie looked at him.

"Tonight?"

"Yep. The military want this Ripper thing sorted in the next couple of days. Just in case he fucks history up and destroys everything."

"You have a remarkable way with words" Thomas replied. Gracie stood up and pushed her chair under the table.

"Well, I guess I'll go get things ready" she said. She walked out the room. Thomas' eyes followed her until the door had closed behind her. Then they moved to Jon, who was watching Thomas with a smile.

"What?" Thomas asked. Jon laughed.

"I know you, Tom" he began. "So, what's the story with you and Gracie?"

"Don't know what you mean mate. We've become good friends." Jon laughed again.

"And like I said Tom, I know you!"

Thomas looked away and smiled. Time to change the subject.

"Come on, there's work to do" he said and stood up. He walked past Jon and out of the room. Jon put his arm around Thomas.

"What are you doing?" Thomas asked, shrugging the arm off.

"Sorry, would Gracie be jealous?" Jon said, and laughed out loud.

CHAPTER 4

"September 30th 1888" Jon said to the scientist who was standing near the control station. "Put us near Dutfields yard, Berner Street. At about midnight." He looked at Thomas, who had joined them. "Is that right?"

"Yeah, that's cool" Thomas replied, and they both walked up the steps to join Gracie. The agent wasn't going along this time as he said he had other things to do. As the three of them stood there the huge barrel of the machine started to spin and the sound of crackling and humming was almost deafening. After the countdown, with smoke bellowing from the burning orange platform, they were gone. There was a loud bang and a crack and they appeared in what seemed to be an old derelict house. The jump had destroyed a wall and the rubble was everywhere. Looking around, there was no furniture or anything of value.

Thomas waved his hand in front of his face to try and clear the dust and debris away from the jump. Jon, who was wearing the old coat again, walked to the smashed window and looked out. It appeared that the old house was in a street. There was a brick archway just to the right of the house outside the window, and a sign on it: Berner Street.

"This is the right place" Jon said, still peering out.

"Yeah, but it's a good job that nobody lives here" Thomas said, still dusting himself down. Jon looked down at the display screen on the inside of his arm.

"Its just after midnight" he said and turned away from the window.

"The first victim was Elizabeth Stride, she was found at about 1 am" Thomas said. "In Dutfields yard. It shouldn't be far from here." He checked the mini map on the device, which lit up bright blue. "Yeah, out of here, take a right and we're there."

At that Jon heard a noise behind him in the street. He turned around to see a man standing with his back to the window. They all ducked down quickly and quietly. The man was talking to a woman and they could hear the conversation clearly. The woman stepped to one side and Thomas could see her easily through the broken window. She was slim and must have been in her forties. It was Elizabeth, he thought. And the man, obviously, was the murderer.

"So, you like grapes?" he said, very well spoken.

"I love 'em sir" the woman replied and placed her hand on his arm. He stroked her face with his gloved hand and ran his finger across her lips.

"We could make this a more permanent arrangement" the man continued.

"I'd like that" she answered. Thomas could see that she would have been quite beautiful in her youth.

"Shall we?" the man said and put his arm around

her as they started to walk off. Jon got to his feet and tiptoed to the window to see them disappear under the archway.

"Was that the victim?" he asked Thomas.

"Yes, I think so" he answered. Jon stuck his leg out of the gap where glass would once have been and stepped outside.

"Wait" Thomas whispered, and he got up and went to the window, followed by Gracie. Jon had already got to the archway and Thomas stepped out to get to him. Jon looked around the corner, not seeing anything but hearing a noise coming from an opening a few feet away. He glanced up at the sign above the entrance - Dutfields. This was it, he thought.

He stepped out of the shadow of the arch and made his way to the opening, putting his back flat against the wooden fence. He heard the rustle of clothing and a gurgling sound. Plucking up his courage, he peered around the fence. All he saw was the back of the man squatting over what was clearly the woman.

"Jon!" Thomas whispered down the passage. "Come back!" Jon turned to face Thomas and as he did so he stumbled to one side. The killer looked round and got to his feet. He still had a long, curved blood-soaked knife in his hand. Jon knew the killer must have heard him and decided to run back to Thomas, who was under the archway peering out. As he reached him, Thomas grabbed Jon and pulled him into the darkness. Just as he disappeared around the corner, the killer came out of the yard and looked in both directions. He wiped the blade with a cloth, tucked it away into his long coat and put the cloth in his pocket. He stared in Jon's and Thomas' direction for a few seconds and then strode off the other way.

"Don't do that again" Thomas said, holding Jon by the old coat he was wearing. Gracie came over to them.

"Has he gone?"

"Yes" Thomas answered. "To the next victim, Catherine Eddows. He clearly killed her because he was disturbed here and couldn't finish what he started. Now we have to get to Mitre Square." He looked round to Gracie.

"It's OK Thomas" she said to him, touching his hand. "This is how history remembers it. And that's what we're here to do. We have to make sure that history doesn't change. Not even a bit."

"I know. Thanks Grace" he said, then turned to Jon. "Its all right Jon. You did good."

"I did?" Jon replied.

"Yes" Thomas said and patted him on the arm as he walked past. Gracie followed him down the alley and towards the Dutfields yard. Jon quickly came up behind her and they made their way down the passage. As they approached the entrance to the yard, Thomas turned to Gracie. "Just look forward and keep going. Don't look in the yard, and don't stop."

She nodded her head and walked past Thomas to the end of the alley without taking her eyes from where she was going.

"Go on" Thomas said to Jon, and gestured for him to do the same. Jon put his head down and stared at the ground, then walked quickly towards Gracie, who was waiting for them both. Thomas stepped forward and stopped at the entrance. He couldn't help himself. He slowly moved his head to the right and his eyes took in the lifeless body of the woman. With an overwhelming sense of sadness he whispered quietly, "I'm so sorry". Then he turned and walked on.

Jon had activated the map on his arm. "Mitre Square isn't that far really" he said, tapping away on the glowing blue panel. "If we stick to the alleyways and the side streets we stand a good chance of not being seen."

"OK, you lead the way Jon" Thomas said. Jon closed down the device on his arm and peered out of the passage. There was another alley straight opposite them, but the street was getting busy. Three men and a woman walked past, clearly drunk. They were followed by a group of soldiers wearing red military jackets.

"OK" Jon said. "It's clear." Jon gave one final look both ways and then ran to the cover of the opposite alley.

"OK, go!" Thomas said to Gracie, and she ran to join Jon. Thomas checked to his right and began to run out. As he got to the centre of the street he looked to his left and suddenly saw two of the soldiers standing right next to him. Thomas stopped in his tracks. The military men were very drunk. They looked Thomas up and down. He stared back.

"What the fuck are you wearing?" one said to him.

Thomas didn't answer. He was thinking quickly. Jon drew his pistol and clicked off the safety switch.

"Are yer stupid or something?" the other man said to him. Again Thomas didn't reply. The soldier to the right had a bottle in his hand and he gripped it tightly. The other pulled from his belt a large knife. Without thinking, Thomas kicked the man with the knife in the knee, while the other man swung the bottle at Thomas' head. He ducked and punched the man in the side of the ribs. The man bent over double. Thomas gave him another punch to the jaw and he fell back flat to the ground, out cold.

The other man hobbled towards Thomas and thrust the long blade forward. Thomas stepped to the side and struck the man in the throat, then dropped the knife and held his neck. Thomas drew back his fist and planted a massive haymaker right on the soldier's nose. The blood spattered up his face and he fell down to the floor and lay next to his comrade, both out for the count.

Thomas stepped over them and walked to the shadows, where Gracie and Jon had watched the fight with awe. Gracie laughed.

"That was amazing!" she said to the victorious Thomas.

"Yep, pretty cool Tom" Jon said, placing the gun back in its holster. "Those combat classes came in handy then."

"Yes thanks. But I think we should leave here before someone else comes or they wake up" replied Thomas.

"This way" Jon said. Thomas and Gracie followed him though the maze of alleyways and poorly lit back yards. Suddenly Jon stopped.

"Did you hear that?" he said. They listened intently. The sound came again. A high pitched whistle.

"It's a policeman's whistle" Thomas said. The noise came again and again, and there was more than one whistle this time. There seemed to be at least four or five.

"They must have found the victim" Gracie said.

"Yes" Thomas replied. "We can't hang around. We're almost at Mitre Square." He walked quickly past Jon to the end of the alleyway. There was a sign opposite saying "Mitre Square". Thomas looked in both directions and ran for it. He got to the street and pushed his back to the brick wall. Jon and Gracie followed him.

"Look" Thomas said, pointing to another street sign. "Goulston Street. That's the street" he said and walked quickly over to it. He peered down the lantern-lit street. There was nobody around. Thomas stepped into the street and began to walk down it slowly and quietly, followed shortly by Gracie and Jon. There were doorways on either side and oil lanterns hung around the walls. A pile of clothes lay just outside one of the houses. A wooden sign hung above the door saying 119 Wentworth Dwellings, and they walked towards it carefully. Thomas knew that this was the location of the next murder. As he got closer he saw what appeared to be a pile of clothing on the floor.

"My god" he said. He turned to Gracie and said.

"Don't look." But it was too late, she had already seen. It was not a pile of old clothes but the badly mutilated body of Catherine Eddows. There was a bloody piece of cloth next to her, with a few coins and what looked like part of her anatomy. Thomas had to fight the vomit back as he surveyed the crime scene.

Suddenly a noise came from the other end of the street. They all ran to the end and hid behind a fence. They could hear police officers talking.

"It's all right" one officer said to the other. "Abberline's on his way. He reckons he knows who the murderer is."

"So, we'll catch that bastard tonight then?" his colleague replied.

"Definitely" the first officer said. The two men walked off in the direction of the first killing. They clearly didn't know about the second yet. Thomas looked at Jon.

"We can't let them catch him tonight, or at all" Thomas said desperately. "If they catch him it'll change history. We can't allow that. We have to stop him and take him back home."

"We need to put them off the trail" Jon replied.

"I know what to do" Thomas said. "Grace, you stay here and keep a look out. Jon, follow me." They both hurried back to where Catherine's body lay.

"Have you still got those things from the man in the Ten Bells?" Thomas asked.

"Yeah, I didn't take them out" Jon replied. Thomas

held out his hand. "Give me the chalk" he said. Jon reached into the pocket and pulled out the small piece of chalk and gave it to Thomas. Thomas started writing on the wall just above the victim. After he had finished, he stepped back. Jon looked at the words.

"You've spelt Jews wrong" he said to Thomas. Thomas just stared at the graffiti on the wall.

"I know" he whispered. "Because history tells it that way." They gave the corpse a final glance, then ran back to where Gracie was waiting.

"What have you been doing?" she said impatiently.

"Making history" Thomas simply replied. In the distance they could see a group of policemen running towards them blowing their whistles.

"Come on, this way" Jon said. The three of them ran across the crowded street, nobody taking any notice of them. They were all probably too drunk. They got to the street opposite and ran to a back yard, where they stopped for breath.

"OK" Thomas said. "I think it'll lay out now the way history tells it."

"Our work for the time being is done" Gracie said, patting Thomas on the arm.

"Let's go back" Jon said, touching the blue panel on his arm. "We could do with the rest." Thomas and Gracie followed suit and activated the recall buttons on their arms. With a loud bang and a blue flash, they were gone, leaving the wooden fence that stood next to them in pieces on the floor and the ground underneath them smoking and glowing orange.

★ ★ ★ ★ ★

Thomas spent much of the next two weeks studying the theory and practice of time travel. Jon happily gave his friend class after class on dark matter and how to use it to create a wormhole through time. Thomas took notes and examined the machine in detail. Gracie helped him of course, for there was nowhere else she would rather be.

On the evening of the 30th July 2027, Thomas returned to his dorm after a long and busy day. He hadn't told anyone that it was his birthday. He would rather have been doing his work and studying than celebrating just another day getting older, and besides, he didn't want the fuss. After having a long shower he went back to the main dorm and switched on the TV. He lay on his bed staring at the screen, not really taking in the programme. His mind was on other things, like the machine, catching the Ripper, the next jump. And of course, his delightful assistant. He was just starting to nod off when he heard a knock at the door.

"Who the hell is this?" he muttered to himself as he got up.

"Hey Thomas!" Gracie said as he opened the door.

"Oh, Gracie, it's you! You OK?" he said. She looked at him confused, with her head cocked to one side.

"Do you really think that nobody knew it was your birthday?" she said, handing him an envelope with his name written on the front. He smiled at her as he opened it. It said "To the best boss ever, happy 37th birthday. lots of love, Gracie x".

"Thank you" he said, still looking at the card. "Do you want to come in?"

"Actually, I've come up here to fetch you" she said. He looked at her in confusion, and with a certain amount of dread.

"What do you mean, Grace?" he asked.

"I'm warning you because I know you don't like surprises" she started. "Jon has organized a party for you in the mess hall."

"Really?" he said. "You are joking?"

"No I'm not. Come on, they're waiting, even Agent Summers is there. It won't be that bad anyway." He looked at her as he slipped his shoes on.

"You've never been to one of Jon's parties, Grace" he said. They walked out and got into the elevator. At the next floor down, the doors opened slowly and they walked out towards the mess hall in front of them.

"Now act surprised" Gracie said as they got to the door. He closed his eyes and prepared himself. Pushing open the door he was greeted by a shout of "Happy birthday!". He put on a surprised expression and walked in.

"Well, you! This is a surprise" he said. Jon stepped forward and hugged his friend tightly.

"Many happy returns, Tom" he said.

"Thank you Jon, did you sort all this out?" he asked, looking to Gracie and giving her a wink.

"Of course I did" Jon replied. "Couldn't let my friend go through his birthday without celebrating it, could I?"

Everyone came over in turn to wish him a happy birthday, and even the stern looking Agent Summers shook his hand. "Happy birthday Dr Long" he said.

"Thank you" Thomas replied. Jon led Thomas further into the room. There was an array of different foods set up on one of the long tables and on another vast quantities of alcohol. Jon took a plastic cup from a stack and started to pour Thomas a drink.

"Thank you" Thomas said, taking the full cup from Jon.

Hours later, after much food and drink had been consumed, most of the staff were either drunk or had to go back to their dorms. Jon was slumped in a chair, his head tilted right back and snoring loudly. Thomas was sitting on the balcony with his feet resting on the rails. The door opened and Gracie walked out. Thomas looked round at her with a smile, taking his feet down. He leaned forward and pulled out a chair for her.

"Thank you" she said. "So, that didn't go too badly did it?"

"No. I guess not."

"I'm kind of nervous about the jump tomorrow" she said.

"We'll be fine" he answered. "It's not like we haven't done it before"

"I know. But tomorrow we'll be catching the Ripper" she said, staring out towards the city.

"We'll be fine Grace, I promise."

"But if something bad was to happen, I kind of want you to know something. You're much more to me than a boss now. You're my friend, my best friend. And what I'm trying to say is, that I care about you."

She took in a deep breath and waited for his reply. For what seemed like ages he stared at her, eyes fixed on hers and taking in every word she spoke. He so desperately wanted to tell her that he felt the same, but he found it hard conveying his feelings to others; he always had. Which was why none of his past relationships had lasted.

He stared at her. "I know what you mean Grace" he said, and swallowed. "I mean. I won't let anything happen to either of us. You have my word." She smiled at him, knowing full well how he felt about her. She knew him better than most other people. She got to her feet "Happy birthday, Thomas" she said. He smiled and touched her hand, and she walked to the door.

"Thank you Grace" he called after her. She turned back and smiled, then she was gone and the door swung shut. "For everything" he muttered under his breath. He stared back out to the lights of the city, a broad grin on his face.

★ ★ ★ ★ ★

The next morning Thomas was up early, and by the time everyone else had stirred from their beds he had got his equipment together and put his suit on. He walked out into the large room, where a few of the scientists were walking around, checking the machine over for the all-important jump.

"Is everything OK?" Thomas said to one of them as he approached. The woman turned to him.

"Oh yes sir. Ready when you are" she said. Thomas smiled and nodded and walked to the machine. He crouched down and looked at it closely.

"Morning doctor" came a voice behind him. He turned to see Agent Summers all dressed up in his conduit suit and ready to go.

"Oh, I didn't know that you were joining us this time" Thomas said.

"I have to be there if we are capturing the test subject today" said Summers. "I am a law enforcement officer, and only I can arrest him." Thomas noticed that the agent had his hand on the butt of the pistol in the holster.

"I see" Thomas replied. "Well, let's hope it goes smoothly"

"If you'll excuse me doctor, I have things to do" the agent said. He nodded to Thomas and walked towards one of the side rooms.

Then Gracie appeared. She had just got ready.

"Morning Thomas" she said.

"Hi Grace" he said, not taking his eyes off the agent. She turned to see what he was looking at.

"Something wrong?" she asked.

"I don't trust him" Thomas said. "People like him tend to be volatile and unpredictable at best. We'll have to keep an eye on him."

"I agree" Gracie answered. At that the door opened and Jon walked in.

"Sorry I'm late everyone. Didn't feel too good this morning. I'm fine now though" he said, walking past the scientists.

"I don't suppose that would have anything to do with the drink last night, would it?" Thomas said, grinning at Jon.

"No, no. Just a headache" he said, tapping Thomas on the shoulder. Thomas looked at Gracie and they both laughed.

"What's so funny?" Jon asked.

"Nothing Jon. Are we ready now?" Thomas asked.

"We most certainly are" Jon replied.

"You know that Agent Summers is coming this time?" Thomas said, looking concerned.

"Yeah, I know. He has to come, apparently" Jon replied. At that the agent came strolling back to them, still with his hand on his gun.

"Ready Dr Walker?" he asked.

"As I was just saying agent, we're ready to go" Jon said. The humming of the power filled the room and blue sparks were shooting from the spinning barrel. The four of them walked up the few steps and on to the platform.

"One more thing agent" Jon said, turning to

Summers. "You are in charge of the arrest of the subject only. Everything else is down to us."

Summers said nothing. He was staring at the barrel as it spun faster and faster. Jon turned to Thomas and winked. The room seemed to shake and the humming became louder. Blue sparks shot between the machine and them, and as the countdown got to one, there came the loud bang and flash.

★ ★ ★ ★ ★

"Where are we?" asked Agent Summers.

"I'm not quite sure" Jon answered. Looking around, they seemed to be in an old, dark building of some sort. Gracie took out her torch and shone the beam around the room. There was rubble lying around from the jump, but nothing else gave them any inclination of where they were.

"Look, there's a door" Thomas said, pointing over to the corner of the room. Jon walked over to it and put his head next to it. He couldn't hear anything the other side, so he decided to open it. It creaked open easily and Jon peered around. He saw coffins lying around the room, some stacked on top of one another. He peered into one. There was the body of a man inside it.

"I think we've landed in an undertakers" Jon said.

"Oh great" Thomas said. Jon walked into the room, quietly followed by Thomas and then Gracie. Summers came in after them, pistol drawn.

"Would you please put that away? All the people in here apart from us are dead, so you won't be needing it" Thomas said, feeling quite irritated by the agent's presence. Summers glanced at Thomas and clicked his weapon back into its holster. Gracie walked over to another door, which was locked.

"Use the cutter on the lock" Jon whispered. She took out the small device and clicked it open. She pointed it at the door handle and pressed the button. The searing red beam cut through the old metal with ease, and she pushed open the door to reveal the shop entrance.

Jon walked past her and went straight to the window. The undertakers seemed to be in a side street. There were oil lamps every few yards. A man and a woman passed, followed by two scruffy-looking men. Thomas activated his arm panel; it was the 9th of November 1888, 2 am.

"The killing could happen any time now" he said. "The fifth victim, Mary Jane Kelly, was found at about 10:45 in the morning, so there's no exact time for her death. We have to get there soon, if we want to catch the subject."

"I agree" Summers said. "How do we get there from here?"

Thomas turned his attention back to the panel on the inside of his arm.

"It's not very far from here" he said, still looking down at the blue-lit device. "It's about a mile away. There are a few alleyways we can use to get there, but this area is quite busy at night time."

"We'll get there" Jon said, still looking out the window. Gracie went over to the external door that lead out to the street. It was locked. Again she pointed the cutting device at the handle and the beam melted its way through. She opened it carefully and peered out. The two scruffy men had stopped at the end of the street. One was speaking to the other while he pissed against the wall. She crept out slowly and pushed herself flat to the wall just outside the doorway. Thomas followed her.

"They're going" he said, peering past her.

"Look, over there, near the street lamp" she whispered, pointing over to what looked like a side gate that stood open. The street was fairly wide but they thought they could make it if they were careful. Jon came out, followed by Summers.

"OK, I'll go first" Thomas said. He looked both ways and saw nothing. He ran as fast as he could. Reaching the gate, he looked round to see if anyone had seen him; it was clear. Gracie followed him, then Jon. But as Summers was about to run, the man and woman came back. The agent slipped back inside the undertakers. The others slipped into the yard and behind the wooden fence.

Summers looked through the window of the shop. The scruffy men had returned and were following the man and woman, gaining in speed. This looked like trouble, he thought. Then one of the men ran forward and took out a knife.

"Give us yer fucking money!" he hissed. The man pushed the woman behind him to protect her, but the other attacker came up from behind. He grabbed the woman and pulled her close to him, holding a short blade to her throat. He laughed out loud.

"Whatcher gonna do now, hey?" he said. The woman was crying and trying to get away from the man, but he held her tightly.

"Please, please. We don't have any money!" the man was pleading.

"Oh, that's a shame" the first man said, running the knife down the man's face. The woman began to cry uncontrollably.

Just then Thomas ran out. The first man looked to his right to see Thomas coming at full pelt towards him. He raised the knife, but it was too late. Thomas was on him. He punched the man hard on the jaw and the man dropped like a felled tree. Thomas turned to his right, drew his pistol and aimed it straight at the other man, who suddenly dropped the woman and ran the other way.

Thomas put the safety back on the gun and clicked it back into the holster. The man helped his woman to her feet and held her close to him. He looked at Thomas, at the way he was dressed and the strange-looking weapon. He had never seen anything like it before.

"Thank you, friend" the man said. Thomas nodded, and the man and woman hurried off towards the city. The agent ran out.

"What the hell was that?" he said furiously. "I

thought we weren't meant to interact with people in this time?" he said. Gracie and Jon came out.

"I'm sorry, I couldn't let that happen" Thomas said. Jon walked over to him.

"We have to be careful, Tom. You know this!" he said.

"I know, sorry Jon." Jon shook his head, but he was smiling. They all walked back to the yard leaving the injured attacker lying on the ground. Gracie held on to Thomas' arm, and he turned round.

"I thought that was brave and the right thing to do" she said. Thomas smiled at her. Then Jon called over "This way". Thomas and Gracie walked over. There was an alleyway that lead to the street.

"We can nip through here" Jon said. The alley was only wide enough to go in single file. They made their way to the end, Jon first, followed by Gracie, then Thomas and finally the agent. Jon looked around the corner to see a tavern at the end of the street and a large group of people outside, laughing and talking loudly. In the other direction, there was a black two-horse carriage coming their way. Jon ducked his head back inside the alley and watched the carriage go past. Just up the street he could see a row of houses and flats. Next to them was a gate, Jon checked the digital map on his arm.

"There" he said to Thomas. "That gate leads to the backyards of those houses. At the end we can jump the fence, and then there's a back street opposite."

"OK" replied Thomas. "We need to go quickly, and

all together this time." Jon nodded and looked round at Gracie and Summers.

"Ready?" he said. They all ran out at once. Jon got to the gate first and pulled it open, then Gracie ran straight through and Jon followed her. Thomas looked around to see Summers stumble and fall. Thomas instantly stopped and ran back to help him back to his feet. They both ran back and got to the gate just before a large group of men walked round the corner next to the yard.

"That was real close" Jon whispered. They made their way through the maze of back yards and outhouses until they got to the end fence. Thomas peered over to the street. He could see an unhorsed carriage, but nothing else.

"It's clear" he whispered.

"Give me a hand" Jon said. Thomas held his hands together for Jon to step on and he pushed him up. Scrambling over the fence, Jon jumped down to the other side. Gracie followed him and he helped her land. The agent put his hand on Thomas' shoulder.

"I want to thank you for coming to my aid earlier" he said.

"That's OK" Thomas replied. He was surprised that the agent had even mentioned it.

"You go now" Summers said, and held out his hands. Thomas placed his right foot on them and the agent pushed him up. He landed and Summers gripped the top of the fence and pulled himself up. Thomas and

Jon reached up to help the agent over. Thomas looked around and saw what he was looking for.

"There" he said and pointed to a street sign – 'Dorset Street'. He looked around the corner and saw nobody. The others followed him down slowly, looking in every nook and cranny. Thomas noticed an archway to the left with a sign saying 'Millers Court'.

"There" he whispered. "That's where Mary was killed." Opposite there was an opening to another property. Thomas walked over to it and peered round the corner. There was a yard and a building that was clearly not being used. Thomas walked in and shone his torch around. Gracie followed.

"We can hide in here until the killer comes" Thomas said. Gracie nodded and gestured for Jon and Summers to come inside. Thomas had already forced the door open. It was a single-room flat with no furniture. The others came in and Gracie closed the door behind them. One of the window panes was missing, so the slightest noise could be heard from outside.

"Now what?" asked Summers.

"We wait" replied Thomas, standing at the window with his arms folded.

★ ★ ★ ★ ★

Jon looked down at the time on his arm; 4 am. Thomas was sitting under the window, listening intently. Summers was sitting against the far wall, repeatedly clicking the ammunition clip in and out of his gun. Gracie was nodding off to sleep.

"It could have happened already. We might have missed him" Jon whispered over to Thomas. There was no reply. All Thomas' attention was on the outside. He could hear footsteps from the street, and they were getting closer. Thomas got to his knees and peered out of the window. He could just make out the entrance to Millers Court. The footsteps got even closer; two people. He stared out into the dark alley, and then suddenly two people walked past and into Millers Court. They stopped briefly just inside the entrance and Thomas recognized the man's voice. It was their target.

"You have beautiful blonde hair, my dear" the voice said. Thomas gritted his teeth. He knew the fate of this poor girl, but could do nothing to stop it. But he could bring the monster to justice, and soon.

"Why, thank you sir" she replied. Thomas listened to her voice. She was so young. Next he heard a door close, and the sadness flooded his soul, for he knew very well what would happen to her.

He sat back against the wall below the window. Jon came over to him. He put his hand on Thomas' shoulder. "Soon, my friend" he said.

Gracie was now wide awake, and she came and sat right next to Thomas. Looking at him, she held his hand tight.

"Come on you bastard!" the agent said, standing at the window now, his weapon drawn.

Two hours passed. Jon checked the time; 6 am.

"Could he have got out another way?" he asked Thomas.

"He's still in there" Thomas replied, his mood darkening.

"We should prepare ourselves" Summers said. "Get into position. I'll wait at the entrance to the street round the back to cover there. Thomas, I want you round the side of the girl's flat, so he can't get out that way. Gracie, you stand in this yard here and cover us with your pistol."

He turned to Jon. "As it was you who sent him here, Dr Walker, I think it should be you who confronts him and brings him down" he said. Jon smiled and nodded.

"Everyone ready?" Summers, said looking at them in turn. They all nodded. "Good. Move out."

They all took their positions as instructed and waited. Jon was standing just inside the archway, and could see the front door to number 13, the girl's flat. A dim light could be seen through the covered window. He looked to the side of the building; Thomas was there, looking impatient. Jon looked at the time: 06:27. He must come out soon, he thought, it'll be getting light in the next hour or so.

At that he heard a noise from the front door. It opened slowly. A man stepped out, a tall man in a long black coat. It was their target. The man turned slightly and took one final glance inside, smiled knowingly and closed the door. Now's the time, Jon thought. His heart was racing and he could feel his arms and legs shaking with the rush of adrenalin.

Now! He stepped out of the darkness. The man turned round, looking shocked to see someone there. Jon took a step closer. The man stared at him, smiling in recognition.

"Ah, Dr Walker. What a pleasant surprise to see you here" he said.

Jon took another step forward. "We know what you've done, and we're here to take you home" he said. The man looked around. He saw Thomas walk from the side of the building and then behind him, Agent Summers. Then Gracie walked slowly out of the yard with her gun pointing straight at the killer.

He looked back to Jon.

"This was my destiny Dr Walker, you must realize this" he said. "Who would have known that I would become the most famous killer of all time, the feared Jack the Ripper? And of course, it's all thanks to you. You sent me here, after all."

"That's enough!" Jon said.

The killer laughed. "Touched a nerve have I, doctor?"

"We're leaving now" Jon said. "We can do this the easy way or the hard way."

"Oh, Dr Walker. Do you not want to admire my work first before we go?" the killer said gesturing to the door of the flat.

"The world knows what you did in there" Jon said, and he reached for his pistol.

"Don't worry doctor, you won't be needing that" he

said, and turned to Gracie. "And you won't need yours either, my dear" He pulled his arm up. He was holding a small bunch of grapes, about five or six of them.

"Do you like grapes?" he said to her, and with that he was knocked to the floor, and Thomas was standing over him with his fists clenched tight. Thomas drew his foot back and kicked him in the stomach and chest, again and again. Thomas' teeth were bared and spit was flying from his mouth with every kick,

Suddenly Gracie grabbed him and pulled him back. She held Thomas' face and pulled it to look at hers.

"Thomas!" she yelled. "No more!"

He began to calm down. She pushed him back against the wall, still with her hands on his face. His colour had started to return. He stared into her eyes.

"It's OK" she said. "It's over." She cradled his head close to hers. She looked back to the Ripper. Summers was putting on the handcuffs. Jon had his gun trained on him, but the Ripper just lay there laughing although blood was spraying out of his mouth and his eyes almost closed from the beating.

Jon clicked his pistol back into the holster and helped Summers lift the Ripper to his feet. They dragged him into the yard opposite Mary's flat.

"Come on" Jon called over to Gracie and Thomas. They followed behind, Gracie holding Thomas' hand tight.

"Ready?" Jon asked.

"Wait. He's not wearing a suit. The jump back might

kill him" Summers said, still holding the killer by his arm.

"Agent Summers" Jon began. "This man is responsible for one of the most horrific serial murders of all time. I really don't give a shit if he survives or not."

Summers looked at him, and then to the killer. Blood was still coming from his wounds. He looked back to Jon.

"Fair enough" the agent said. Jon nodded and clicked the panel on his arm and the others did the same.

"Ready?" Jon said. Thomas gave the door to Mary's flat one final glance, knowing full well what horror was inside. The blue flashes came. Sparks shot from them to the walls of the yard. The ground under their feet started to heat up and then they were gone, leaving Victorian London and the brutal history of the Whitechapel murders behind.

CHAPTER 5

It had been almost three months since the jump back to 2027. The Ripper had been incarcerated, and the general mood in the facility was good. Thomas looked forward to jumping to a time where he could study the people instead of hunting down a psychopath. Jon had promised him that they could go to one of Thomas' specialized times, the Middle Ages or the Dark Ages.

Thomas sipped his drink. The lighting was dark and the sound of the soft jazz in the background was relaxing. A man and a woman walked past him, laughing, and his mind went back to Whitechapel, and the couple who he had saved from being mugged, or worse. They would have been dead now many years ago, he thought to himself. Then his mind went back to the victims of the Ripper. He couldn't have stopped that. History must remain the same. But the realization that in fact it was he who was responsible for some of the historical facts in the Ripper case got to him. He thought about it frequently, finding it both remarkable and disturbing. He drank down the last of his beer and put the empty glass back on the bar.

"Another one please" he said to the barman. The

man nodded and started to pour a fresh one from the pump. He scraped off the white frothy head and slid the glass to Thomas.

"Thank you" he said and took a sip.

"So what part of England are you from?" asked the barman. Thomas just looked at him.

"Your accent?" the barman said.

"Oxfordshire" Thomas replied with a smile. The barman's eyes lit up.

"Oh, do you know Robert Smith?" he asked excitedly. Why is it that because England is small, people think we all know each other? Thomas thought.

"No, no I'm afraid not" Thomas replied politely.

"Oh, no matter" the barman said and walked off. Thomas took another sip from the cold glass, and suddenly his mobile started to ring. He took it out of his pocket and looked at the screen. It was Jon. Thomas clicked the button and held the phone in front of him. Jon appeared on the screen, looking in a panic.

"You OK Jon?" Thomas asked.

"Well, not really Tom" Jon answered. "Can you get back to the facility as soon as please. I need you."

"Why, what's happened?" Thomas asked, confused.

"We've had a security breach. Please just get here Tom" said Jon. and hung up. The screen on the phone went black and Thomas slipped it back into his pocket. He took another sip of his beer and got up off the stool. Taking a 20 dollar bill from his pocket, he left it on the bar and walked out. It was dusk and the lights of the big city lit up the night sky.

"Hey" Thomas called waving his hand to a taxi. The cab pulled over and he got into the back seat.

"The military facility, just outside of town" he said to the driver, who was confused and unsure where the facility was. Thomas gave him directions, and within forty minutes they pulled up at the front gate. Thomas handed over the money and got out. He reached inside his jacket and pulled out his ID card, which he held up to the security guard standing outside the hut. Thomas walked in and made his way over to the main building, and at that a man came running over to him. It was one of the scientists.

"Dr Long" he said, out of breath. "Please, Dr Walker is expecting you. This way" And the man ran back towards the large building. Thomas quickly ran after him. What sort of trouble Jon had got himself into this time?

The scientist had made his way to a door Thomas had never been through before. He turned around and waved for Thomas to go in. As he approached, Jon came out of the door and closed it behind him. He glanced up at Thomas and shook his head.

"What's wrong?" Thomas asked him eagerly. "You said something about a security breach."

"Yeah" Jon started. "Something bad has happened."

"What?" Thomas asked.

"I'm afraid our trip to the Dark Ages will have to wait, Tom. We found out this afternoon, just after you left, that a few of the security officers had been planning something. Agent Summers and I went to question them."

"And?" Thomas interrupted.

"They were already gone."

"Gone where, Jon? What's happened?" Thomas was desperate.

"Apparently, they came up with a get-rich-quick scam. They planned to jump to another time and steal gold and treasure. Bring it back here and live like kings."

"And they've already jumped?"

"I'm afraid so" Jon said, leaning back against the wall now. Thomas looked at him.

"How do you know this?" he asked.

"One of the scientists heard them talking about it in one of the dorms. We managed to capture the officer who helped them. He operated the controls while the others jumped." He gestured to the door. "He's in there. Agent Summers is questioning him."

"Do we know where they've gone?" Thomas asked. Jon looked down at the floor, his face quite grim.

"To Germany, 1943. We think they've gone looking for stolen Nazi gold" he said.

Thomas took in a deep breath and shook his head. "Jon" he said. "I'm no expert on wartime Germany I'm afraid. I wouldn't be much good to you there. I take it you are going after them?"

"Yes we are" Jon said. "And Gracie says she's coming too, to help."

Thomas looked at Jon with anger in his eyes.

"Gracie doesn't know a lot about wartime Germany either" he said. "So please don't drag her into yet another one of your mistakes!"

Jon moved away from the wall and stepped closer to Thomas. "She's coming because she wants to help. I didn't even ask her" he replied. "And besides, like you've said before, we can't let history change. At all. And these fools that have jumped might do something to change history." He opened the door. After taking a final glance at Thomas, he walked in and closed the door behind him. Thomas leaned against the wall and stared at the ceiling.

"Hey" he looked round to his right. Gracie was standing there. "You OK Thomas?" she asked.

"Not really Grace. What's this I hear about you going with Jon to catch yet more crooks?" he said sarcastically.

"We have to stop them, Thomas. They could do some real damage where they are." She took a step closer.

"We're not the goddamn time police, Grace. We're scientists. Archaeologists! We were meant to jump to different times to study, not catch every nutter that Jon decides to send back."

Gracie looked at him disappointedly.

"I thought you wanted to make a difference" she said.

"I'm a scientist, Grace, not a fucking superhero!" he snapped. She stopped for a second and took a breath.

"Back in Whitechapel, when we caught the Ripper, the way you attacked him, the anger, the passion you put into every blow. You did that because you cared about what that monster had done. You wanted him punished."

Thomas closed his eyes and calmed himself. "I know Grace. But I also did what I did because of the way he looked at you" he said. He began to walk off in the direction of the elevator towards the dorms. She watched him all the way, right until the doors had slowly closed. Taking a step forward, she knocked on the door of the interview room.

"Enter" came the voice of Agent Summers. She opened the door and walked in. Summers was sitting in a chair opposite the handcuffed security guard. Jon was leaning against the wall at the back of the room. Jon looked at her. She could see in his eyes that he wanted to hear that she had persuaded Thomas to go with them. She shook her head, and he looked back at the handcuffed guard.

"So, officer Smithfield" the agent said. "You have no more to tell us?"

The guard shook his head. "No sir. I've told you all I know."

"And, of course you were going to be paid by the others for your part in all of this" the agent said.

"Yes sir" the man replied.

"How much?" Jon said. The guard turned in his chair to face him.

"I'm not sure doctor. Depends how much the others got" he said.

"So, it's only the five of them involved?"

"Yes sir."

"And the names?" the agent said.

"Carter. Ford. James. Bolton, and" the guard took a breath. "Lt Mackenzie." The agent glanced up at Jon, and they made eye contact for a moment.

"Thank you Smithfield" the agent said and stood up. He opened the door and gestured for two officers to come in.

"Take him to the cells!" he said. The two guards took an arm each and lifted him up. Gracie stepped to the side as they dragged the man out and down the corridor. She looked over at Jon.

"Now what?" she asked.

"We go after them before they cause too much damage" the agent interrupted.

Jon looked at Gracie. "Tom isn't coming, is he?" he asked.

"I'm not sure" she answered. Jon walked past her, not being able to hide his disappointment.

"When do we leave?" she asked the agent.

"The machine will be ready first thing in the morning" he replied, and followed Jon down the corridor. She stepped out of the room and watched them go their separate ways.

She walked into the mess hall and went over to the coffee machine. She took a full cup, went out on to the balcony and took a seat. Thoughts were racing through her mind, about Whitechapel, the jump to wartime Germany tomorrow. And of course Thomas.

"You OK?" A voice came from the door. She glanced round. It was Jon. She looked back towards the city with disappointment.

"Yeah, I'm fine" she answered.

"The machine will be ready by seven am tomorrow" he said, taking a chair next to her and looking out to Washington.

"Good."

"I know you want Thomas there tomorrow but…"

"I need him there Jon!" she broke in. He looked back out to the lights of the big city. "Me too" he said.

She put her cup down and stood up. "Well, early start tomorrow" she said and walked to the door.

"Good night Gracie" he said as the door closed.

After an hour or so of contemplation, he went back to his dorm for much needed sleep. Tomorrow after all, was another big day.

★ ★ ★ ★ ★

"We're ready to go whenever you are, Dr Walker" the scientist said, walking over to him. Jon nodded at the man. He had his suit on ready and clicked his pistol into place.

"Do we have the coordinates, doctor?" the agent asked him as he approached Jon.

"Yes agent. The last place and time used on the

machine are automatically saved. The last place was the Eiffel region of West Germany. The date used was 1943" Jon said. The agent nodded, and at that Gracie walked over to them, all suited up and ready to leave.

"No word from Thomas?" Jon asked eagerly. She shook her head with disappointment.

"OK, are we ready then?" Agent Summers asked, starting to walk over to the platform. He was carrying an assault rifle.

"Do you really need that?" Gracie asked him. The agent turned, looked at the rifle and then up to Gracie.

"We're going to Germany, in the middle of the Second World War. So yes, I think I might need it." he answered her sarcastically.

"OK" Jon said. "Let's go." the three of them walked up the steps and on to the platform.

"Start the countdown" Jon called over to the man standing at the control station. And at that the door to the elevator opened and Thomas stepped out. He was wearing his conduit suit. He walked over to them and up the steps.

"Glad you could make it" Jon said, hardly able to control the relief in his voice. Gracie just looked at him, with the biggest smile. He looked back at her, returning the smile. She took a step closer to him and gripped his hand.

"Ready!" Jon said. The countdown started, the blue sparks shot from the machine barrel. The humming became louder, and then came the familiar bang.

★ ★ ★ ★ ★

"Where are we?" asked Summers. They looked around. All that could be seen were trees. The ground beneath them was glowing from the heat of the jump, and the trees closest to them were burning.

"Looks like we're in the middle of a forest" Thomas said, looking around warily. Jon took a few steps from the burning crater and shone his torch.

"What time is it?" Gracie asked.

Thomas looked at the display panel on his arm. "02:14 am, 4th August 1943" he answered.

"Look" Jon said suddenly. "Over there!" he ran a few feet to their left. There was another crater. The ground was blackened from the burning, but cold.

"It's at least a day old now" Jon said.

"They could be anywhere" Thomas said, looking around. Jon put the beam of the torch on the ground. There were footprints leading away from the crater and up to a hillside.

"That way" he said. They started to run up the slope and towards the hill. As they approached the top they heard the sound of marching.

"Get down" Thomas whispered. They all lay flat on the ground. The sound became closer, and then it stopped. They heard talking, very clear, and in German.

"Sie, kam das Schiessen vom Schloss" said the first voice.

"Sie dienen nicht dazu die Ausbildung heute Abend. Ist etwas falsch?" came the reply. "Jetzt gehen. Schnell!" the second voice said again.

The men started to march away again, in the direction of the hill. Thomas looked up. He could see the soldiers walking up a muddy pathway, and in the distance a large stone building could be seen.

"What did they say?" Gracie asked Thomas. He was good at languages and fluent in many European dialects.

"They said something about there being some shooting at the castle. And that it's not training and to hurry up there" he answered her. The agent came over to them and sat down next to Thomas.

"That could only be the rogue security man" he said. "We're going to have to be extra careful now, if those German soldiers are on their way up there."

"Yes" answered Thomas. "We're going to have to try and not be seen. The last thing we want is to get into a fight with them."

Summers nodded and turned to move up the hill to get a better look. Jon followed him, and they lay close to the ground and looked up towards the towering stone walls of a castle.

"I'm so glad you're here" Gracie whispered to Thomas. He looked round at her.

"I wouldn't be anywhere else" he said, and smiled at her. He helped her up and they made their way over to where Jon and Summers were. The agent pointed over to a row of trees along the right-hand side of the footpath.

"We can go that way" he said. "Move along the tree line and stay out of sight."

Thomas nodded. "I can go first, make sure the coast is clear" he said.

"OK" the agent replied.

"Be careful though Tom" Jon said.

Just as he was about to move up the hill and towards the trees, Gracie gripped his arm. He turned and looked into her face.

"I'll be fine Grace. Promise" he said. "I'll see you in a sec." He turned around and ran for it, up the hill and into the trees. The hill was a lot steeper than he had thought and the muscles in his legs burned. He got to a large tree and knelt down. The castle was close now. He could see the main gate. It was large. Two of the soldiers were standing outside holding their rifles up close to them. The left-hand side of the gate was open. He moved up to the next tree and lay down so as not to be seen.

"Ich frage mich was zum Teufel ist denn da?" said one of the soldiers.

"That was 'I wonder what the devil is going on in there?' Thomas whispered to the others.

The other soldier answered him.

"Ich furchte zu denken" he said.

"I dread to think" translated Thomas. He slowly moved back down the treeline and out of earshot of the two men. He switched on his communicator and spoke into it.

"Thomas to Jon" he whispered.

"Go ahead Tom" Jon answered.

"Stay where you are, we're not getting in this way" Thomas finished.

"OK, received that Tom." Thomas switched off and turned around, but just then he heard something right behind him. He turned quickly and saw the two soldiers standing next to the tree. They looked shocked and bewildered. Probably at what Thomas was wearing.

"Stoppen!" the one said. Thomas did as he was told and put his hands in the air.

"Nicht bewegen!" the younger one said. Thomas wasn't about to move. The men's rifles were pointing straight at Thomas. The younger man walked behind him and pushed him forward.

"Bewegen!" he said. Thomas followed the other soldier up towards the castle, the other man just behind him, pushing him every now and again. Jon, Gracie and Summers watched in horror.

"What the fuck are we going to do now?" Jon said, holding his head in his hands.

"We go after him!" Gracie said, and she got up and ran towards the tree line.

"Oh shit!" Jon said. He had no choice but to get up and run after her. Summers got to his feet and lifted his rifle up. He turned it on its side and pulled back the slide. A bullet clicked into the chamber and the blue-lit display appeared on the side. He grunted and ran up the hill after them.

The soldiers led Thomas through the huge gate and into a courtyard. There were other soldiers there, and they turned to look at him. They began muttering to each other, and pointing over to him. A tall man stepped forward, he was wearing a long black coat and a flat hat with a skull in the centre. This man was clearly in charge. He walked up to Thomas, his eyes wandering all over the suit. He prodded Thomas' chest, and felt the material of the strange uniform.

"Guten Tag" the man said as he circled Thomas, looking at the suit with intrigue and wonderment.

"Hello" Thomas said in a low hushed tone. The man stopped in front of him.

"Ah. You are English?" he said in a rough German accent. Thomas nodded.

"Yes sir" he said.

"And you are a spy?" the German officer said, still not taking his eyes from the suit.

"No sir, I'm no spy" Thomas replied. The officer turned to one of the soldiers next to Thomas.

"Nehmen sie ihn in das Büro nur in der Seitenansicht der Eingang" he said, Thomas knew he had asked the soldier to take him to an office inside the entrance of the castle. The soldier pushed Thomas and he started walking, the barrel of the soldier's gun in his back.

"Do not push our guest around so" the officer said in English, clearly for Thomas' benefit, not knowing of course that Thomas could speak German. The soldier looked back at Thomas, then gestured with his rifle for him to walk forward. They walked through a large wooden door and into a main hall. There were portraits hanging on the walls and large tapestries. A shiny suit of medieval armour stood next to a grand staircase. Thomas looked around. There were bloodstains on the floor and bullet holes in the walls. The soldier opened a door just to the left of them.

"In there" he said. Thomas walked inside. The large office had a desk placed under the barred window, and to the left, a display case with swords on display. The soldier pulled out a chair and gestured to Thomas.

"Sitzen!" he said, and Thomas sat down. The soldier walked out of the room and stood with the door wide open. What the fuck was he going do now?

At that the German officer walked in. He took off his cap and then his coat and put them down carefully on a chair next to the door. He then waved his hand for the soldier to move away, and as he did so the officer closed the door. He walked past Thomas and over to a cabinet, then opened it up and took out a glass and a bottle of what looked like port.

"Would you like a glass?" he said to Thomas. Thomas shook his head. The officer shrugged and started to pour himself one. He took a sip and then placed the glass on the desk. He then gestured to Thomas.

"Please to remove your weapon. We do not want accidents" he said. Thomas reached to his side and undid the catch holding his pistol in place.

"And, please don't do anything brave!" the officer added. Thomas glanced at him. He could shoot the man dead right now if he wished, but then he would have to fight his way through the rest of the troops. Thomas clicked the gun out of its holster and placed it on the desk next to the glass of port. The officer stared at it. What kind of a weapon was this? It was far more advanced than anything he had seen before. He looked back at Thomas, and of course, the suit he was wearing.

"Who are you?" the officer said. Thomas looked up at him.

"Nobody, sir" he said. The officer stared at him, and then looked down at the gun. He picked it up and his eyes moved all over it. He flicked the safety catch off. It beeped, and the neon blue light came on at the side. He moved the gun around with wonder.

"It is a remarkable weapon" he said. Then he looked at Thomas. "The armour you are wearing, and this pistol. What kind of technology is this?" Thomas didn't answer. He did not know what to say. The officer sat down on the other chair, right opposite Thomas. He placed the pistol back down on the desk and then leaned on his hands. For a moment he just stared at Thomas. Thomas stared back.

"Are you an alien?" the officer asked. Thomas looked at him. He almost smiled, but resisted it.

"From out of space?" the officer asked.

"No sir, I'm no alien" he said.

The officer stood up quickly and yelled at him.

"Then what are you?" he shouted.

Thomas looked him in the eyes. "I'm from the future" he said softly. The officer stared at him. His eyes moved back to the gun, and then back to Thomas.

"How is this possible?" he asked.

"I'm not really sure myself" Thomas said.

The officer sat back down again. "And are you responsible for the deaths of every soldier who was stationed in this castle?" he asked.

Thomas looked at him. He knew it must have been the security guards that had done it.

"No sir. I am not" he said, and at that there was a gunshot from outside, then another. Then all hell broke loose. The officer got to his feet and pulled his Luger pistol from its holster, then ran to the door and opened it. The soldier had gone.

Thomas saw his chance. He jumped up from the chair and grabbed the gun from the desk. The officer turned quickly round and pointed his pistol at Thomas. There was a ringing gunshot and a muzzle flash, and the officer dropped to the floor.

Thomas stood there for a few seconds, the barrel of his pistol smoking. He moved slowly over to where the German officer was lying. A pool of blood had started to spread from his chest. This was the first time Thomas had ever had to take a life, and he didn't like it. He felt guilt mixed with anger, as well as relief that it was he who was still alive.

More gunshots sounded from outside, as well as the

louder sound of a fully automatic weapon. He peered around. He ran quickly to the door and pushed his back right against the wall, his gun ready. The shots were coming from the courtyard just outside. As he looked around the door he saw Nazi soldiers desperately trying to get a better shot at their enemies. As one man tried to run across the yard the automatic weapon went off again and the soldier was cut down, blood spraying from large wounds in his chest. Thomas tucked his head back inside. There was a scream as another of the soldiers went down. Jon, Gracie and Summers must have come for him, he thought.

He looked round the door again, trying to get a glimpse of them. He stared out across the battlefield of the courtyard. Another Nazi took a shot to the head, went down and was quiet. The shooting had stopped. Now there was just the smoke from the guns and the bodies of the soldiers. Thomas walked out slowly, his gun still at the ready. But then he heard voices, and not the voices he wanted to hear. He looked around frantically. There was a side door open just to his left, and he ran for it.

"Carter, check the perimeter!" said a voice. Thomas peered round the door. Five men came into view, wearing conduit suits. Shit! It was the rogue security team. He pulled his head back inside the cover of the door.

"Yes sir!" Carter answered, and he ran off towards the main gate. Thomas watched him, and then, seeing some movement just to the right of the gate, his eyes moved across. It was Gracie, Jon and the agent, peering up from a trench along the side of the entrance.

"Sir, there's nothing here" One of the security men said. Thomas moved back in as the voice sounded closer.

"I'm aware of that, thank you Bolton" came the answer. "They must have moved it elsewhere."

"Lt Mackenzie, there's still one alive." Thomas looked round, seeing one of the security guards standing over one of the Nazi soldiers, the young one who caught him earlier. The young soldier tried to crawl away, but the man put his foot down on his back to stop him moving. The huge lieutenant walked over to him.

"Well well" he said, towering above the soldier. He bent down and turned the soldier on to his back. His shoulder was pouring out blood. Mackenzie bent down.

"Where is the gold, boy?" he said holding the soldier by the collar. The young man looked terrified and didn't answer. Mackenzie grunted and threw the man back down.

"What shall we do with him sir?" the security guard asked. Mackenzie looked down at the young man, who was now crying with pain and fear.

"Prepare to leave" Mackenzie said, and the guard walked off to the others standing over by a truck. Mackenzie didn't take his eyes from the young soldier. He clicked his gun from his belt, pointed it at the man's head and fired. Thomas closed his eyes at the sound of the gunshot. Poor boy, he thought. He opened them to see the lieutenant walk towards the truck. He got into the passenger side and the truck started. Fumes shot out of the exhaust and the vehicle began to move off, through the large gate and down the muddy path.

Just then Thomas saw Jon, Gracie and Summers get out of their hiding place. Summers looked out of the gate to make sure the truck was leaving. Thomas walked out of the door and over towards them. As Gracie saw him she ran over to him and threw her arms around him. He held her tight, as Jon walked over to them.

"Thomas, are you all right?" he said. Thomas nodded, letting Gracie go.

"Yeah, I'm fine Jon" he answered. At that the agent came over.

"Dr Long, I'm so glad you're OK" he said and shook Thomas' hand.

"Thank you Summers" Thomas replied. They stood there for a few moments looking at the carnage around them.

"My god!" Jon said. "They've killed everyone."

Thomas shook his head. "I know" he said.

"Did they hurt you?" Gracie asked Thomas, looking up at him.

"No, I'm fine" he said. "They did question me though, asked me where I was from, even asked if I was an alien." Jon looked at him and smiled.

"And what did you say?" he asked.

"Told them the truth" Thomas answered. Jon laughed, and Gracie smiled. Agent Summers turned around.

"We need to be extra careful now" he began. "I wasn't aware of the firepower they had brought with them."

"We could jump back" Thomas said. "Get a larger team together, and then come back?" But the agent shook his head.

"The last thing we need is to draw even more attention to ourselves. The smaller our group the better, we just have to plan our move and be careful."

Jon nodded in approval. "I think Summers is right" he began. "We'll look around this place first, there must be some indication of where they sent the gold. And where the gold is, Mackenzie will almost certainly be."

"Yes, Mackenzie isn't stupid, he'll find the gold. And when he does, we'll be there to take him down" the agent said.

"OK, well we better start searching this place if we're going to find out where the gold has been taken" Thomas said, looking at each of them in turn.

"We should split up into pairs" Jon said. "Summers and I will start on the upper levels, Thomas, you and Gracie start on the main floor, keep in touch with the communicators and inform one another if we find anything." They all nodded and made their way into the main hall. Jon and the agent walked up the huge staircase as quietly as possible. After all, someone might still be up there.

"Shall we start in here?" Gracie asked, walking over to the office where Thomas had been held.

"Wait" he said, there's something in there."

"What?" she asked him, just stopping outside the half closed door.

"Gracie, I had to kill someone." he looked her in the eyes. "I had no choice, he was going to kill me."

She walked closer to him. "Thomas, it's OK, I understand. You or him" she said, then looked over to the door. "Is he in there?" she asked. Thomas just nodded. "Come on" she said and took his hand. They approached the door and she pushed it open slowly. The body of the Nazi was lying where he had fallen. She walked around him and into the room.

"I'll try the desk Thomas, you try the cabinet over there" she said, pointing over to the far wall. Thomas walked over and pulled open the door to the large cabinet. There was a drinks decanter, a Luger pistol and a pile of paperwork. He took out the papers and moved over to the desk where Gracie was.

"I'll start sifting through this" he said. She nodded, going through the drawers. All the paperwork, Thomas noticed, was invoices from prisoner of war camps and train times.

"Anything?" Gracie asked him.

"Nothing about gold" he answered. She handed him a piece of paper with handwriting on it.

"Can you translate this?" she asked. He took the paper from her and scanned through it.

"It says that the train to Leipzig will be there at 15:00, yesterday" he said. "I wonder what that's about?"

"It may be important, better hold on to it" she said. They took one final look around the room, and deciding it held no more secrets they walked out, leaving the dead Nazi where he was. Thomas closed the door after them and they walked out to the grand staircase and looked around.

"Over there" Thomas said, and pointed over to another door. She looked over. It was quite a large door with heavy brass fittings.

"Come on" she said and they walked over to it. Thomas tried the handle, but it was locked. Of course it would be, he thought.

"The cutter" she said. Thomas looked down to his belt and clicked off the little device. He switched it on and pointed it at the lock. The red beam did its job and the handle glowed and popped open.

"Stand back" he said and drew his pistol. He took a step back and then kicked the door wide open, it was dark inside. Gracie took out her torch and shone the beam into the room. There were boxes and crates stacked up, and along the far wall, row after row of rifles. Thomas stepped in, reached around the corner and switched the light on.

"Wow" he said. "Looks like an armoury." They both walked in. There was a large table just to the left with boxes of what looked like paperwork in them.

"Better get to work" Thomas said, and they walked over to start sifting through the documents.

"Do you see anything?" asked Jon.

"No" the agent replied, scanning the hallway and pointing his rifle straight in front of him. They walked down a bit further. There was a doorway just to the left of them. Summers moved round and stood with his back to the wall, his gun held close to him. He signalled for Jon to open the door, he drew his pistol and pushed it open. The moon was shinning through the window which lit up the room. On the far wall was a portrait of Hitler, and on the wall opposite a flag of a swastika. Summers walked in, his weapon still pointing forward, and Jon followed him.

"The switch by you, flick it on" the agent said. Jon turned round and switched on the lights. There was a desk just below the portrait. Summers moved over to it. His eyes glanced at everything sitting on the wooden desk, but nothing stood out. As he was about to move away, he noticed that there were hinges on one side of the portrait. He looked at it closely.

"Hold this" he said to Jon and handed him the rifle. He ran his fingers along the other side of the picture and found a switch. He flicked it up and the portrait swung slightly away from the wall. He looked at Jon and smiled. Pushing the portrait open, they saw that there was a small safe planted in the wall.

"This'll get through it" Jon said and took out the cutting device from his belt. The beam melted through the lock and the door popped open. Summers waved the smoke away and moved the door to see the contents of the hidden safe. There was more paperwork in there, plus a small box and a bar of what could only be gold.

"Wow!" Jon said as the agent took out the bar. "Is that real?"

"I think so doctor" replied the agent. He took the papers and the box and placed them on the desk next to the gold. Jon picked up the documents and held them up.

"It's all in German" he said. "Thomas will have to translate." Summers picked the small box up and looked at it. It was a wooden box covered in black velvet. He opened it. Inside was a large key, made of gold by the look of it.

"I wonder what that's for" Jon said as the agent handed it to him. It was heavy, and there was German lettering down the side.

"I'll call Thomas" Jon said and gave the key back to Summers. Then he switched on the communicator on his arm and spoke into it.

"Thomas, I think you'd better come look at this" he said.

""Yeah, received that Jon" came Thomas' reply.

"Where are you?" Thomas whispered down the hallway. Jon's head poked out from the doorway.

"In here" he replied. Thomas and Gracie walked into the room. Thomas glanced up at the portrait of the dictator. "Charming" he muttered to himself. He walked over to the desk and Summers handed him the key. He held it up to the light.

"Wow, is it real gold?" he asked.

"Looks like it" Summers replied. "Can you read the

writing on it?" Thomas held it close to his face, the words were clear. 'DEM REICHTUM DER JUDEN!'

"It says 'to the riches of the Jews'" Thomas said and handed the key back to Summers. Jon looked at Summers and then to Thomas.

"It has to be a key to a safe, or something like that" he said.

"Is that gold?" Gracie asked, looking down at the bar of gold sitting on the desk.

"It certainly is" Jon said, picking up the heavy bar. He handed it to her and she stared at it.

"Wow" she said simply. Summers picked up the papers on the desk and gave it to Thomas.

"These papers were also in the safe" he said. "Can you translate them?" Thomas took the pile of papers from the agent and sat down at the desk. He began flicking through them. There didn't seem to be anything of significance until he got to one piece. He held it up and read it closely.

"Anything?" Summers asked.

"Yeah, maybe" Thomas said, and he took the paper from his belt which he and Gracie had found early.

"On this piece, which we found in an office downstairs, it says that a train left here yesterday going to Leipzig, and this document from the safe is talking about a large underground bunker in the Leinawald forest."

The agent looked at him. "And?" Summers asked.

"Leinawald forest is near Leipzig" said Thomas. The agent nodded.

"OK" he said. "Looks like we've found our next destination."

At that they heard a sound coming from the hallway. Summers picked up his assault rifle and moved round the desk, pointing the weapon at the open door. Thomas stood and drew his pistol, then put his hand on Gracie's arm and pulled her behind him. Jon walked quietly over to the door, his gun held up. He nodded at the agent, who then moved straight out of the door and into the hall. He checked both ways, but could see nothing.

Jon followed him out. The agent gestured for him to move down the corridor. Jon walked slowly down towards the large staircase, followed by Summers, and then the sound came again, from a room to their left. Thomas and Gracie came out to see what was going on, and Summers pointed to Thomas to move against the wall. He did so and Gracie followed him.

As Jon walked over to the door, the noise came again. He looked back at Summers, who pushed himself flat against the wall next to the door, nodding at Jon. Jon reached down and tried the handle - locked. The agent nodded again and moved to where Jon was standing, then took a step back and kicked the door wide open. He and Jon ran in, their weapons pointing forward, scanning the room. It was dark and nothing out the ordinary stood out. Thomas peered around the corner, Gracie holding his arm tightly.

"See anything?" he whispered. Summers put his hand up to signal for silence. They could see movement behind a curtain. Summers pointed over to it and Jon slowly and quietly walked over. Jon stood next to the curtain, his hand on it, ready to move it. He looked back at Summers, who was standing right in front of it, his rifle aimed forward. He nodded to Jon and Jon pulled the curtain back as fast as he could and took a step back.

Behind the curtain was a girl. She was crouching down and covering her head with her arms. Jon took a step closer and reached down. He gently touched her arm, and suddenly she started screaming and shouting.

"Nein, nein, bitte nicht weh!" she shouted out. Jon turned around to Thomas, who walked over to the girl. She was young, maybe 17 at the most.

"Beruhige dich, wir werden dich nicht verletzen. Ich verspreche es" Thomas said to her calmly.

"What did you say to her?" Jon whispered to him as the girl began to calm.

"I told her to calm down, and that we won't hurt her" Thomas said, still not taking his eyes from her. She looked up at him, and he gave her a warm smile.

"You are English?" she said in a German accent. Thomas nodded to her.

"Yes I am, and my friend over there" he said gesturing over towards Gracie.

"And these two men are American." She stared at him, looking at the others and the clothes they were all wearing.

"Who are you?" she asked. "You don't look like soldiers."

Thomas shook his head. "No, we're not soldiers" he said. "We're here to take some men back to where we live, the men that are responsible for killing everyone in this castle."

"Your clothes are strange" she said, still looking at them. Thomas just smiled at her. What's your name?" he asked her.

"Edda" she said quietly.

"Nice to meet you Edda, my name is Thomas" he said. "You can come and sit on the chair if you like?" she nodded her head and got to her feet, Jon pulled out a chair, and she sat down and pulled her skirt down to cover her knees.

"You speak very good English, Edda" Thomas said to her, taking a seat opposite her.

"My father taught me" she replied.

"And is your father here?" Thomas asked.

She shook her head. "Nein - I mean, no sir" she answered.

"And what are you doing here Edda?" Thomas asked her. She looked away and a tear rolled down her cheek.

"The soldiers took me" she said, wiping her face. "My father owed the general a lot of money and couldn't pay him, so he took me." Thomas looked at Gracie.

"Where do you live Edda?" Gracie asked her.

"In the next village, it's about five miles away, but I can't go back, the general will kill my family" she said with terror in her voice.

Thomas shook his head. "Everyone here, including

the general, is dead now Edda, there's no one to stop you going home" he said and smiled at her.

"Really?" she said enthusiastically, smiling at him. Summers came over to Thomas and whispered in his ear. Thomas nodded, then looked back to the girl.

"We can take you home, we are going that way" he said.

She smiled. "That would be wonderful, thank you sir, thank you" she said. Thomas gestured towards Gracie.

"Stay with this lady, she'll look after you" he said and the girl walked over to where Gracie was standing. Gracie put her arm around the girl's shoulder and they walked out the room. Jon patted Thomas on the back.

"Regular hero aren't you?" he said and laughed. Thomas smirked at him.

"Yeah yeah" Thomas replied.

"Look" Summers said. He was looking through the window. Thomas and Jon walked over to him. There was a long black car parked around the side.

"We can use that" Summers said. Thomas nodded. "Yeah, let's get down there before more Nazis come."

They made their way out and walked down the staircase, Gracie still with her arm around the girl. The agent led them out and into the courtyard. "It's this way" he said, and they ran towards the end of the building. As they turned the corner, they saw a gate which was slightly open.

"I'll get it" Thomas said and he ran over to it and

pulled it fully open, the agent was crouched down, his rifle at the ready.

"There's the car" Jon said and ran over to it, followed by Thomas and then Gracie and the girl. Summers stayed where he was to keep a look out. Jon lifted the handle of the door and it opened.

"Bit of luck" he said. Thomas opened the back door.

"Get in" he said to Gracie. she gestured for the girl to go first, then climbed in. Thomas walked around the other side and got into the seat next to Gracie and the girl.

"Can you start it?" Thomas asked, leaning forward to ask Jon, who was sitting in the driver's seat.

"Yeah, no problem" he said, the concentration visible on his face. The engine started.

"Got it" Jon said. He turned the vehicle round and drove it out of the small gate and into the courtyard. Summers got up and ran to the car, opening the passenger side door and getting in.

"OK, go" he said. Thomas turned on the device on his arm and the mini map was activated.

"Go out of the main gate and follow the road" he said. "We'll pass through the village on the way." Jon put his foot on the accelerator and they sped out of the large gate and down the muddy road, The lights of the village could be seen through the trees.

"There" Edda said, pointing. Jon took a right turn at a crossroads and soon enough they were entering the little village.

"I live just down there" the girl said, pointing down a side road. They could see the lights of a house about half a mile away. Jon drove the car slowly as they approached. The front door opened and a man stepped out, obviously curious to see who was visiting him at such an hour. He had a shotgun in his hands. The car slowly came to a stop and Thomas got out. the girl quickly followed and ran over to her father.

The joy on his face was obvious. He dropped the gun and held her close to him, then they spoke for a few moments and he looked over at the car. He nodded and put his hand up to Thomas. Thomas raised his hand and got back into the car.

"OK, let's go" he said. Jon moved the vehicle off slowly, back down the narrow road and to the village, then took a right and drove through the centre of town. It was quiet, and nobody was around.

"OK, we're going the right way" Thomas said, looking down at the digital map. They had driven about six or seven miles when Jon suddenly stopped the car.

"What is it?" Gracie asked him. He pointed down the road.

"A road block" he said, and sure enough, just at the bottom of the road there was a hut, with a barrier across, blocking the way.

"Shit, now what?" Thomas said. Two Nazi soldiers stood there. They had noticed the car and one started to walk up towards them.

"What shall we do?" Gracie said. Summers clicked the

safety off his rifle. "Jon" he said. "Put your foot down."

Jon looked at him. "What?" Jon said.

The agent opened his window all the way down. "I said, drive. Fast. Go through the barrier!" he said. He hung out of the window, his rifle gripped tightly in both hands. The Nazi soldier stopped and raised his gun. Shots rang out and two bullets went through the windscreen, missing their targets. Summers returned fire, with his much more advanced assault rifle. The soldier went down, riddled with bullets, and the other Nazi took cover behind the hut and started shooting. Jon slammed his foot down, the wheels spun round, flicking mud up, and then the car shot off, racing towards the barrier.

"Get down" Thomas said to Gracie, holding her close to him and ducking down, keeping as low as possible. Summers was still firing, the bullets ripping through the little hut like paper, and then with a loud crash the barrier was smashed into pieces. Jon kept his foot firmly on the pedal and they screamed down the road, the soldier firing his rifle at the rear of the car. The agent came back in, clicked the ammunition clip out of the gun and replaced it, slamming it into place. He looked at Jon, and smiled.

"Well done doctor" he said. Jon glanced over at him but didn't answer. He was too busy keeping the car on the road.

"Everyone all right?" Thomas asked. Gracie lifted her head back up.

"Yeah, I'm good" she said. Thomas nodded to her and gave her a smile.

"We'll have to find somewhere to rest, it's a long drive" he said, looking back at Jon and the agent.

Summers turned to face him. "Agreed, anywhere safe on the map?" he answered. Thomas looked at the neon panel.

"Yeah, about ten miles away there's a side road, it leads to a wooded area, we can rest there" he said, and shut down the device.

CHAPTER 6

The sun had started to appear above the horizon.

"We're almost there" Thomas said. Houses could now be seen across the fields, and there was a church just down the road, Jon noticed.

"The turning should be around here somewhere, keep an eye open" said Thomas. The road had begun to get narrower; if a vehicle had come the opposite way, it couldn't have passed. They drove on. The trees to the left of them had become fewer and more spread out and a rocky cliff could be seen in the distance.

"Here" the agent said, and pointed to the left. They saw a muddy pathway. Jon turned the car and drove down the path.

"Take it slow, we don't want to get stuck in the mud" Thomas said, tapping Jon on the shoulder.

"No worries" Jon answered and he carried on down the winding dirt track. The cliff was now getting closer and the wood was becoming denser, the trees blocking out the sunlight. The path began to get wider and soon opened up to a large area where the road was blocked by the towering cliff before them. Jon stopped the car and Summers got out to take a look around. The area seemed very remote. The only sound came from the wind blowing through the trees and occasional bird song.

"It looks safe enough" Summers said, and the others got out.

"Looks like a path over there" Jon said, pointing over to a small pathway that appeared to lead up the cliff.

"I can go and check it out" Thomas said. "Get a better view from up there."

Jon nodded. "Do you want me to come with you?" he asked, but before Thomas could answer, Gracie butted in.

"I'll go" she said. She took hold of Thomas' arm and began to lead him over to the rocky pathway. Thomas glanced at Jon on the way past and gave him a smirk. Jon smiled.

"OK then, we'll wait here then. Set up camp or something." Thomas raised his hand as he and Gracie walked away. The agent pointed over to the base of the cliff, where there was an alcove with some boulders dotted around.

"We can rest over there" he said.

Jon looked over. "Yeah, should be OK, I don't think many people are going to be coming through this way anyhow" Jon said as they walked over towards the cliff.

"Be careful Grace" Thomas said, as Gracie ran up the rocky slope. "The last thing we want is for you to fall."

She looked back at him. "Come on, it's perfectly safe" she said, smiling. They made their way up the narrow, steep slope. Thomas looked down. They were about thirty feet up. The black car could be seen and the tops of the trees were just becoming visible. "We're almost there" Gracie said, and they scrambled up a bit further.

Thomas looked down from the top of the cliff. It didn't seem as high as it had from the bottom, but the whole area could be viewed from where they stood. There were houses dotted around, farmhouses, Thomas thought, and in the distance a town could be seen. The wood seemed to go on for miles. The cliff ran down to a river.

"We'll definitely see if anyone comes from here" Thomas said, still surveying the area. Gracie nodded.

"It is beautiful though" she said and glanced at him. He turned his head slightly and gave her a smile.

"We can sit down for a bit" Gracie said, gesturing to a flat rock. She stepped over to it and sat down. Thomas followed and sat down on the floor just by her feet.

"You didn't really want to come here, did you?" she asked him. He glanced up at her.

"Not really. I was kind of looking forward to visiting the Dark Ages, or somewhere I know about" he answered.

"But you came anyway" she said. "You're a good friend to Jon, you came when he needed you, and I know he thinks a lot of you."

Thomas looked out over the countryside. "I came because of you, Grace" he said. There was silence for a few moments, and she looked down at him with a warm smile and put her hand on his shoulder.

"What do you mean?" she asked him softly. He turned to her, his eyes looking straight into hers.

"You know what I mean" he answered, reaching to take her hand. She leaned down towards him, not taking her eyes from his. Their lips touched. The kiss seemed to last forever, and they would have both happily remained like it for an eternity. They moved their heads back, and again their eyes met. She smiled at him and he touched her face with his hand.

"You know how I feel" she said, flicking her blond hair away from her face.

"I know" he answered. "I feel the same."

"I'm starting to get hungry" Jon said to Agent Summers, who was sitting on the floor and leaning against a boulder, his rifle on his lap.

The agent looked over at him. "There's not too much we can do about that at the moment" he said. "We'll try and get something later, when it gets dark again. Try one of the houses maybe."

"I was thinking" Jon said. "Maybe we should jump back. We can freshen up, get something to eat and then jump back to Leinawald forest. It'll be a lot easier."

The agent looked at him. "You're right" he answered. "We'll leave when Dr Long and Miss Stevenson come back down." He looked up at the cliff. Gracie was now sitting on the ground next to Thomas, her head resting on his chest and his arm around her, holding her tight. Then Thomas noticed something along one of the lanes.

"Did you see that?" he said, sitting up.

"What?" she answered, and she moved her head up to look out. Thomas got to his feet and scanned the area. He pointed.

"Over there" he said, and sure enough, over to the north, there was a small farmhouse and on the lane that led to the house was a convoy of what were obviously Nazi trucks. The red, white and black swastikas could be seen clearly on the sides of the vehicles.

"I wonder what their doing?" Gracie said.

"I'm not sure" said Thomas. "I don't imagine for a second that it will be good news for the occupants of the house though."

"We should go back down, let Summers and Jon know what we've seen" Gracie said, holding Thomas' arm. He nodded and they made their way down the steep and narrow pathway. It didn't take as long coming down as it had going up, and before they knew it they were at the bottom. Jon walked over to them.

"Hey, we've thought that maybe we should go back home to get freshened up and return to the forest later, what do you think?" he asked them as he approached.

"Yes, I agree" Thomas said. "We saw a few Nazi trucks going towards a farmhouse, it's not far from here."

Summers came over to them. "Really?" he said. "How many?"

"About five or six" Thomas said. The agent looked at Jon.

"OK, we should definitely jump back, they could come this way and we wouldn't stand a chance" he said.

Jon nodded in agreement. "Yeah, we should get the hell out of here" he said. "You two cool with that?"

At that the sound of gunshots rang across the whole area, birds were startled out of the trees and the shots echoed around them. Thomas looked back at Jon.

"We should go now" he said.

"I guess" Jon replied, and they made their way over to the clearing, all switching on the devices on their arms.

"Ready?" said Jon. They all nodded. "Now!"

But nothing happened. Thomas looked over at Jon.

"Try again" Jon said. They all pressed their recall buttons on the panels but again, nothing happened.

"Why the fuck aren't they working Jon?" Thomas said, getting frustrated.

"I don't know" said Jon, panic in his voice. "The devices are working, so it must be some problem back home."

Thomas walked over to his friend. "Jon, can we communicate with the lab back home, send a signal or something?" he asked.

Jon looked around, thinking hard. "Yes, sure we can. I can just reprogramme my device to send a signal, and they should be able to send one back and let us know what's happing there." There was more optimism in his voice.

"OK, do that then" Thomas answered.

"I'll do it now, it might take a few minutes" Jon said. He went over to the car.

"Thomas, what are we going to do if we can't get back?" Gracie asked.

"Try not to worry, Jon will sort it" he said, glancing over at his friend, who was tapping away on his arm panel.

"I have every faith in Jon" she said. "But we don't know what's happened at home, in our own time. Something bad might have happened"

"Try not to worry, we'll get back."

"I think we should go up to the top of the cliff" Summers said, looking up. "We'll be safer up there and we can see what's coming."

Thomas nodded. "You're right" he said, and ran over to Jon. "Jon, we're going up there" he said, pointing up to the cliff. "It'll be safer." They quickly made their way up the rocky path towards the top, followed by Jon.

"See anything?" Gracie asked as they stepped on to the top.

"Looks like the Nazis are leaving that house" Thomas said, pointing over towards the convoy going back down the lane away from the farm. Summers came and stood next to Thomas.

"I wonder what they were doing?" the agent said, looking out at the vehicles.

"I dread to think" Thomas replied. He looked over at Jon, who had perched himself down on a rock and was still working on the device on his arm.

"Any luck Jon?" Thomas asked him. Jon just shook his head. "Not yet, almost there" he said. Gracie sat down, and Thomas looked over at her.

"Are you OK?" he asked.

She glanced at him and smiled. "I'm good" she replied.

"There!" Jon suddenly shouted. "I've done it, the message is sent. We just have to wait for a reply now." He looked up at Thomas, pleased with himself, and Thomas patted him on the shoulder.

"Well done mate, I knew you could do it" Thomas replied. Gracie hadn't reacted to Jon's news, and Thomas wondered if she was really OK. He walked over to her and sat down.

"What's up?" he asked. She looked round at him.

"He's sent the message back home, yes, but what if they don't answer?" she said, the worry almost getting too much. She looked away from him and he put his hand on her face, making her look at him once more.

"Gracie, we'll get back. You have my word" he said, and gave her a smile. She smiled back and then placed her head, again on his chest.

"I'm so glad you're here Thomas" she whispered softly. He rested his head on hers. "Me too" he answered.

Jon looked up at the agent and gestured over towards Thomas and Gracie. Summers looked round at them, then turned back to Jon and smiled. Jon's stomach had started to rumble.

"This couldn't have happened at a worse time" he said to Summers. "I'm starving."

The agent rested his rifle against a rock and sat down next to Jon.

"It'll be dark soon" he said. "If the lab hasn't been in contact soon, I think we should go looking for food. And I know just the place." He pointed over towards the little farmhouse the Nazis had left. Jon looked back at him.

"What if someone is there?" he asked.

"I'm guessing there won't be anyone to see us. We'll go straight across the field."

Jon nodded and glanced back down at the device, hoping that a message would come soon. Thomas put his head back down and glanced at Gracie's face. Her eyes were now closed, fast asleep. She was so beautiful, he thought to himself. He rested his head on hers once more.

An hour went past, two hours, then three, and still no word from home. It was now almost dark and a steady breeze was blowing through the trees. Summers got to his feet and stretched his legs.

"We should go soon, give it another half hour" he said.

Jon stood up next to him. "Yep" he replied.

Gracie started to wake. Her eyes opened slowly and she glanced up at Thomas and smiled.

"Hey" he said softly.

"Hey" she replied.

"Good sleep?"

"The best, with you to lean on. I listened to your heart and it sent me to sleep" she answered with one of her warm smiles.

At that Jon came over. "Sorry to disturb you guys, but we're going to go down to the farmhouse, see if we can get some food" he said, crouching down next to them.

"Oh great, I'm starving" Gracie said, stretching her arms.

"Tell me about it" Jon answered.

"I got a feeling nobody will be home anyway" Thomas said, getting to his feet.

"Yeah, Summers said the same. We're not going to know what the Nazis have left behind, so prepare yourselves" Jon said. He turned around and the agent came over to them.

"We'll go soon" he said.

"Yeah, we're up for that" Thomas replied. "We're starving."

"What time is it anyway?" Gracie asked. Summers looked down at the panel on his arm.

"Six thirty."

"Well, I reckon it's dark enough" Thomas said. He took Gracie's hand and they walked over to the narrow pathway. The agent picked up his rifle and followed them, Jon walking down behind them, checking the device every now and then, just in case the message had come through. Twenty minutes later they reached the bottom.

"OK, the house is straight through those trees and

across the next field" Summers said, pointing. "It won't take long to get there."

"Good, but we should be careful and watch our backs" Thomas replied. Summers nodded in agreement and walked over to the tree line, Thomas and Gracie following, Jon catching up behind. It was getting dark quickly, so Summers turned on his torch. He looked round at the others.

"Just have the one torch on, we don't want to bring any attention to ourselves" he said. The others nodded and followed the agent through the trees and towards the road. The sky was clear and the moon full, casting a radiant light across the whole area.

Soon they came to a small fence along the roadside, and Summers turned off the torch and clipped it back on to his belt. He raised his head over the fence and looked both ways, but nothing was coming. It was so quiet that they would easily have heard a vehicle approaching. Summers stepped over the wooden fence and on to the road, and Thomas followed. They stood there for a while, looking and listening, but nothing came.

Summers ran across the road and over the opposite fence into the field, and Thomas signalled for Gracie and Jon to follow. They stopped for a while on the other side, crouched down in the long grass and waited, still listening. Summers turned around to face Thomas.

"OK, we run the whole way towards the house, keep going and keep low" he said. Thomas nodded and looked around at Gracie.

"Ready?" he asked.

"Yes" she replied, Jon took one final glance down at the device; still nothing. Summers called "Go" and they all ran forward towards the house, keeping as low as possible. Finally they came to a low white fence. Summers and Thomas crouched down, and Thomas signalled to the others to do the same.

Summers got closer and looked across the fence. There was a small yard and a shed in the one corner. Nothing could be heard. He scanned the area; no movement, no sound, nothing. He looked over towards the front door, which was open slightly. Inside, the house was dark. He stepped over the fence and signalled for the others to stay put. As he got closer he looked into every corner, his rifle pointing forward. He put out his hand towards the others and gestured for them to come over.

"It's so quiet" Thomas whispered to him.

The agent stood up. "I don't think there's anyone here" he said. "We should still be cautious though." he walked over towards the front door, then looked to Thomas and gestured to his pistol. Thomas looked down and unclipped it from its holster. The agent moved over to the one side of the door and Thomas moved up behind him, then turned round to Thomas and pointed at the open door. As Thomas moved in front of it, he noticed that something had been carved into the wood; a mark or symbol of some kind. It was the star of David.

Thomas looked at Summers and then back at the

door. The agent moved in front of the door, while Thomas moved round to the side and Summers took a step forward. Pushing the door open, he looked into the darkness. A kitchen table could be seen, and a stove in the corner. He took a step inside. Thomas was right behind him now. Jon and Gracie had moved up and stood just outside. Thomas looked round at them.

"Wait out here, we'll check inside and you keep a look out" he whispered, Gracie nodded and stroked his hand. he gave her a tender glance and stepped inside. Summers tried the handle of the kitchen door, which swung open slowly with a creak. He turned and gestured over to Thomas. Thomas walked over to him.

"See anything?" he whispered. The agent shook his head as he looked down the hallway towards another room. It was too dark to see, so Thomas switched on his torch and shone it over the agent's shoulder. They made their way slowly down the hall. Thomas looked up; there was a staircase to their right, he shone the torch up; no sound, nothing. Summers gestured for them to keep going forward and they walked carefully in front of the door. The agent pushed it open gently with his foot and Thomas pointed the beam of light into the room. It was the sitting room. The furniture had been knocked over. There was a seat next to the door and Summers stepped over it, followed by Thomas. Over to the left a cabinet was lying on the floor, its contents scattered everywhere. Thomas moved round, past the agent and then the torchlight caught something in its beam; the body of a man. Thomas moved closer and Summers followed. Thomas leaned down slightly. The man had a bullet hole in his head, and two more in his kneecaps.

"Poor man" Thomas whispered.

"They must have made him suffer first" Summers replied.

"I wonder if there are any more" Thomas said, looking around the rest of the room.

"We'll check upstairs" Summers said, and moved back over to the door. Thomas glanced back down to the dead man, and followed him. They walked out and back into the hallway. Thomas shone the beam up the stairs once more - still nothing. The agent went first, his rifle held up. The steps creaked as they walked up slowly. On the landing there were two doors. Summers looked round to Thomas.

"I'll take this room, You take that one" he said. Thomas nodded and moved over to the door on the left. The agent moved to the other, and they both pushed together. Both doors swung open.

"Anything?" Summers shouted to Thomas.

"Nothing" same the reply. They returned to the stairs.

"I'll go and cover up the body if you go and tell the others it's safe" Summers said, and walked into the sitting room. Thomas moved back down the hallway and in the kitchen.

"Grace, Jon?" he called. They both put their heads round the door.

"Is it clear?" Jon asked.

"Yes, all clear" Thomas said, and they both walked in. Jon closed the door behind them. Gracie looked at Thomas. She could see sadness in his face.

"You OK?" she asked, walking over to him.

"There's a dead man in the sitting room. He's been shot" Thomas replied.

"Oh" Gracie said. "I thought something would be wrong, I noticed the mark on the door."

"Yeah, looks like they must have taken the rest of the family" Thomas said.

"Well, maybe we should bury him."

"Summers has covered him up, but you're right, we should bury him." Thomas looked up at Jon.

"Well, you'd better look for some food" he said. Jon nodded.

Thomas and Gracie walked down the hall and into the sitting room. Summers was standing near the window, looking out. The man on the floor was covered with a table cloth. Blood had started to seep through the white fabric. Thomas walked over to the agent.

"We're going to have to bury him" he said. Summers looked round.

"OK, well, we can do that while Gracie and Jon get some food together" he replied, glancing over to Gracie for approval. She nodded and walked back into the kitchen.

"OK, let's get it done" Thomas said, and they both walked over to the man's body. Soon enough they had managed to wrap the whole of the body with the cloth. Thomas took hold of the man's shoulders and Summers took the legs. They lifted him up and made their way down the hallway, passing Jon and Gracie, and went out of the door into the yard.

"Round here" Summers said, and they walked around the side of the house to a garden.

"Over there" Thomas said. They walked a little further and placed the man down gently.

"There must be a spade in the shed over there, I'll go check" Summers said. He walked over to the little wooden shed. On the door he noticed little drawings which had clearly been done by a child. A wave of sadness filled him. He shook it off and opened the door, to find a neat row of tools and gardening equipment, he picked up the spade and walked back over to Thomas.

"Let's do this" he said, looking down at the body.

"We can take it in turns to dig" Thomas answered. The agent smiled and nodded. He slammed the spade into the ground and began to dig. Their only light came from the moon.

★ ★ ★ ★ ★

"Can you get it working?" Gracie asked Jon, who was crouched down in front of the stove.

"Yeah, just put the wood in and light it I think" he answered. Gracie looked around. There was an oil lamp on the side and she moved over and picked it up.

"There, a bit of light" she said and turned it on. The kitchen was now filled with a warm, dim glow. She placed the little lamp on the kitchen table next to the food they had managed to salvage.

"There" Jon said, the stove lit. He placed a pot of water with some chopped vegetables on top, then sat at the old oak table.

"The veg shouldn't take long" he said. "Be nice to have a proper meal."

"Sure will, I'm starving" Gracie replied, and started cutting up a loaf of bread. Jon looked at her for a few moments. He was dying to ask her something.

"So then. You and Tom?" he began. She looked round at him and smiled.

"Me and Tom what?" she asked, still smiling.

"I take it you've finally managed to - get it together, so to speak?" he said, with a smirk on his face. She laughed out loud.

"Well, it's early days" she answered. "There." She placed the plate of bread out in the middle of the table. "There's some butter over there." She gestured to the side. Jon stepped over, picked the butter up and placed it next to the bread.

"Well, I'm very pleased for you anyway, Thomas is a good man."

"I know that" she answered, glancing over to him and smiling. At that, Thomas and Summers walked back through the door. She looked over at Thomas.

"OK?" she asked.

"As well as can be expected" he answered.

Summers walked over to the stove. "Smells good" he said.

"We're eating a proper meal, there's some bread on the table too" Gracie said. He came over and took a slice off the plate, then sat down and started to spread some butter on it.

Two hours later the food was all gone. They stayed at the table, chatting and discussing things, mainly the time project and its implications.

"Surely now, you can see how things can go so horribly wrong?" Thomas said to Jon, leaning over the table.

"I know, I never said it would be risk free. But nothing good in life was ever easy" Jon answered.

Thomas moved his chair back. "And the Ripper?"

Jon shrugged. "The whole Whitechapel thing was caused by the time project."

"I agree. But that became a part of history, so it had to happen. You yourself said this."

Thomas nodded. "I know, I'm just saying we need to take more care. It's a lot of responsibility, Jon. Plato once wrote that the measure of a man is what he does with power. Remember that."

Jon smiled. "I do like our little debates, Tom" he said. Thomas laughed, and at that the panel on Jon's arm lit up, the blue light filling the room. He looked down at it.

"Is it home?" Gracie asked excitedly.

"Yeah, something happened there" Jon answered.

"What?" Summers asked.

"The security guard that helped the others to get here escaped and sabotaged the machine."

"Have they caught him?" Thomas said, leaning forward.

"No, he got two other guards to help him and they got away. The machine is being repaired now. They'll send another message when we can jump back."

"Did they say how long?" Thomas asked.

Jon shook his head. "No, hopefully not too long" he said, glancing up at his friend.

Summers looked around; he had heard something. He stood up and walked over to the window. In the distance a vehicle was approaching down the lane. Summers could see the headlights clearly.

"Shit" he said, and picked up his rifle.

"What is it?" Thomas said, getting to his feet and moving over to the window. The vehicle was getting closer, winding its way down the narrow lane towards the house.

"It looks like a truck" Thomas said. Summers watched closely, holding his weapon close to his chest. "It's Nazis" he said. "They must have seen the light coming from the house." he pulled the slide back on his gun to put a bullet into the chamber. Thomas pulled his pistol from its holster.

"What are we going to do?" Gracie said, beginning to panic.

"Stay calm" Jon said, drawing his gun. The truck pulled up in the driveway to the house and a soldier jumped out of the passenger seat, his machine gun in his hand. He scanned the property, looking for any signs of movement.

"Stay down" Summers whispered to the others, who were crouched down, Thomas near the window with Summers, Jon and Gracie just behind the table. Thomas looked over at Gracie.

"It'll be fine" he whispered. She looked at him, eyes fixed. The Nazi soldier walked over to the house. He went right up to the kitchen window and peered through. Thomas was still crouched just below it. Summers signalled to him to move across. He did so and Summers crawled past him and knelt in front of the door. He looked around at the others.

"We're going to have to fight our way out of this" he hissed. "There will only be about six of them. Stay low, and prepare yourselves" he whispered and looked back to the door, his rifle fixed forward. The soldier turned around to the driver of the truck, then shrugged his shoulders and turned back round to the house. He stepped forward to the doorway, placing the strap to his machine gun over his arm, and reached for the handle. It clicked open. Summers held up his rifle, aiming straight for the door. The Nazi pushed it open slowly and Summers fired. The shot ripped through the Nazi's chest and he dropped to the ground. Summers kicked the door shut again as the other soldiers jumped out of the truck, their weapons at the ready.

"Fuck!" Thomas shouted as bullets started to smash through the window just above him. "Stay down!" he called to Gracie. Summers got to his feet and pushed himself against the wall next to the door, his gun up. The door had opened under the impact of the bullets. He quickly peered round the door frame. Two Nazis were crouched behind the front of the truck.

The firing stopped as the soldiers reloaded their weapons. The agent
leaned out, rifle up, and gently squeezed the trigger. The bright muzzle flash lit up the yard. The two Nazis at the front of the vehicle fell.

Summers leaned back inside the house, smoke curling from the barrel of the weapon. "Two down" he said over to Thomas.

But then the gunfire began again, bullets ripping through the widow again and tearing up the kitchen. Gracie lay flat on the floor, her hands over her head. Jon lay against the back wall, his weapon held up.

"Summers!" Thomas called over to the agent. "I'm going to try and make it upstairs, get a better position from up there." The agent nodded.

"I'll cover you" he said. He looked around as the firing stopped once more. Leaning out, he started shooting at the truck, the bullets ripping through the cab. He turned to Thomas. "Go!"

Thomas got to his feet and ran down the hallway to the staircase, then sprang up the wooden steps to the top and into the first bedroom facing the yard. He could hear the sound of the soldiers reloading their guns, clicking the magazines into place. He popped his head up and looked out. He could see two soldiers kneeling at the rear of the truck and three or four moving towards the side of the house. They were trying to surround the place. He leaned out, his pistol pointing forward, aiming at one of the Nazis.

"Come on Thomas, you can do it" he said to himself. He squeezed the trigger and the gun went off. The slide kicked back and the flash lit up the room. The soldier fell forward, a hole in his forehead.

Something caught Thomas' eye in the background; more headlights were coming down the lane. They must have heard the gunshots, Thomas thought. He ran out of the room and jumped back down the stairs.

"Summers, there's more coming!" he shouted as he ran into the kitchen. Once again, bullets started to rip through the house. "They're also moving around the back." He pushed himself against the wall next to the agent.

"Now what are we going to do?" Gracie shouted. Outside two new trucks pulled up, the Nazi soldiers jumping out to join their comrades in the firefight. Thomas leaned out of the door and fired a few shots off, then darted back inside as the bullets started to hit the door. Jon looked down. The panel on his arm had lit up, bright neon blue. He pressed buttons, then sat up.

"One minute and we can jump back" he shouted.

"We've still got to hold them off!" Thomas called

back to his friend. Jon ran over and crouched under the window.

"We can do that" he said and got to his feet. He aimed his pistol out of the window and started firing, shot after shot, hitting the trucks. One bullet ripped through the leg of one of the Nazis and he fell to the ground. Jon quickly ducked down again as the soldiers fired back. The men round the back of the house had made their way to the sitting-room window. There was a loud smashing noise as a soldier thrust the butt of his gun through the glass.

"What was that?" Jon called out.

"They've made it round the back!" Thomas shouted. Summers moved to the hallway and peered down. He could see the shadows of the soldiers moving around as they clambered through the window. He pointed his rifle forward. A soldier started to run towards him, and he opened fire and the man dropped to the floor, blood splattering up the wall. Thomas leaned out again and fired his pistol, two bullets hitting a soldier in the chest.

"Come on!" Jon said, looking down at the touch panel. "OK, now, activate your recall devices." Gracie switched hers on and it powered up with a hum. Thomas did the same. But as he looked round at the agent he saw him fall back, a bullet in the shoulder.

"Shit!" Thomas shouted and ran to his aid. The soldier was coming down the hallway now and Thomas took him out with a few shots of his pistol.

"You OK?" Thomas said, crouching down next to Summers.

"Yeah, we're getting out of here" the agent said gritting his teeth in pain and fumbling for his panel.

"Everyone ready?" Jon shouted.

"Yeah, let's go" Thomas called out. They all pressed their recall buttons simultaneously. The familiar bright blue sparks shot out and the humming became louder. The Nazi soldiers stopped firing and shielded their eyes from the light. Then, with a loud bang and a crash, they were gone, leaving the wrecked house behind.

The smoke cleared and Thomas looked around, still supporting Summers. "Can we get a medic up here?" he shouted. One of the scientists ran up the steps and on to the platform, crouching down next to Thomas and the agent.

"I'll take over, Dr Long" he said, looking up at Thomas. Thomas got to his feet and moved back. Another man came running up the steps to assist the scientist with helping Summers. Thomas looked round at Gracie, and she looked back at him and smiled.

"You OK?" he asked softly. She nodded. Jon stood up and clicked his pistol back in its holster.

"Wow, got out of that one" he said, looking over at Thomas.

"Only just" Thomas answered. He walked back down the steps, behind two men carrying the agent down on a stretcher. Gracie followed him.

"I've got to get out of this suit" she said, and stroked

Thomas' hand as she walked past him. He watched her walk across the room and into the elevator. Jon walked down the steps and over to his friend.

"Tom, we're fine, we all made it" Jon said. Thomas looked at him with anger in his eyes.

"Fine? Summers was shot, we only just made it out of there Jon" he answered and started to walk away.

"Tom, we got through it because we stuck together" Jon called after him, Thomas just kept walking, ignoring his friend. A scientist came out of a side room and approached Jon.

"Dr Walker…" he began, but Jon interrupted him. "What the hell happened here?" he said. The man took a step back.

"Sir, it really wasn't any fault of ours, two of the security guards helped the other escape from custody. They sabotaged the machine and made a break for it" he answered, almost panicking.

"Have they been tracked down yet?" Jon said, walking over to the machine to check it over for himself, the man following quickly behind.

"No sir, but we believe that they haven't left the complex. We've got several security teams tracking them down."

"Good" Jon answered, still fiddling with the machine. "No more jumps until the bastards are caught." He turned back to face the scientist. "I'm going to get freshened up, then I'll be back to go over the machine properly."

"Yes sir, of course" the man said, and watched Jon walk off to the elevator. The scientist put down his electronic tablet and made his way back to the room he had come from. He swiped his access pass across the little device on the door and it opened. He stepped inside and turned round.

"What did he say?" the security guard asked him.

"It's fine, they think the three of you are hiding somewhere. You'll be safe in here for the time being" the man said. One of the guards walked over to him and took out his pistol, then pushed the barrel under the scientist's jaw.

"How can we trust you?" he said. The man looked terrified.

"I won't tell anyone you're paying me" he said, quivering.

The security guard grunted. Then he took away the gun and placed it back in its holster.

"Good" the other guard said. "Let's keep it that way."

Thomas stepped out of the shower and began to dry himself. He stopped and listened. Again, three little knocks came from his door.

"Hold on" he called out, and quickly pulled on some loose jogging bottoms that lay on his bed, then walked over to the door and opened it.

"Oh, hi Grace, come in" he said, and stepped to one side. She smiled and walked past him into the room. "Can I get you a drink? I've only got coffee I'm afraid."

"Coffee's fine" she said. He gave her a smile and walked over to the little kitchen area.

"I just came to thank you for everything" she said. He walked back over and handed her the cup. She took a sip, not taking her eyes from his bare chest.

"You don't have to thank me, Grace" he said.

"I do" she answered. "You didn't think twice about protecting us, about protecting me" He looked at her bright blue eyes.

"Is that really all you came here for?" he asked. "To thank me?" He placed his hand on her waist. She looked up at him, her eyes moving from his chest up to his face. She moved her head up and closed her eyes, and he leaned forward and kissed her, his other hand moving up and holding her head. The coffee dropped to the floor as they moved over to the bed. They both fell down on to the soft quilt, still embracing, kissing passionately. He reached over to the side of the bed and switched off the light. The room was now lit only by the moon shining through the window.

The next morning Thomas woke to the sound of the intercom system next to his bed bleeping loudly. He looked down at Gracie. She had both her arms wrapped around him and her head was on his chest. He looked to the side, and the bleeping suddenly stopped.

"Morning" Gracie said, glancing up at him.

"Morning, gorgeous" he replied with a smile. She sat up, holding the quilt up to her naked breasts.

"We're going to be late for work" she said, with a huge grin.

"Who cares" he replied, and leaned close to her, giving her a kiss. She put her hand on his chest and pushed him back gently.

"You're a bad influence" she said, and laughed.

"Yeah, but you like it!" Thomas said, and at that the intercom started to bleep again. "god damn it" he said, looking up at the little box on the wall.

"It's probably important, you better get it" Gracie said, getting out of bed and walking naked to the bathroom. Thomas reached up and clicked the switch.

"Yeah, what is it?" he said.

"Morning Tom, it's only me" said Jon's voice.

"Morning Jon" Thomas replied.

"Are we friends again?"

"We're always friends Jon"

"Excellent. come and join me for breakfast in the mess hall" Jon said, and the intercom clicked off. Thomas smiled and got out of bed. He walked over to the kitchen and switched on the coffee machine. He could hear the shower turn off, and a few minutes later Gracie came out of the bath room with a towel wrapped around her.

"Coffee?" he asked her.

"Please" she replied, sitting down on the bed and drying her legs. He took her cup over and leaned down to kiss her.

"Watch your feet" she said. He looked at her, confused.

"Sorry?"

"The cup from last night, it's broken on the floor."

"Oh, yes" he replied and laughed. He picked up the pieces and put them in the bin, picking up his cup, he took a sip and turned back to her.

"Jon's asked me to meet him for breakfast. I'll get a quick shower, then we can go" he said.

"Well, I've got some things to do, and I think he's going to want to talk to you alone" she replied. He walked over to her and bent down.

"OK beautiful" he said and kissed her. She closed her eyes and brought her hands up to his face.

"See you later" he said, and walked into the bathroom. When he was finished he came back out, to find that Gracie had already gone. She had made the bed and left a small piece of paper on the quilt. He walked over and picked it up, read the writing on it, smiled and put it in his pocket. He walked over to the door, picking his ID card up on the way, opened the door and walked out.

Jon was sitting at the end of the large mess hall, staring into his coffee. He looked up to see Thomas standing in front of him.

"Morning Jon, good night sleep?" Thomas asked.

"Not really. Been a bit worried, to be honest" Jon said. He took a sip of his coffee.

"Why, what's wrong?" Thomas picked up his bagel and took a bite.

"Well, apart from worrying about what you think of me, there's the problem with those fucking security guards"

Thomas smiled and placed his bagel back on the plate. "Jon, we'll catch them, don't worry about that, and as for me, well, I think you're one hell of a scientist. You're the cleverest man I know, and apart from that, you're my friend, and I respect you. But we don't always have to agree."

"Thank you Tom, means a lot."

Thomas gave him a smile. "I mean it Jon, you know that" he said. Jon leaned forward and gripped Thomas' hand. "Now" he whispered. "Will you please tell me what the hell is going on with you and Gracie? It's driving me nuts!"

Thomas laughed out loud. "Jon, Gracie and I have got, closer since all this has happened. We get on really well, she's my friend, and much more."

Jon looked at him and smiled. "I can see you're happy" he said. "I'm glad for you." He sat back.

At that his cell phone started to beep. He took it out his pocket and clicked it on. "Hello?" he said to the screen. It was blank, but he could hear noise coming from the other end of the line. "Must be a bad connection" he said. But at that a voice came through.

"No Dr Walker, the connection is fine" the voice said.

"Who is this?" Jon asked, the screen still blank.

"This is the security team that's fucked everything up for you doctor."

Jon gritted his teeth. "Where are you?" he said.

"We'll see each other very soon doctor. You see, we need to meet, to exchange something."

"Exchange what?" Jon asked. Then another voice came over the phone, a voice both Jon and Thomas recognized.

"Please help me!" the voice said. Gracie.

Thomas stood up quickly and grabbed the phone from Jon.

"Where are you?" he screamed.

"Meet us outside the generator building in thirty minutes, just you two" said the voice. The phone went dead. Jon looked up. Thomas' face was red with rage.

"I'm sorry Tom" he said.

"It's not your fault, but I have to help her Jon" said Thomas. Jon nodded.

"Get the guns!" Jon said and they both ran out of the hall. They made their way straight to the equipment room as fast as they could. Jon used his keycard and the door opened. Thomas went over to where his suit hung. Under it, his utility belt was placed on a stand and next to it was his pistol. He picked it up and loaded a clip into the handle, slamming it in hard. Jon picked his up and did the same, then looked over at Thomas.

"We need a plan, Tom" he said and pushed the gun into the back of his trousers. Thomas pulled back the slide on his gun, loading a bullet into the chamber, then glanced at Jon.

"You go to them first, I'll work my way around the back of them, just tell them I'll be there shortly."

"But he said both of us."

"Jon, just keep them talking" Thomas said. Jon nodded. "Let's go" he answered, and they both walked out of the room and down the corridor to the exit. Thomas pushed open the door and walked out, Jon following.

They stopped suddenly. The treacherous scientist was standing in front of them, pointing a gun straight at Thomas.

Jon stepped forward. "What the fuck are you doing?" he said to the man.

"I'm sorry doctor, I don't really have a choice" the man answered, still pointing the gun forward.

"I really wouldn't do this if I were you" Thomas said.

"I don't think you're in a position to be making threats, Dr Long. Besides, Lt Mackenzie is paying me a ridiculous amount of money to help him."

Jon glared at him. "It was you helping them?" Jon asked, raising his voice.

"Of course, you don't think those idiot security guards could think of this on their own do you?" the man answered with a smirk. Thomas glanced at the man's gun, and then back to his face. In a second Thomas shot forward, gripped the man's arm and pushed the gun away. Then he threw a punch, catching the man on the chin. The man dropped to the ground. Jon bent down and picked up the gun. The scientist tried to get back to his feet, but Jon raised the gun up high and brought it down hard on the back of his head.

Again the man went down, knocked out cold.

"OK, bind his hands together" Thomas said. He looked around to see if anyone had seen the scuffle, but no one was in view. Jon had taken the man's belt off and was fastening it around his wrists.

"That should hold him" Jon said, standing straight again.

"Come on" Thomas said, and they both ran towards the generator building on the other side of the complex. As they got nearer, they stopped at one of the small pump house buildings. Thomas pushed himself against the wall and peered round. Sure enough, the three security guards were standing there waiting, Gracie kneeling next to them.

A rush of anger filled Thomas. He gritted his teeth and drew his pistol.

"OK, they're there, I'll go around to the left. Jon, just walk calmly up to them, and remember, keep them talking, I need time to work my way around."

Jon nodded. Thomas started to walk away. "Good luck Tom" Jon said.

Thomas turned around, raised his hand and then ran for it, away from the building and around to the left. Jon took a deep breath and walked out. As soon as he did, the three security guards saw him, and one was holding a rifle. Jon glanced at Gracie, who was looking at the ground. The man in front was gripping her hair. As Jon got closer the security guard stepped forward.

"Dr Walker, where is Dr Long? I did say both of you" he said, looking around.

"He's on his way" Jon answered. He looked down at Gracie and she glanced up at him, eyes wide with fear.

"I sure hope you haven't harmed her" Jon said, glaring at the man before him.

"We haven't hurt her at all, but we need to make a deal" the man said.

"What kind of deal?"

The man stepped closer to him. "You can have the girl back, that's not a problem, but we want unconditional access to the machine, and any other equipment we might need to transport the gold back here."

Jon looked from the man to Gracie and back again. "And what if I say no?"

The man shrugged. "Then I'll kill her now" he answered, and drew his pistol. Jon raised his hands submissively.

"OK, OK. We can do that, just let her go" he said, still holding his hands up.

"Excellent" the man said. "As soon as Dr Long gets here."

"I'm right here" came Thomas' voice from behind the group. As the men turned round, Thomas leapt forward and struck the man holding Gracie hard in the throat. Then he turned his attention to the other man, kicking him in the knee and punching him in the face. He went down, out cold. Thomas turned back to the other man and hit him straight in the nose. Blood spattered over the man's face and he fell back. Jon drew his pistol and aimed it at the last man, the ringleader.

"Don't fucking move!" he said, the barrel of the gun pointing straight at the man's face. The man raised his hands in surrender. Thomas leaned down and picked Gracie up. He held her close to him, his arms around her tight, and she sobbed and gripped hold of him. Thomas looked over the yard to see a group of other security guards running over, alerted by the fight.

"Sir, are you OK?" one said as they reached Jon.

"Yeah, arrest these men, and I want them off the complex. Inform the police" he said, and lowered his gun. Two of the guards grabbed hold of the man and handcuffed him, while two more cuffed the men from the ground, lifting them up and slapping the cuffs on them. One of the security team radioed their control to ask for a transport vehicle. Thomas and Gracie walked over to Jon, Gracie still gripping Thomas tightly.

"Gracie, I'm so sorry this happened" Jon said, putting his hand on her shoulder.

She looked up at him. "It's not your fault Jon, it's over now anyway" she said and placed her head back on Thomas' chest. Thomas put his hand out and Jon gripped it tightly.

"Thank you Jon" Thomas said. "You did good."

"I really wish it hadn't come to this" Jon answered. Thomas shrugged. "As Gracie said, it's over now." At that a truck came roaring towards them and suddenly stopped. The security team dragged the rogue guards inside.

"We'll hand them over to the police" the security guard said as he walked over to Jon.

"Good, I don't want to see them again" he said, the guard bowed his head and walked back to the truck, getting in the passenger side, the vehicle's engine roared and it drove off towards the main gate.

"I'm going to get Gracie back inside, get her some rest" Thomas said, Jon nodded and patted Thomas on the shoulder.

"OK, call me if you need anything, either of you" he replied. Thomas smiled, holding Gracie tight. "Thanks mate" he said.

Jon watched them walk slowly back to the main building. He rubbed his head and made his own way back.

CHAPTER 7

"How are you feeling?" Thomas asked as Gracie sat up in bed. He was perched on the edge of the bed next to her.

"I'm fine" Gracie answered. "Just a bit sore."

"I've been thinking" he said, handing her a mug of coffee. "Maybe we should leave, go back to England. We've still got our work there to finish, the finds from Denmark and the skeleton." She looked up at him.

"That can wait Thomas, we couldn't let Jon down, not now" she said.

"Grace, it's getting too dangerous here, we never signed up for this" Thomas replied.

"You knew it wouldn't be easy."

"I know, but that was before."

"Before what?"

"Before us, before you. I don't know what I'd do if something were to happen to you." She leaned closer to him.

"You have to put those thoughts aside Thomas" she said. "We have a job to do, and we're going to see it through to the end." She looked lovingly into his eyes. "I'm fine Thomas. Really. And besides, don't you still want to see the Dark Ages?"

"Well, yeah" he said. She laughed and gave him a kiss. At that the intercom started bleeping.

"Always at the wrong time" Thomas said, and switched it on.

"Hello, Thomas?" Jon said on the other end.

"Hey Jon" Thomas replied.

"Agent Summers has asked if you could visit him in the infirmary."

"Yeah no problem. When?" Thomas replied.

"Whenever you can Tom" Jon answered. "How's Gracie?"

"I'm fine Jon, looking forward to the next jump" Gracie shouted at the intercom.

"That's great news Gracie. Well, I'll see you both later."

"OK Jon, catch you later" Thomas said and turned off the little box. "I wonder what Summers wants?"

"Who knows? Why don't you go and see him? I'll get up, have a shower and I'll go and meet up with Jon" Gracie said, sitting up.

"Yeah, sounds good, I'll come find you after I'm done with Summers." Thomas got to his feet. "You're sure you're OK?"

"Thomas, I'm fine, now go!" she said and stretched up to kiss him.

"OK, well, I'll see you later then" he said opening the door. She smiled at him as he walked out, then closed the door behind him.

Agent Summers was sitting up in the hospital bed,

staring out of the window. He surprised Thomas by greeting him with a smile.

"Hi" Thomas said, returning the smile. "How are you feeling?"

"I'm doing OK, just a flesh wound, it's healing nicely. Please sit down." He gestured to a chair at the side of his bed. Thomas accepted the invitation.

"You wanted to see me?" he asked.

The agent turned slightly to face Thomas. "When I was shot, back in the farmhouse, you didn't hesitate in coming to my aid. That was the second time you've done that for me. I really just wanted to say thanks." Thomas smiled. For the first time Summers seemed fully human.

"You're very welcome, agent" Thomas said. He leaned over and shook Summers' hand.

"Michael, my first name is Michael" said Summers.

"Nice to meet you Michael" Thomas said. "My name's Thomas." They both laughed.

"I can get the nurse to get you a drink if you like?" the agent said, holding up the call bell.

"I'm fine thank you" Thomas replied.

"How is Miss Stevenson? I heard that something happened regarding those security guards."

"She's fine, thank you. Gracie is, well, very strong" Thomas answered. Summers nodded in appreciation. "That she is, Thomas" he said.

"Do you know when you're going to be able to get out of here?"

"Today, I was told, hopefully soon. I really hate just lying here doing nothing. So, I'll be seeing you later, I imagine. Now those guards have been caught, I would think the next jump to the 1940s is just around the corner."

Thomas shrugged. "To be honest, I'm not sure when we can go back" he said. "Jon's got to check the machine over first, see what damage was done." He got to his feet. "Well, I should really go and find Gracie, we have some work to do today."

Summers leaned forward and shook Thomas' hand. "Again, thank you Thomas" he said.

"Don't mention it, Michael" he answered and gave a smirk. "I still can't get used to calling you that." Michael laughed. Thomas walked out the room and left the infirmary wing of the complex, making his way back to the main building.

Gracie found Jon crouched under the barrel of the machine, adjusting small parts of the huge device, making sure that everything was correct and functional.

"Need a hand Jon?" Gracie said. He looked up.

"Oh, Gracie, hi. I'm nearly done to be honest, and anyhow, I don't like other people messing with my baby." He smiled. "How are you feeling now?"

Gracie moved an office chair over and sat down. "You know, I'm all good. can't wait to jump back, we've still got to stop those other guards" she said, looking under the barrel, trying to see Jon.

"Well, it shouldn't be long now" Jon replied.

"I hope not" Gracie said. "You know, Thomas wanted us to go home."

Jon stopped what he was doing and looked up at her. "I can understand that" he said.

"Don't worry, we're not going anywhere yet" she said with a grin. "It was only because of us being, well, together now. He was worried about me."

Jon moved back under the machine, starting his work once more.

"That's understandable too" he said. "So, how's all that going anyway? I kind of knew you would get it together. I've seen the way he looks at you."

She glanced down at him and laughed. "Yeah, it's going great, it's been a long time coming. Thomas and I have always had a connection, my feelings have grown stronger though with these recent events, and I think he feels the same."

Jon looked up. "Believe me, he does. I've known Thomas for a long time now, and I know he isn't very good at showing his feelings, but with you, a blind man could see how much he cares for you."

She began to blush. "Thanks Jon" she said. She turned round to see Thomas walking over to them from the main door. She got to her feet and went over to greet him.

"Hey" she said as he approached.

"Hi Grace" he replied and kissed her.

"So, what did Agent Summers want you for?" she asked as they walked over to where Jon was still working. Thomas grinned at her.

"Actually, his name is Michael" he replied.

"What?" she said.

"He has a given name?" Jon said, coming out from under the barrel and standing up. "I thought his parents just baptised him Agent."

Thomas and Gracie laughed out loud. "Well, he's actually OK. He thanked me for helping him, back at the farmhouse" Thomas said, leaning against the desk next to the machine.

"He must like you then, I've known him for five years and he's never told me his first name" Jon replied.

"I think that's good, it's bonding. We'll need to trust each other when we go back" Gracie said.

"Speaking of which" Thomas said, "When can we go back?"

Jon turned back to the machine. "She's all ready" he said. "We can leave as soon as tomorrow morning."

"That's great" Gracie said, looking at Thomas, who gave her a wink.

"Yeah, sooner the better" Thomas replied. "What about Michael, I'm sure he'll want to come too, can he with his injury?"

Jon looked at him with a smile. "Oh, so it's Michael now" he said and laughed. Thomas just gave a smirk.

"Yes, can he come?" he said.

"As long as the medics say he's fit enough, then that's fine with me" Jon said. "Well, I'm going to get some food, what about you two?"

"Yeah, I'm starving" Gracie replied, looking up at

Thomas, who nodded. They made their way over to the elevator, the next floor up, got out and walked into the mess hall. They got food from the automatic dispensers and found a table. The hall was full of workers and scientists on their lunch breaks.

"After lunch, I've got something to show you both" Jon said after taking a bite of his burger.

"Really, what?" Thomas asked.

"Something to even the odds when we jump back."

"Sounds intriguing" Gracie said, taking a drink of water.

"You'll see" Jon said, seeming pleased with himself. Gracie looked over to the door.

"Here's your new best friend" she whispered to Thomas. He glanced up to see Summers walking in, his arm in a sling. Thomas stood up and shook his hand.

"Glad to see they finally let you out" he said. "How's your arm?"

"A lot better fellers, thank you" he replied.

"Good, because we're leaving tomorrow morning" Jon said, looking up at him. "Has the medic given you the all clear?"

"Yes, I'm fully mission ready" Summers replied. Jon smiled.

"So, are we on first names now?" he said. Summers looked flustered.

"To tell you the truth, over the past few months you have all become my friends, and I wouldn't have got through some of the situations without your help." He held out his hand to Jon. "My name is Michael" he said. Jon smiled and got to his feet. He gripped Summers' hand.

"Glad you feel that way, Michael." Jon gestured to the seat next to his. "Would you like to join us?"

Summers nodded. "Thank you" he said. He glanced over at Gracie, and she gave him a wink. "I'm glad you're OK Gracie, I did here about your ordeal" he said.

"Thanks, yeah, I'm fine now. Looking forward to the jump tomorrow, and apparently Jon has something to show us after lunch" she said and looked over at Jon, who, just smiled.

"Really?" Michael said, glancing at Jon.

"Oh yes, you're going to love it" he said, and finished the last piece of his burger. Thomas got to his feet.

"Well, come on, I can't wait any longer" he said. Jon laughed.

"OK, OK" he said. "It's in the equipment room."

Gracie and Summers got up and followed Jon and the eager Thomas out of the mess hall and down the corridor back to the elevator. Arriving back on the lower floor, they got out and walked into the main room. Jon took out his ID card and swiped it across the access device on the equipment room door. They walked in. On the centre table was a stand, and placed on the stand was a device that looked a lot like a gun. It had a wide barrel, similar to that of the time machine, and a long straight handle with a red trigger.

"What the hell is that?" Thomas said, staring at the object.

"Whatever it is, I like it" said Summers, also fascinated by the device. Jon smiled, feeling very pleased with the effect his new device was having on his friends.

"This is a proton emitter" he said, running his hand across the black metal.

"What does it do?" Thomas asked, still staring at the device.

"It's an energy weapon" Jon replied. "It fires a superheated energy beam. It overloads the target material with energy, making it disintegrate." He picked up the weapon. "Come on, I'll show you" he said, walking past them and into the testing room. A large metal target was set up at the end of the long room. Jon positioned himself. "I'd stand back if I were you" he said. He pushed a switch down and the device lit up with a humming noise. Jon lifted the weapon up, pointing it straight at the target. He squeezed the trigger gently. The humming got louder and then a bright blue beam shot out of the barrel, hitting the target. The target began to glow, and then it was gone in a cloud of smoke and sparks. Jon switched the weapon off and turned back to face the others.

"I want one" Summers said, his mouth agape.

"Wow!" was Gracie's only answer. Thomas walked over to Jon.

"Does it matter with the size of the object?" he said, looking down to where the target used to be. Jon shook his head.

"Not at all, you may have to hold the beam in place

longer with a larger target, but the results will be the same" Jon answered. Michael walked over to them.

"It will most certainly come in handy when we get back to the war years. We could obliterate tanks and armoured trucks" he said, looking closely at the weapon.

"Yes, but remember why we're going there" Thomas said. "We're going to stop Mackenzie and his men, not fight the war. We still have to try and remain undetected."

"Absolutely" Jon answered. "This is just a precaution." He held the weapon up. "Now, I have some work to finish before the jump tomorrow. Get some rest or something."

Summers turned to Thomas. "He's right, the longer I can rest this arm, the better" he said. "I'll see you both tomorrow."

"Come on" Gracie said, taking Thomas' hand. They walked out and back into the main room, making their way to the entrance door. They walked outside and Gracie made her way over to a car parked just in front of the doors.

"Let's go into town" she said, turning to Thomas and holding up the car keys. He smiled and gestured for her to lead the way. She laughed and walked over to the car, unlocking it with her remote. She got into the driver's seat and Thomas went round to the passenger side.

"Let's go" he said, and she drove slowly over to the main gate. The guard raised the barrier up and the gate opened. Gracie put her foot down and the car screamed off, down the side road and on to the freeway.

Agent Michael Summers was standing in his room, moving his arm around slowly, giving it some much-needed exercise. He walked over to the desk and took some painkillers with a glass of water. He looked up at the mirror opposite, staring into his reflection closely, he brought his hand up and touched the small bullet scar on his shoulder. He turned around at the sound of knocking on his dorm door, threw on a vest top, walked over and opened the door.

"Michael" Jon said, leaning against the door frame.

"Jon, please, come in" Summers said gesturing with his hand.

"Thank you" Jon replied, and stepped in.

"Is there something wrong?" Summers said, closing the door behind him.

"I've just come to make sure you're going to be fit enough for the jump" Jon said. The agent walked past him and went to the kitchen area.

"I'm fine Jon" he said pouring some coffee into a cup.

"I have to check, that's all" Jon answered.

Summers turned back round and handed Jon the cup.

"Thank you" he said. "As the lead scientist, it's my duty to make sure everyone is fit and able to work, you understand, don't you?" He took a sip of his coffee.

"Of course I understand, you can ask the medic if

you like, I really am fine" he said and put down the empty glass.

"Actually, I already did" said Jon. "He said you were fit enough, and the wound is healing nicely." He took a seat next to the desk.

"Well then, why ask me if you already know I'm capable?" Summers asked. Jon smiled.

"It's OK having a positive medical report, but I wanted to see how you are in yourself, you're not acting as you normally do" Jon said.

"How do you mean?" Summers said, sitting down.

"You're usually pretty calm and collected, not really showing emotion, and now, you're having us call you by your first name, and calling us friends. That's not like you" Jon said, placing his empty coffee cup down. Summers looked down. Jon got to his feet and walked over to him.

"Michael, we are your friends, don't get me wrong, I'm just worried about you" he said.

"After we're done with all this, the time jumping and so forth, after you and Thomas and Gracie no longer need me, I'm going to quit being a government agent" Summers answered and looked up at Jon.

"Really, why?"

"Well Jon, being shot kind of puts things into perspective. It makes you value things" he said. "I'm done with all that. But don't worry, I'll do my job to the best of my ability, while you still need me." Jon smiled and patted him on the back.

"OK Michael, well, you'd better get some rest ready for tomorrow" he said, and made his way over to the door. He turned back to the agent. "When you do quit, I can always find you a job here" he said. Summers smiled as Jon opened the door.

"Thank you" he answered, and the door closed.

"Table for two please" Thomas said to the concierge standing at the restaurant's reception. The man turned around to one of the waiters and clicked his fingers, and the waiter came running over.

"Please, this way sir, madam" he said, and led them over to a table near the window, in the corner of the large dining room. "Is this OK for you?"

"Yes, thank you" Thomas said. The waiter pulled out the chair for Gracie and she sat down, Thomas opposite, the man gave them both a menu each and bowed his head.

"I'll be over shortly to take your orders, please call if you need anything" he said, and scurried off.

"Well, this is nice" Thomas said. Gracie smiled and leaned over, taking his hand.

"You, got the note I left you that morning didn't you?" she asked him.

He smiled. "I did, yes" he answered. "I keep it with me, in my pocket"

"Really?" she said, surprised.

"Of course, and I really wanted to tell you that, well…" he stopped, trying to find the right words. "The words, that you wrote, well, I love you too Grace." He was looking straight into her blue eyes. She blushed. "Gracie, I always have." She leaned over the table and kissed him gently on the lips. The waiter came back over.

"Can I get you both something to drink?" he said.

"I'll just have water, please" Thomas said. He glanced over to Gracie. "You can have wine, I'll drive back" he said.

"You sure?" she replied. He nodded and gave her a wink.

"OK, I'll have a dry white wine please" she answered.

"Thank you" the waiter said, and walked off again.

"Can't have too many, we've got to be up early tomorrow" Gracie said.

"Yeah, going to correct another of Jon's mistakes" Thomas answered.

"Oh come on, you like going back really" she said. "And when we go back to the Dark Ages - well, I bet you can't wait."

"Well, maybe I am looking forward to that jump, but do you know what I'm most looking forward to?" he said.

"What's that?" she replied.

"To going back home and finishing our work back at the lab in England. Finding out more about the skeleton we found, where he was from, what he did, how old he was when he died. And doing all that together, just me and you" he said.

"It'll be sooner than you think" she replied as the waiter brought over their drinks.

"Are you ready to order now?" he asked them.

"I'll have the steak please, cooked well done, no pink bits" Thomas said. Gracie laughed. "I'll have the gammon please" she said.

"Thank you" the waiter said and took the menus from them. Thomas raised his glass.

"Here's to us" he said, and Gracie tapped her glass gently to his.

"To us" she said.

* * * * *

The next morning, Jon was up and ready to go by 6 am. He made his way to the main room, suited up ready. The new weapon was placed on a desk next to the machine, and Jon walked over to check it.

"Morning Jon" Summers said as he approached. Jon turned round.

"Hi Michael, you sleep well?" he said.

"Yeah, not bad" Summers replied. He turned around to see Gracie and Thomas walk out of the elevator and into the equipment room. "So, are we ready to go?" Summers asked, Jon put down the weapon.

"We sure are, as soon as Thomas and Gracie are suited up." He turned to one of the scientists working on the machine. "Have you entered the time yet?"

"Yes Dr Walker" the woman answered. "The 6th of August 1943, at 05:30. We'll aim you for the Leinawald forest."

"Good, thank you" Jon answered. He turned back to see Thomas and Gracie walking over to them, their suits on, ready to go.

"Hey!" Jon said as they approached. Thomas raised his hand.

"Morning" Gracie said.

"We all set?" Jon asked them.

"Yeah, all good" replied Thomas.

"Good, we'll be landing in the middle of Leinawald forest, 1943. There's an underground Nazi bunker there, so we'll have to be careful and keep our eyes sharp." He picked up the energy weapon. Summers took out his pistol and pulled the slide back, loading the weapon.

"Let's go" he said, clipping it back in its holster.

"OK, remember, be careful, Mackenzie and his men are heavily armed" Thomas said as they all walked over to the platform.

"We've got this baby" Jon said, turning round and holding up the proton emitter. Summers laughed. Jon walked up the steps first, followed by Thomas and then Gracie, Summers last.

"Start the countdown" Jon called over to the scientist at the control station.

"10, 9, 8," the voice over the tannoy came. "7, 6, 5, 4…" Thomas looked over at Gracie and smiled. "See you on the other side" he said.

"3, 2, 1" the noise became louder, electrical sparks started shooting from the large barrel of the machine, and then, the flash. The sound faded, the humming stopped and the smoke cleared. They were gone.

* * * * *

Thomas moved his hand around to try and waft away the smoke. The smell of burning wood filled his nostrils.

"Is this the right place?" he asked. Jon looked down at the inside of his forearm, the touch panel activated.

"Yep, this is it" he said. "Leinawald forest. We're about five miles from the bunker, according to this." The smoke had almost cleared and they could see around them. It was still dark, but the sun was not far from rising. The trees around them were burned from the energy from the jump, and there was a smouldering crater beneath their feet. Summers looked down at the device on his arm.

"It's north from here" he said. "If the gold is in the bunker, that's where Mackenzie will be." Thomas reached into his bag and pulled out the strange golden key they had found at the castle.

"And we have this" he said, holding it up.

"Good, keep it safe Tom, we might need it" Jon said. He looked around. The sun was just coming up over the horizon. "It's pretty remote around here, we should be OK."

"Come on" Gracie said, and started walking away from the smoking crater. "We can't waste any time." They quickly followed her through the trees, and away from the jump site. They had walked about a mile through dense forest when they heard a sudden noise. They all stopped dead in their tracks.

"What was that?" Thomas asked, looking around.

"It sounded like an engine" Summers answered, and sure enough, over to their right the sound came again – motorbikes. They all hit the ground fast.

"Over there" Gracie said, pointing to a clearing, Thomas crawled over to her to get a better look. They could see four bikes, soon joined by a fifth. The riders were in Nazi uniform. They were clearly patrolling the area and using motorbikes for speed.

"Stay down" Thomas said, turning to Gracie. "They should move on."

Four of the soldiers started their bikes up again and rode off, heading north. The fifth stayed behind. It seemed something had gone wrong with his machine, as he was crouched down fiddling with the engine. Thomas and the others watched him for a few moments. Finally he gave the bike a kick, picked up his machine gun and started walking over towards where they were hiding.

"Shit, now what?" Thomas said, turning round to Jon. Summers got to his feet and drew his pistol. The soldier stopped in surprised. Thomas got to his feet and did the same, unclipping his gun and aiming it at the Nazi.

"Stoppen!" Thomas said. The man raised his hands and Jon got up and walked over to him. The soldier stared at him, unable to take his eyes from the suit and the weapons these strange people carried. Jon quickly grabbed the gun from the man and threw it over his shoulder; it hit the ground behind him.

Thomas moved slowly over to the Nazi. He lifted his gun up and struck the soldier hard on the head. He fell to the ground, out cold.

"Tie him up" Thomas said, Summers walked over, took off the man's belt and tied it around his wrists.

"Now what?" Jon said.

"We're going to have to leave him here" Summers said.

"OK, come on, before any more turn up" Jon said, and they made their way quickly over a small hill and through the trees. An hour later they got to a small ridge which looked over one of the entrances to the bunker. There were five or six soldiers standing outside, with two large trucks parked up and three motorbikes. Thomas got down and crawled over to the edge of the ridge to look over, followed by Jon and then Summers. Gracie crouched down and got close to Thomas, moving right in next to him.

"Now what?" she whispered.

"We wait" Thomas said, not taking his eyes from the bunker. An hour passed, two hours, and then, in the distance, they heard the sound of a truck approaching. "Look, over there" Jon said, pointing over to a vehicle making its way up a muddy road through the trees and towards the bunker. The soldiers watched it approach.

One man picked up his rifle. Clearly these men were not expecting company.

"Stay down" Summers whispered to the others. The truck came to a stop a few feet from the entrance. One of the soldiers had walked over to talk to the driver when there was a sudden gunshot and the Nazi dropped to the ground, the back of his head blown away. The other soldiers ran to cover as the driver of the truck, along with the passenger, got out. It was Ford and James, two of the rogue security guards. James stood in front of the truck, raised his assault rifle and started firing at the soldiers. The rounds from the automatic weapon ripped through their bodies as if they were made of paper. Ford stood there laughing, holding a shotgun over his shoulder. Bolton and Carter got out of the back of the vehicle, followed by Mackenzie.

"We can take them now!" whispered Jon.

"No, not yet, they're ready for combat, they'd be too alert" Summers said. "We have to take them by surprise."

"Ford, James, stay out here and keep a look out" Mackenzie said, walking past them, his pistol drawn, ready for action.

"Yes sir!" they both answered.

"Bolton, you first and Carter, you stay at the rear" the lieutenant said. He pulled the slide back on his gun and walked over to the door. "Ready!" he shouted and opened the door, pulling it towards him. Bolton threw in a grenade and took cover behind the metal door.

There was a loud bang and the sound of screaming. Mackenzie laughed out loud. "Go on, get the bastards!" he shouted and Bolton ran in, his rifle firing. Carter pulled the bolt back on his assault weapon and went behind the lieutenant.

"Ready sir" he said, Mackenzie ran in, followed by Carter. The sound of the gunshots and screaming could be heard, and Thomas gritted his teeth.

"We have to stop this!" he said, turning to face Summers.

"Not yet" replied the agent. The sound of the firing got further away and James leaned against the truck, becoming more relaxed. Ford sat on one of the motorbikes, trying it out for size.

"OK, we can take those two" Summers said. He pulled out his pistol and loaded a bullet into the chamber. "Jon, I want you and Gracie to work your way down and round the back of them. Thomas and I will keep them occupied this end."

"Right" Jon said, and started to crawl down the bank, Gracie looked at Thomas and he kissed her on the lips.

"Be careful" he whispered, she nodded her head and followed Jon.

"Ready, Thomas?" Summers asked him. Thomas loaded his gun and switched off the safety catch.

"Let's do it!" he replied. He got to his feet and pointed his weapon straight at James. Summers did the same, holding his gun towards Ford.

"Don't move boys!" Summers shouted down to them. They both looked up, surprised.

"Agent Summers, is that you? And Dr Long too" James said, moving off the truck.

"I said don't fucking move" Summers said, and gripped his pistol with both hands. "You're both under arrest."

"For what?" James said, and took another step forward.

"For mass murder, for starters" replied Summers. James looked over at Ford, Ford glanced at him and then back to the agent, then suddenly Ford drew his pistol and opened fire. A bullet hit the tree next to Thomas and another went straight past Summers' head. James ran behind the truck and Thomas took a couple of shots at him but missed, hitting the vehicle. Summers crouched down and fired three shots. The first hit Ford in the shoulder, the second blasted a hole through his leg and the third hit him straight in the chest. He fell to the ground, dead. James raised his assault rifle, aimed it at Thomas and Summers and started firing.

"Get down!" shouted Summers, and they both hit the ground fast, the bullets hitting the trees around them. One small tree fell to the ground with a crash, and there was a bright blue flash. The truck next to James started to glow, sparks started shooting from it. Then it disintegrated in a burst of blue flames.

James stood there, hardly being able to believe his eyes. Summers got to his feet and pointed his gun. Jon and Gracie walked out from the cover of the trees. The energy weapon in Jon's hand was smoking and Gracie had her pistol out, aiming forward. James threw down his gun and raised his hands. Thomas and Summers made their way down the small ridge and towards the beaten security guard. Summers took out a pair of handcuffs and slapped them on James.

"On the ground!" Summers said, James stared at him and sat down. Summers leaned over and bound his feet. Jon walked over to them.

"There are five more agents waiting back home for them, trusted men" Summers said. "We can send them back now, along with Ford's body. We can't leave it here, with the technology of the suit he's wearing."

"OK" Jon said. "I'll arrange for them to jump back." He opened up the display screen on his arm.

"You OK?" Thomas asked Gracie.

"I'm fine, I was worried though when he started shooting at you" she replied. Thomas gave her a wink and said.

"I'm fine."

"OK, in ten seconds, step back" Jon said, and they all walked away from James and the body of Ford. Flashes of lightning hit James and his dead partner. Then there was a loud humming and another flash. The two men were gone, leaving behind a smoking crater.

"Well that came in handy" Thomas said, gesturing towards the energy weapon in Jon's hand. Jon smiled.

"I told you it would even the odds" he said.

Summers made his way over to the bunker and looked inside. There were six or seven Nazi bodies dotted around the main passage. The lights were flickering and gunsmoke filled the area. He waved his hand for the others to come over to him.

"We should take extra care inside, there will be many places that they could ambush us" Summers said as he stepped in. Thomas followed close behind, his pistol at the ready. Jon walked in and went to Thomas' side.

"I'll go first" he said, and pointed the large energy weapon forward.

"Jon, I really wouldn't fire that in here if I were you!" Thomas said, putting his hand on Jon's shoulder.

"Why?" he said.

"Because if you hit one of the supporting walls with the beam, you could bring the whole bunker down on us" Thomas replied.

"Shit, didn't think of that" Jon said and switched off the weapon. Summers ran over to a stack of crates and ducked down behind them. Down the long passage way were more dead Nazis. Thomas ran to his side.

"Now what?" he said. "They could be anywhere."

"Just follow the trail of bodies" Summers replied and got to his feet, stepping out past the crates. Thomas followed him. In the distance there was the sound of screaming. Gracie ran to catch up with Thomas. "Stay close" he said. Jon walked behind, his pistol drawn ready.

They made their way down the corridor, stepping over blood-soaked corpses as they went. They reached a corner where a passage ran off to their right. The sound of a man crying and shouting something in German came from the smaller side passage. A gunshot silenced him.

"This way" Summers said. The passageway opened up into a larger room, which was quite well lit. Summers crouched down behind a stack of artillery shells. "They're over there, in the corner next to that door" he whispered, Thomas leaned round the side and peered over. The three security guards were standing in front of a massive door cut right into the rock. Thomas looked back at Summers.

"What's the plan?" he asked. Summers turned to Gracie and Jon and gestured for them to come over.

"You and Jon make your way round to the side of them while we move forward. We'll stay in the cover of these weapons and crates and approach them head on."

Thomas looked at Gracie, and then back to Summers. "She'll be fine" Summers said, knowing exactly what Thomas was going to say.

"I can take care of myself, Thomas" Gracie said, pulling out her pistol and loading it. Sneaking from cover to cover, they made their way closer to Mackenzie and his two lackeys.

"Come on" Thomas said, turning to Jon. They kept as low as possible, moving round to the right to get a good position on their targets. They were now within earshot of the security and could make out every word.

"It won't fucking budge!" Carter said, turning to the other two.

"Maybe there's a mechanism around here" Bolton

answered. Mackenzie leaned towards him and grabbed his neck.

"I don't care how it opens, just get it fucking open, I haven't travelled through fucking history for nothing" Mackenzie said. "We'll blow it open if we have too!"

"Yes sir, of course" Bolton said. He ran over to the massive door and began to study it. He switched on his arm device and a thin blue beam of light came out of the panel. He used the beam to scan the door until the device bleeped and he looked down.

"It needs a key" he said, turning to Mackenzie. "It has a complex internal locking mechanism." He pointed to a small hole in the centre. "The key would go in here, you wouldn't even have to turn it. The mechanism reacts to the key being pushed in, it'll open automatically."

Mackenzie walked over to him. "Well, we haven't got the fucking key, have we?" he shouted. "Now get it open another way!"

Summers caught Thomas' eye and signalled to him to get ready.

"OK Jon, this is it" Thomas said, clicking off the safety catch on his gun. Summers got to his feet.

"Now!" he said, and he and Jon got up quickly, their pistols pointing forward. "Don't move lieutenant!" Summers shouted. The three guards turned round in surprise.

"Well, I really didn't expect any of you to have the balls to come and stop me" Mackenzie said.

"You didn't give us much choice" Summers replied. "Now, this doesn't have to get messy."

The lieutenant gave a faint smile. "Oh, I'm afraid it does agent" Mackenzie answered. He looked over to Carter, who raised his weapon.

"Get down!" Summers shouted, grabbing Gracie. They hit the floor as the assault weapon roared into life, blasting the crates and boxes around them. Thomas and Jon raised their guns and fired. Carter took cover, while Bolton returned fire with his pistol. Gracie peered out of their hiding spot to see Mackenzie running down a side passage. She got to her feet and aimed her pistol, firing four or five shots without hitting him.

Bolton turned round and aimed his gun at her, but just in time she spun round and fired. Bolton fell to the ground, blood flowing from a chest wound.

"Shit!" Carter shouted. He got to his feet, firing his weapon. Gracie got down, the bullets just missing her. Thomas ran out from cover just as Jon fired. Carter dropped to the ground.

"Thomas, not on your own!" Summers shouted as Thomas ran past in pursuit of the lieutenant. He made his way down the passage, and finally saw Mackenzie at the top of some steps. It was a dead end. He turned around to face Thomas.

"Come on!" the lieutenant shouted and ran towards him. Thomas crouched slightly, and as Mackenzie drew his fist back he ducked and returned the punch, striking Mackenzie hard in the ribs. The lieutenant smiled.

"Is that it, little man?" Mackenzie said, and began to walk forward. He drew his huge arm back and swung at Thomas' face. Thomas moved his head and tapped the lieutenant's hand away, throwing another punch, which landed on Mackenzie's jaw. As the big man staggered back, Thomas kicked him in the knee, and the leg buckled. As Mackenzie slumped down Thomas struck again, aiming at the cheekbone. Mackenzie dropped, blood spattering from a cut.

"No, that's not it" Thomas said.

Mackenzie got to his feet once more.

"I taught you well doctor" Mackenzie said. Quick as lightning he punched Thomas straight in the stomach. Thomas went over, the wind knocked out of him. The lieutenant lifted his arm up and dropped his elbow down on Thomas' back. Thomas hit the ground and Mackenzie kicked him in the side.

"Thomas! Thomas, where are you?" he could hear the others shouting. He raised his body up slightly to see the lieutenant still standing over him, drawing his pistol. Thomas glanced away for a second and then struck, punching Mackenzie hard in the knee cap and feeling it dislocate under his knuckles. Mackenzie screamed in pain as he fell to the floor. Thomas got to his feet, drew his gun and pointed it at the lieutenant.

"Don't move" he said. Mackenzie gritted his teeth with pain and anger. Summers, Jon and Gracie ran in to see Thomas standing over the huge man.

"Well done Thomas" Summers said, taking out some handcuffs. Gracie ran over to Thomas.

"You OK?" she asked.

"I'm good" he answered, not taking his eyes from the beaten lieutenant, his pistol still trained on him. Summers pushed Mackenzie on to his side and put the cuffs on, then turned to Jon.

"Ready!" Summers said, Jon activated the device on his arm.

"OK, stand back" he said. Blue sparks shot from Mackenzie and the humming noise started, getting louder and louder. Then he had gone, back to his own time to face his punishment. Thomas waved the smoke away. The ground where Mackenzie was sitting was glowing from the heat of the jump. He turned to Jon.

"We should take the bodies back home" he said.

"Agreed, we can take a look at that door too" Jon replied, and made his way back to the main chamber of the bunker, the others following.

"We'll have to be quick" Summers said. "We don't want more Nazis showing up."

"OK, Summers, give me a hand" Jon said as they approached the two dead men. Summers gripped Carter by the legs and dragged him over to the body of Bolton. "Clear!" Jon shouted, and tapped away on the touch screen panel. Blue sparks flashed and the bodies were gone. Thomas walked through the smoke, taking the golden key from his bag. Gracie came over and stood by his side.

"Go ahead" she said, Thomas gave her a smile and stepped forward, clicked the key into position and pushed it in. The door seemed to take it from him with a loud clunk. The mechanism inside could be heard clicking and snapping into place. Then, there was a loud bang and the door started to open. They could see the inside of a huge vault.

"My god!" Thomas said, taking a step forward. Piled up in boxes and crates were thousands upon thousands of gold bars, just like the one found at the castle.

"Holy fuck" Jon said, walking in, his eyes wide, Summers picked one of the heavy bars up and stared at it.

"All this wealth was stolen from different people in different countries, then melted down to make these bars" he said, not taking his eyes from the gold in his hand.

"What shall we do with it?" Jon asked.

"We do nothing with it, it's blood money" Gracie replied. She stepped forward and took Thomas' hand. "We should go now, lock it up again and leave it to history."

Thomas looked down at her and smiled. "She's right" he said, turning back to the others. "It's not ours to do anything with."

"Not even a little?" Jon asked, sounding disappointed.

"Not even a little" Thomas replied. Summers put the bar back where he had found it.

"They're right, we should leave now" he said. They stepped out of the massive vault and Thomas removed the key. The huge door started to close and they stood there, watching the vast store of wealth disappear into the darkness once more.

"We did what we came to do" Thomas said, and at that the sound of running could be heard coming from the corridor, Summers stepped forward to listen.

"We should get out of here, now" he said.

"Shit, more Nazis!" Jon replied. He switched on his panel. "Quick, press your recall buttons" he shouted, and they all activated the devices on their arms. "Ready?" Jon said. They nodded, and at that, soldiers ran into the room. "Now!" Jon shouted. The blue electrical sparks started blasting. The crates and ammunition boxes were pushed aside by the energy. The humming became louder. The Nazi soldiers aimed their weapons, but it was too late. Thomas, Gracie, Jon and Summers were gone, leaving behind a burning and smoking crater.

The smoke began to clear. Standing in front of them were two of Summers' colleagues.

"Sir" one man said as Summers walked down the steps. "Mackenzie and James are in custody and the bodies you sent back have been taken to the mortuary."

"Thank you agent" Summers replied. Jon followed him off the platform. Gracie suddenly stopped dead and looked around.

"Where's Thomas?" she said, in a panic. Jon walked back up the steps and looked.

"Tom?" he said. "Shit!" He ran back down the steps and over to the control panel. "Something's wrong!" he said. Pushing aside the scientist, he tapped away on the control station. Summers came running over to him.

"Jon, where's Thomas, what's happened?" he said.

"There must have been a glitch with his recall device" Jon answered, still tapping on the buttons.

"And what does that mean?" Summers said. There came no answer. "Jon?" Summers shouted grabbing hold of him. "What's happened to him?"

"He's jumped somewhere else, I'm not sure where" Jon answered. Summers turned away and walked back up the steps on to the platform. Gracie stood there, white as a sheet.

"We'll find him" Summers said, bending down to her. She looked up at him, crying softly. He helped her to her feet and they walked down off the platform, Summers glanced over to Jon, still working on the control station. Summers and Gracie walked out the room and the door slammed behind them.

CHAPTER 8

Thomas looked around. All he could see were trees. The ground under his feet was burning from the jump. He hoped he wasn't still in Germany, but it looked as if he could well be.

He walked off the smouldering crater, keeping an eye out for any Nazis. Eventually he reached a muddy footpath, where he looked in both directions. Nobody could be seen. What had happened? Why the fuck was he still in Germany?

He held up his arm, pressing the panels buttons, but the screen was blank. Shit. It looked as if he was stuck. But just then he heard something coming from further down the pathway. He froze, drawing his pistol, and then he saw someone walking towards him; a man. He dived off the path and into the trees, pushing his back against one of the larger oaks.

The man got closer, and Thomas peered round the tree. The man walked past holding a dog on a lead, but as they drew closer the little dog began to bark. Clearly he could smell Thomas.

"Come on!" the man said, pulling on the lead. He spoke English, not German, and in an accent Thomas thought he recognized. He looked round the tree once more to see the man walking on, the dog still barking. The man was wearing jeans and a red coat with a beanie hat, most certainly not a Nazi uniform.

Holy shit – this was England. He was home.

He stepped out, back on to the path. The man was now out of sight. Thomas walked on, eventually coming to a gate. That was when he realized that he truly was not only in England, but back home in Oxford.

He read the familiar sign which was fixed on a post near the gate: 'Bagley Wood.' He was close to his parents' house, the place where he had grown up. He walked out on to a tarmac pathway to see a bus stop opposite him. A woman was walking with a child on the other side of the road, and a smile came to his face. Of all the places he could have jumped to, he was home.

A man approached, walking down the path towards the bus stop. "Morning" he said, staring at Thomas and the strange suit he was wearing. Thomas nodded.

"Morning" he replied. The man stopped.

"What you got on there mate?" he said, pointing at the suit with a smile on his face.

"Oh, er, I'm a sewage worker, it's just protective gear we have to wear" Thomas answered, struggling to think of a lie. The man nodded.

"Must be some mighty shit down there" he said, and began to walk off. Thomas laughed and raised his hand as the man walked over to the bus stop. He was about to walk away when a bus came down the road. He stopped for a second and then ran over to the man.

"Excuse me" Thomas said. "Does this bus go to South Hinksey?"

"Yes, well, it goes through it" the man replied, looking Thomas up and down. "I don't suppose you've got any change in that suit though, have you?"

"No, I haven't. I've got family there you see, just wanted to pop in, say hello."

The man smiled and patted Thomas on the back. "Come on, my shout" he said.

"Thank you so much. I can repay you" Thomas said as they took their seats.

"Oh, don't worry about it" the man replied. "My name is Ken, Ken Diggins." He put out his hand, Thomas shook it and then thought for a second.

"I think I remember you, Ken" he said. "Oh, sorry, I'm Thomas Long."

The man looked at him. "Really? I know a Thomas Long" the man answered. "My friend's son. He's only about ten years old though."

Thomas smiled as he sat back in his seat. He did know this man. Ken Diggins was his father's friend from golfing. But he had died in 2013.

"You OK son?" he asked Thomas.

"Um, yeah, I'm fine" Thomas said. "Tell me Ken, what's your friend's name?" The man turned back to him with a smile.

"Gordon Long, he works for the government, an agent or something, he's not allowed to talk about what he does" said Ken. Thomas looked shocked. "Are you related to him them, is that who you're visiting?" the man went on.

Thomas just stared in disbelief.

"Hey, are you sure you're OK?" said Ken.

"Oh, yes, sorry. Um, no, I'm not related" Thomas replied. Ken gave him a smile and looked forward. Shit, Thomas thought, he wasn't really back home. He was 27 years in the past.

"This is your stop, son" the man said, nudging Thomas' arm.

"Oh thank you" Thomas said. He got to his feet and pressed the bell for the driver to stop, then turned back round to face his father's friend. "Thank you for your kindness, it is most appreciated."

"Your very welcome" Ken Diggins replied with a smile.

Thomas stepped off the bus and looked around. This was somewhere he really did recognize, his old neighbourhood, and just around the corner was his street, the street where he had grown up.

* * * * *

Jon walked into the mess hall. Gracie was sitting there with Summers; they were now both in their normal clothes. He walked over to them. Gracie shot up out of her chair.

"Have you found Tom?" she asked with desperation in her voice.

"Not yet, well, not exactly" Jon said, taking a seat next to Summers.

"What do you mean, not exactly?" Summers asked, turning to face him, Gracie sat back down, disappointed.

"Well, I have a theory as to what happened, and I think I'll be able to find him, if my theory is correct that is."

"Well, go on?" Gracie answered.

"Well, you see, a few years ago I was working on a project when there was some kind of meteor strike in New York. It destroyed a whole building. There was only one survivor in the rubble, a disabled guy. After some time in hospital it was discovered that not only had he survived the meteor hitting the building, it had altered something about him. His DNA was changed. He could manipulate matter, dark matter, and create a hole through space around his body, giving him the ability to teleport anywhere he wished."

"Really?" Gracie asked. Summers looked at her. "It is true, the government got involved in it to as I remember" Summers said. Jon nodded.

"Yes, it was kept from the public, for obvious reasons" Jon added. "After all, nobody wants someone like that around, someone who could just teleport anywhere he wanted. He could appear in a bank vault, people's houses, anywhere. It was too dangerous to let people know. There would have been panic."

"What happened to him? And more importantly,

how does this help us find Thomas?" Gracie asked, getting impatient.

"Well, not only could he teleport, he could charge up the energy of the dark matter around him and use it to smash things apart. I mean, he became so powerful, but whenever he got stressed or frightened, the dark matter would automatically send him somewhere safe – at least, somewhere he felt safe. With him, it was his local church. And what I was thinking is, that maybe, when Thomas' recall device failed, the dark matter did something similar and sent him somewhere safe."

"OK, well, I kind of know what you're saying Jon, but do you know this for sure?" Gracie asked. He shook his head.

"Not for definite, no, it's just a theory. But I really do think the dark matter may have reacted to Thomas' state of mind, and therefore sent him to a safe place."

"OK, we just need to find out what that safe place is" Summers said, looking from Jon to Gracie.

"Well, it wouldn't have been his uni days, he hated that" Jon said.

"He loves his work, I mean the archaeology" Gracie said. "But that's still just work, I'm guessing it'll be somewhere personal."

★   ★   ★   ★   ★

Thomas walked down his old street. There was a row of garages on the right next to some small houses, and on the opposite side of the road, the larger houses where his family lived. He walked down further and took a seat on a bench next to a grassed area. A few doors away from him sat his old house. His father's car wasn't on the drive. He must be working, Thomas thought.

Then he saw the woman walking up the path. It was his mother. She had died in 2017 of breast cancer. A tear rolled down Thomas' cheek.

"Mum" he whispered under his breath. She was holding a young boy's hand. It was himself as a child. The woman and the child walked up the path to the house and disappeared through the door. Thomas was about to walk away when he had a sudden thought.

"This is really stupid" he muttered under his breath, as he walked quickly over to the house and down the pathway to the front door. He paused for a moment, took in a deep breath and pressed the doorbell. Then he changed his mind. "Forget it, it's stupid" he muttered and had started to walk back down the path when the door opened.

"Hello, can I help you?" His mother's voice came from behind him, a voice he had almost forgotten. He turned back round slowly and gave her a smile. She looked at his suit, up and down.

"Can I help?" she said again. She was looking at him oddly.

"Er, I'm a sewage worker madam, I just needed to know if you have had any problems with the drainage around here?" he asked her, feeling ashamed that he was lying to his own mother.

"No, no problems around here" she said. Thomas smiled at her. "Thank you" he said, and turned back round. As he started walking down the footpath, she spoke again.

"Thomas!" she said. Thinking she must be calling the younger version of himself, he ignored her.

"Thomas!" Again came her voice.

Thomas turned back to face her. She was standing there, staring at him. He stopped dead and stared back. She smiled at him.

"I don't know how this is possible, but do you really think that I wouldn't recognize my own son?" she said. A tear rolled down Thomas' face as she smiled at him, a smile he remembered so well, a warm comforting smile. He slowly made his way back, stopping in front of her, and looked her in the eyes.

"Hey Mum" he whispered. She smiled and gripped him tightly and he held her close to him. Still more tears came down his cheek. He had missed her death, working away, he had never got to say goodbye, but now he had been given another chance.

"Come inside" she said and took his hand. They walked in and made their way to the sitting room. "Would you like something to drink?" she asked him, he smiled and shook his head.

"No thank you, I can't stay long."

"How is this possible?" she asked him suddenly. He paused for a second.

"At university, I met a man called Jon" Thomas

began. "He became a great scientist and a good friend, he invented time travel, and here I am." His mother smiled.

"You go to university?" she asked.

"Yeah" he answered, taking her hand. A tear fell from her face.

"How old are you?" she asked.

"I'm 37 now Mum" he answered. She gripped his hand tightly.

"Am I still....?" He shook his head, and began to sob, interrupting her. "It's OK, it's OK" she said. "And your father, is he still alive in your time?" she asked.

"Yes, he still lives here, alone, I try and visit him as often as I can" Thomas answered, still with tears rolling down his face. She forced back her tears and wiped her eyes.

"I always knew you would do great things Thomas" she said, and reached up to wipe away the tears from her son's face.

At that the young boy came running in from the garden and suddenly stopped, seeing Thomas standing there. Thomas smiled.

Thomas actually remembered this scene from his childhood, the strange man standing there, talking to his mother.

"Thomas, go and play, I won't be long" his mother said. The young Thomas smiled and ran back out with his ball. Thomas turned back to his mum.

"I have to go now" he said. She smiled and nodded

her head. As he was about to leave, he stopped and turned round.

"Mum?" he said.

"Yes son?"

"I never got the chance to say goodbye last time, I was too late" he said. She gave him one of those warm smiles.

"Say it now then" she whispered. He looked at her, straight into her tearful eyes.

"I love you Mum" he said. "Goodbye."

"I'll always love you Thomas. I was always so proud of my little boy" she said. He leaned down and gave her a kiss on the cheek.

"Don't tell Dad about this" he said. She shook her head. "I won't, I promise" she replied. He stepped away from her, still holding her hand.

"Bye Mum" he said, and released her. She gave him a wave as he walked back down the path, out of the front gate and down the street. She watched him the whole way.

"Bye son" she murmured softly, and went back inside.

★ ★ ★ ★ ★

Gracie came running out of the elevator and over to Jon.

"Jon, Jon!" she shouted, out of breath.

"What is it Grace?" he asked her, trying to calm her down.

"He's gone home" she said.

"Home?"

She nodded her head. "He's talked about when he was younger before, how it was the happiest time in his life, when his mother was still alive" she said. "He's gone to that time." Jon nodded, then looked at the control station.

"What are you doing?" she asked.

"If I can put a time in and a place, I should be able to lock on to him, and if the recall device is working, then I'll be able to jump him back" Jon answered, tapping away on the brightly-lit screen. "What sort of age would you say he was happiest?" Jon asked, not taking his eyes from the station.

"Try ten years old" she said with a smile. Jon selected the time and date on the screen.

"OK then, Oxford, the year 2000" he muttered under his breath. The screen suddenly made a beeping noise, and Jon smiled.

"What is it?" Gracie asked eagerly.

"I've got him" Jon answered. "He's there." Summers walked in, and could sense the excitement.

"What's happening?" he said as he approached them. Gracie turned round and threw her arms around his neck.

"We've found him!" she shouted. Summers smiled, holding her arms.

"That's wonderful" he answered.

Jon turned round to face them. "I'll bring him back" he said.

Gracie smiled frantically. "Hurry!" she said.

"OK, OK. I just have to hit the recall switch" he said, and pushed the button. The loud humming started, but then, it stopped again. No Thomas.

"What's happened?" Gracie asked. Jon was tapping away on the control station.

"His recall device isn't working, that must be why he was sent there" he answered. He turned to face Gracie. "I'll have to go and get him" he said.

"I can go!" she shouted as he walked off towards the equipment room.

"I'm the only one who'll be able to repair the device" he answered. He carried on, opening the door and walking in. Summers took hold of her hand.

"It's OK, Jon will get him back" he said. She moved forward and hugged him. The door to the equipment room opened and Jon came walking out, doing his suit up.

"Gracie, when I say hit that button, hit it, OK?" he said. She nodded.

"OK" she said and Jon made his way up the steps and on to the platform. He turned round to face the others, then smiled and put his thumb up.

"OK, Grace, now" he shouted over to her. She raised her hand to him and pushed the button in, and the countdown started. Within seconds, Jon was gone in a cloud of smoke and sparks.

★ ★ ★ ★ ★

Jon stepped off the burning crater and activated the touch screen on his arm. The mini map came up, and sure enough, the little red flashing dot representing Thomas appeared. He's only a few streets away. Jon thought, and ran over to the main road, looking in both directions. A police car was approaching, and on seeing Jon dressed so oddly, the driver slowed down to have a better look at him. Shit, he thought, and walked off quickly down the road. He glanced down at the digital map on his arm. There was an alleyway just a bit further down on his left. He looked back to see that the police car had turned around and was coming back in hiss direction. He began to run, almost falling over a trash can. He stumbled, but carried on running until he had reached a block of garages. The police car screeched to a halt and two officers got out and ran down the alley. Fucking hell, Jon thought. He ran over to a garage, lifted the door up and slid inside, closing the metal door quietly behind him. Glancing under the door, he could see the shiny black shoes of the officers looking around the area.

"He's had it away" one said.

"Come on, the station canteen's closing in 20 minutes and I'm starving" the other replied. Both officers made their way back down the alleyway. Jon stayed where he was for a second, and on hearing the police car start and move off, he came out of his hiding place. That had been close.

Just then a young man came round the corner and

gave Jon a smile. Jon politely smiled back and was about to walk away when the youth spoke to him.

"Saw yer 'iding" he said.

Jon stopped and turned around.

"Saw the pigs looking for yer too, didn't tell 'em where you was though" he said, walking over to Jon. He lifted his baseball cap up slightly and stood right in front of Jon. Jon smiled.

"Thanks for that" Jon answered and went to walk away again, but the young man seized Jon's arm.

"Oh, you're a Yank are yer, explains the clothes" he said. "I reckon you owe me a little something for helping you out there."

Jon turned back round to face him.

"Well, I don't have anything" Jon answered. The youth gritted his teeth and stared at Jon. Then he pulled out his hand from his pocket, producing a small knife. Jon took a step back.

"Well, that's a real fucking shame ent it!" the youth said. As he took a step closer to Jon, Jon leaned forward, gripping his hand tightly and turning it. The wrist snapped with a sharp cracking noise and the knife fell to the ground. Jon released him and he fell to his knees, crying in pain. Jon walked away, leaving the crying bully where he was.

He walked out on to a side street and he looked down at the map. Shit, Thomas was just round the corner. He ran down the street and on to yet another main road, looking around frantically. Then he saw him, just down the road sitting on a bench. Jon smiled and made his way over to his friend.

Thomas was sitting fiddling around with the device on his arm, the screen still blank.

"Hey Tom" said Jon. Thomas looked up to see Jon standing next to him, smiling. He stood up and hugged his old friend tightly. Jon gave a little laugh and hugged him back.

"What's all this, why the hugs?" asked Jon. Thomas moved back and looked at him, a tear in his eye. "Thank you Jon" Thomas said.

Jon smiled. "What for?" he answered. "For coming to get your ass back home?"

Thomas smiled and shook his head.

"No, my friend" Thomas replied. "For creating the time device." Jon looked confused. "It allowed me to say goodbye to my mother."

Jon put his hand up and wiped Thomas' tear away, smiling at him.

"You're welcome Tom" he replied. "Now, let's have a look at that device." They both sat down on the bench. Jon took out his tool set from his belt and removed the screen from Thomas' arm, exposing the wires and lights. Jon glanced up at Thomas.

"So, you actually went to see your mum?" he asked. Thomas smiled.

"Yeah, I had too. I was given another chance, thanks to you."

"Well, glad to hear that it's had a positive outcome at last" Jon answered.

"It's a wonderful gift you've created Jon, as long as it's used wisely" Thomas said, still holding his arm out for Jon.

"I didn't know if you would have visited her or not, after all, it could have changed history" Jon replied.

Thomas shook his head. "She won't tell anyone, not even me" he answered with a smile. Jon glanced at him.

"So, did you see yourself?" he asked, Thomas had a big grin on his face.

"Yeah, I did" he answered.

"Wow, that must have been weird" Jon said, looking back to the device.

"The funny thing is that I do actually remember it from when I was 10, this man talking to my mum" Thomas answered, and Jon glanced at his friend once more.

"That is weird" Jon said, and at that the device started to bleep. "There, give it a few seconds to reboot" Jon said, and fixed the screen back over the wires. "I'll have to check them all over when we get back, make sure this doesn't happen again." The device lit up. "There, it's ready" Jon said. "OK Tom, press the recall button in three seconds."

They both switched on the devices and Jon started the countdown.

★ ★ ★ ★ ★

As the smoke cleared, Thomas could hear Gracie

calling. "Thomas, Thomas!" she shouted as she ran up the steps and straight into his arms. He closed his eyes and gripped her tight.

"Hey baby" he whispered, as she hugged him.

"Hey" she replied and moved back, looking at him straight in his eyes. "I was worried" she said softly. He gave her a smile. "Sorry about that" he said. She grinned and embraced him once more. Jon walked down the steps to be greeted by Summers.

"Well done Jon" he said, and patted Jon on the back.

"He was OK" Jon replied and looked over at Thomas. "I'm going to have to take a look at the recall devices, all of them, make sure this doesn't happen again. I think everyone should take some time off, just a few weeks, maybe a month."

Summers nodded. "I take it no more jumps for a while then?" he asked Jon, Jon gave a faint smile.

"Like I said, just a few weeks" he said, and walked over to the equipment room. Summers walked over to Thomas and Gracie, who had came down now, off the platform.

"Glad to see you're all right Thomas" he said. Thomas leaned forward and shook his hand.

"Thank you Michael. Yeah, I'm good, better than good actually." Gracie looked up at him.

"What do you mean, better than good? What happened there?"

Thomas gripped her hand and smiled at her lovingly.

"I saw my mum" he answered. Gracie looked shocked.

"Did she see you?"

"Yeah, and she knew who I was too" he replied.

"Really?"

"We talked for a while. I even saw myself, as a boy." He grinned at the memory of seeing the younger Thomas.

"And what did you say?"

"I got to say goodbye to her, I was given another chance Grace." She leaned up and gave him a kiss. "That's good darling" she answered stroking his face.

"I'm going to go back home for a bit" he suddenly said.

"Really? For how long?"

"I just kind of need to see my dad" he replied. "Not for long, a week maybe."

"OK, well, I'll be here when you get back" she said. But he shook his head.

"Come with me" he said. "I'd like Dad to meet you."

"OK, that'll be nice" she answered. At that Jon came over, back in his everyday clothes again.

"Hey you two" he said walking up to them.

"Hi Jon" Thomas answered. "Listen, Jon, me and Gracie are going back to England for a week or so, if that's OK with you?"

Jon smiled and patted Thomas on the shoulder. "Of course Tom, I've got things to do here anyway, check over the devices, and give the machine a once over too, so there'll be no jumps for about a month anyway" he answered. "And, it'll get you two love birds out of my way for a bit." He smiled.

"I've got to get this suit off" Thomas said.

"OK, when do you want to leave for home?" Gracie asked him.

"As soon as" he replied.

"OK, you get freshened up and I'll organize the flight."

"That would be wonderful" he said, bending down and kissing her. She watched him walk over to the equipment room and go through the door. Then she gave a little smile to herself and made her way out to make the necessary arrangements.

★ ★ ★ ★ ★

Jon had all the suits lined up on racks in front of him. He was starting the long process of taking each suit and device apart, looking for any faults, and finding ways to improve the high tech devices. The door slid open and Summers walked in. Jon glanced over with a smile.

"Ah, Michael, what can I do for you?" he said.

Summers came over to him and took a seat next to the workstation.

"Well Jon, I was wondering if you had anything that I could do, I'm a tad bored to be honest" Summers replied. Jon laughed.

"It's only been two days and your bored already?"

Jon said, still taking small pieces off the devices and looking at them closely. Summers looked over to him with a smile.

"Yes I'm bored" he answered.

"OK, well, you can give me a hand if you like" Jon said.

"OK, that'll be great" Summers replied with a smile.

★ ★ ★ ★ ★

On arrival in England, Thomas and Gracie first went to her parents house in Worcestershire, where Thomas, met her mother and father for the first time. He thought how normal they were. After all, the things that Thomas and Gracie had experienced together were far from normal. It was nice to just sit there, talking about normal things, drinking tea, and of course, eating a proper English roast dinner.

After a delightful few hours, they stood at the front door saying their goodbyes.

"Don't leave it so long next time, Grace" her mother said, kissing her on the cheek.

"I'll try not to, Mum" she answered. Her father shook Thomas' hand.

"It was nice to meet you Thomas" he said. Thomas smiled. "And you, Mr and Mrs Stevenson, it was a pleasure" he replied. Gracie's mother leaned up and gave him a hug and a kiss. "You're always welcome here Thomas" she said.

Thomas and Gracie got into the car and slowly began to pull off, waving at her parents as they did.

"Next stop, your house" Gracie said. Thomas smiled, and they began their journey to Oxfordshire.

* * * * *

"So, where does this go?" Summers asked, holding up a small piece of golden metal. Jon took it from him. "Michael, just pass me things, please, we can't make any mistakes with this" he answered. Summers gave a slight grin.

"Sorry Jon" he said.

"It's OK, it's just very important that we get it right" Jon replied. Summers got to his feet.

"Listen, I'll leave you to it" he said. "I'll go into the city I think, have a break."

"Are you sure?"

"Yes, of course, I could do with a drink" replied the agent with a smile, walking out. Jon picked up his tools and started working again, able to fully concentrate once more.

* * * * *

Thomas and Gracie pulled over outside his parents' house. It hadn't really changed since he had been a child. The front door opened and his father came out to greet them. Thomas got out the car, followed by

Gracie, and he walked over to him.

"Tommy" his dad called out and embraced him.

"Hey Dad" Thomas replied and hugged his father. "This is Gracie."

"Gracie, it's so nice to meet you" his father said moving towards her. She smiled and went to shake his hand and he hugged her tightly.

"Mr Long, hello, it's good to meet you, I've heard so much about you from Thomas" she said.

"All good I hope?" he answered and gave her a wink. "Oh, and call me Gordon" he added. He picked up Gracie's bag for her and they made their way inside the house. "So, how about a cup of tea?" he asked as they got into the sitting room.

"Yes please, that would be lovely" Gracie replied as he walked into the kitchen. "Milk, one sugar please."

Thomas stood there, looking around the room. The furniture had changed, and the wallpaper, but he could almost still smell his mother's perfume. He walked over to the mantlepiece and picked up a photograph of her. She must have been in her thirties when it was taken, about the same time that he had visited her with the device. He stared at it, and the thought came to him that, his whole life, his mother knew that he would do this remarkable thing, this time travel, and she had kept her word, she had never told a soul. A smile crept onto his face and he put the picture back where it belonged.

"Still taking two sugars son?" his dad asked as he came back in the room, handing Gracie a cup.

"Yeah, still two Dad" Thomas replied. "We'll stay for a couple of days, if that's OK."

His father grinned. "Of course son, as long as you like" he answered, and handed Thomas the cup of tea.

"And how have you been, Dad?" Thomas asked.

"Oh, I'm fine son, you know me" he replied. At that Gracie came into the room and Gordon looked at her.

"And I'm so glad my Tommy has finally found himself a nice pretty girl" he said with a smile. She giggled and Thomas laughed. His dad turned to him. "So, you two met through work then?" he asked.

"Yeah, he was kind of my boss" Gracie said. Gordon laughed out.

"Tommy, you haven't been making inappropriate advances on staff, have you?" he said with a huge smile. Gracie laughed out loud. "No Dad, well, maybe a little" he answered.

"Good boy" his father said and patted Thomas on the back. "So, how is work going, you went to America didn't you, to work with that strange friend of yours?"

Thomas glanced over at Gracie, and she smiled at him.

"Um, yeah, you mean Jon. Yes it's going great, doing some really good work over there" Thomas replied, taking a sip of tea.

"That's good son, I'm very proud" his father said, with a warm smile. "So then, how about a takeaway tonight? I was thinking maybe Chinese or pizza?" He looked at them.

"Chinese would be great" Gracie replied.

"Excellent, I'll get the menus" Gordon replied and walked back into the sitting room. Gracie came over to Thomas. She put her cup down and put her arms around his waist.

"I really like your dad" she said. "He's lovely." Thomas smiled.

"Thanks, you wouldn't think he used to be an MI5 agent would you?" he replied.

"Well, look how nice Summers has turned out to be" Gracie answered. Thomas laughed and leaned forward, kissing her. That evening they ate a wonderful Chinese feast, and after several glasses of wine and great conversation, they all went to bed, Thomas and Gracie in his old room.

★ ★ ★ ★ ★

Summers stepped out of the taxi and after paying the driver he walked into the bar and took a stool. "Whiskey please, make it a double" he asked. He looked round at the entrance. A man had walked in, quite rough looking, with a full beard. He took a seat next to Summers and ordered a drink.

"Vodka!" he said, in a low Russian accent. Summers felt suspicious of the man and kept glancing at him. After several more vodkas he turned to Summers.

"You Summers?" he asked. Summers turned to look at him.

"Who are you?" he replied, the man smiled.

"I take it that's a yes" he said, and got to his feet. Summers sensed something was wrong and stood up quickly. The Russian hurtled forward, straight at Summers, his fist clenched tight. Summers, having no time to react, took the punch right on the cheek bone and fell to the floor, his face bleeding. The man stood over him.

"My name is Vladimir Sharkov. My benefactor, Lt Mackenzie, sent me" he said. "I've been instructed to hunt you all down." From the back of his jacket he pulled out a huge hunting knife. The girl behind the bar ran out to the back. The Russian turned to the other people in the bar.

"Get out!" he yelled at them. They all ran out the bar into the street, Summers managed to get to his feet, still a little dazed from the punch.

"You are making a very big mistake my friend, you won't get away with this" Summers said, taking a napkin from the bar and wiping his face. The Russian smiled and again lunged at Summers, this time with the knife. But Summers stepped to one side, and as the blade went past his face he struck the Russian hard in the throat. The man dropped to his knees, holding his neck. Summers stepped away calmly.

"Like I said, a very big mistake" Summers said. The Russian got to his feet, still with the knife in his hand. He turned to Summers and gritted his teeth, swiping out with the blade, once, twice. Summers dodged and then aimed a kick straight at the man's knee cap. The leg broke with a loud snap and the Russian fell to the floor, crying out in pain.

Summers turned to see two police officers run in, their weapons drawn.

"Freeze!" one shouted. Summers put his hands up.

"I'm a government agent" he replied. "This man attacked me."

"Let's see some ID!" the other officer called out, still with his gun trained on Summers. The agent pulled his badge from his pocket. One of the officers took it from him and looked at it. Then he handed it back.

"Sorry sir" he replied. "What's happened here?"

Summers looked down at the Russian, still gasping in pain. "This man came in looking for me, a grudge attack by the looks of things" Summers answered. The second police officer holstered his weapon and handcuffed the Russian.

"We'll take care of it, sir" the first officer said.

Summers nodded. "Good, make sure you do, I don't want to see him again officer, understand?"

"Yes sir" the policeman answered. Summers walked over to the bar, taking his glass from the side, and knocked back the rest of his drink. Then he walked out of the bar.

Jon had put back together the final suit and hung them all back in the equipment room with the rest of the gear. He walked out and went over to the machine, then smiled and stroked the cold metal, recalling the time back at university when he had had the idea of time jumping. The first project he had worked on involving the manipulation of dark matter, enabling him to travel anywhere he wished. Jon often wondered what had happened to that man.

He crouched down and took off one of the panels. There was a glowing blue orb in the centre, in amongst the wires and lights and micro chips. This orb was heart of the machine. It controlled the dark matter and manipulated it to form wormholes through space and time.

He took from his pocket a small device and held it up to the orb. The device bleeped a couple of times.

"Nice and normal" he said. He placed the device back in his pocket and fixed the panel back on, covering the glowing orb and fastening it into place. One of the workers came over to him, in a hurry.

"Dr Walker, Agent Summers just called, something happened to him in the city" he said. "A man attacked him."

Jon looked shocked. "Is he all right?" he asked.

"Yes sir, but he said the man who attacked him was working for Lt Mackenzie."

"Really?" Jon said. He put down his tools and started to walk away. "Contact Agent Summers, tell him to come back" he called back.

Jon walked through a door and made his way down the corridor. At the end of it was a large red door made of solid metal with a security key code on the side. He punched in a number and a small compartment opened up. Jon leaned forward and a beam shot out, scanning his retina. The door made a loud clunking noise, jets of steam shot out from the corners and it began to open slowly. Jon stepped inside a large white room. A security guard was standing on the right-hand side, next to a control station.

"I'm here to see Mackenzie" Jon said. The security guard nodded. He pressed a button on the panel and the wall on the opposite side of the room opened up with a loud clanking noise. A row of cells slid forward and began to rotate. Jon stepped over to a red line painted on the floor and waited. The cells moved round and then suddenly stopped. One cell came forward and the shutter covering it slid open to reveal Mackenzie sitting there. He looked up at Jon and smiled.

"I trust you have all begun to die?" the lieutenant asked with a smirk. Jon stepped over the red line and walked right up to the solid plastic glass separating them.

"I'm afraid Summers stopped your assassin" Jon said, with a sarcastic smile. The lieutenant got to his feet and thumped on the plastic barrier.

"I will have my vengeance Walker!" he said, spit flying up the plastic glass. The security guard was about to come over when Jon put his hand up to halt him.

"Well, you'd better get someone more skilled than your last thug then, hadn't you?" he said to Mackenzie and stepped away from the glass. The guard pressed the button once more and the lieutenant's cell moved back again, the metal shutter closing behind it.

"Thank you" Jon said to the guard and walked back out, the large red metal door slamming shut behind him.

★ ★ ★ ★ ★

Thomas was standing outside the front door to his father's house. "It was nice to see you Dad" he said. His father smiled and embraced his son.

"Tommy, you're always welcome, and please, don't leave it so long next time" Gordon replied, still holding his son.

"I won't Dad, I promise" Thomas answered with a smile.

"And you young lady, you're welcome here any time" Gordon said, hugging Gracie.

"Thank you Gordon, it was lovely meeting you."

"You too my dear. Barbara would have loved you, god rest her soul" he replied with a sad smile.

"I would have loved to have met her, I've heard so much about you both from Thomas" she answered, and gave him a kiss on the cheek. Thomas had loaded the car with their luggage and walked back up the path.

"Bye Dad, see you soon" Thomas called out. His father grinned. "See you son, good luck with your work" he replied and Gracie and Thomas got into the vehicle. One final wave and they set off to the airport.

★ ★ ★ ★ ★

Summers walked into the mess hall. Jon was sitting alone at one of the tables, a cold cup of coffee in front of him.

"Jon" Summers said and took a seat opposite him.

"Michael, are you OK? I heard about the attack" Jon replied.

"Yes, I'm fine, just a little scratch." He tapped a small wound on his cheekbone.

"I've spoken to Mackenzie, he practically admitted his involvement in the attack" Jon said. Summers sat back and frowned.

"Well, what I'm concerned about is how many of these assassins he's sent out after us all. Knowing Mackenzie, these people won't be very nice" Summers answered. Jon looked up at him.

"Shit!" he suddenly said. "We should warn Thomas and Gracie. They may be in danger."

Summers quickly got to his feet. "OK, I'll do that" he said, and ran out of the hall as fast as he could. Jon took a sip of the coffee and pulled a disgusted expression. He stood up, threw the plastic cup in the trash bin and walked out the room.

An hour later Summers came over to Jon, who was working in the main machine room again.

"I can't get hold of Thomas or Gracie, they must be in the air already" he said. Jon stopped what he was doing and turned to Summers.

"Well, we'll have to leave it a few hours then, try again after they land" he replied.

The flight was a pleasant and comfortable one. Thomas got to his feet as the plane came to a halt at the Ronald Reagan National Airport. He reached up and handed Gracie her bag. After leaving the arrivals section, they walked over to a small café and ordered two coffees.

"Can't beat American coffee" he said and handed Gracie her cup.

"Thanks" she answered with a smile. They sat there for about an hour, chatting about their trip back home, the time project, and of course, each other, the whole time. Thomas had noticed a woman sitting at the other end of the café. She hadn't taken her eyes from them, and Thomas was becoming suspicious of her.

"See that woman over there, the one in the leather jacket?" Thomas said to Gracie. She carefully glanced round.

"I see her" Gracie replied.

"She's been watching us the whole time we've been here" Thomas said.

Gracie grinned. "Maybe she fancies you?"

Thomas smiled. "No, I don't think so, something's wrong."

"Well, let's leave, see if she follows" Gracie suggested.

"OK." Thomas picked up his rucksack, throwing it over his shoulder. Gracie stood up and took the handle of her suitcase. They left the café and walked down the wide corridor, shops on either side of them. Thomas paused for a minute and bought a newspaper. When he glanced round, sure enough, the woman was following.

"Maybe she works for Jon?" Gracie asked. Thomas looked at her and shook his head.

"No, she would have came up to us" Thomas said. They carried on to the main area and out of the doors, where a row of taxi cabs waited. Thomas quickly went over to one and spoke to the driver. Gracie opened the rear door and got in while Thomas helped the driver load the trunk with the luggage. Soon they were on their way back to the facility.

"Well, we lost her" Thomas said, putting his arm around Gracie, They were driving through a section of the city with skyscrapers on either side, and the air buses travelling just above them. Gracie held Thomas tight.

Then she glanced over her shoulder and through the rear window to see a black car approaching fast. The driver was the woman from the airport. The car gained on the taxi with great speed and soon it was on them. The front bumper of the black car slammed into the cab hard, shunting Thomas and Gracie forward.

"Shit!" the taxi driver yelled.

"No, don't stop, keep going!" Thomas shouted to the man. Gracie turned round to see where the car had gone. There was also a passenger. Thomas took out his pistol and leaned out the window.

"Get down!" Gracie called out. Shots rang out and

bullets started blasting through the windows. Glass scattered everywhere.

"Keep going, put your foot down!" Thomas yelled at the driver.

"Haven't got to tell me twice!" he replied and put the pedal down to the floor. The taxi raced off down the freeway followed by the black car, shots still ringing out. It pulled alongside the cab and the female driver slammed it into the side. At this point the taxi driver lost control and the vehicle shot across the lane, hitting another car and sliding down a bank into some trees.

"Grace, are you OK?" Thomas asked, glass all over him.

"Um, yeah, I'm fine" she answered. They looked at the driver. He wasn't moving, but he was still breathing. Thomas kicked his door open and scrambled out, then turned round and helped Gracie. Just then there was a crack as another shot rang out. Thomas grabbed Gracie and pulled her to the ground.

"Fuck!" Thomas said, holding Gracie close to him. He glanced up, peering through the broken window of the taxi to see a man coming down the bank. The woman was waiting at the top.

"Stay down" Thomas whispered to Gracie, then moved across and picked up a broken piece of glass from the cab window. As the man jumped down, his gun held up, Thomas threw the glass. It hit the man in the face, and blood spattered down his jacket. Thomas ran over to him and punched him full on the nose. He fell to the ground, knocked out cold.

Then a shot rang out, and Thomas looked up to see the woman aiming a pistol at him. Another shot just missed him. Thomas picked up the man's gun and fired back as they ran back behind the taxi.

"Who are they?" Gracie yelled out.

"I'm not sure" Thomas answered and fired another shot, missing the woman. In the distance, they heard sirens. Thomas looked up to see the woman look round. Blue flashing lights could be seen now, getting closer and closer. The woman got back into her car and sped off.

Thomas and Gracie got to their feet to see a police car pull up, and Thomas raised his hand to them.

"Are you guys OK?" An officer called down to them.

"Yeah, the driver's hurt though" Thomas yelled back.

"There's a man down here too, tried to kill us" Gracie called up to him. He waved his hand and his colleague came down the bank, slowly. Thomas and Gracie walked over to meet him, and Thomas handed the man's gun over.

"He used this gun" Thomas said. The officer looked down at the still unconscious man.

"OK, thanks" he said and bent down. The man started to stir and kick out at the officer, who quickly cuffed him.

"We need paramedics down here" the officer said down his radio.

"We can get up ourselves" Thomas said to him. He and Gracie made their way back up the small slope to the road, where several police officers were waiting to meet them. An ambulance pulled up, followed by another, and Thomas and Gracie were seen to straight away.

"Only cuts and bruises, you're very lucky" the paramedic said, cleaning a small cut on Gracie's arm. Thomas looked round to see a grey car pull up next to a police vehicle. It was Summers. He got out and spoke to the officer for a few minutes before coming over to Thomas and Gracie.

"Michael, am I glad to see you" Thomas said, shaking the agent's hand.

"We did leave a message on your answering machine" Summers replied. "Something's happening."

"Clearly!" Thomas answered. "I haven't turned my phone on since England, sorry." Summers patted him on the back.

"At least you're safe. And Gracie, are you all right?"

"Yeah, I'm good" she said. "But who were those people, and why try and kill us?" Summers frowned.

"It's Mackenzie, he's had some of his associates try and hunt us down" Summers replied. Thomas looked over at Gracie, then back to the agent.

"I thought Mackenzie was locked up" Thomas said.

"He is, kind of" Summers answered, looking down to the ground.

"What do you mean?" Gracie asked.

"He is locked up, but not in prison. He's in a secure incarceration block held at the facility. He was allowed one phone call, that must have been when he arranged these hit men."

"And you didn't think to tell us about this cell block?" Thomas asked him angrily.

"It was on a need-to-know basis. The block is used only to hold criminals that have time-jumped, to study any effect the machine might have had on them. The Ripper is there too."

Thomas stepped away from him. "Oh this is great" he said. Summers came closer to him.

"They have to be kept somewhere safe, out of the way of the public" he said. "The cells were designed ages ago, just in case this sort of thing happened."

"Did Jon know about this, or just the CIA?" Thomas asked. The agent looked away. "Jon knew, of course he knew, it's his project" he replied.

"I've heard enough, can we leave now?" Thomas said, walking over to Summers' car. He opened the passenger door and got in. Summers glanced at Gracie.

"Gracie, I'm sorry" he said. She smiled.

"He's just angry that he was kept out the loop, that's all, he'll calm down" she said. She walked over to the car with Summers, and they began the rest of their journey back to the facility.

After what seemed like a long drive, in deafening silence, they pulled up outside the main building. Jon came out to greet them, walking over to the vehicle and opening the door.

"Thomas, Gracie, are you all right? We heard about

the car chase over the police scanner, figured it was you guys" he said. Thomas stepped out the car.

"Jon, I know about Mackenzie and the secret cells you've got here" said Thomas. Jon looked in shock at Summers. "Yes, Summers told us everything, why the fuck didn't you tell me?"

"Tom, please, it was for security reasons, the fewer people know about it the better" Jon answered.

"I need a shower" Thomas said. He picked up his bags and walked through a door leading to the dormitories.

"He'll be fine" Gracie said, and quickly followed Thomas, pulling her suitcase behind her.

Jon walked into the mess hall, hoping to find Thomas there. He was about to leave when he saw Gracie sitting outside on the balcony.

"Hey Jon" she said.

"Is Thomas still mad with me?" he asked, taking a seat next to her.

"Not really, he's in his dorm, got a headache. He's just lying down for a while."

"Grace, I'm truly sorry about not telling you about the cell block" he said. She glanced at him. "Don't worry Jon, we understand."

"Does Thomas?"

"Yeah, he's fine, he just doesn't like being lied to" she replied.

"Grace, I didn't lie, I..."

"Just didn't tell the whole truth" she said, finishing

his sentence. "Listen, you should go and see him, not me." He stood up and pushed his seat back under the table.

"You're right, thanks Gracie" he answered, and walked back inside and out of the mess hall.

He found Thomas lying on his bed, a pillow over his head, his head pounding. "What do you want Jon? I've got a headache" he said.

"We need to talk, Tom" said Jon, closing the door behind him. Thomas sat down on one of the armchairs next to the window.

"Jon, I just don't like being kept from important things, and finding out you've got a room full of psychopaths was a bit of a shock" Thomas replied.

"Well, Tom, they have to be kept there, for their own good if anything. They couldn't go to a public prison, the time project is strictly classified. Someone would inevitably find out about it."

"I see where your coming from Jon, I really do, I'm just saying I thought we were a team" Thomas replied.

Jon smiled. "We are Tom, I couldn't have done any of this without you, and besides, it was the CIA that wanted it kept top secret, not me" Jon said, almost beginning to plead with his friend. Thomas glanced at him.

"We're cool Jon" he said with a smile. Jon leaned forward and shook Thomas' hand, grinning.

"I promise Tom, no more secrets" he answered. Thomas whacked him on the arm.

"There'd better not be Jon!" he said, then laughed as Jon rubbed his arm.

"Anyway, how's the equipment looking? Will there be a jump soon?" Thomas got to his feet and walked over to the kitchen. Jon got up and followed.

"Actually, my work's done, all the checks are complete, we can jump as soon as the day after tomorrow" Jon answered. Thomas looked round at him as he poured a drink from a juice carton.

"Really? That's great. Sorry, drink?" he said holding the carton up.

"No, I'm fine, thank you" Jon replied. Thomas sat down at one of the stools at the breakfast bar and took a sip.

"So, where are we going then?" Thomas asked.

Jon smiled at him. "To the Dark Ages" Jon answered. Thomas almost dropped his glass. Then a big grin crept across his face.

"Yes, at last, no more chasing psychos through time, we're going to do some proper research, in your time of expertise" Jon said. Thomas leaned over and hugged him, and Jon gave a small laugh.

"That's great news Jon" Thomas said.

"You're welcome Tom" Jon replied. "Now I'll leave you to get rid of your headache, oh, and get your stuff together, we'll leave soon." Jon walked over to the door. "And don't forget that tatty old notebook of yours."

The next day the whole place was abuzz with excitement. The scientists ran around, engineers checked the machinery over and Jon walked among them, doing his own final checks. Summers and

Thomas tried on their new and improved suits, while Gracie made sure the rest of the equipment was ready to go.

"Feels kind of tighter, wouldn't you say?" Summers said, zipping up the suit. Thomas smiled.

"Yeah, well, maybe Jon's into something that we don't really want to know about" Thomas answered. Summers laughed out loud as Jon walked in.

"What's all this?" Jon asked with a smile.

"The suits are great" Thomas said. Again Summers laughed.

"I don't see what's funny" Jon answered. "Anyway, there's a couple of new features to the suits."

"What, apart from being tighter?" said Thomas.

"The armour has been improved, it's lighter now" he said. "The control panel on the left arm has a new function too." He walked over to Thomas, took hold of his arm and pointed to a new red button. "Pressing this will activate a laser which ejects from this side compartment. The laser is quite powerful and will replace the portable cutting devices, making the belt lighter." Thomas smiled and switched the red button, and the small laser sprang out.

"Nice" he said, and pressed the button next to the red one. The laser hummed and a thin beam of light shot out and cut through the cabinet over on the other side of the room.

"Shit, be careful Tom, it's not a toy!" Jon said, hitting the button. The laser clicked back inside the panel.

"Sorry" Thomas said with a smirk.

"Never mind" Jon answered. "The objective was to make every thing more compressed. The belts will now only hold the pistols. The suits do everything else."

"Well, it all seems very efficient" Summers said after recovering from his laughing fit.

"Yes, that's what I was aiming for, Michael" Jon answered. At that, one of the security guards came in. Jon turned to him as he approached them.

"Dr Walker, someone has asked to see you" he said.

"Who?" Jon replied. The guard looked at Thomas and then back to Jon.

"Someone from the cell block" he said, Jon looked at Thomas and then back to the guard.

"Mackenzie?" he asked. The guard shook his head.

"No sir" he answered. Jon looked at Thomas. "Take off the suit Tom, I want you to come with me" he said.

"Why me?" Thomas replied, as Jon was walking out the room.

"No more secrets, Tom!" Jon shouted to him as he left, the door closing behind him. Thomas looked at Summers and started to take off the suit.

Thomas waited for Jon at the entrance to the corridor leading to the cell block.

"Jon!" he said on seeing his friend come round the corner.

"Tom, follow me" he replied and they walked through the door and made their way down the long corridor to the red door at the end. Jon punched in the key code and the scanner read his retina. The large door slowly opened and Jon walked in, followed by a curious and slightly nervous Thomas. The security guard came over to them.

"Sir, he's been asking for you for about a week now" he said.

"Well, let's get this over with" Jon said. He waved his hand and the guard went over to the control station. He pressed a few buttons and again the wall opposite opened, the cells began to move round and then stopped. One came forward and the shutter slowly opened, and Jon walked over to the red line, Thomas just behind him.

"What do you want?" Jon said. The Ripper looked up at him, and his dark eyes seemed to pierce into Jon's soul. The Ripper got to his feet and slowly walked over to the Perspex barrier. He stared at Jon and Thomas and a faint smile crept over his face.

"Dr Walker, and I see you've brought your friend with you, how charming" he said.

"Why have you called me here?"

"Doctor, I did so enjoy my time in Victorian London, I could express myself, so to speak" he replied. Thomas felt disgusted at the thought of what this monster had done to those poor women.

"That doesn't answer my question!" Jon said. The Ripper glared at him with soulless eyes.

"Dr Walker, I'm giving you my permission" he answered.

"For what?" Jon replied. The Ripper laughed softly.

"To experiment on me" he said.

"I still don't know what you mean."

"Let me loose on the world, let me go through time. I will ravage every era that I set foot in, but you doctor, will be spared. You can study me, my behaviour, my actions, my hunger" he said.

He seemed in a state of euphoria at the thought of committing more of his bloody acts of violence. Both Jon and Thomas felt shocked and disgusted. This was a monster, a devil. The crimes he had committed in Whitechapel were among the most barbaric known in history, and the idea of letting this creature free to act out his fantasies for the purpose of studying him was disgusting at best.

Jon was about to speak until Thomas raised his hand to silence him. He stepped past Jon and over the red line and went straight up to the plastic barrier. The Ripper inside his cell stared at him as he approached. Thomas stopped in front of him.

"We would have to be as insane as you to let you out" he said. "You will never see the light of day again, you disgusting piece of shit!"

The Ripper glared at him, his black eyes staring straight at Thomas. His lip began to curl up, exposing a few teeth.

"I remember you. Thomas isn't it?" he said in a whisper. Thomas stared back at him, refusing to show any signs of fear. "Yes, you protected that pretty girl back in Whitechapel with your blows. The passion with which you saved her from me was, well, beautiful." The Ripper gave a cruel smile as he got closer to the glass. "I could see then how much you cared for her, that pretty blonde girl, you love her don't you? May I give you some advice, Thomas? Do you know the quickest way to a woman's heart?"

Thomas said nothing. The Ripper got closer still, almost touching the plastic. "The quickest way to a woman's heart, Thomas, is through the rib cage!" he said and a huge grin crept over his face. Thomas thumped the plastic with anger as the Ripper started to laugh, louder and louder.

"I will kill you, you bastard!" Thomas yelled. The Ripper just continued to laugh, then moved back and sat down on his bed. Jon approached Thomas and put his hand on his shoulder.

"Tom, he can't hurt anyone any more, he's done" he said. Thomas turned to face his friend.

"He's a monster!" he yelled.

"I know, I know Tom, but this is what he wants, don't let him get to you. He's behind there forever now, you and Gracie are fine and we're going to do great things now, going back in time to study. Imagine the knowledge we'll gain from it all."

Thomas looked back at the Ripper as the shutter began to close once more, then looked back at Jon.

"You're right" he said.

"Of course I'm right, now, come, we've got work to

do" he said and they walked out the room, the big red door slamming behind them.

Back in the main room, they found Gracie writing notes for their jump tomorrow. Thomas walked over to her, put his arms around her and kissed the top of her head. She looked up at him with that beautiful smile of hers.

"What's all this?" she said. He looked back at her warmly.

"I love you" he said softly. She smiled and leaned up to kiss him.

"I love you too Thomas" she answered.

CHAPTER 9

Thomas woke up early. He was showered and ready to go down to the main machine room by the time Gracie opened her eyes.

"Hey, morning Thomas" she said. "You're up early, it's only five thirty." He sat next to her, perching on the side of the bed, then leaned down and kissed her.

"I couldn't sleep, too excited" he said.

"Well, you go down then, I'll catch you up."

"OK, see you in a bit" he said, picking up his bag and moving over to the door. He turned round to her once more. "This jump will be something amazing, Grace" he said calmly. He was holding back the excitement inside.

"Go on!" she answered with a smile. He gave her a wink and disappeared through the door.

Thomas walked out of the elevator and into the main room to see Jon again looking over his machine, making sure everything was ready and perfect for the jump. Thomas walked over to him and patted him on the back.

"Morning Tom" he said, Jon was already suited up, his pistol strapped on and ready to go.

"Today's the day my friend" Jon said. Thomas smiled.

"Jon, I can't wait to see the Dark Ages. We can learn so much from this" Thomas said, putting his bag down on the side. Jon smiled at him.

"Well, better go and get your suit on then." Thomas grinned and ran over to the equipment room.

"Morning Jon" Summers said, stepping out of the elevator.

"Morning agent!" he replied with a cheeky smile.

"Are we all ready to go?"

"We certainly are Michael, as soon as everyone is ready, we'll have a briefing and then get going" Jon answered.

"Excellent, well, I'll get suited up then" Summers replied, as he began to walk over to the equipment room, Jon called him.

"Is your arm all right Michael?" he asked, the agent turned round, held his arm up and answered.

"Absolutely fine Jon" he said and opened the door. Walking in he saw Thomas fastening the straps and doing the zipper up on his suit.

"Morning Thomas, bet you're looking forward to this jump" Summers said, taking his suit down from the stand.

"I've hardly been able to sleep" Thomas replied. Summers laughed.

"Well, soon my friend, we'll be there, in your time of expertise" he answered, slipping into the suit.

"See you out there" Thomas said. He walked out of the room, leaving the agent to get ready. Gracie was talking to Jon by the machine, and Thomas waved to her and made his way over.

"As soon as everybody is suited and ready, we'll have a quick meeting and then we can go" said Jon.

Thomas picked his bag back up and checked it. Everything he needed was there, a bottle of water, his old notebook, a pen, and a small penknife he carried with him. Summers and Gracie came over to Thomas and Jon. "OK then, everyone ready?" Jon asked. They all nodded. "Excellent, come on then." They followed him over to a large table set up in the corner of the room.

"OK then, a suggested landing site?" Jon said, looking around them all in turn.

"That's easy, I would say Denmark" said Thomas. "It's the area most of my knowledge is based on."

Gracie glanced at him. "I knew you would say that" she said.

"OK then, you want to see Vikings do you? That's fine" said Jon.

Thomas laughed. "That's OK, the new suits have a translator built into the arm panel. It holds over a thousand languages as well as a few dead languages, so ancient Danish will be fine" he said.

"Michael, do you want to add anything?" Jon said to Summers.

"Yes, the safety aspect is critical. This is a brutal time

in human history, people there would kill you as soon as look at you, so stay together and above all else, try not to be seen."

Thomas nodded. "Yes, we must stay anonymous. We're just there to observe life, not interact with it" he said.

Jon smiled and patted Thomas on the shoulder. "This is it, my friend" he said. He looked back at the others. "OK then, let's jump" he said. "Denmark 789, here we go!"

★ ★ ★ ★ ★

As the smoke began to clear and the glow from the crater started to fade, they all looked around. It was quite dark and the only noise was a constant dripping of water. Thomas stepped out of the smouldering crater.

"Where is this?" he said. Gracie switched on her torch, which was now positioned on the chest of the suit, just to the right. She shone the beam around, but all that could be seen was rock.

"We're in a cave" she said.

"Look, over there" Jon said. He pointed over to a small opening, where a shaft of daylight was creeping through. Thomas made his way over to the opening, slipping on the wet rock a few times. He glanced through the little gap.

"I think we can get through here, I can smell fresh air too" he said. Jon tapped away on his arm panel.

"The devices won't work in here, must be all the rock" he said. The screen on his arm was making nothing but white noise.

"I'll go first" Thomas said and began to crawl through the gap. A toad jumped out of his way as he slid along the narrow space, which suddenly opened up into a wide cavern. The entrance to the cave could be seen now up a slight incline. He put his hand up to shield his eyes from the bright sunlight. Gracie came through after him.

"Come on" she said with a beaming smile, and they made their way up towards the light. The rays of the sun felt warm on their faces, mixed with a cooling breeze They stood at the entrance looking out over a vast landscape. A large hill could be seen in the distance and a small wooded area just to the east of them. Thomas stepped out of the cave and into the Denmark of the Dark Ages. There seemed nothing dark about this time; it was beautiful and colourful. Gracie walked over and took his hand and they stepped out and on to a rocky area. There was a small natural pathway leading down from the small cliff.

"The view's amazing" Gracie said, still holding Thomas' hand. Jon and Summers stepped out to join them.

"Wow" Jon said, looking over the land. Summers stepped past him and peered down. "We can get down there" he said, and started making his way down the path, Thomas and Gracie eagerly following him. They reached the bottom to find a few trees dotted around, mixed with huge rocks, and a short distance away they saw a massive standing stone, a monument of some kind. Jon walked over and stared at the huge stone. There was some kind of inscription on it, with strange symbols.

"What's this mean?" he said, Thomas stepped in front of him, rubbing his hand across the stone with a smile. "I've seen this before" he said. He looked over to Gracie. "On the dig site, remember?" She came over and looked at it closely.

"Oh my god" she said. "It looks so new."

"We saw this stone back in our own time, over 1300 years ago, our dig site was close to it" Thomas said with excitement.

"But what is it?" Jon asked, Thomas looked at him and then back to the standing stone.

"Its called rune scripture, ancient Danish writing" Thomas answered him, still staring at the massive piece of rock. "This was a sacred site, a site of worship."

"There's another one over there" Summers said. Thomas turned around to see him pointing over to a smaller piece of stone. Thomas went over to it. "Wow, this is long gone in our own time" he said. He took out his notebook and started to copy down the runes. Jon came over to him and switched on his arm panel.

"Tom, you can just scan it, it'll copy it all down in seconds" he said. Thomas glanced up at him. "I like to do it the old fashioned way" he said with a smile, Jon laughed and shook his head.

"OK Tom, as you wish" he answered.

"There are burn marks over here too" Summers called over to Thomas. He was bent down, examining the marks.

"They would be lit to mark the way to the cave. They must think the cave leads to an underworld, a spirit world" Thomas replied, still scribbling away. Gracie sat next to Thomas.

"You know our dig site wasn't far from here" she said. "It was in and around a Dark Ages village, including their cemetery. That means we're close to the village now. There are people around here."

"We could take a look at them" said Tom.

Jon came rushing over again. "Wait, Tom, don't run before you can walk, this is only a short visit. We've got plenty of time to be looking for really old people" he said. "We're going to be making more than one trip here, let's just spread it out a bit, OK?"

Thomas got to his feet. "I know Jon, but just a quick look, it won't take long" he said.

Summers came over to them. "It wouldn't hurt, we can stay for another hour or so Jon" he said. Summers gave him a wink. Jon looked back at Thomas.

"Have you finished copying?" he asked.

"Yes, all done" Thomas replied.

Jon smiled. "OK then, Michael and I will remain here, you and Gracie go find your village, stay in radio contact, and don't get seen" Jon said.

Thomas grinned. "Thank you Jon, we won't be

long" he said, picking up his bag and throwing his notebook back inside.

"Make sure you're not, and stay in contact" Jon called out as Thomas and Gracie made their way through the trees and out of sight.

"They'll be fine" Summers said. Jon glanced at him.

"I hope so" he replied.

Thomas and Gracie walked down the small slope towards a gathering of trees. A stream ran through the area, and Thomas noticed three or four wicker fish traps had been set up. He knelt down and inspected them.

"Grace, look at these" he said. Gracie bent down next to him.

"Wow, the workmanship is excellent. We must be close" she replied.

Thomas got to his feet and looked over to the east. Something had caught his eye.

"Look, smoke!" he said and pointed at a stream of smoke rising from just over a small hill. They both made their way towards it. "Keep down" Thomas said and they ducked down and slowly crept over to the edge. Below them, less than a mile away, they could see a small settlement. It consisted of a few small wooden buildings and a larger, rectangular building in the centre. It was the same village he and Gracie had been excavating, the place where they had discovered the skeleton.

"My god" Thomas said quietly.

"It's beautiful" Gracie replied. They were both staring down at a distant gathering of Dark Ages people.

"Jon to Thomas, come in" came a voice from Thomas' communicator. He quickly pressed the button on his chest and answered.

"Jon, we've found it" he said.

"Tom, that's great, but we need to leave, come back straight away!" Thomas looked at Gracie with disappointment.

"Come on" she said. "We can come back." They both got to their feet, making their way back to the cave. Jon came over to meet them as they got closer. He looked stressed and a little worried.

"Thomas, come, we need to leave" he said.

"What is it?" Thomas asked as they made their way back over to Summers, who was standing there with his pistol drawn.

"We were seen Tom. A woman and a child came up and put some beads down next to the standing stone. We tried to hide, but they saw us,"

"And what happened?" Gracie asked.

"Nothing, they ran off, but we need to leave before more come to investigate" he replied.

"OK, let's go" Thomas said.

"We can come back in a couple of days Tom, it'll be fine" Jon said and switched on the recall device. They all followed suit and the devices lit up, bright blue. "OK, now" Jon said, looking at them all in turn. They all pressed the recall buttons at the same time, the loud humming started up, the blue sparks shot from them. The humming became louder and then in a shower of sparks and flames, they were gone.

From their hiding place behind an old tree, the Dark Ages woman and her little girl watched the scene wide eyed.

★　★　★　★　★

The smoke cleared and Thomas stepped off the platform. He turned to look at the others with a huge grin.

"It was wonderful, Thomas" grinned Gracie. Jon turned back to them, unsmiling. "We're going to have to have a debriefing" he said.

"OK Jon" Thomas replied and walked over to him.

"In the board room, ten minutes."

Thomas, Gracie and Summers were already waiting when Jon walked in, pulled out a chair and sat down.

"We have a problem" he said. "Today, the jump was good, but we got ourselves seen. This could have a devastating effect. It could change history."

Thomas looked confused. He leaned forward and rested on the table.

"Jon, it wasn't that bad, no one was hurt, and I truly believe that we could make contact with these people" Thomas replied. "Surely they are far enough away in time for there to be no effect on the future?"

Gracie nodded. "Yes, I agree" she said. "It really wouldn't affect these people, in fact it would probably strengthen their belief system. They would see us as astral beings, as gods."

"Yes, particularly as we appeared near their site of worship" Thomas added.

"Gods. Interesting" Jon said, almost to himself. "OK then, well if you think it'll be safe, and if what you say is true, we'll jump back again the day after tomorrow."

"OK, that's fine with me" Thomas replied. He looked at Gracie, who nodded in agreement.

Jon smiled. "Well, OK then. Get some rest, I'll see you tomorrow." He got to his feet and walked out of the room.

"Well, he seemed strange" Gracie said as the door closed.

"Yeah, I wonder what was up?" Thomas added.

"We should keep an eye on Jon on the next jump" said Summers. "The thought of being considered a god may be too tempting."

Back in their room, Gracie asked Thomas what she had thought of Jon's behaviour.

"He was acting a little strangely, after you mentioned about the Dark Ages people thinking of us as gods" Thomas replied. He reached into his bag and removed his notebook.

"Well, I'm kind of worried about Jon now" Gracie said. Thomas opened up the book and started to look over what he had copied.

"I wouldn't worry Grace, Jon isn't the type to be filled with self-importance. He was probably just worried about being seen by the natives" Thomas replied. He put the book on the table and slid it over to

Gracie. "Look at those markings on the other stone" he said.

She picked up the notebook and scanned the strange symbols Thomas had copied from the smaller standing stone. "I was right" he said. "Those runes suggest that the native people there believe that cave system is a gateway to the spirit world. And that would mean that you were right too." He leaned forward. "If they saw us there, the way we're dressed, our advanced technology, they would probably think of us as gods."

"We'll have to take care then. We don't know how they would react to us" Gracie replied.

Thomas smiled. "Yes, but if they think of us as their gods, that would protect us. They wouldn't harm their own gods, would they?"

"Well, if that is the case, and what Summers says is correct, then maybe we'll have to watch Jon after all" Gracie replied.

"It'll be fine Grace, Jon will be fine. I think Michael is reading too much into it." Thomas got to his feet. "Now then, we should get some rest."

* * * * *

Meanwhile, Jon was sitting in his room at his desk, looking at images of Danish gods and mythical beings from the Dark Ages. He scanned the long list of names. There seemed to be a different god for everything. He copied some of the details down on his electronic tablet, just the interesting stuff and the more powerful gods, like Odin and Thor. A sly smile crept over his face as he typed it all in.

There was a knock at the door. Jon got up and walked over to open it.

"Hello Jon" Summers said, standing in front of him.

"Michael, are you OK?" Jon asked. "I am a bit busy, but please, come in." Summers closed the door behind him and walked into the room.

"I just came to check that you're all right Jon" Summers said, looking around the room. He noticed the laptop on Jon's desk.

"Michael, I'm fine, why do you ask?" Jon replied.

"Well, as an agent of the law, I have to make sure there are no security risks" Summers answered. Jon glanced down at the computer and closed down the lid.

"And what sort of security risk do you think I would know about?" Jon said, starting to get defensive.

"Jon, I just have to check. This time travelling project is a gift, a powerful gift. We all need to remember to use it responsibly."

"Yes Michael" Jon answered. "It is a gift, a gift I created. It is my project and I will not be judged by you."

Summers got to his feet. "Jon, I'm sorry, I didn't mean to offend you" he said. Jon stood up and moved over to him.

"Michael, really, it should be me apologizing. I overreacted" Jon replied.

"OK, Jon well, I'll leave you to your work" Summers said and opened the door. Jon watched him leave via the elevator and then returned to his studies.

Summers got out on the floor of Thomas' dorm, walked over to the door and gave it a gentle knock.

"Oh Michael, hi" Gracie said. "Come in, Thomas is in the shower, he shouldn't be long."

Summers smiled as he closed the door behind him. "That's OK, I just need a quick word, with both of you really" he said.

"Really?" she said. Summers, seemed more serious than usual.

"Yes" he replied and at that Thomas came out of the bathroom, his hair still wet.

"Michael, you OK?" he said as he threw on a vest top.

"Hello Thomas" Summers answered. "And, well, I've been to see Jon" he continued.

"And, is he all right?" Thomas asked taking a seat next to his desk.

"I'm really concerned about him. He was looking at Danish gods on the internet" Summers said.

Thomas smiled. "Michael, that doesn't mean anything, he could have just been researching it for our next jump" he answered.

"That's what I'm worried about, he can't let this power go to his head, I can't allow it either."

"Michael, listen" Thomas said, turning back to Summers. "I've known Jon for years, we went to university together, and I'm telling you, he's not the type to let power go to his head."

"Thomas, power can do things to people, it can change people. All I'm saying is that we need to keep a close eye on Jon, that's all."

"We will Michael" Gracie said. She glanced at Thomas with a concerned look.

"That's all I ask" Summers answered with a smile. "Well, I'll leave you both to it, it's getting late." He made his way over to the door.

"Goodnight Michael" Thomas said as the door closed.

"It's true that Jon was acting a bit strange earlier" she said.

"I know" he muttered. "I'll keep an eye on him."

She smiled. "Come, let's get ready for bed" she said.

★ ★ ★ ★ ★

Meanwhile, Jon was still hard at work studying the myths and legends of the ancient world. What if these Vikings did look upon three modern human visitors as gods? He thought of the possibilities it would open up. A smile crept over his face as he stared at the images on the screen. Then he glanced up at the clock; midnight, time for some rest.

★ ★ ★ ★ ★

Thomas woke up suddenly to the sound of the intercom blasting out a loud bleeping. He leaned over and switched it off, but almost straight away it started again.

"It must be important" Gracie said. Thomas sat up and pressed the answer button. It was Jon.

"Thomas, get down here straight away!" he shouted down the intercom.

"Why, what is it?"

"Quickly, I'm outside the main building" Jon answered and the intercom went dead. Thomas looked round at Gracie, who was now sitting bolt upright.

"Thomas, it sounds urgent" she said. He got up and slipped on his jogging bottoms and vest top. "Gracie, stay here" he said and ran out the room.

Jon was standing just outside the main building talking to Summers and a security guard. A body lay on the ground, a puddle of blood around it. It was one of the scientists.

"My god" Thomas said. "What's happened?"

"He was found early this morning by this security guard who was patrolling the area" Summers said. "He's been murdered."

Thomas stared at the lifeless man. "Has the culprit been caught?"

Summers shook his head. "No, we believe it's one of Mackenzie's hit men, a least that's what Jon seems to think" he said. Thomas walked over to Jon and placed his hand on his shoulder. "Jon, are you OK?" he asked.

"I'm fine Tom, me and Summers are going to pay the lieutenant a visit, see if he'll tell us anything" Jon replied.

"Sir, shall we remove the body now?" the security guard asked.

Jon nodded.

"Yes, do it straight away." Thomas was confused.

"Jon, the police need to be called, this has to be dealt with properly."

"Yes Jon, you can't sweep this under the carpet" Summers said.

Jon took a step closer to Summers.

"I'm pissed off with you, mister interfering agent" he said. "This is my facility, my project, I am in charge here!"

"And I am an agent of the law" snapped Summers. "A man has been murdered and I am placing myself in charge." He turned to the security guard. "Leave him where he is" he said. The guard nodded. Summers walked away, taking out his cellphone. Jon looked at Thomas.

"Tom, if the police come here, it could ruin everything" he whispered. Thomas patted him on the back.

"Jon, it'll be fine, listen, go and talk to Mackenzie, see if you can get some answers out of him" he said. "Michael and I will sort this out."

Jon nodded. "Yes, if we can find the killer, then the police won't need to stay here long" Jon replied as he walked back inside. Thomas watched him in.

"Thomas, the police are on their way" Summers said as he came back over.

"Michael, you're a CIA agent, you can sort this with the police, we can't let the time project be shut down, not now" Thomas said, almost in desperation.

"I'll deal with this, don't worry, the project will not be shut down" Summers replied. Thomas smiled.

"OK, thank you Michael" he said. "I'm going to take a shower and get dressed. Please wait here for the police to arrive"

"Of course Thomas" Summers replied. He watched Thomas walk back inside the main building.

★ ★ ★ ★ ★

Jon walked into the large white room as the red metal door opened. "Mackenzie" he said to the security guard standing at the control station. The guard nodded and pressed buttons. The loud clanking noise started up and the cells moved round. Then they stopped and the panel slid open, revealing Lieutenant Mackenzie sitting on his bed. On seeing Jon he gave a cruel smile. Jon approached the cell.

"Where are they?" he asked. Mackenzie got up and moved over to the Perspex shield.

"Dr Walker, nice to see you" he said.

"Don't fucking play games with me! Your hit man, where is he?" Jon shouted at him.

Mackenzie looked over Jon's shoulder. "He's behind

you" he replied. Jon looked round to see the security guard standing there, his pistol drawn and aiming it straight at him. Mackenzie started to laugh.

"Well doctor, looks like you're fucked" he said. The guard walked over to Jon and struck him on the head with the gun, knocking him out cold.

★ ★ ★ ★ ★

Jon's eyes started to open. His head was pounding and a trickle of blood ran down his face. He looked up to see Mackenzie standing over him, along with the security guard. Jon tried to move his hands but they were cuffed. He could feel the cold metal on his wrists.

"You don't have to do this" Jon said quietly.

"Oh yes I do Walker" smirked Mackenzie. "You fucked up my last mission, my last chance of getting wealthy, you and that little prick of a friend of yours."

The guard leaned over to whisper something in his ear, and Mackenzie nodded.

"Well, my next mission awaits doctor, and this time you're not going to fuck it up" he said. The guard handed him the gun. He pointed it straight at Jon's head and clicked the safety catch off. Jon closed his eyes. There came a loud GUNSHOT, then another, but he felt nothing. He opened his eyes to see Mackenzie taking cover behind the control station. He looked around. Two security guards had appeared; it was obviously their shots he had heard.

As Jon dropped and started crawl over to the door, a shot rang out and a bullet whizzed past him, hitting one of the guards in the head. The man fell to the floor. The other security guard took another shot, dropping Mackenzie's guard with a hole in his chest. He heard Mackenzie shout out in a rage, and then came gunshot after gunshot as Mackenzie fired at the guard. The man fell backwards, riddled with bullets.

Mackenzie slowly walked over, smoke still coming from the barrel of his pistol. He glanced down at Jon and lifted his arm up, aiming the gun at him.

"Shit" Jon whispered.

There was a click. No more bullets.

Mackenzie snarled and threw the pistol down, then ran towards Jon and kicked him hard in the head. The room seemed to spin, and then - blackness.

* * * * *

Jon awoke to see Thomas next to him. He looked around to find that he was now in the infirmary, lying in a bed. He tried to sit up, but pain filled his head.

"Jon, stay still" Thomas said, getting to his feet. Jon looked up at him.

"It was Mackenzie, he's escaped, I have to find him" he said.

"I know, he's gone" Thomas replied. Jon looked up at him.

"Where? he couldn't have got far."

"He used the machine again, he's jumped."

Jon looked at Thomas, devastated "Where?" he asked.

"We're not sure yet, they're working on it."

"I can find him quicker" said Jon. Thomas put his hand on Jon's chest and gently pushed him back down.

"Jon, you need to rest, your skull was fractured. I'll find Mackenzie, you have my word. Get some rest now, I'll keep you informed, I promise."

Thomas got up from the bed and left the room. "Keep an eye on him" he said to the medical doctor as he walked out of the infirmary.

"Sir, we think we've got a trace on Mackenzie" one of the scientists called out. Summers quickly walked over to the man standing at the control station.

"Really, where is he?" the agent asked. The scientist tapped a few more buttons and then replied "1718 sir, in North Carolina".

"Good, keep working, try and get an exact fix on him."

"Any news?" Thomas said as he approached them. Gracie came running over from one of the other stations.

"Yes, we're closing in on him" Summers replied.

"Excellent, where?" Thomas asked.

"For some reason, he's jumped to North Carolina in the year 1718."

Thomas' face dropped. "Thomas, what is it?" Gracie asked. Thomas moved over to the scientist. "He wouldn't be on Ocracoke would he?" Thomas asked. The man looked at him.

"Yes Dr Long, but, how would you know that?" he replied. Thomas stepped away from the control station.

"Thomas, do you know something?" Summers asked eagerly. Thomas took a seat at one of the desks. "I take it you've heard of the pirate, Blackbeard?" he asked quietly. Gracie looked at Summers, confused. She turned back to Thomas.

"Yes, of course, why?" she replied.

"Because that's where Blackbeard was caught and killed on the 22nd November 1718" Thomas answered. "He was quite a successful pirate, and I would imagine Mackenzie has gone looking for him. I fear that if the lieutenant saves him, history will change."

"Shit" said Summers. His head was in his hands.

"We have to go after him, Michael" Thomas said. Summers nodded.

"Good, I'll get the equipment ready" Gracie said. She was about to walk away when Thomas spoke.

"No" he said. She stopped and looked round. "Not you Grace, not this time" he said. She stomped over to him.

"What do you mean, why not?" she asked. He stood up and held her arms.

"Grace, this is too dangerous. Mackenzie is getting desperate and Blackbeard was a psychopath. I will not let you get into danger." She pushed his arms away and strode off towards the elevator. Summers got to his feet and put his hand on Thomas' shoulder.

"She'll calm down" he said and walked over to the equipment room. Thomas followed behind him.

★ ★ ★ ★ ★

"Dr Long, we've got Lt Mackenzie's jump site" the scientist said as Thomas and Summers walked over, suited up and ready to go.

"Good, where is he?" Thomas replied.

"November 15th 1718 sir, on the island of Ocracoke" the man answered.

"Excellent, put us there" Thomas said. He turned to Summers. "Ready?" he asked. The agent nodded, clipping his pistol into its holster. As they both walked up the steps and on to the platform, Gracie came running out of the elevator and over to Thomas. She gripped him tightly.

"Be careful" she whispered. He leaned down and gave her a kiss.

"I will" he replied with a smile. She stepped away from the machine as the countdown started up.

CHAPTER 10

As the smoke cleared and the sound of the humming faded, Thomas stepped out of the burning crater to see a man standing in front of him with a look of shock and fright on his face. So much for not being seen.

Thomas moved towards him, his hands held up.

"Please, we won't hurt you" Thomas said. The man backed into a wall.

"What are you?" he answered Thomas.

"We're human, like you" Thomas replied. "We're looking for someone." The man quickly pulled from his back a flintlock pistol and aimed it straight at Thomas.

"You're not human!" he cried. "You're devils!"

Quickly Summers moved forward and drew his gun, aiming it at the frightened man. "Please, you don't want to do that, we really will not hurt you" he said. The man looked at Summers and then back to Thomas. Then he slowly lowered his weapon.

"Who are you?" he asked quietly.

"Well, you probably won't believe us if we tell you" Thomas began.

"Please tell me" the man replied. Thomas looked at Summers, who nodded. He turned back to the man.

"We're from the future" he said. The man tucked his pistol back inside his belt.

"I see. What do you want?" he replied simply.

"We're here to find a criminal from our time, a man called Mackenzie" Thomas said. The man nodded.

"Well, plenty of criminal folk around here, what's this future man look like?"

Summers stepped forward and held up his arm. He pressed a button and the screen lit up, displaying a digital picture of Mackenzie. The man stared at the brightly-lit panel, his eyes fixed on the image.

"Truly this is a miracle" he said.

"It's just technology" Summers answered. The man looked blank. "Now, have you seen him?" The man's eyes moved from the screen to Summers' face. He nodded slowly.

"Yes I have seen him" he said.

Summers looked round to Thomas and smiled. "Good, where is he?"

The man smiled. "Not on shore" he replied.

"What do you mean?" Summers answered. The man walked slowly past them, wearily.

"He's taken up with Teach, he's on his ship" the man said.

"Teach?" Summers replied.

"Edward Teach" Thomas said. Summers looked round at him.

"Better known as Blackbeard" Thomas continued.

"Aye, that's right, he's on the *Queen Anne's Revenge*"

the man said, Summers looked round at Thomas yet again.

"Blackbeard's ship" Thomas said.

"Oh great" Summers said. "How are we going to get to him now?"

The man stepped forward. "Well sir, just as it happens, you're in the company of a spy" he said with a huge smile on his face.

"Go on?" Summers said.

"Well, I was sent ashore by none other than Robert Maynard, he's planning to bring that scum, Blackbeard to justice, I'm a mate on board the *Pearl*" said the man.

Summers glanced at Thomas, and Thomas nodded. The man continued. "I was to gather intelligence for the coming assault, and it would now appear that our interests are aligned" he said.

"OK, you help us get to Mackenzie, and we'll help you get Teach" Thomas said. The man smiled, spat on his hand and held it out to Thomas. Thomas looked at Summers and then gently shook his hand.

"Deal then" the man said. He stepped away from Thomas and looked him up and down. "Can't be dressing like that though" he said.

"And what would you suggest?" Summers replied. The man held up his hand. "Give me an hour, I'll be back with more suitable attire" he said with a grin. He slowly moved over to the door of the shed, not taking his eyes from Thomas or Summers until he was out of the door. Thomas moved over and slammed the door shut behind the man.

"Oh great, do you think we can trust him?" Summers said, sitting down on the chair.

"We have no choice" Thomas replied, looking through the small window.

★ ★ ★ ★ ★

In the captain's cabin on board the *Queen Anne's Revenge*, Mackenzie was sitting opposite the feared Blackbeard, sipping on a large tankard of ale. The captain stared at the man with his piercing eyes.

"So then, Mr Mackenzie, you say there is a plot to kill me?" the man said, in his broad Bristol accent.

The lieutenant put the tankard down on the captain's table. "Yes captain, and I can help you" he replied.

"For a price, I imagine?" Blackbeard answered.

Mackenzie smiled. "Yes, for a price" he said, Blackbeard leaned forward, placing a very large flintlock pistol on the table in front of him.

"And why, pray tell, would I need your help?" he said.

Mackenzie gave a grin and pulled from his belt a weapon he had brought with him from the future. The captain stared at the strange gun.

"What in the devil's name is that?" he asked.

"This captain, is a weapon the likes of which you have never seen" Mackenzie replied.

The captain leaned back in his high back chair. "Prove it" he said with a smile.

The lieutenant picked up the gun and stood up. Blackbeard gestured to the door and they both walked out on to the main deck. Blackbeard pointed to one of his crew.

"Him" Blackbeard muttered. Mackenzie smiled and aimed the gun at the man, who straight away stopped what he was doing and raised his hands.

"Captain, not me sir" he pleaded. A trickle of urine ran down his leg and made a puddle by his feet. The captain laughed out loud.

"You have to let them know who is in charge" he said. "Do it."

Mackenzie looked back at the frightened man, then clicked off the safety catch. A cruel smile crept over the face of the captain.

Mackenzie squeezed the trigger, again and again. Round after round blasted through the man's body. When the smoke had cleared, there was hardly anything left of him.

Blackbeard walked forward, his mouth agape, eyes fixed on the remains of the unlucky sailor.

"Well well Mr Mackenzie, looks like I've found myself a new first mate" he said. He walked back to the lieutenant and shook his hand. "Welcome aboard." He gestured back towards his cabin, and both of the men stepped inside, leaving the rest of the crew to clean up the mess.

★ ★ ★ ★ ★

The door opened slowly. Thomas and Summers both drew their guns as their new friend's head peered round the corner. "'Tis only I" he said. Walking inside, they clicked their weapons back into their holsters. The man was carrying a large sack, and he now turned it upside down, spilling clothes and garments over the floor. "These are all I could get" he said. Thomas picked up a pair of breeches and held them next to him.

"They'll be fine, thank you" Thomas said. "And what should we call you?"

"My name is William Lockwood, at your service."

A few minutes later Thomas and Summers were dressed and ready to go out into the 18th century.

"I feel like a right dandy" Summers whispered to Thomas, who smiled.

"You look fine, we'll fit in this way" Thomas answered.

"Ready?" said William, standing at the door. Summers nodded.

"Yeah, let's go" Thomas said. William smiled and opened the door, and the three of them walked out. The dock seemed huge. Gulls squawked over head, massive galleon ships were lined up on the dock, and in the distance was another ship, bearing a black flag. William pointed over to it.

"There, that's the *Queen Anne's Revenge*" he said. "The *Pearl* and the other vessels we've managed to acquire will attack from the east, they'll be here in the morning of the 22nd."

Thomas nodded. "Good, is there anyone else here that knows this?" he asked. William smiled.

"Yes sir, I have two other men at hand to help, we're here to try and break Teach's defences from here" William replied. "Come, I'll take you to them," Thomas and Summers followed the man through the busy dock area and into a market place. There were stalls set up in every direction, fish stalls, bread stalls, stalls that sold tools, even clothing stalls.

"Wow" Thomas muttered to himself. William turned round to Thomas and Summers, who were lagging behind.

"Come, we must hurry" he said. They quickly made their way through the busy market. "It's just up this street" William said. They walked up the narrow street until William stopped at a doorway. He gave it three knocks, and a few seconds later the door opened. A scruffy man with a huge grey beard was standing before them.

"Bobby, these are the men I told you about" William said. The man looked them up and down and then gestured for them to go inside. Despite the warm weather, there was a fire burning in the little house. Another man was sitting at a desk loading a pistol.

"Sorry, I don't know your names" William said, trying to introduce them.

"My name is Thomas and this is Michael" Thomas replied. The scruffy man came forward and shook their hands.

"All right, I'm Bobby" he said. The other man stood up and made his way over. "Connor" he said. "So then, William tells us you can help us to catch that brigand pirate?"

"Yes, there is also a man on board his ship called Mackenzie, it's him that we're after" Thomas said. "But we will help you to bring Blackbeard down." Bobby smiled and nodded.

"Good, well, I hear that some of the pirates crew are ashore, in a tavern called the King's Crown" Bobby answered. "I reckon we should go there, see what we can find out." Connor sat back down and gestured for the others to take a seat at the table. He poured them some ale in small goblets.

"Well, maybe just a couple of us should go, we don't want to draw suspicion to ourselves" Connor said, after taking a sip of the strong beer.

"I agree, we should try and stay as low key as possible" Thomas replied. Summers nodded.

"OK then" Bobby said standing up. "Thomas, you and William will go to the tavern, myself, Michael and Connor will head to the docks, see if we can find anything out there" he said, looking at them all in turn, Summers glanced at Thomas, and Thomas nodded.

"OK, agreed" Thomas said getting to his feet" Bobby smiled.

"Well, no time like the present" he said and picked up his flintlock pistol and pushed it into his belt next to his cutlass sword. "Do you two have weapons?" he asked. Summers looked at Thomas, who smiled.

"Yes sir, we do" he replied.

"Excellent, let us away then" he said and opened the door. they all walked back out into the narrow street.

"The tavern is this way Thomas" William said pointing down to the other end of the street. Summers, along with Connor and Bobby went back towards the market place. "The tavern isn't far" William said as he and Thomas strolled down the street.

"Tell me William" Thomas began. "Do Bobby and Connor know where Summers and I are from?" William looked at him with a smile.

"Well sir, to be honest with yer, I'm not too sure myself. All I knows is that you're both a bit special. I saw you just appear in front of me in a flash of lightning, so, in answer to your question, no, I didn't tell them anything like that."

Thomas glanced at him. "Why not?"

"Because Connor is real superstitious" William replied with a smile. "I don't think he would like it too much if I told him what I saw. He might think you're wizards or devils or somethin'."

"Thanks" smiled Thomas, and then he looked up. The street was getting wider. There were shops and taverns on either side, and at the very bottom of the street was a lighthouse, sitting on the shore line. William laughed and Thomas turned round to him.

"What's so funny?" Thomas asked.

"Your face" William replied. "Come over here." He walked off down the busy street, followed by Thomas.

William stopped outside a large building. The sign hanging above the door read 'King's Crown'. William pushed open the door and walked inside. Thomas went in after him. The sound of instruments filled the building. Men staggered around drunk, groping after the serving wenches.

"Welcome to the King's Crown, Thomas" William said. his eyes scanned the room and he spotted the three men from the pirate crew. "Over there" William said, gesturing towards the men. "Come, let's get a drink, don't want to be out of place now do we?" He took a seat at a table next to the three crew members. A woman came over to them, her breasts almost spilling out of her dress. "What can I get you two?" she said with a wide grin.

"Two ales" William said and the woman flounced off. Thomas and William listened carefully to the men talking.

"So then, that's twenty-two of us all together now including that new man, the big guy" the first said. He took a sip from his tankard. Thomas leaned in close to William. "The big guy must be Mackenzie" he whispered. William nodded.

At that the woman returned and placed two large tankards of ale down on the table.

"Anything else and you just call me" she said and gave Thomas a wink.

"So then, this new guy reckons that there's gonna be an attack on us shortly" the second man said.

"Yeah, the Royal Navy are coming for us apparently" the third replied.

"The captain's too smart for them, he'll blast them out the ocean" the first answered.

"They're on to us" William whispered. Thomas nodded. "Now what?" he muttered. William winked at him, then got to his feet.

"What are you doing?" Thomas asked.

William took from his belt his flintlock and pointed it at the men. "Gentlemen, by order of the British Crown, you are under arrest for piracy and murder" he said.

The three men looked at each other and the first got to his feet. William pulled back the lock on his pistol, loading the weapon ready to fire. "Don't move, brigand!" William shouted. Thomas got to his feet and stood next to William.

"Like he said, don't move, we have questions for you" Thomas said. The serving woman came running over to them.

"No trouble in here boys, take it outside!" she yelled. At that, using the woman as a distraction, the first man leapt forward at William, punching him straight on the jaw. He fell backwards, smashing through the table. Thomas stepped forward and struck the man hard in the throat. he went down, gripping his neck. The second man drew his short sword and came at Thomas, but there came the sound of a shot and he dropped to the ground. Thomas looked round through the gunsmoke.

William had got to his feet and fired his flintlock.

"You bastard!" the third man cried and took out his own pistol. He pulled back the lock ready to use it, but Thomas fired first. The man dropped to the floor, blood flowing from his wounds. William stared at the gun.

"By the heavens" he said. Thomas gestured to the man holding his neck.

"Get him up, we can question him" Thomas said. William heaved the man to his feet and dragged him out of the tavern. Thomas clipped his pistol back under his coat and walked outside.

"We can take him to the house" William said.

"Good, let's go, before more trouble finds us" Thomas replied, and he took hold of the man's other arm. They dragged him back to the hideout and shoved him down on a chair. William bound his hands together.

"The others should be back soon" William said and poured a drink of ale. He held out the goblet to Thomas. William knocked back the drink and then moved in front of the bound man.

"Tell us what you know about your captain, Edward Teach" said William. The man glanced up at him, his eyes fixed on Williams. "Get fucked" he spat.

William grimaced. he pulled back his fist and struck the man hard on the cheek. The man looked back at William and spat out some blood. "Like I said, get fucked" he said again, and again William punched him, this time hitting his nose. Blood splattered over the man's shirt and his head slumped down. Thomas moved forward and held William's arm.

"Not too much, we need information" Thomas said. William looked back to the man.

"Tell us, or I'll shoot you like a dog right now" William said, and he drew his flintlock from his belt. The wounded man looked back up.

"OK, OK, I'll tell ye everything I know" he said, blood still flowing from his nose and mouth. William took a seat, placed it in front of the man and sat down. He leaned forward. "Go on then" he said. The man looked right in his eyes.

"The captain's taken up with some big feller, and he knows of your attack too" he said. "You'll never beat the Blackbeard." He grinned.

"Oh, I beg to differ my friend, Now how many men does Teach command?"

"Nineteen now, you killed two of us at the tavern."

"And weaponry?" The man laughed. "Blackbeard has more guns than the whole of the Royal Navy" he replied. At that, Connor, Bobby and Summers came through the door.

"And who's this?" Bobby asked, walking up to William, who got to his feet.

"This is one of Teach's men. Me and Thomas here felled two of his mates at the tavern" William replied. Bobby got close to the man and grabbed his throat.

"I hope you're spilling your guts to these fine men, or I'll be spilling your guts over the floor" Bobby said, taking from his belt his cutlass and holding it to the man's face.

"Yes, yes sir!" the man cried.

"Good!" Bobby said and released him.

"Has this big man said anything else to your captain, other than about the attack?" Thomas asked the man. He glanced at Thomas.

"I don't know. They stay in the captain's cabin all the time, don't know what's said" he replied.

Bobby looked back at him and held up his sword. "But we know he's got some kind of fancy weapon" the man said desperately.

"What kind of weapon?" Connor asked.

"Some kind of pistol, real loud and powerful, and you can keep firing it without reloading" the man said.

Thomas looked over at Summers, who shook his head to indicate that he should not say anything.

"There is no such weapon" Bobby answered the man, moving forward, his cutlass held up high. The frightened man tried to move back.

"I'm telling the truth, God be my witness, I am sir!" he cried, and Bobby halted, staring at the man.

"He's telling the truth" Summers said. Bobby quickly turned round to face him. "How do you know?" he asked.

"Because we've seen the man with this weapon" Thomas said.

Bobby's eyes moved back to the crying man. "We keep him here, prisoner, at least until the attack has taken place, then he'll hang" Bobby said, and moved away from the man, placing his sword back in its sheath.

"How can we get on board the *Queen Anne's Revenge*?" Thomas said, bending down in front of the man.

"You can't, they'd spot ye coming, blow ye out the water" the man replied quietly.

Then a man stepped out of the shadows. "I can help with that" he said. Thomas stood up straight again and looked at the man. He was wearing full 18th century Royal Navy uniform.

"Sir, these men have been helping us to bring the pirate to justice" Connor said, moving over towards the man. he held out his hand to Thomas and Summers. "Sir, this is Thomas and this is Michael Summers" he began. "Boys, this is first lieutenant Robert Maynard of His Majesty's ship the *Pearl*."

Thomas' mouth gaped to see such an influential figure of the 18th century standing before him. He moved forward and shook Maynard's hand. The officer smiled.

"Thomas, I have heard about your kind offer, and indeed, your effort in helping us to bring down that brigand pirate Teach" he said. "It is an honour sir."

"Sir, the honour is mine" replied Thomas. Maynard moved over to Summers and held out his hand.

"Agent Summers, I am pleased to meet you" he said. Summers shook his hand.

"Sir, we are pleased to help you" Summers said. "But our true goal is to find and stop the man called Mackenzie, who has taken up with Blackbeard."

Maynard nodded. "Ah, yes, I have heard about him also" he said. "Do not worry, we'll catch your criminal too." He moved over to the prisoner. "And you, you will hang for crimes to the crown" he said.

He turned to Thomas. "Thomas, may I have a word in private?"

Thomas looked shocked. "Yes sir, of course" he replied. Maynard moved over to him, put his hand on Thomas' shoulder and led him out through a back door and into a small yard. The view of the ocean was amazing, Thomas thought to himself. For a moment Maynard just stood there, staring out into the sunset. Thomas stood just behind him.

"Sir, you wanted to talk?" said Thomas.

"No need for secrecy Thomas, William has told me everything" Maynard replied, still looking out over the water. "Is it true, what William saw? That you appeared before him in a blast of lightning and sparks?"

Thomas struggled to find the words to answer.

"Don't worry Thomas, I won't say a word to a soul" Maynard said.

Thomas looked him in the eyes. "Yes it is true" he said. "Michael and I are from another time, many, many years from now."

Maynard smiled. "And I take it this Mackenzie fellow is also from your era?"

"Yes sir, we need to stop him" Thomas said.

Maynard put his arm around Thomas. "And we will my friend, we will. Now I must get back to the *Pearl*.

She's anchored around the other side of the island, out of sight. there are plans to be made, but, we'll see each other again very soon."

They both walked back inside the little house. William looked at Thomas and smiled.

"Connor, Bobby, come with me to the *Pearl*, we have things to discuss" Maynard said as he opened the front door.

"Yes sir" they both answered. Bobby then turned to William.

"Don't let this bastard out your sight" he said, gesturing to the prisoner. William smiled and nodded, and the three men, including Robert Maynard, walked out the house, leaving William, Thomas and Summers to watch their prisoner.

* * * * *

Jon was making a full recovery. He had been discharged from the infirmary and had soon got back to work. Gracie came down to the main machine room to find him sitting next to the machine, on the computer, double-checking that the programming was all as it should be.

"Jon, shouldn't you be resting?" she said as she approached him. He turned round to her and smiled.

"Hi Gracie, no no, I'm fine. I've rested enough as it is, I need to do something" Jon replied. she took a seat next to him.

"Just don't want you overdoing it" she said. He turned round, facing her.

"I wonder how Thomas and Michael are getting on?" he asked. She glanced up at the large screen that displayed the stats of the jumpers, including their heart rate. "Well, they're still alive" she said.

"I want to go there, to help them" Jon said suddenly.

"The doctor said you shouldn't jump yet, the pressure might crack your skull again, it's not properly healed" Gracie replied. He looked back at the machine.

"I know, I just feel so helpless" Jon answered. she leaned forward and put her hand on his shoulder.

"Me too Jon" she said with a smile.

★ ★ ★ ★ ★

Thomas got to his feet and walked over to William, who was standing by the window, leaving Summers to watch the prisoner.

"William, Lt Maynard told me that you told him about me and Michael" Thomas said. William looked at him, and then patted him on the arm. "The lieutenant can be trusted Thomas, you have no fear there" he replied.

"It's OK William, I understand, he is your commanding officer, he should know" Thomas answered with a smile. they both leaned against the side and looked over at the prisoner.

"What will happen to him?" Thomas asked. William sighed.

"Oh, he'll hang for his crimes" he said, still staring at the man sitting in the chair. Thomas felt sad at that thought. Maybe this man had had no choice but to serve Blackbeard. These were hard times after all, and some people had to resort to such crimes in order to survive.

Thomas was disturbed from his thoughts by a knock at the door. William picked up his flintlock and moved over to the door.

"Who is it?" he called out.

"Tis a messenger, from the *Pearl*" came a voice. William opened the door slowly. A boy stood there, holding a folded piece of leather.

"Come in" William said. The young man walked in, wet from the rain outside. He handed William the piece of leather. William walked over to the table, unfolded it and took out the piece of paper within.

"What does it say?" Summers asked, as he stood up and moved over to William. The prisoner's eyes watched Summers as he left his side. He glanced over at Thomas, and then to the open door. Without anyone knowing, he had managed to unbind his hands. Now was his chance to get out. He leapt forward, pushing the boy out of the way. Thomas tried to grab him, but too late, he was out. Summers ran after him down the street.

"Stop him!" cried William. Thomas too took off in pursuit.

As Summers gained on the man, he looked round, and then suddenly stopped. He threw a punch at

Summers, but the agent deflected the fist with his hand. Moving to the side, he struck the man hard in the ribs. The man went down and Summers gave him one more hit, just to make sure, striking the man on the cheek. Thomas reached them and drew his gun.

"Get him up" Thomas said. Summers gripped the man's arm and they walked him back to the hideout.

"Good, well done chaps" William said. Summers threw the man back down on to the seat and bound his hands again.

"You OK?" Thomas asked, glancing at Summers.

"Yeah, no problem" Summers replied. The young man stared at Thomas' pistol. William noticed this and moved over to the boy. "OK, that'll be all, thank you George" he said and led the young man out, back into the rain.

"William, what did the letter say?" Thomas asked. William looked concerned as he took a seat next to the table.

"Teach and a few of his crew are on shore, looking for the three men who were at the tavern, including this gentleman" William said, gesturing over to the prisoner.

"And what of Mackenzie?" Summers asked. William looked over at him.

"He's still on the *Queen Anne's Revenge*" William said. "But if Teach finds out that the *Pearl* is anchored on the other side of the island, then I fear our attack in a few days will be futile."

"Then he must not find out" Thomas said. "We'll

have to give him a reason to return to the safety of his ship."

William leaned forward. "What do you have in mind?" he asked with a smile, Thomas glanced over at Summers.

"We'll go and find them, and try and arrest them" Thomas said. William laughed. "We'll stand no chance" he said.

"I know, but they'll quickly go back to the ship won't they?"

Again William leancd forward, looking deep in thought.

"OK then, yes" he said getting to his feet. "But we'll need to go now, find them as soon as possible."

Thomas walked over to Summers. "Summers, you'll have to stay here, watch him" he said, gesturing to the prisoner.

"Yes, that's fine Thomas, he's not going anywhere" Summers replied. He leaned close to Thomas. "Be careful my friend" he whispered. Thomas smiled and patted him on the back. William opened the door and turned to Thomas.

"OK then Thomas, away with us" he called out, and both men walked out into the rain, closing the door behind them.

They walked up the street. The night was getting quite dark now. A few oil lamps lit the street and the walkways, but the rain was coming down harder and Thomas pulled up his collar around his jaw.

"We'll try the tavern first" William said as they walked out on to the main street. A few people were out, despite the weather. Two men came out of a nearby tavern and started to squabble.

Then a woman came out of one of the alleyways. "Fancy some?" she said, pushing her chest out. Thomas smiled and carried on, following William down the street until they were standing outside the King's Crown tavern. William pushed open the door and they both walked inside. Music was playing and the whole place seemed rowdy.

"Come Thomas, this way" William said. Thomas followed him to the back of the tavern, where there was a small yard area. William looked around but could see nothing.

"Damn!" William said. "Where are they?"

"They're not here" Thomas said as they walked back inside, out of the rain.

"They must have moved on." He thought for a moment, then looked up at Thomas. "The Redcoat Tavern, it's down by the docks" he said.

"Come on then" Thomas replied and both men walked out, back into the rain and down the street towards the lighthouse.

"Stop!" William suddenly said, putting his arm across Thomas' chest. He pointed down to the bottom of the street, where a group of men were coming out of a tavern, shouting and calling out.

"That's Teach" William said. Thomas stared at the

tall man. He wore a long black coat, a black hat and his trademark black beard. He had with him five other men. Thomas and William were outnumbered, but not outgunned.

"Come on" Thomas said and drew his gun. William smiled and unsheathed his cutlass. They ran down towards the men, stopping a few yards in front of them. Thomas aimed his gun straight at Blackbeard.

"Stop there, Teach!" Thomas called out. The pirate stared at him, cocking his head to the side.

"I've seen a weapon like that before my friend" he said.

His men had fanned out. William got ready for combat.

"I know you have Teach, and I want the man who had that weapon" Thomas said.

Blackbeard smiled. "Well, you can't have him" he said.

Thomas held up his gun higher, aiming straight at Teach's face. At that Connor came running around the corner from a nearby alleyway. He drew his flintlock ready for action. Again Blackbeard smiled.

"Do you think I don't know about the *Pearl* around the other side of the island ye fools?" he said, with a laugh.

William turned to Thomas. "How would he know?" he whispered.

"And do you think I don't have spies of me own?" Teach called out.

Connor turned round and aimed his pistol at William and Thomas. "Drop your weapons, boys" he said. William glanced at Thomas. Both men threw down their weapons, Thomas' gun hitting the ground with a clank.

Blackbeard strolled over to them. He looked Thomas up and down, then moved his shirt aside, revealing the conduit suit beneath. Teach's eyes moved up to Thomas'.

"The same as my man" he whispered, and stepped back. "I don't think meself wise enough to know where ye came from." He glanced down to the gun. Picking it up, he continued, "But I like the weapons." He gave a little chuckle, looking over at Connor. "Mr Wright, dispose of these men and return to me on the *Queen Anne's Revenge* would you?"

Connor nodded. "Aye sir" he answered. Blackbeard stepped forward and patted Thomas on the face.

"Goodbye gentlemen, I'll be keeping this" he said and held up Thomas' gun. He gestured for the rest of his men to follow him, and they all walked back down the street and out of sight, leaving William and Thomas with the traitorous Connor. William turned round slowly to face his old friend.

"Connor, why?" he said. Thomas stood just behind him, glaring across at Connor.

"Because he pays well" Connor answered. Then, with his other hand, he drew his cutlass. William raised his hands in submission. The rage began to build in

Thomas. These men were meant to be friends, fighting injustice together, but Connor had turned now, seduced by the wealth that Blackbeard could offer.

Thomas took in a breath, closed his eyes for a second, then opened them. Leaping forward and pushing William aside, he struck Connor hard in the face. Connor he fell backwards. His flintlock went off, the ball shooting high in the air. Connor recovered quickly and swung his sword at Thomas, but Thomas moved back, the blade just missing his chest.

"No, Thomas!" William shouted. He handed the cutlass to his old friend. "Move aside Thomas" he said. Thomas looked back at Connor, who threw down his empty, fired pistol to get ready for combat. Thomas moved back and William stepped forward, his sword held out.

"We don't have to do this Connor" he whispered.

"Oh we do William, I'm not going to hang" Connor answered. He lunged forward, his cutlass smashing against the blade of William's. William staggered back and again Connor came forward, his sword held high. Before he could bring it down, William moved aside and slashed his blade across, catching Connor on his leg. Connor stumbled aside, blood now flowing from the wound. William was clearly a much better swordsman than his opponent. He held up his cutlass, pointing it at Connor.

"Do you yield, my friend?" William asked softly. Connor looked up at him.

"I will not hang William, never!" he shouted and darted forward. William deflected Connor's sword once more and inflicted yet another cut, this time deep in his side. Connor dropped to the ground, holding the wound. William stood by, his blade held up ready.

"Connor, please!" he said, but Connor, still reluctant, got to his feet, his sword up. William shook his head, knowing full well that his friend was about to die. Connor moved forward and swung his sword hard at William's head. William ducked and thrust the tip of his blade forward. The sword went straight through Connor's stomach. Blood began to trickle down the blade. Connors' eyes stared into William's.

William withdrew the sword and Connor dropped to the ground. William threw down his sword and knelt down beside his friend, Connor gripped William's hand and looked into his eyes.

"William, I'm sorry my friend… please… please forgive me" he groaned. William held him close and put his hand on the wound, blood flowing through his fingers.

"Of course Connor, my friend" William replied, a lump beginning to form in his throat. Connor smiled and reach up, touching William's face. Then his hand dropped and his head flopped down.

"I'm sorry" William whispered. Thomas moved over to him, placing his hand on William's shoulder.

"You had no choice William" Thomas said.

"Come, we have to go" William said. He picked up

his sword, wiped the blood off the blade with a rag and sheathed it once more.

"What about Connor?" Thomas asked, gesturing down at the body. William stared down at Connor for a moment.

"Leave him, people will think the pirates have killed him" he said. "And I won't correct them."

The men started to walk quickly back down the street towards the safe house.

* * * * *

"Thomas, what happened?" Summers said, getting to his feet as the two men walked through the door, dripping wet from the rain. William walked straight out to the back of the house, while Thomas took off his coat and hung it up next to the door.

"Thomas?" Summers asked once more. Thomas sat down at the table and poured himself a drink of strong ale.

"Connor was a spy for Blackbeard" Thomas muttered. Summers frowned and took a seat opposite. "What happened?" he asked. Thomas took a big gulp of his beer, putting the goblet down, he replied.

"We confronted Teach and his men, then Connor turned up and pointed his pistol at us. Blackbeard escaped and William killed Connor" Thomas said.

"Shit" Summers said, leaning back in his chair.

"William had no choice" Thomas said. He looked

towards the back of the house. The back door was open and he could see William sitting there, under a canopy, just staring at the ground.

"Does Lt Maynard know?" Summers asked. Thomas looked back to him. "No, and William wants it to stay that way" he said.

"Why?"

"So Connor isn't dishonoured" Thomas replied softly. Summers nodded. Leaning forward, he asked quietly "I take it Blackbeard knows of the attack?"

Thomas took yet another gulp of beer. "Yes" he said.

"We'll have to tell Maynard this. He'll need to know Teach is aware of what's going to happen."

"He will." Summers turned and saw William standing in the doorway. "I'll tell him that Teach has found out about the attack." He walked inside and sat at the table next to Thomas.

"I can tell him if you want" Thomas said, pouring William some of the beer.

"No Thomas, I'll go to the Pearl at first light" William said.

"OK, we'll watch him then." Thomas gestured at the prisoner.

"Thank you Thomas, and you Michael, the help you have given to us is admirable, and wherever you are from, the future, the heavens, you both truly are a blessing" William said.

Summers got to his feet and patted William on the shoulder. "You are most welcome William, but we are just men, just human" he said. William glanced up at him with a smile.

"Well, you had both better get some rest, been a busy day for you, and we must be up early" William said. He looked over at the prisoner. "We'll take it in turns to watch him, two hours each, I'll go first."

But William could not sleep. He sat there thinking about the death of his friend by his hand, wondering what on earth he was going to tell Robert Maynard the next day.

★ ★ ★ ★ ★

The *Queen Anne's Revenge* bobbed on the waves. The night was black, but the ship was lit up with candle and lantern light and the sound of merriment and laughter could be heard coming from the captain's quarters. All nineteen crew members, including Mackenzie, were sitting around the huge table placed in the middle of the room. Blackbeard himself sat at the head with Mackenzie next to him.

"Well, Mr Mackenzie, I've met one of your friends today" Teach said, leaning towards the lieutenant.

"What do you mean?" Mackenzie asked. The captain smiled and placed on the table the gun he had taken from Thomas.

Mackenzie stared at the weapon. "Where did you get that?" he asked and Teach laughed out loud.

"Someone like you. He had one of those suit things on too" Blackbeard answered.

Mackenzie sat forward, still looking at the gun on the table. "They have followed me" he said.

Blackbeard smirked. "Aye, and they want you Mr Mackenzie" he said.

"And what did you say to that, captain?" Mackenzie asked.

"I said that you were mine" Teach replied with a grin.

Mackenzie smiled and picked up his tankard of ale. He took a large gulp, then slammed the empty tankard down. Teach laughed out loud and Mackenzie did the same. One of the other crewmen turned to the captain.

"Captain, does yer wife know where you hid yer treasure?" the man said.

Blackbeard laughed. "Only the devil and me knows where that treasure is" he said, and laughed again. Mackenzie stared at Teach. *I will know it soon my friend,* he thought to himself, and smiled from ear to ear.

"I wonder what this Maynard is planning then? I was once a military man myself, and if I were him, I wouldn't be taking you on alone" Mackenzie said and took another sip.

"What do you mean?" Teach asked, beer dripping from his beard.

"He won't be alone Captain, he'll have help, they'll surround your ship" Mackenzie replied.

Teach scoffed and leaned back. "Let the bastards try" he said.

★ ★ ★ ★ ★

The next day, after a disturbed sleep, Thomas and Summers woke early and made their way downstairs. William was already up and about. Bobby and another man were standing in the room. William smiled as he walked over to Thomas and Summers.

"Good morning gentlemen" he said. "Bobby and David here have come to take the prisoner to the *Pearl* for us. And Lt Maynard has invited you two men to join us and come aboard." Thomas looked at Summers with a big grin.

"Aboard the *Pearl?*" Thomas asked, looking back at William, who just smiled.

"Yes Thomas, a carriage is waiting outside for us" William replied.

Bobby had moved over and picked up the prisoner by his arm. The other man, David, opened the door and Bobby dragged the man outside, loading him into the carriage.

"Well, let's go then" Summers said and they all left the little house. William closed the door behind them and locked it. The carriage set off down the street towards the other end of the island. Thomas sat next to William with Summers opposite and Bobby and the prisoner next to him, while David drove the four-horse carriage. The weather was warm, but the streets were still wet from the downpour the night before.

Forty minutes later the carriage arrived at a small

bay, where a long wooden jetty stretched out into the ocean. Beyond it was the *Pearl*. Thomas stepped out of the carriage and stared across at the massive vessel.

"She's beautiful, isn't she?" William said, standing next to him.

Thomas smiled. "She is" he whispered. They all walked down the jetty to the very end, Bobby holding the prisoner tight. A large rowing boat was tied to the post. William got in, followed by David. Then Bobby handed the bound man down to them.

"After you, gentlemen" Bobby said to Thomas and Summers, gesturing towards the boat. They got in and Bobby followed. David and William took the oars and they began to row out towards the ship. Ten minutes later they were being helped on board. The prisoner was instantly taken below deck. Thomas looked around at the huge masts, the gleaming white sails and the brass fittings to the wood.

"Hello Thomas." Thomas looked round to see standing before him the ship's commander, First Lieutenant Robert Maynard. "Welcome on board the Pearl" he continued. Thomas smiled and approached Maynard.

"Sir, it is an honour to be asked here, it really is" Thomas replied.

Maynard grinned and shook his hand. "You are welcome my friend. Please, come to my quarters" he said, leading the way. Summers followed behind.

"Now please, take a seat" Maynard said and sat down opposite them.

"Sir, something has happened" William began.

"Mr Lockwood, don't worry yourself, I have heard about the pirate finding out about the attack, all is in hand" Maynard said before William could explain further. "And I have also heard about Mr Wright's death at the hands of the pirate." William gave Thomas a worried look.

"That's right sir" Thomas said, answering before William could.

"You were there, Thomas?" Maynard asked, Thomas nodded.

"Yes sir, Connor fought bravely" Thomas replied.

Maynard nodded. "Yes, well, I would expect nothing less from a man of this ship" he said. He glanced at William.

"I am sorry for your loss Mr Lockwood, I know you and he were friends" he said. "We have recovered his body, and we will give him a proper seaman's funeral later this day."

William looked down. "Thank you" he muttered.

"Now, to business" Maynard said. He pulled out a map of the island and laid it flat on the table. "Now, the other ships will arrive in the next couple of days. The *Pearl* will move round the bay to the east, the other ships from the west. We'll trap that brigand and blow him out the water."

"I'm afraid Blackbeard took my gun" said Thomas.

Summers unclipped his own weapon and placed it on the table. "It was like this one" he said. Maynard looked at it with wonderment, then glanced up to Summers.

"May I?" he asked. Summers nodded, Maynard carefully picked up the gun and examined it. His eyes moved to Thomas.

"You truly are from a different time?" he asked.

"Yes we are" replied Thomas. Maynard handed the gun back to Summers with a smile.

"Well, no matter, let him keep the gun, I have you two" he said. "Now, come, William, show Summers here our fine store of weapons, see what a man of the future thinks of them."

"Yes sir" William said. He and Summers got up and moved over to the door of the cabin. Summers turned to Thomas.

"Are you coming?" he asked. Maynard answered for him. "No no, Thomas and I have things to discuss" he said. Thomas sat down again and Summers and William walked out, closing the door behind them.

Maynard smiled at Thomas. "May I see the suit William has told me about?" he asked.

"By all means" Thomas replied. He stood up, undoing his shirt and pulling it agape. Maynard got up and stepped forward. With his finger, he touched the black shiny material. Small pieces of the harder black armour could be seen underneath. Maynard stared at it.

"You are a miracle Thomas" he finally said. He moved over to a cabinet, gesturing for Thomas to do his shirt back up. "As I said, I will never tell a soul of this, and for your help that you are offering to us, and have already given, I would like you to accept this." He had produced a fine sword. The sheath was made of black leather with bright brass fittings, as were the hilt and guard.

"Sir, you really don't have to give me this" Thomas said.

Maynard shook his head. "I want you to have it" he replied. Thomas took the weapon, which was surprisingly light. He drew the blade from its sheath and the metal shone brightly.

Maynard smiled. "Here, let me help you" he said. He fastened the sheath to a strap which he fixed to a belt, placing it over Thomas' shoulder so it hung on his left-hand side.

"Thank you" Thomas said, and he placed the sword back in its sheath. Maynard patted Thomas on the shoulder.

"You are welcome Thomas, come, let's see how your friend is getting on." Both men stepped out on to the deck, Summers was standing near one of the large cannons talking to a group of men.

"Nice sword" he said, seeing Thomas' proud smirk.

"I have prepared cabins for you both on board the Pearl" Maynard said, placing his hands on both men's shoulders.

"We're staying on the Pearl?" Thomas asked eagerly.

Maynard chuckled. "Yes my friends" he answered, and he gestured for the two men to walk with him. They moved up some steps on to a higher platform. The wheel stood before them and Thomas stared at the huge wooden and brass object, Maynard took hold of it with one hand and gestured to the ship.

"Again gentlemen, welcome on board the *Pearl*!" he called out, and the crew cheered with pride.

★ ★ ★ ★ ★

Gracie awoke early and made her way down to the main machine room. She stepped out of the elevator and glanced up at the large monitor displaying the heart rates of the time jumpers. Over the days since Thomas and Summers had gone this had become a ritual for her. She might not be able to see Thomas, but she could at least watch his heart rate.

"Morning Gracie." She turned around to see Jon standing next to her.

"Hi Jon" she said with a smile. He looked concerned.

"Jon, what is it?" she asked.

"Did Thomas tell you about the secure sector, the cells?" he answered.

"Yes, he did" she replied with a frown. "Why?"

"Because today, all the security guards are to be replaced by CIA agents, to prevent any more, well, security risks."

Gracie shook her head. "And? Surely that's a good thing?"

"I'm worried that the cells will be closed down for security reasons and the prisoners moved elsewhere."

"Oh, I see" she said. "Worried that your guinea pigs will be taken away from you?"

He looked at her sharply. "Not at all, but those people can't go to normal prisons for obvious reasons" he replied.

"Yes, I know, I'm sorry Jon" she said. He gave her a smile and began to walk away.

"Well, I have things to do Gracie, speak to you later" he said and made his way through one of the doors. It closed behind him and she was alone once more. She quickly went over to a computer and activated the vault, as Jon called the heart of the facility, the memory and the database. She pressed a few buttons and brought up the schematics. She looked at it intently until she saw what she was looking for; the cells. She quickly switched off the computer and moved over to a door, a door she had never been through before. Because the security was being changed today, there was nobody to stop her. She opened the door slowly, revealing a long white corridor and at the very end, the big red door. She walked down as quickly as possible and looked at the panel next to it.

"Shit" she muttered. It was a retinal scanner. She took out of her pocket a small device, pressed a button and it opened, revealing a touch panel screen and a thin plug device attached to it. Taking out the little plug, she clicked it into a small slot next to the scanner. The touch screen lit up and she started tapping away on the little device.

"Come on" she whispered to herself. At last the little light on the scanner turned from red to green and the door made a loud clanking noise. Steam hissed from the corners and the massive door slowly started to open. Gracie stepped inside, not sure what to expect. The room seemed huge, at least as big as the main machine room. A small control station sat on her right hand side, unmanned. She moved over to it and looked at the panel. Along the side of the screen was a list of names, and next to each, a category. Most said 'low risk' next to them, but one stood out; 'cat A' - extremely dangerous. There was no name, just a number. She pressed the button next to it and the panel suddenly lit up.

To her surprise, the wall opposite her started to move. A row of red panels came forward and started to rotate, then one came forward and stopped.

She walked over slowly as the large red metal panel started to open up. A thick Perspex shield could now be seen behind the panel, and on the other side of that, in a tiny cell, sat the Ripper.

He looked up at her and a cruel smile crept over his face.

"I didn't know you were being held here" she said quietly. He smiled.

"Where else would I be, my dear?" he replied. She shrugged, moving up to the red line on the floor. The Ripper got to his feet and moved over to the Perspex.

"You can come closer, I can't get to you, after all" he whispered, touching the plastic glass. She glanced down at the line and then took a step over it, making her way to the Perspex barrier. The Ripper leaned against it and turned away, his back now facing Gracie.

"What happened to you?" she said. He did not reply. "You couldn't always have been this man, my mother always says that people aren't born bad" she said.

"Well, maybe your mother is wrong" he said softly, still not looking at her.

"What you did to those women in 1888 was horrendous and unforgivable" she said, taking another step closer. He turned his head slightly, still not making eye contact. He replied in a very low tone, almost silent.

"This is what I am my dear" he said. She dared herself to get closer.

"I don't believe that, everyone can change if they wish" she said. He finally looked round and his dark eyes stared right at her. To her surprise, a tear rolled down his cheek.

"Not me" he whispered. For a moment, a strange feeling of sadness and sympathy overwhelmed her.

"What happened to you?" she said softly. He paused for a moment, and then replied.

"I was born a monster. This is what I am, what I will always be" he answered. She tried to look into his eyes to see if she could find a trace of humanity again, as she had just witnessed from him.

"No one is born a monster" she said. His dark eyes moved up and glanced at her.

"Tell me my dear, if this plastic wasn't separating us, do you think that I wouldn't harm you, that I wouldn't rip you to pieces?" he said calmly. "You see, I am a monster and I would kill you given half the chance." She looked straight back at him, staring right into his eyes.

"You are just a man, a human, nothing more" she said. "I thought I was getting through to you, that I saw a trace of what seemed like normality, but maybe I was wrong." He looked away, and Gracie saw another tear come from his black eyes and roll down his cheek.

"There" she said. "You are just a man, and you can be healed." he glanced up at her and smiled, but it was not a cruel smile. There seemed to be no trace of evil in this monster any more. He who had done a terrible thing, but he was a man nonetheless. His soul had been damaged, twisting him into the devil that he now was, but the human side was now coming through. Gracie looked at this pathetic man, this damaged man. Neither she nor anyone else would ever know what had happened to him to change him, but there was hope there, a sign that evil can never take hold of anyone completely. She gave him a smile, and smiled back.

"You can go now, my dear" he whispered and stepped back over to his bed. He lay down and faced the wall, his back to her once more. Gracie walked back slowly to the control panel, taking one final glance at him. She pressed the button, the cell moved back and the red metal panel came down again, covering the Perspex. The Ripper was now out of sight. She walked out of the large room, the huge door closing behind her. A tear came to her eyes as she thought of what had become of the Ripper, and why he was now the way he was.

"What were you doing in there Gracie?"

She looked round and saw Jon standing there with two agents. She moved over to him, gritted her teeth and gave him a slap across the face.

"You are no better than the men you have imprisoned!" she yelled at him. He held his face, which was now throbbing. The agent to his right, looked at him.

"Dr Walker, we need to go, please show us the containment room" the agent said. Gracie gave him one last glare and stormed off back to her dorm, leaving Jon and the agents to study his collection of psychopaths and criminals.

★ ★ ★ ★ ★

Thomas awoke to the sound of the waves hitting against the hull and the gulls screaming above. A knock came on his door. He stood up and stepped across the tiny cabin.

"Hey Thomas" Summers said, as Thomas opened the door.

"Morning Michael" Thomas replied,

"Lt Maynard has asked to speak with you, he's waiting on deck" said Summers. Thomas quickly turned around, threw on his long coat and placed the sword strap over his shoulder. He and Summers made their way out through the lower deck space. A few of the sailors were about, doing little jobs below deck. The cook could be seen at the far end, in the galley. They walked up a narrow staircase and the daylight hit them. Thomas closed his eyes as the warm sun touched his face. He took in a deep breath, taking in as much fresh air as he could.

"Goon morning Thomas, did you sleep well?" Thomas turned and saw Maynard standing before him.

"Yes sir, thank you, best one yet to be honest" Thomas replied. The first lieutenant gave a little chuckle and answered.

"Well, the ocean does that to a man" he said as he and Thomas made their way up the steps to the wheel. "Gets under your skin." He looked out to the rest of the ship. The sailors were running around, going about their business, doing their daily routines. It had now been a few days since Thomas and Summers had joined the crew of the *Pearl*. Each night they would sit in Maynard's cabin, talking of tactics, bringing down the pirate, and of course, catching Mackenzie. The day of the attack was now tomorrow, and there was a buzz in the air. The whole crew seemed excited at the approaching battle. Sailors would sharpen their swords every night and check that their firearms were in working order and the cannons had been cleaned.

Maynard turned to Thomas with a smile.

"Tomorrow Thomas, we will have victory, and you will have your man" he said. Thomas nodded. He too felt a sense of excitement at the thought of the battle tomorrow, this fight that he had read so much about in the history books. He knew full well of course that the *Pearl* would win; history told it that way. He hadn't told Maynard this, nor any of the crew, as they might get over confident and end up changing history. He kept this knowledge to himself. The focus had to be on Mackenzie; he must be caught and taken back home.

Maynard turned back to Thomas once more after giving a sailor an order.

"I take it that you and Summers will be returning to your own time after the battle?" he asked quietly.

"Yes sir, we will" he said. Maynard nodded. "Well, we had better give you a battle to remember, hadn't we?" he replied, and he walked back down the stairs and on to deck. *History remembers what happened*, Thomas thought to himself.

"Good morning gentlemen." Thomas and Summers turned to see William standing there. Thomas moved forward and shook his hand. "How are you finding life on board?" William asked, looking out over the huge deck of the ship.

"It's invigorating, William" Thomas answered. William glanced at him, a big smile across his face.

"I am pleased" he replied. "We now have 35 sailors at hand and Blackbeard has only 19. We will win this fight, I feel." Thomas patted him on the back.

"Yes we will my friend" Thomas said. William looked at him with a smile and at that, Maynard returned, walking back up the steps. A young man was standing next to him.

"Gentlemen" Maynard said. He looked concerned.

"Sir, what is it?" William asked. Maynard gestured to the young man to speak.

"I am a messenger from the town of Ocracoke" he said. "I've been sent to give word that the first mate of the *Queen Anne's Revenge* is ashore, trying to gather more help for the battle tomorrow. He has two other men with him, but…"

Thomas moved forward. "Yes?" he asked.

"He is a very tall man, sir" the young man said. Thomas looked at Summers. This must be Mackenzie.

The young messenger continued. "They are taking men as slaves" he said, Thomas looked at Maynard. "Thank you" Maynard said to the messenger and he moved off quickly back down the steps.

"We have to stop them sir" William said, moving closer to the first lieutenant.

"I know, Mr Lockwood, and we will" Maynard replied, looking deep in thought.

"We will go sir" Thomas said. Maynard's eyes moved up and looked at Thomas. He nodded.

"So, there'll be three of them, all together" Maynard said quietly, almost to himself. He looked back at Thomas and Summers. "Gentlemen, would you go with William on shore?" he said. Summers nodded. Thomas gripped the handle of his sword tightly.

"Yes sir" Thomas said. Maynard smiled.

"Good, stop them, free the slaves they are catching, send them back to Blackbeard empty-handed" Maynard replied.

"Yes sir" the three of them answered, and they moved off, on to the deck.

* * * * *

An hour later they had reached the jetty. The sailor from before, David, had rowed them from the *Pearl*. William got out, followed by Thomas and then Summers.

"I'll wait for you here" David called to them. William held up his hand to acknowledge him and they made their way down the jetty.

"We'll cut through the woodland, it'll be quicker" William said. Thomas and Summers followed him up the sandy beach and into the woods. The day was hot and the trees gave some much-needed shade.

"It's this way" William said as he clambered over a huge rock. The sound of people could now be heard in the distance. They reached a small ledge and moved through the trees slowly.

Quietly Thomas looked down on the town, now so close.

"Come" William said, and they made their way down the steep hill and towards the town of Ocracoke. As they stepped into a narrow street, a woman ran past them, crying.

"They must be this way" Summers said. They ran

down to where the woman had come from, and at the end of the street they stopped dead.

"Wait" Summers said. He peered around the corner to see a large group of people. Mackenzie was standing on a market table. Two of his men were grabbing men at random and throwing them to the ground. Mackenzie shouted over the shouting and screaming.

"If you were to volunteer, then we wouldn't have to force you!" he cried.

Summers unclipped his pistol and clicked off the safety switch. Thomas grabbed his arm. Summers looked round and Thomas shook his head.

"We can't use those weapons, not yet, not with so many people around" Thomas said. Summers looked back towards Mackenzie. He gritted his teeth and holstered the gun once more.

"Here, take this" William said, and he handed him a huge flintlock weapon. Summers looked at the massive gun. "It's a blunderbuss" William said. Summers took the weapon and peered back round. A group of men had now joined Mackenzie and his two crew members, and William pointed over to them. "Look, there" he said.

"Who are they?" Thomas asked, looking at the five men standing next to Mackenzie.

"They are local ruffians, thieves, criminals. Your Mackenzie must have hired them to join the crew or gather slaves" William replied. Thomas frowned and gripped the handle of his sword, staring at the armed men.

"Well, we'll have to stop them too" he said. He moved out into the crowd.

"Wait!" Summers called after him. But Thomas was already in the crowd. William smiled and moved out after them. They kept their heads down. Mackenzie was still shouting.

"We just want one man from each family to help bring down this Maynard" he said. "He will control you, rule your lives for you, kill you if necessary. Edward Teach will protect you. He will stop Maynard, give you your freedom, but we need your help!"

But the people were having none of it. One shouted back in rage, "It is you and your captain that wish to control us, why else would you enslave us?" One of Mackenzie's men stepped forward and struck the man hard with the butt of his musket. The man fell to the ground, blood flowing.

"That's it!" Thomas shouted. He pushed his way through the crowd to the front.

"Mackenzie!" he shouted out. The old lieutenant looked down at him.

"You!" he replied. "You have followed me here to die, have you?" Summers and William pushed the people away, trying to get them to leave the area. Mackenzie glanced at one of his hired goons and the man came forward, an axe in his hand.

"Goodbye Dr Long" Mackenzie shouted. He and his two men strode off down the street and back to the safety of the *Queen Anne's Revenge*.

Thomas drew his gleaming sword. The hired thug came forward, his axe ready, his men surrounding Thomas. Thomas looked around, getting himself ready for the coming attack, when he heard a shot. He turned around to see that the men on his left had hit the ground. Then he saw Summers with his blunderbuss, smoke coming from the muzzle. He had taken both men out with one shot of the scattergun.

As Thomas turned, he saw William jump from a platform and hit the other two thugs, all three of them falling to the ground. The man with the axe shouted and started to run forward, coming straight at Thomas, the axe held up above his head. Thomas bent his knees slightly, getting himself ready. The man swung the axe, but Thomas moved to the side and punched him on the cheek. The man staggered back and looked up at Thomas. Then he hefted the large axe up once more, gripping it tightly with both hands. Thomas held up his sword.

William dodged out the way of one of the man's sword, the blade just missing his head. He turned and saw the other man come close, a sword in one hand, a dagger in the other. He stepped back out of the way of the knife blade as it came down. The sword followed, but William deflected it with his cutlass. At that Summers came running over. He struck the man with the sword hard on the head with the now empty blunderbuss, and the man dropped to the ground.

The other man shouted out in rage and came at William with both weapons, but William stepped back, knocking the dagger away easily and then the cutlass. He then slashed his own sword to the right, making a large gash in the man's chest. He dropped both weapons and looked at William. William pulled back his sword and thrust it straight into the man's stomach. The man gripped his stomach and fell to the ground.

Thomas slashed with his sword, striking the man's arms. Blood began flowing down his arm and dripping off his hand. He glared at Thomas as he lifted the axe up once more. Thomas got ready, holding his sword up and pointing it at the man. The thug ran forward, swinging the axe round. It hit Thomas' sword, knocking it away. The man then hit Thomas hard in the face with his fist, knocking him to the ground.

"Shit" he muttered to himself. He looked up just in time to see the man lift the axe above his head. Thomas glanced at his sword and then back to the man. He reached out and grabbed the weapon by its hilt. Lifting it up, he thrust it forward, the sharp blade sliding easily through the mans stomach. The man froze and his eyes glazed over as Thomas withdrew the sword.

Summers came running over. "Are you OK?" he asked as he helped Thomas to his feet. Thomas smiled.

"Yeah, I'm fine Michael" he replied. He glanced round to see William walking over, sliding his own cutlass back into its sheath.

"Thomas, you are now truly one of us" William said. "You have used your cutlass, the blade has now been baptised with the blood of your enemy." He handed

Thomas a cloth, and Thomas took it and wiped his blade clean.

"It wasn't something I wanted to do" Thomas said as he slid the sword back inside its sheath. William patted him on the back.

"That is good, killing should never be something you want to do, but sometimes you need to do it to survive" William replied.

"I think we have company" Summers said. They looked around to see the crowd of people returning once more.

"Now what?" Thomas said, looking from face to face as the people began to surround them.

"We just saved them" Summers replied, getting ready to defend himself. William moved forward and placed his hand on Summers' chest.

"And they know it" William said with a smile. One man started to clap his hands, followed by a woman, and then someone else until the whole crowd were applauding. A woman ran forward and hugged Summers. "Thank you sirs, thank you" she cried. Summers smiled as the woman moved away and a man came forward.

"Sir, we owe you a debt of gratitude" he said, shaking Summers' hand. William laughed as the people were touching him. Cries of thanks came from all over the marketplace.

William turned to Thomas. "We have done a good job today my friend" he said. He climbed up on to the table Mackenzie had been standing on earlier. "My friends, listen, listen!" he called out. The people turned round, looking at him. "People, HMS *Pearl* and its crew are here to destroy Blackbeard and his pirates" William began. "On the morrow, we will attack the *Queen Anne's Revenge*. I urge you to stay in your homes, stay safe. do not come out until the pirates are brought to justice!" The crowd once more started to cheer.

William jumped down from the table and walked back over to Thomas and Summers, Summers put his hands up to the crowd as they left the marketplace, walking back down the street and into the woods once more.

On the walk back to the *Pearl* through the dense woodland, Summers and Thomas talked over what had happened.

"Looks like we're heroes" Summers said with a big smile.

"I know. Did you see the way the people thanked us?" Thomas replied.

"I could get used to this" Summers said.

Thomas turned to him. "Michael, remember, we're not staying here, we have a job to do and then we go home." Summers nodded.

"I know, I know Thomas, it is nice to be appreciated like that though."

Back at the ship, Maynard approached them eagerly.

"Mr Lockwood, what happened?" he asked William.

"There were three members of the *Queen Anne's*

Revenge ashore sir, including the man that Thomas and Summers seek. They were trying to gather help, by any means necessary, even enslaving the people" William said. Maynard frowned.

"And what happened?" he replied.

William smiled. "We stopped them, sir" he answered. He turned to Thomas and Summers standing just behind them. "These men fought well."

"Many thanks. Thomas, Summers, you are invaluable to the *Pearl*" Maynard said, patting Thomas on the shoulder and shaking Summers' hand.

"You are welcome sir" Thomas replied with pride. Maynard smiled and gestured towards his cabin.

"Come now, the attack is now a few short hours away, there are things to discuss" Maynard said, and they made their way over to the wooden door. They stepped inside and Maynard closed the door behind them. He gestured for them to take a seat and hung up his coat.

"So then, the smaller and faster sloop ships will be here by dusk, and the attack will commence at first light" Maynard said, after taking his seat opposite Thomas and Summers.

"Yes sir, but we cannot forget that Blackbeard and Mackenzie have two weapons from our time" Summers replied with concern. Maynard simply held up his hand.

"Fear not Michael, we will have the advantage, not the pirates" he answered with confidence. He gestured to Thomas' sword.

"I trust your weapon came in useful?" he asked, Thomas gripped the handle and smiled.

"Yes sir, it did, thank you" he replied.

"Excellent" Maynard answered. He got to his feet and peered out of the window. The day was going fast and the sun was now low on the horizon. "Well, better get some rest, tomorrow will be a good day" he said, still looking out to sea.

"Yes sir" Thomas said, and he and Summers got to their feet. Summers opened the door. Thomas stopped for a second, then turned back to face Maynard.

"We will not fail you tomorrow sir" he said. He followed Summers out of the room, closing the door behind them.

★ ★ ★ ★ ★

The following day Jon walked into the mess hall to see Gracie sitting alone in the corner of the room. He made his way over to her.

"Gracie, are you OK?" he asked.

"Yes" she muttered. He pulled out the chair opposite her.

"May I?" he asked. She nodded and Jon sat down.

"I'm sorry for hitting you Jon" she suddenly said. He smiled.

"I understand. It must have been a shock, seeing the prisoners like that" Jon replied. Gracie looked up at him and he gave a shrug.

"Have you heard?" Jon asked her. She was confused.

"No, what?" she answered.

"I have had word today from the CIA that the prisoners are to be moved to a maximum security compound, off site" Jon said.

"No, I didn't hear that" she replied. "And what of your studies?"

"They will end now, my work will concentrate on the time project." He leaned forward and managed to force a smile. "It's for the best, I'm sure. There are only two prisoners left anyway, James the security guard and the Ripper."

Gracie looked down. "What is it?" Jon asked.

She sighed. "I think I was getting through to the Ripper" she said. "He seemed to regret what he had done."

Jon snorted. "Gracie, please, don't be so forgiving, you know what he did, what he's still capable of."

"I didn't say he should be forgiven, did I? All I meant was that I saw another side of him."

Jon leaned back once more. "OK, OK. Sorry, well, it matters not, they're leaving today" Jon said. He looked at his watch. "In an hour's time, actually." He got to his feet. "Excuse me, I have to go and meet the agent in charge in my office. See you later Gracie."

★ ★ ★ ★ ★

"Ah, Dr Walker" the agent said, greeting Jon with a handshake.

"Agent" Jon replied. He opened the office door and was about to walk in.

"Dr Walker, there is no need to go in, what we want is in your cell block" the agent said. Jon turned back to face him.

"So, we do not need to discuss this?" Jon asked.

The agent shrugged. "No doctor, I have three agents waiting for us outside the cells as we speak, let's not keep them waiting." He turned back to make his way down the corridor. Jon gritted his teeth and slammed the door closed again, quickly following the agent into the elevator. The agent opened the door that led down the corridor to the cell block, Jon following behind. The three other agents were waiting outside the red door.

"Sir" the one said as he walked up to greet the agent with Jon.

"Let's get this done shall we doctor?" the agent said, turning to Jon. Jon pushed past him and punched in the code. The retinal scanner opened to read Jon's eye and the door opened with a clank. Jon was about to walk in, but one of the agents put his hand on his chest, stopping him.

"We'll go first Dr Walker, thank you" the agent said. Jon gritted his teeth; this was his facility after all. Two of the agents walked in, their pistols drawn. Jon followed in behind. The first agent gestured to the control panel, and Jon glared at him as he walked past. He pressed a few of the buttons and the wall started to open up. The cells moved forward and stopped, revealing the Ripper.

The first agent stepped forward, looking at the murderer.

"Is this him?" he asked quietly.

"Yes" Jon answered.

The agent smiled. "Get him out" he said to the other agents. He turned back to Jon. "If you would, please doctor?"

Jon pressed another button and the Perspex started to move up. The Ripper got to his feet and the agents ran over, guns aimed at him.

"Get down!" one shouted. The Ripper lay on the floor, his hands behind his head. The other agent ran over to him and cuffed him. They lifted the Ripper up and dragged him out of the cell.

The first agent turned once more to Jon. "The other one, doctor" he called out. Jon pressed another button, and the cells began to move round once more to reveal James, the security guard who had helped Mackenzie. The Perspex slid away and the agents moved in.

At that, Gracie came in.

"What are you doing here?" the agent said. Jon looked at her.

"Gracie, you have to leave" he said.

But James saw his chance. He punched the agent standing next to him hard in the face and the man fell down, knocked out cold. The other agent turned round, pointing his gun, but James had already picked up the pistol the first agent had dropped as he fell. He raised the gun and shot the agent twice.

James walked out of his cell slowly. The first agent aimed his weapon, but James was faster; two down. On seeing Jon, James fired again. Jon ducked behind the control station, and sparks flew out from the panel as the bullet hit.

With a smile, James turned to Gracie and raised the gun, aiming it straight at her head. She closed her eyes, terrified.

A shot rang out.

Gracie opened her eyes. Why was she still alive?

Then she looked down to see the Ripper lying on the floor, blood flowing from a bullet hole in his chest. He had thrown himself in front of her, a final act of redemption. Jon scrambled forward, grabbed one of the dead agents' guns and aimed it at James.

"Drop it James!" he called out. But James gritted his teeth and aimed his own weapon. Jon squeezed the trigger and James slumped to the ground.

Gracie bent down next to the Ripper, whose hands were still handcuffed behind him.

"Do not weep for me, girl" he murmured. Gracie held him tight. His colour was fading, his lips turning blue. He stared into her eyes. "I am truly sorry for what I was" he said. Then his eyes closed.

Gracie looked down at him. This creature had been responsible for some of the most horrific murders of all time, and yet, as he lay in her arms dying, she could only feel pity for this lost soul. After all, she owed him her life.

"Gracie, are you all right?" Jon said. As he spoke, the door burst open and more agents came running in. Jon leaned down next to her, placing his hand on her shoulder and looking at the Ripper.

"It was a brave thing he did" Jon said softly. Gracie looked back at the Ripper's face. Then she released him gently and he slumped to the floor.

"Are you OK?" one of the agents asked, standing over them, Jon looked up at her, nodding. The agent stepped away, joining her colleagues.

"Come on Gracie, let's get out of here" Jon said and helped her to her feet. He put his arm around her as they walked out of the room, leaving the carnage behind them.

★ ★ ★ ★ ★

November 22nd, 1718, Ocracoke, North Carolina. Thomas was up very early, trying to prepare his mind for the attack later on that morning. A knock came on his cabin door, and he took a sigh and stood up.

"Thomas" Summers said, Thomas stepped out past Summers as he placed his sword strap over his shoulder. "Come on, you should see this" Summers said. Thomas patted him on the shoulder and they walked up the steps and on to the main deck. Thomas walked over to the port side of the ship and looked out. There stood eight or nine small ships, sloops, each with a crew of about 19 men, and each ship with seven or eight cannons on board.

Thomas felt a hand on his shoulder and turned to see Robert Maynard standing there, smiling.

"We cannot lose today Thomas" he said.

"When do we leave, sir?" Thomas asked.

"We'll depart in about an hour. With the wind on our side, we should reach Blackbeard's ship in about twenty minutes" he replied. He gestured to the sloops. "They will go around the other side of the island. We'll trap that brigand like a rat in a trap." Just then William came walking over from the other side of the ship, carrying a long object wrapped in a cloth. He looked at Thomas and smiled.

"Weather report, Mr Lockwood?" Maynard said.

"Sir, the wind is steady east and there is a layer of fog on the other side of the island. It should take us about forty minutes to reach the pirates" William said. Maynard looked disappointed.

"No matter, we'll leave soon then" he replied. He looked down at his pocket watch. "Say in twenty minutes."

William saluted. "Aye sir, I'll let all vessels know" he answered.

William signalled for one of the crewmen to come to him, and the man came running over and saluted him.

"Mr Smith, make sure all ships know that we leave in twenty minutes" William said. The man saluted again and ran off.

Thomas approached William. "What's that?" he

asked, gesturing at the long package in William's hand. William smiled and carefully unwrapped the cloth to reveal a huge broadsword. He held it up and took out the massive blade from its sheath.

"This, Thomas, was my great-great-grandfather's sword" William said, holding the weapon out with pride. "He was a Scotsman, and a warrior. I will use it today at the battle to honour my family name."

Thomas smiled. "I'm sure you will my friend" Thomas replied.

"Look" Summers said, coming over to them, after speaking with other crew members. Thomas and William looked out, back to the sloop ships. They were all raising their anchors and preparing to set sail.

"The time is now my friends" William said and quickly moved off towards the first lieutenant to receive his orders. Summers glanced at Thomas, who was visibly nervous.

"You all right Thomas?" Summers asked.

"I'm fine Michael, let's get this done, catch Mackenzie and help stop Blackbeard" Thomas replied. "We are now apart of history."

Then came a call of "Raise anchor!" and the loud clanking of the metal could be heard. Crewmen darted around pulling on ropes. The sails splayed out, catching the wind and moving the vessel forward.

"Turn to starboard" Maynard said as he walked past Thomas and Summers, making his way up the steps to stand in front of the helm. The *Pearl* was under sail.

★ ★ ★ ★ ★

The trip around the island took longer than expected, due to the wind changing course and a fog that was now before them, but an hour later they were drawing close to the *Queen Anne's Revenge*. Maynard called down from the helm for a longboat to be launched. Two men were to row out and find the exact location of the pirate vessel. Within twenty minutes the rowing boat was coming back in haste; the pirates had fired upon them with one of its cannons.

"Move her forward" Maynard called out, and the *Pearl* began slowly to creep forward, waiting for the fog to clear so the pirates could be seen.

"Sir, they're raising anchor" William called up to Maynard.

"Full sail!" Maynard's response came. The *Pearl* quickly went forward, gaining in speed as she got nearer the pirates. Now the crew of the *Queen Anne's Revenge* could be seen on deck. Blackbeard stood at the helm.

The pirates started to move off towards the land, but the *Pearl* was quickly upon them. Blackbeard moved over to the port side of his ship and called out "Who the hell are ye?"

Maynard walked calmly over to the side and gripped the wooden rail.

"I am First Lieutenant Robert Maynard of His Majesty's Navy, and as you can see by our flag, we are no pirates" Maynard replied, and pointed up towards the Union Jack flying high on the central mast. Blackbeard spat over the side of his ship and gave Maynard his two fingers, holding them up high. He then appeared to call down to one of his crew. Thomas walked up to Maynard and stood by his side.

"What are they doing?" he asked. Maynard stared out.

"They are going to fire upon us, Thomas" Maynard replied. To the left, the smaller sloops had now appeared and were moving in fast, blocking the pirates escape route. Maynard smiled. "And here is our cavalry" he said.

Thomas moved over to the side and looked over towards the *Queen Anne's Revenge*. Mackenzie was looking straight back at him. Thomas gritted his teeth.

"We have to get them now" he said. Maynard placed his hand on Thomas' shoulder. "We will Thomas, we will" he replied. He turned to a man who was at the helm. "Get closer" he said, and the *Pearl* moved in.

Then the pirates fired one of their cannons, and the blast hit the *Pearl* dead on. The charge was not a round shot but shrapnel, small pieces of metal, old coins, bits of wood, anything the pirates could get their hands on. One man fell down to the deck, pieces of metal protruding from his body.

"Everybody, arm yourselves, and get below deck, hide anywhere!" shouted Maynard.

Thomas moved over to him. "What are you doing?" he asked. Maynard smiled.

"Setting a trap, Thomas. Now get down!" Maynard

replied. Another shot came from the pirates, this time aimed at one of the smaller sloops. Screams could be heard. Then the *Queen Anne's Revenge* turned round and started coming straight towards the *Pearl*. Maynard smiled. His plan was working. As the pirate ship drew closer, Blackbeard's orders could be heard.

"Board!" he called out. Several grappling hooks came over, thrown by Blackbeard's crew, and the two vessels pulled together. Thomas glanced up to see Blackbeard standing there, his cutlass in his hand, and the burning fuses under his hat that he wore to make himself look even more terrifying. He had several flintlock pistols placed around his body and belt.

He held up his sword and screamed "Attack!" Then he leapt from the helm and over the side, landing on the deck of the *Pearl*. Other pirates followed him, weapons in hand. The pirates, believing that the crew of the *Pearl* were killed or had fled after the first shot, boarded the ship, ready to finish off the rest

"Now!" cried Maynard, and the crew came running out from their hiding places. Blackbeard looked shocked, but not deterred.

"Kill 'em!" he shouted out, and his crew, loyal to the end, ran forward. The *Pearl*'s crew did the same, and battle was joined.

Thomas drew his sword and ran out. He cut down a man who ran towards him, slashing him across the stomach. He glanced up to see Mackenzie, a sword in one hand, the automatic pistol in the other. He swung the blade at any man who came near, and shot after shot rang out as he blasted his way through the rest.

"Mackenzie!" Thomas called out.

Summers looked over at him. "Thomas, be careful!" he shouted. Thomas did not hear, or chose not to. He ran forward, his blade ready. Mackenzie saw him, but too late. He raised the gun, but the shot missed. Then Thomas was upon him. He slashed out with the sword, catching Mackenzie across the arm. Mackenzie dropped the pistol. Thomas slashed again, but this time Mackenzie deflected it with his own sword.

"You will die here, Dr Long!" Mackenzie said, holding the blade out. Thomas held out his own sword, his arm straight.

"Not today" Thomas replied. Mackenzie snarled and lunged forward. Thomas moved to the side as the sharp blade went straight past his head. He moved his own sword down with great speed, cutting Mackenzie once more, this time across the leg. He fell against one of the masts, blood flowing from his arm and his leg.

"I can take you back alive, Mackenzie" Thomas said, lowering his sword. Mackenzie smiled, weakened by the blood loss.

"We both know it won't end up like that" he said. He began to climb to his feet. Thomas took a step back and again raised his weapon.

"As you wish" Thomas replied. Mackenzie leapt forward, his sword held high, screaming in defiance. Thomas stepped aside and made another cut across

Mackenzie's stomach. Then he turned and from behind, he pushed the sword straight through Mackenzie until the tip of the blade appeared from his chest. Thomas withdrew the sword and Mackenzie dropped to the deck. His eyes closed.

Thomas looked over to see Summers raise a hand to Thomas. He looked around the deck. The pirates were all either dead or had abandoned the fight, except for Blackbeard, who was locked in combat with Maynard.

William came running over to Thomas and Summers, his huge broadsword red with blood. He glanced at Mackenzie's lifeless body.

"Got your man then?" he said, looking back to Thomas. Then they heard a shout of anguish from Maynard. Blackbeard had cut Maynard's hand and knocked his sword to the deck. Maynard scrabbled for his sword and held it up, pointing it straight at Blackbeard.

"Think you're winning do ye?" said the pirate with a smile. "You may kill my crew, take 'em prisoner even, but I'll kill you this day Maynard!" He lunged forward with his sword, but Maynard quickly parried the attack and thrust his own sword forward, the blade sliding into Blackbeard's stomach. The pirate captain looked down as Maynard withdrew the sword. Blackbeard looked back at Maynard, and to Maynard's surprise, he smiled. Again he leapt forward, knocking Maynard's sword from his hand.

Maynard drew his flintlock pistol from his belt. He cocked the lock, aimed it and fired. The shot went straight through Blackbeard's chest, but again, Blackbeard smiled. He began to walk slowly forward. Then another shot came, this time from one of Maynard's crewmen. The ball hit the pirate in the shoulder, but still he kept coming.

"I've had enough of this devil!" William said. He ran straight up the steps and on to the helm deck, where he stood in front of Maynard and Blackbeard, his broadsword ready. The pirate captain glared at him, still coming on, his cutlass held up. William took a step forward and slashed out with his huge sword. The blade just caught Blackbeard's neck. The pirate staggered back and lifted his hand up to the wound. He looked at the blood on his hand and turned to William.

"Good job lad" Blackbeard said with a smile.

William moved closer, his sword still ready. "Well, if that is a good job, I will have to do better, won't I?" he said. With all his strength he swung the massive broadsword. The blade sliced right through the pirate's neck. His head came clean off, fell to the floor and rolled, stopping just by Maynard's feet. Blackbeard's dead eyes stared up at him. The pirate's body stayed where it was for a few short seconds, and then it too fell to the floor, blood gushing from the neck.

Maynard bent down and gripped the dead pirate's long, straggling black hair. He lifted it up and held it high for the crew to see. Blackbeard's own surviving crew did not dare to look, fearing the same fate for themselves. The crew of the *Pearl* cheered and shouted at the sight of the head of the pirate, knowing victory was theirs. Maynard placed the head next to the helm and turned to William.

"Mr Lockwood, well done, well done. And thank you" he said, shaking William's hand. He then turned to Thomas and Summers. "You have gotten your man too?" he asked.

Thomas nodded. "Yes sir" he replied.

Maynard patted his arm. "Then we are all victorious this day." He put his arm around Thomas and walked with him to the side rail. A dozen pirate prisoners were now chained up and kneeling.

"What will happen to the prisoners?" Thomas asked.

"We will set a course for Virginia. They will probably hang for their crimes there" Maynard replied. Thomas stared at the doomed crew of the *Queen Anne's Revenge*.

"And you Thomas, what will you do now?" Maynard asked, Thomas glanced at him.

"We must go ashore" Thomas replied.

"Ashore, why?" Maynard asked. Thomas turned to face him.

"Because sir, we have to return home soon, and if we do it on board the ship, then I fear the power of the jump back will damage the *Pearl*."

Maynard looked rather shocked at this, but nodded. "I understand" he said. "Prepare a long boat!" he shouted down at his crew. Four men ran over to the port side and began lowering a dinghy into the water.

Maynard turned to William. "Will you join us?" he asked.

"Yes sir" said William, still looking at Thomas with a smile.

"I will return shortly" Maynard said to his crew as he climbed aboard the boat. He took a seat next to Thomas, with Summers sitting opposite, and William began to row to the beach.

"Do you have the firearms from Teach and Mackenzie?" Maynard asked. Summers lifted up a parcel of cloth and unwrapped it to reveal the two automatic weapons. Maynard stared at the guns. "I must say, I wonder how your departure will appear" he said.

Thomas smiled. "And do we have your word sir, that you will never speak of it again?" he asked.

Maynard looked straight at him. "Of course Thomas, I will take it to the grave" he replied.

Ten minutes later they had reached the shore. Summers and William dragged the small boat up on to the beech, while Thomas and Maynard walked up towards some rocks. Thomas took off the sword strap and undid his shirt, revealing the conduit suit beneath. Summers did the same as William and Robert Maynard looked on in wonder. Thomas walked over to the pair, the sword in his hand. He lifted it up and held it out to Maynard.

"Thank you" Thomas said, but Maynard put his hand against it and pushed it back.

"Keep it Thomas, you have earned it" Maynard replied with a smile.

"It is a great gift, thank you" Thomas said. Summers put his hand on Thomas' shoulder.

"We must leave" he whispered.

Thomas nodded, then turned to William, who now had a tear in his eye. "William, you are a good friend, I'll miss you" Thomas said. William moved forward and gripped Thomas' hand tight, the tears now rolling down his face.

"Thank you for all your help, I will never forget you" William said. Thomas then clasped William to him.

"Goodbye my friend" Thomas said as he released him. Maynard put his hand on Thomas' shoulder. Summers had turned on his arm panel, which lit up, neon blue.

"Goodbye sir" Thomas said, shaking Maynard's hand. He walked over to join Summers. "Ready Thomas?" Summers asked. Thomas nodded.

"Ready" he replied. He raised his hand, giving his new friends a final wave. Then both men pressed their recall buttons

Maynard and William stepped back as the humming started and bright blue sparks shot from the two men from the future. Then with a loud bang, they were gone. All that was left was a smoking crater and a burned patch of sand. Maynard and William stared for a moment, then walked back towards the little boat.

CHAPTER 11

Jon ran into the mess hall, almost slipping over in his haste. It was lunchtime and the room was full. He spotted Gracie and ran over.

"Gracie, Gracie, they're back!" he shouted out as he got nearer to her. She looked up, surprised, and then, without saying a word, she got to her feet, running through the door, Jon following behind her. The elevator doors slowly opened and Gracie and Jon ran out into the main machine room. A tear came to Gracie's eye as she saw Thomas. He looked over, and then, pushing the scientists aside, he ran over to her. She gripped him tightly, her arms wrapped around him.

"I've missed you, Dr Long" she said. He moved his head back to get a look at her face, a face he had so wanted to see.

"I've missed you Miss Stevenson" he replied. Summers came over and raised his hand. "No hugs" he said. Jon laughed. "Welcome back, Agent Summers" he said.

"Did you get Mackenzie? What happened?" Gracie asked eagerly as the four of them walked out of the room, heading for the meeting room for a debrief.

Thomas laughed. "There's so much to tell, but yes, we got him. He's dead" Thomas said as they walked into the large room, the door closing behind them.

* * * * *

"Wow" Gracie said. "You actually met Robert Maynard! I had to do an essay on him at college." Thomas smiled and nodded, and then placed the sword given to him by Maynard on the desk.

"And that's the sword?" Gracie said, picking it up and looking at it intently.

"You say that the CIA have taken over completely?" Summers said turning to Jon.

"Yes, and the prisoners are dead, a failed escape" Jon replied. Thomas leaned forward.

"And the Ripper?" he asked, Jon frowned as he looked at Gracie.

"He's dead too. He died saving me" Gracie said, turning to face Thomas.

"He saved you?" Thomas asked.

She smiled and nodded. "Yes, James had me in his sights and he pulled the trigger, but the Ripper jumped in front of me to take the bullet."

Thomas reached over and held her hand. "You could have died" he said.

"And for that, I owe the Ripper. He died for me. I saw a glimmer of humanity in his eyes as he died. He was sorry for what he was."

Jon stood up. "I guess it's all for the best, no more prisoners. I mean we can concentrate on the time jumping alone now, no more distractions" he said, and moved over to the door. "Well, you should get some rest now, you two deserve a break. In a few days, we'll be jumping back to the Dark Ages." He smiled and disappeared through the door. Summers moved over to sit next to Thomas and Gracie.

"How has he been?" Summers asked, looking at Gracie. She leaned back in her chair.

"Well, you know Jon, the same I guess" she replied.

"If he's that keen on jumping back to the Dark Ages, we should still keep a close eye on him" Summers said.

"It'll be fine Michael" Thomas said and stood up. "Michael, we'll see you tomorrow" he said.

Summers smiled at them as they walked through the door. He was thinking hard. After pursuing Mackenzie through time, the last thing he wanted to happen was for Jon to end up the same as Mackenzie, the power going to his head. If that happened, he would stop him - by any means necessary.

★ ★ ★ ★ ★

15th June 2028. Summers came down from his dorm and walked into the mess hall. It was early, and hardly anybody was up, but Jon was sitting there alone.

"You're up early Jon" Summers said as Jon passed him over a cup of coffee.

"Well, you know, can't sleep very well lately. I'm excited about returning back to the Dark Ages I think" he said, and grinned. Summers took a sip of his coffee and leaned back in his seat.

"And how is it that you're suddenly excited about that era Jon? Thomas is the expert."

Jon leaned forward. "I've done a lot of research on it, and Michael, it was a very interesting time, it really was. I'm just looking forward to going back there and learning more about it and its people."

Summers stared at him for a moment before answering. "Are you sure you're not just looking forward to being treated like some sort of god?"

Jon stood up. "Michael, this is my project, my idea, my planning. If it weren't for me, there would be no time travel. Do you not think I deserve some recognition?"

"This is what I mean Jon, this idea that you want people to worship you."

Jon struck the table with his fist. "I have brought time travel to the world. I deserve some appreciation!" he shouted. He walked out of the room, slamming the door behind him.

Summers thought for a second, took a sip of coffee and got to his feet. He made his way back over to the door, threw his empty plastic cup in the trash bin and walked out.

That evening, after a long day planning and organizing everything for the jump tomorrow morning,

Summers walked into the main machine room. Thomas was there, along with Gracie, going over their notes and research.

"Michael, you OK?" Thomas asked, moving back over to his notes and his precious writing book.

"It's Jon" Summers replied.

Thomas stopped and looked at Summers. "Is he all right? What's happened?" he asked.

Summers sat down next to Gracie. "He is becoming more obsessed with this idea of being worshipped" he said. "This power he's gained by creating the time machine is truly a gift, but it's going to his head."

"Are you sure?" Gracie asked, placing her notes down on the table.

"I'm sure. His reaction to me this morning was one of anger, and I haven't seen him at all the rest of the day" Summers replied.

"I can speak with him if you like, find out for sure what he's thinking?" Thomas asked. Summers glanced up at him.

"Well, he is your friend, he might talk to you better than me" Summers replied. Thomas nodded and put his notebook back inside his bag. "He's been in his dorm all day, I'll go and see him now" Thomas said, and gave Gracie a kiss.

"See you later babe" she said as he walked away. She turned to Summers.

"Thomas will sort it" she said. Summers didn't answer. He just watched Thomas step into the elevator.

The doors closed. Summers stood up, turned to Gracie and replied "I hope so".

Thomas made his way to Jon's dorm and knocked on the door. No answer. He knocked again. Then the door quickly opened.

"What?" snapped Jon. Thomas moved back, surprised at his anger.

"Oh, sorry Tom" Jon said and moved out the way, allowing Thomas to walk in.

"You all right Jon?" Thomas asked as he stepped into the dorm. The room was very dark. The blinds were drawn and only a small lamp was on, along with the bright computer screen of Jon's laptop.

"Yeah, fine Tom, just busy doing research for the jump tomorrow" Jon answered. "Sorry about being short with you, I thought you were Summers."

"Oh right, has he upset you then?" Thomas asked, trying to get a look at what was on the laptop screen. It was a website dedicated to Viking stories and the myths of the Scandinavian gods.

"Well, he has pissed me off a bit" Jon replied, flicking the screensaver on.

"Really, why, what's he done?" Thomas asked, taking a seat at the kitchen bar.

"He keeps going on about me thinking I'm a god" Jon replied.

"And are you?" Thomas answered.

"Please, don't you start Tom" Jon said.

Thomas put his hands up. "I'm not mate, really I'm not. But you are acting a bit, well, strange lately."

"I don't want to be worshipped Tom, I just want to be known for what I've accomplished, what I've managed to do, something that nobody has ever done before. To be honest it feels like I'm just a worker here. The fucking CIA have taken control of the project, but this is my baby Tom! I created it, I deserve to be known for it. And if we go some place where people will recognize my ability, my gifts, my..."

"Power?" Jon looked at him and sighed.

"I know you may think the same as him Tom, but believe me, the power isn't going to my head, trust me Tom, please. I need you on my side!"

Thomas felt sorry for his friend. He looked defeated, worn down by the government's control over his project. And after all, why shouldn't he be known for what he had done. Thomas got to his feet and made his way over to Jon, putting a hand on his shoulder. Jon looked up at him.

"Jon, I'm always on your side my friend, you know that" said Thomas. Jon reached up and held his arm.

"Jon, get some rest, big day tomorrow" Thomas said.

"Goodnight Tom, see you in the morning, good and early" Jon said. Thomas grinned and walked back down the corridor, heading back to his dorm. He and Gracie would have a quiet and relaxed evening before their jump tomorrow.

Jon switched his laptop screen back on.

* * * * *

"So, what did he say?" Gracie asked Thomas as he walked through the door. Thomas placed his keycard down on the side and made his way over to the kitchen area to pour a cup of coffee.

"I don't think there's anything to worry about Grace" he said. "The man just wants some recognition for what he's done."

"Really? Michael thinks it's more serious than that" she answered, walking over to him. He leaned next to her and kissed her softly on the lips.

"I'll still keep a close eye on him, but I really think it'll be fine" he said.

"If you're sure Thomas?" Gracie said, still with concern in her voice. He reached up and touched her face. "Don't worry darling, it'll be fine" he answered. "Now, what about an early night?"

She grinned, kissed him gently and then moved slowly over to the bed. "Come on then" she whispered with a wink.

* * * * *

The next morning everybody, even the scientists, was up early. Thomas and Gracie came out of the elevator and into the main machine room. Summers was already there, suited up and checking his equipment. Jon was standing over by the control station, talking to a group of scientists and engineers.

"Morning Michael" Thomas said. Summers greeted him with a smile.

"Good morning Thomas" he said. "Did you have a word with Jon?"

Thomas placed his hand on Summers' shoulder.

"I did, we'll keep an eye on him, but I think he'll be fine" Thomas said. "He was looking at websites about Vikings and pagan gods. A bit strange, unlike him."

Summers frowned and glanced over to where Jon was still talking to the scientists. "Well, I'll be keeping a very close eye on him" he said.

"I'm going to suit up" Gracie said. Thomas made his way over to Jon. "Morning Tom, you OK?" said Jon.

"Morning Jon, yeah, I'm good, excited about the jump" Thomas replied with a warm smile.

"Excellent" Jon answered. "Well, you better get yourself ready, get your conduit suit on, we'll be leaving within the hour." Gracie had just finished fastening her suit up and clipping the gun belt into place when Summers walked in.

"I'm not disturbing you, am I Gracie?" he asked. She looked over at him, and he could see the concern on her face, despite Thomas' reassurance that all was well.

"Are you OK?" Summers said, taking a seat on one of the benches.

"Not really" she said.

"Is it Jon?" She looked away.

"Gracie, if you're worried about something you have to tell me. It is my responsibility to protect the time jumpers from harm, no matter where that harm may come from" Summers said.

"Yes, it is Jon" Gracie said. She took a seat opposite him and leaned forward. "Thomas thinks that all is fine with Jon, and I don't want to go behind his back."

Summers placed his hand on her shoulder. "Gracie, you won't be betraying him, we all have that responsibility to look out for each other, and that's all you'll be doing" Summers said.

"I do think that all this power might be going to his head. I'm worried, let's put it that way" she said.

"Has he said anything to you? Do you know anything for sure?"

"No, nothing for sure, just women's intuition I guess."

"Gracie, will you help me to keep an eye on Jon? Anything you see, anything you hear, please report it to me straight away." She looked at him for a few moments, then nodded.

"Yes, OK."

At that, Thomas walked in. "Hey, what's all this?" he asked with a smile. Gracie looked up at him.

"Nothing, I was just worried about the jump today" she said and looked back at Summers.

"Yes, I was just reassuring Gracie here that all will be fine" Summers said. Thomas came over and put his arm around her.

"This isn't like you, you never get nervous about the jumps" he said.

She looked up at him. "Well, first time for everything I guess" she replied. She got to her feet. "Well, I'll wait for you out in the main room."

Thomas watched her walk out, then turned to Summers.

"So, do you want to tell me what that was really about?" Thomas asked.

"As I said, she's nervous" Summers replied.

"Please Michael, don't treat me like I'm an idiot, I know her, and I know you" Thomas answered sharply. Summers got to his feet and leaned against the wall next to Thomas.

"If you must know, she's worried about Jon's behaviour, as am I, and with good reason" Summers said.

"Yes, but I've already said..."

"You've already said that all is fine with Jon, but it is not. You're wrong about him." He went over to the door and pressed the button to open it, turning once more to face Thomas. "If I see anything, anything at all that makes me question his ability, or something that's going to put us in danger, I'll drag him back to this time myself if I have to" said Summers. Then he went through the door, and it closed behind him, leaving Thomas alone.

Maybe Summers was right, and Gracie too. After all, he trusted her judgment over anyone else's.

* * * * *

"OK everybody, the jump will take place in ten minutes" Jon called out from the platform. Gracie turned around and looked at Thomas as he came through the equipment room door. He raised his hand and smiled, and she smiled back at him. Thomas walked over to where Gracie and Summers were standing waiting. Summers was about to walk away, worried that he had upset him, but then Thomas gripped his arm.

"OK, I'll help you, we'll watch Jon's behaviour together" Thomas said. Summers smiled and nodded.

"Thank you Dr Long" Summers replied. Then Jon came over to them.

"Hey, everybody ready?" he said eagerly, looking at them all in turn. Gracie smiled.

"Yeah, let's do this" she said. The four of them made their way over to the platform, walked up the steps and stood there waiting.

Jon put his hand up. "Ready" he called out. The scientist signalled and pressed the button. The machine started up, humming louder and louder. The sparks started to shoot from the barrel on to the time jumpers. The humming became louder, the sparks more violent, and then, as the smoke cleared, they were gone.

* * * * *

Jon flicked on the torch fixed to his suit, and the others did the same. They were back inside the cave. As the smoke cleared, Thomas switched on the panel on his arm.

"We're here" he said.

"What time?" Gracie asked moving over to him, he smiled and replied.

"Thirteen hundred hours, 16th July, 798AD" he said. Gracie grinned and threw her arms around him.

"Come on you two" said Jon. They all squeezed through the gaps in the rock and slowly made their way out of the dark cave and into the warm sunlight. It took a few minutes for their eyes to adjust to the bright light, but when they did, the time travellers saw a beautiful sight. The whole area had been decorated with flowers, pieces of coloured fabric and small offerings. Baskets of fruit and vegetables had been placed around the standing stones.

"Wow" Gracie whispered to herself. Thomas looked round at her with a smile.

"Maybe the natives did all this after seeing us, they probably thought we were their gods" Jon said. He made his way down off the rocks and on to the grassy area below. Summers glanced round at Thomas and Gracie, concern in his eyes. Thomas gestured for him to move on, and carefully Summers stepped down, followed by Thomas and then Gracie, helped down by Thomas. Jon had already walked on, looking at the wonderful gifts.

"Hold up Jon" Thomas called. Jon looked round, hearing the sound of rustling from behind one of the large trees. Summers drew his pistol but Thomas moved in front of him, placing his hand on the gun and pushing it down.

"Do you see anything?" Thomas called over to Jon. Jon raised his hand, signalling for the others to hold their positions. A skinny, tall young man came out of the bush and stepped towards them slowly, spear in his hands. He wore a simple tunic with a large leather belt around his slim waist. Jon activated the translator device on his suit and then turned, signalling for the others to do the same. The man stepped a little closer. Jon gestured for Thomas to come over.

"You should be the first to make contact, my friend" Jon said as Thomas approached him. He smiled gratefully at Jon. Thomas moved closer, and the young man backed away slightly.

"We mean you no harm" Thomas said. The device translated his words into ancient Danish. The man looked around, frightened. He grasped his short spear tightly in his hands.

"Can you understand me?" Thomas said. The man froze and then nodded. Thomas smiled and held out his hands. The man started to relax. He lowered his spear and then ran, fast, in the direction of the village.

"Damn it" said Thomas. Gracie moved over to him and took his hand.

"Well done Thomas, at least they know we won't harm them" she said.

"Yeah, I guess" Thomas replied. He took out his notebook. He moved over to the large standing stone and began to scribble down what he saw.

"There's plenty of time for that" said Jon. "We should go down to the village." The village could be seen from where he was, and he could tell that there was excitement in the air.

"I'm sure they'll be back" Thomas replied, still taking notes. Gracie knelt down next to him and started to type away on her arm panel, assisting with the logging.

"They'll be back" Summers said as he leaned against the rock. Jon's attention moved back to the valley. He could see a line of people moving across the fields, coming back towards them.

"Well, I don't think we'll have to wait long" Jon said. Thomas got to his feet and slipped his notebook back inside his bag. Sure enough, within ten minutes, they could hear voices getting closer.

"Get ready, they may not be friendly" Summers said and unclipped his gun.

"They won't harm their gods, will they!" Jon snapped. Thomas looked over towards Summers, and Summers raised his eye brows.

Soon enough, the group of people could be seen coming up the small hill. They slowed down as they got closer and saw the time jumpers. Their leader, a tall and powerfully-built man, stepped forward. A skinny man standing next to him whispered something in his ear and pointed at Thomas. The big man came forward, his hands raised, and Gracie pushed Thomas forward.

"Hello, my name is Thomas, we mean you no harm" Thomas said. The device translated every word as he spoke. The man looked around as the device echoed around them. He glanced at Thomas and the others and then looked round at his people and gestured for them to get down. The big man and his followers all got on one knee, bowing to Thomas and the others. Thomas looked over at Jon, who was smiling to himself.

"There, you see, we are gods to these people" Jon whispered over to him. He stepped closer to the group of natives.

"Jon, be careful" Thomas said. Jon ignored him and walked towards them, hands held out.

"We mean no harm" Jon said. Thomas came over quickly and pushed past Jon, who glared at him. He bent down in front of the big man, put his hand on his shoulder and looked him in the eye.

"It's OK, you don't have to bow" Thomas said. The man looked at the others kneeling behind him as the words got translated, and slowly got to his feet. His people did the same.

"My name is Thomas" Thomas said. The man stepped forward. He was wearing a long leather tunic, leather trousers and a belt around his waist, and attached to that was a massive Viking broadsword. The man raised his hands, pointing to Thomas.

"Odin!" he said.

Thomas smiled. "No, Thomas" he replied. Jon leaned in, close to Thomas.

"Let them believe we are their gods" he whispered. Thomas ignored him.

"Thomas" Thomas said again. The man smiled under his huge beard. "Ragnar Lodbrok" he said, pointing to himself. Thomas smiled and moved forward, holding out his hand, but the huge man just looked at it. Thomas moved forward a bit more and took the man's hand, shaking it. The man smiled once more, then he turned to his people and raised his other hand. The crowd cheered and then the man hugged Thomas. "Odin" he said as they embraced.

Again, Jon leaned in. "He still thinks you're Odin" he whispered with a smile.

The people gathered around the strangers, welcoming them and giving them gifts, small colourful beads, fruit, small metal finger rings. Gracie received a beautiful golden necklace. Thomas had heard Ragnar's name before. He had been a powerful Nordic leader of the Dark Ages.

Ragnar came over to Thomas, put his arm around him and led him over to the edge of the hill. He gestured over the valley and the village below them.

"This is my land" he said. The device translated every word for Thomas.

"It is beautiful" Thomas replied, Ragnar looked at him and smiled.

"I am pleased that the gods like my home" Ragnar replied. Thomas looked up at him.

"Tom, it may be safer to let them think of us as gods, they might attack us if they think we are just strangers" he whispered. Thomas glanced at him. Maybe Jon had a point. This way they were being welcomed; if the villagers thought they were mere mortal intruders, they might not be so friendly. He nodded reluctantly.

"Please, come" Ragnar said and gestured for them all to follow him back to the village. They all made their way down the hill and into the valley, which was a beautiful sight. Thomas had never seen grass this green before. The trees grew wild, and a little stream ran through, leading to a river. Now, before them, was the village. Ragnar stepped out in front of the others.

"Welcome to our home" he said and led the way into the small town. The buildings were quite long, made of timber with wattle and daub plastering the walls. Some of the more and more luxurious houses had beautiful ornate decoration carved into the wooden beams.

The town had a well right at the centre, with buildings around it in a circle. Ragnar moved over to Thomas and pointed up a small bank. At the very top was a very long building, with green and red decoration going the whole length.

"Yours?" Thomas asked.

Ragnar smiled and nodded. "Yes, my house" he replied and started to make his way up the bank towards his home. He turned and gestured for Thomas and his friends to join him.

"Come on" Gracie said. They all walked up,

following Ragnar. The big Dane pushed open the large wooden door and walked in, the others following him. Thomas looked around the massive room. The ceiling was very high, with huge wooden beams. Along the left of the house a long table was placed, and at the centre was a hearth, with a small hole in the roof for the smoke to escape.

A woman came from the back of the house. She saw the strangers and straight away got down on one knee. Ragnar smiled and walked over to her, holding her arm and pulling her to her feet. She was tall and beautiful.

"My wife, Lagertha" he said. She bowed to them once more. "She is just as good a warrior as I am" Ragnar said with a chuckle. He then gestured for Thomas to follow him. Thomas walked past the flames of the hearth and over to where Ragnar was standing. Below him, lying on a bed of straw, was a child, about four or five years old but small for his age and clearly disabled. "This is my son, Ivar" Ragnar said.

"What's wrong with him?" Thomas asked. Ragnar looked at him for a moment before answering.

"Well, you, and the rest of the gods saw fit to make him so, we cannot question the choices of the gods" Ragnar replied. Thomas frowned. These people really did think they were gods, even to the point where Thomas and his friends would get the blame for making this poor child disabled.

"May I?" Thomas asked. Ragnar nodded. Thomas got down next to the child and studied him. The boy's legs were immobile and his spine was crooked. There had to be some spinal damage. If they were back home, in their own time, something might have been done to help him, but here in this time, there was no way for him to be healed or mended.

"It is OK, he is how he is" Ragnar said as Thomas got up. Lagertha came over with food and placed it on the table. There was bread, fruit and pieces of meat.

Thomas moved over to Gracie. "What is it?" she asked as Summers and Jon sat down at Ragnar's invitation to eat the food.

"I believe this child is Ivar the boneless, as he will later be called. He becomes a great leader" Thomas said. Gracie smiled, and they both made their way over to the others to tuck into the food Ragnar and Lagertha had provided.

★ ★ ★ ★★

Over the next few hours, they sat and chatted to Ragnar and his wife, while entertainment was provided for them in the form of dancing girls. Ragnar told them of his ongoing conflict with a rival group of Vikings called the Vali, led by his old adversary Alrik Vali. They lived on the side of the valley, near the river mouth, which made it difficult sometimes to sail through to the sea. But Ragnar and Lagertha were fearsome warriors, and would never give into the Vali.

"It is getting late, we should go home, return

tomorrow" Summers whispered over to Thomas. Thomas nodded. "Yes" he replied. He stood up, and Ragnar got to his feet.

"My friend, we must leave, but we will return, if we have your permission?" Thomas said to him.

Ragnar bowed his head. "Of course, the gods do not need my permission to do anything they wish" he replied. Thomas then turned to Gracie, who had several children around her, touching her hair and stroking the suit she wore. The shiny black material was a wonder to these ancient people. She looked up at him with a smile.

"Maybe a little longer" Jon said as he got to his feet. Thomas shook his head.

"No, there's plenty of time to get to know these people" Thomas answered. Jon, desperate to show his power to the ancient people, wanted to stay longer, to show them what he could do. He looked round at Ragnar, and then noticed a metal brazier. He flicked on the built-in laser in his arm, aimed it at the brazier and pressed the button. The bright red beam shot out and melted its way straight through the metal. Ragnar and the other people moved back in fear.

"What the fuck are you doing?" Thomas said, grabbing hold of Jon by his arm.

"Showing them true power" Jon said. He snatched his arm back and walked slowly out of the large longhouse, the ancient people lowering their heads as he went past.

"I am truly sorry Ragnar" Thomas said, turning around to face their host.

"You do not have to apologize, the gods do as they wish" Ragnar replied and bowed his head. Thomas looked round at Summers, who was equally unhappy with what Jon had done. They walked out of Ragnar's house to find the moon full and the night sky clear. Jon was standing over by the well, and from where Thomas and the others were standing, it looked as if a group of people were worshipping him.

"I'm not having this" Summers said to Thomas.

"Ragnar, thank you for your kindness and welcoming us to your home, we will return soon" Thomas said and shook Ragnar's hand. Ragnar bowed his head as Thomas and Gracie walked down the bank towards Jon and Summers.

"We need to go" Summers said to Jon as he passed him. Jon gave a sly smile, watching Summers walk past.

"Come on" Thomas said and he grabbed Jon's arm. Jon tried to struggle but Summers came over quickly and took hold of the other arm. Then he turned over Jon's left arm and hit the recall button.

"Now" Thomas said, turning to Gracie. She pressed her button and the humming began. The villagers looked around, confused by the noise. Then came the sparks and with a bang, the visitors were gone, leaving the bewildered ancient Danes gaping at the space they had left behind.

* * * * *

The smoke began to clear, the humming ceased and Jon shot forward, pushing Summers and Thomas away from him.

"What the fuck are you doing?" Jon turned, shouting at them.

"I should ask you the same question!" Thomas yelled back, pointing his finger.

"I was showing them what our technology can do" Jon replied, raising his voice.

"You're getting out of control, doctor!" Summers stepped in.

"And you, you've had it in for me from day one" Jon shouted at the agent.

"Michael's right Jon, you're losing it, getting obsessed with all this power" Thomas said, getting up close to Jon. Jon gritted his teeth and pushed Thomas back. The scientists stood there, not knowing what to do

"Please, everybody calm down" Gracie said, getting in between Jon and Thomas.

"You too, you're all against me!" Jon yelled and gave her a push. She fell backwards, hitting Summers, who managed to catch her. Thomas' rage built up immediately on seeing Gracie get pushed by Jon. He leapt forward and punched Jon on the jaw so hard he fell back, hitting the ground, Summers moved in and took Thomas' arm, his fist still clenched.

"Calm Thomas, calm" Summers said, Thomas glanced at him, and then at Gracie.

"Come on" Thomas said. He took Gracie's hand

and they headed towards the elevator, their conduit suits still on. One of the engineers helped Jon up, but he got to his feet and then pushed away the man who had just helped him. His jaw was bruised, but other than that he was fine. Summers approached him calmly.

"I can't say you didn't deserve that, doctor" Summers said. Jon stared at him. Summers continued "I am afraid, after what I saw in the Dark Ages, I have no choice but to ground you from any future expeditions until further notice."

Jon glared at him. "This is my project, my work, you cannot exclude me!" he replied.

"Yes I can Jon, I am a CIA agent, and the CIA are now running this project" Summers said. He slowly walked back to the equipment room to get changed. Jon stood there, the scientists and engineers looking at him. "What are you staring at?" he yelled. "Im still in charge here!" But the employees started to walk away, paying no more attention to him.

★ ★ ★ ★ ★

"Im sorry about that, Grace" Thomas said as they got into their dorm. She placed a hand on his shoulder.

"It's fine Thomas, not your fault" she replied. Thomas started to unclip his suit. "I can't believe what's happening to Jon, it's not like him" she said.

"I know, I didn't think he was like that. I've known him for years, he's my best and oldest friend, this isn't like him." Thomas walked over to the kitchen area and poured out two glasses of wine.

"Maybe the dark matter from the time machine is affecting him" Gracie suggested, taking a glass from Thomas. He shook his head. "Or maybe some people just can't handle power" he said.

"Well, either way, I wonder what will happen to him?" Gracie replied. At that, the intercom started to buzz. Thomas nodded to her to answer it and she pressed the little button. "Hello" Gracie said.

"Hi Gracie, this is Summers, would it be possible to visit you and Thomas please?" Gracie glanced over at Thomas, who nodded again and took another drink of his wine.

"Yes, that would fine" Gracie replied.

"Thank you, I'll be there shortly" And the intercom went dead.

"I wonder what he wants" Gracie said as she slipped on her joggers and a vest top.

"Well, I guess we'll find out what's going to happen to Jon" Thomas answered.

There came a knock at the door and Thomas walked over to open it.

"Hi Michael, what news do you have?" said Gracie. Thomas lifted up the bottle of wine. "Drink?" he asked.

Summers smiled. "No thank you" he replied. Gracie sat down at the kitchen bar, Summers next to her.

"I have had no choice but to ground Jon" Summers said.

"That will break his heart, Michael" Thomas said, moving over to stand next to Gracie.

"I know, but I have no option, he is getting unpredictable, dangerous even. I simply cannot allow him to go on any more jumps, not until I have proof that he has changed his ways."

"That's a shame" Gracie said, looking up at Thomas.

"Yes it is, and now we need a new leader. Thomas, it should have been you from the start anyway, you are the historian after all." Thomas looked shocked.

"Me?" he said. "I really don't think..." but Summers interrupted. "You're perfect for the job Thomas."

"Well, I was only meant to be an advisor, but, I guess I'll do it" Thomas said. Summers leaned forward, shaking his hand.

"Excellent, I'll let everybody know straight away." Summers got to his feet.
"See you tomorrow Thomas, we jump at first light."

"Well, I guess that makes you my boss again" Gracie said as Summers left. She put her arms around his neck, and he leaned down and kissed her.

"I've always been your boss" he replied with a smile.

* * * * *

"Jon, I'm telling you, you're confined to this facility until further notice" Summers said.

"Michael, please, this is my life, my work, I created

this, for fuck's sake!" Jon was getting angry and desperate.

"I know Jon, but I can't take any chances" Summers replied, Jon glared at him for a moment and then punched the door as he walked out of the equipment room.

★ ★ ★ ★ ★

"So, today's the day you're in charge" Gracie said as they left their dorm, making their way to the elevator.

"Yeah, feels wrong though, this is Jon's project, not mine" Thomas answered. He pressed the button and the doors opened.

"Yes, but you said yourself last night, some people can't handle the power, or responsibility, so, it must come down to people like you, people who are responsible" Gracie said. The elevator doors opened and they stepped out into the main machine room. The scientists and engineers looked over at them. Thomas took a deep breath.

"Well, here we go" he whispered to Gracie and they both made their way over towards the control station. "Is the machine ready?" Thomas asked the woman standing at the controls.

"Yes Dr Long, the time and date are set, ready to jump you" she replied. Thomas smiled at her.

"Good, thank you" he answered, and he and Gracie walked over towards the equipment room.

Thomas and Gracie already had their suits on, kept in their room overnight, they opened the door to the equipment room and walked in to get the rest of the gear they might need. It was time for their jump.

CHAPTER 12

As the smoke cleared Thomas switched on his torch, and Gracie and Summers did the same. They were back inside the cave. Gracie moved first, Thomas and Summers following behind her. Then she suddenly turned.

"Can you smell that?" she asked.

Thomas took in a deep breath. "Wood smoke" he said.

"The villagers have probably got a fire going" Summers said. Slowly they made their way out of the cave. It was night time, but the glow of the fire could easily be seen over the hill. It was coming from the village.

"Quick!" Gracie said and she ran down the rocky path to the grass below. She made her way over to the edge of the hill and looked down. Some of the houses and buildings of the village were on fire, and the sound of screaming and shouting could be heard.

"What's going on?" Thomas said as he approached her.

"I think they're being attacked" Gracie replied.

"Alrik Vali" Thomas said. "Ragnar's enemy."

"We can't let this happen, these people welcomed

us, gave us food and drink, we can't just let them be butchered" Gracie said, turning to Summers.

"We should help them" Summers replied. They all ran down the hill as fast as they could, the smell of the fire getting nearer until they could feel the heat. As they approached a man saw them, then raised his axe and ran towards them. Thomas unclipped his pistol, aimed the gun and fired. The man dropped to the ground. Another came from behind a house, a woman screaming in his arms as he dragged her out. He looked up just as Summers fired again, dropping him with a single shot to the head.

"Come on!" Gracie shouted and ran over to the woman. "Are you OK?" she asked, and the device translated.

"Yes, thank you, o mighty ones!" the woman cried as she gripped Gracie.

"Look out!" Summers shouted. A man was running towards them, sword in hand. Thomas aimed his gun again and the man fell.

"Look, there" Thomas said, pointing towards the well, Ragnar was there, battling away with his broadsword. "Stay here, both of you" Thomas said to Summers and Gracie. Three more shots rang out and three of Vali's men fell. Ragnar looked shocked.

"The gods come to aid us!" Ragnar said with a smile.

"Erm, yeah, kind of" Thomas replied. He fired again, and another man dropped to the ground. Vali's men stopped and stared.

"Yes, that's right, go, tell Alrik that the gods fight for Ragnar" Ragnar called out to them. They turned and ran, back out towards the woods where they had come from. Gracie and Summers came over, still with their weapons drawn.

"Thank you, thank you so much" Lagertha said as she came over. She too had a bloody sword in her hand.

"You're welcome" Gracie replied, clipping her pistol back in its holster.

"The gods are great!" Ragnar shouted out and his warriors started to cheer and raise their weapons high in the air.

★ ★ ★ ★ ★

After a few hours of helping the wounded, putting the fires out and moving the dead, Ragnar invited Thomas, Gracie and Summers to his home, which had not been damaged by the attack. He pushed open the door to see a man inside holding a short sword and standing next to a woman with a long spear.

"That's all, thank you Gunnar" Ragnar said. The couple bowed to him and they made their way out of the house. "They were here to protect my little Ivar" Ragnar said as he went over to check on his disabled son. Lagertha went over and picked up her child, holding him close. Ragnar sat down at his long table. "Well, the gods truly are great!" he said, grinning at Thomas.

"We had to help" Gracie replied, Ragnar glanced at her and smiled.

"Well, we are truly grateful, our prayers to you were worth every word" Ragnar replied. Thomas walked over and took a seat next to him. He smelled of sweat and blood and Thomas held his hand to his nose.

"I don't suppose Alrik or his men will return soon, not now they know that the gods favour us" Ragnar continued with a grin. Thomas smiled.

"Well, let's hope not" he said. Ragnar got to his feet and saw his wife's face, she looked frightened and worried.

"What is it woman?" Ragnar said, moving over to her. She walked up to him holding the child. Sweat was running from his brow and he was shaking violently.

"My boy" Lagertha said. Ragnar grabbed the child from her.

"Ivar, Ivar!" he called, but the child did not respond. Gracie moved over and looked at the boy.

"May I?" she asked. Ragnar handed the child over to her. She could feel his high temperature, even through her conduit suit. She looked at Thomas sharply. "He has an infection" she said.

"At the back of the suit, on the belt, are several vials of antibiotics" Summers said. Gracie reached round and felt the small plastic pouch. She unclipped a vial from it, snapped off the end and injected the small needle into the boy's leg. "Now we wait" Summers said, placing his hand on Ragnar's shoulder.

The child lay in his bed, and hour after hour passed. His mother and Gracie sat next to him. Ragnar just sat there next to the hearth, staring at the flames. At length Gracie took from her medical kit a small thermometer and placed it into the boy's mouth. Sure enough, the medicine was working. His temperature was slowly coming down. Gracie clipped the thermometer back into the small plastic pouch and clipped it back on her belt.

"He should be fine by tomorrow" she said as she got to her feet. Lagertha looked at her son, who was now sleeping soundly.

"Thank you, thank you!" she said and gripped Gracie's hand.

"You're welcome" Gracie replied. Ragnar came over quickly, looked at the boy and then to Gracie. "Thank you so much" he said and bowed his head to her.

"You don't have to bow" Gracie replied, placing her hand on his shoulder.

"I do, I really do" Ragnar answered. "Not only did you save my village and my people from those damn invaders, but you saved my son too. I will tell all that our gods are great, and are to be worshipped. Every man, woman and child will know of your greatness."

Thomas came over and placed his hand on Ragnar's shoulder. "We have to leave soon" he said. The sun was rising over the valley.

"Will you return?" Lagertha asked eagerly. Gracie smiled.

"Yes, we will, we still have much to learn from each

other" Gracie replied. Lagertha got to her feet and took from her neck a beautiful beaded necklace with golden runes hanging from it. She placed it over Gracie's head, so that it hung down at her breast.

"Please, take this as a gift from me" Lagertha said with a smile.

"Thank you, it's beautiful" Gracie replied, and then embraced Lagertha.

Ragnar took from his belt a long knife and he held it out to Thomas.

"This is my scramasax, it has served me well, I give it to you" he said. He handed over the knife to Thomas, who took it. He stared at the beautifully decorated weapon.

"Thank you Ragnar" Thomas replied. Ragnar smiled and then moved over to Summers. Hung on a post at the side of the wall was a short spear, and Ragnar lifted it off its hooks and turned to face Summers.

"Here, I made this last summer, for boar hunting. I give it to you now" Ragnar said. Summers took the spear from him and held it up. The blade was wide with razor-sharp edges.

"Thank you" Summers said. Ragnar stepped back to the centre of the room and raised his hands.

"These are simple gifts to you, the gods, but please, accept them with our thanks" he said, looking at them all in turn.

* * * * *

They walked with Ragnar, out of the village, leaving Lagertha to watch over the child. They made their way up the hill and back to the standing stones.

"Ragnar, we will return soon" Thomas said, and held out his hand. Ragnar looked at it for a second, and then raised his hand up, gripped Thomas' and shook.

"We will pray to you" Ragnar said and then stepped away.

"Ready?" Thomas said, turning to the others, Gracie nodded and Summers put his thumb up. Thomas pressed the recall button.

★ ★ ★ ★ ★

As the smoke cleared, Thomas, Gracie and Summers walked slowly down from the platform, holding their gifts from Ragnar.

"I wonder if it's him?" Gracie asked Thomas as they went into the equipment room. Thomas looked round at her, confused.

"Who?" he replied. She smiled.

"Ragnar, do you think he's the skeleton we found?"

Thomas smiled and sat on one of the benches.

"Maybe. The rest of the graves we found were cremations. The skeleton was the only burial, so that would indicate that the person was of high status. Which of course, Ragnar is" Thomas replied.

"It's so exciting isn't it? To think we actually knew him, spoke to him and he is over 1700 years old" Gracie said as she slipped out of her suit.

"Well, that's the gift Jon has given to us" Thomas replied. Then he stopped what he was doing for a moment and thought, *Poor Jon. It's because of what he has done, what he has created, that all this is possible.*

"You OK?" Gracie asked him. He turned round, still in thought.

"I'm going to see Jon. It's not right that he's being left out of all this, he should be with us."

"But Michael said he needs to change his ideas before he can come again" Gracie replied.

"I know what he said Grace, but it really isn't fair, is it?" Thomas answered. "Listen, I need to go and see him now. He's my friend Grace, I have to." He walked over to the door, glancing back at her with a smile.

Summers came into the room. "Where's Thomas going in such a rush?" he asked Gracie.

"To speak to Jon. He feels guilty about him not being able to join us on the jumps" she replied. Summers unclipped his belt and placed it on the display cabinet.

"This is Jon's own doing though" Summers answered.

"I know" Gracie replied. "But they are friends."

★ ★ ★ ★ ★

"Jon, are you OK?" Thomas said as he entered Jon's room.

"I am now Tom" Jon replied with a strained smile.

"I've come to see how you are."

"I feel much better now, and you know, I've been thinking" Jon replied as he pulled his chair round from the other side and sat next to Thomas. "You and Michael are right, I was letting it get to me."

"That's good Jon" Thomas replied. "I'm going to try and get you back with us. As you said, it is your project."

"That would be great Tom, really" Jon replied.

"I'll sort it Jon" Thomas said, Jon moved back and tapped Thomas on his shoulder.

"Thank you Tom, thank you" Jon replied.

"Well, I'd better get back, Gracie will be waiting."

★ ★ ★ ★ ★

"How was it?" asked Gracie.

"It went well. Jon seems better. And tomorrow, I'm getting him back on the team." Thomas took off his jacket and hung it up on the back of the door.

"Do you think it might be a bit soon?"

"No Grace. Jon should be there, no matter what time we jump too, this is all his."

"I'm just worried about his behaviour, that's all" Gracie said.

"I know Grace, but it'll be fine, he's learned his lesson. Now I'm getting a shower, I have to speak to Michael tomorrow, so I want an early night."

Tomorrow, he thought, he would persuade Summers to allow Jon back on the jumps or quit himself.

$\star \quad \star \quad \star \quad \star \star$

It was getting close to lunchtime and Thomas still hadn't seen or heard from Summers. Where the hell was he?

"Have you seen Agent Summers today at all?" Thomas asked one of the engineers as he walked past.

"No doctor, but I did hear that he had business today at the Pentagon" the man replied. Thomas frowned.

"OK, thank you" he answered. The man smiled and carried on with his duties. Shit, why hadn't Summers told him he wasn't going to be on site today? But Summers had put him in charge of the expeditions. It was now up to Thomas who went and who didn't. And as far as he was concerned, Jon was back on the team.

He went over to the counter and ordered a coffee, taking two of the little sachets of sugar from the side, ripping them open and pouring them in. He made his way over to a table, stirring his drink as he went.

"Tom?" A voice came from the doorway. Thomas turned round to see Jon.

"Have you spoken to Michael yet?" Jon asked as he took a seat opposite Thomas.

"No, he's not here, business at the Pentagon" Thomas answered.

Jon looked disheartened. Thomas leaned forward and touched his arm.

"Listen, I'll clear it with him tomorrow morning, before the jump. But he did put me in charge, so, you're back with us" Thomas said.

Jon's face lit up. "Tom, thank you so much" he answered and suddenly got to his feet. "Well, I'll have to get some things ready for the jump, get an early night too" he said. Suddenly he was like a child at Christmas.

"All right Jon, well, I'll meet you at the equipment room at seven, don't be late" Thomas replied.

Jon laughed out loud. "Tom, when am I ever late?" he said with a huge grin.

As Thomas went back to his coffee, he glanced around the room. Some of the scientists and engineers on their breaks were looking oddly at him. Maybe they thought he had made a mistake. Maybe they knew something he didn't. But it was his choice to allow Jon back, not theirs. After all, he knew him better than anyone else and there really wasn't any danger.

★ ★ ★ ★ ★

"Morning Thomas" Gracie said as he started to open his eyes. He glanced up at her and smiled.

"Hey" he said, Gracie was already up and showered. He reached up to kiss her, but she smiled and put her hand up to his face.

"Sorry lover boy" she said. "Michael has left a message, he wants to see you, urgently."

He knew what about too, Thomas thought as she

walked over to the kitchen. "Shit" Thomas said to himself. Gracie looked over.

"I think he might have found out about you letting Jon back" she said.

"Yeah, I guess" Thomas said quietly. He stood up, took a sip of the coffee that Gracie had made for him and then walked into the bathroom.

Ten minutes later and Thomas was ready. He gave Gracie a kiss and walked over to the door. "Wish me luck" he said. She smiled and gave him a wink.

As he stepped out of the elevator, Summers was waiting near the control station, talking to the scientists. He had his conduit suit on, ready to go. He turned round, seeing Thomas walking over.

"Thomas" he said and shook his hand.

"I know what this is about Summers, but you did put me in charge, and I want him with us" Thomas said. Summers didn't reply for a few moments.. Then he folded his arms and looked at Thomas.

"I know Thomas, I agree with you."

"Really?"

"Yes, really" Summers said. "But I will be watching him." He smiled.

"OK, fair enough" Thomas replied.

Summers gestured towards the equipment room. "You'd better get ready then doctor" he said. "Jon is waiting for you."

Thomas turned round and saw Jon standing outside the room with a huge smile on his face.

"Morning Tom" he said as Thomas approached him.

"Morning Jon" Thomas replied. "Shall we?" He gestured inside the room. Jon smiled and walked in, followed by Thomas.

"What did Michael say?" Jon asked as he took down his suit. Thomas reached up and took hold of his.

"He's fine with it" Thomas replied.

"Really?" Jon asked, thrusting his legs into the black suit.

"Yeah, my team now" Thomas answered and started to put his suit on. Jon looked away in anger. It was his project, his machine, his gear, his suits, all created by him. He should be the one in charge.

Summers walked over to meet Gracie as she came out of the elevator, before she had a chance to go into the equipment room.

"Gracie" he called as he approached her. She quickly turned round.

"Michael, hi."

"Did you know about this?" Summers asked her. She glanced over to the equipment room door, checking it was closed before she replied.

"If you're referring to Jon being back on the team, I found out last night. Thomas told me."

"What do you think of it?"

"I think that I'll support Thomas in whatever choices he makes" she said, and then she stopped for a moment. "But I'll still be keeping an eye on Jon." Summers looked relieved.

"Thank you Gracie" he replied and without saying another word, Gracie swiped the access control of the door and it slid open.

"Hi Gracie" Jon said as she stepped into the room. She glanced over at him. He was standing next to Thomas, who looked over and smiled at her warmly.

"Morning Jon, glad to see you're back on the team" Gracie replied diplomatically.

"Thank you, I'm very excited about going back" Jon answered. Secretly, he knew deep down that she was just as suspicious of him as Summers was. At that moment, the door beeped and slid open, and one of the scientists popped his head in.

"We're ready" he said. Thomas raised his hand.

"OK, ten minutes" Thomas replied and the man went back out as Jon and Thomas walked over to the open door. "See you in a minute" Thomas said to Gracie as he passed her. She glanced up at him with a smile and he and Jon walked out. Jon stopped for a moment when he saw Summers walking over to greet them.

"Oh great" Jon said under his breath. Thomas looked at him.

"We've all got to get on, so I suggest you and Summers kiss and make up" Thomas answered.

"Yeah yeah" Jon muttered just as Summers reached them.

"Jon, how are you?" Summers said, standing before him.

"I'm fine Michael, and you?" Jon replied with a forced smile.

"Very well, thank you" Summers said, also with a forced smile. He then turned to Thomas and placed his hand on his shoulder. "Everything is ready for…" he began, but Thomas interrupted him.

"We'll have a briefing first I think, get some things clear before we jump. I don't want anything going wrong" he said. Summers smiled his approval and simply nodded.

The door to the equipment room opened and Gracie came out, suited and geared up. Thomas raised his hand and gestured for her to come over.

"I'm ready" she said as she got to them. Thomas put his hand on her back. "Briefing first" he said. Jon looked at him.

"Briefing, really?" Jon said, Thomas glanced at him for a second and then looked back at Gracie.

"Yes" he replied, and made his way over to the large table set up in the corner of the large room.

"So, what's this about?" Jon asked as they all stood around. Thomas looked at them all in turn and then looked down at his tatty notebook.

"On this jump, we will be honest with our new Viking friends" Thomas began.

"What do you mean?" Jon said. Thomas lifted his hand up for silence.

"I will explain to Ragnar that we are not gods but humans, just as they are." He looked at Jon, waiting for him to object, but he said nothing. Maybe he had changed his ways after all.

"I will try to explain to him that we are from another time, not some spirit world" Thomas said. Gracie touched his arm, a smile on her face.

"I agree" she said softly.

"Me too" Summers added and all three of them looked at Jon. He could see they were waiting for him to object, but he decided not to give them the satisfaction.

"I agree, we should not deceive them" he said and a smile slowly crept across his face.

"Excellent" Thomas replied, glad that his friend was once again back on side. Summers however, suspicious as always, knew deep down that Jon was lying, and if he could lie to his friends, he should be watched even closer.

"Let's do this" Thomas said with a smile. He picked up his notebook again and placed it back inside his bag, then quickly followed the others over to the platform, where the scientists were waiting impatiently.

"We're ready now, sorry" Thomas said as he walked past the control station. He walked up the steps and stood next to Gracie.

"Ready?" Thomas asked, looking at them in turn, to which Jon just nodded, Summers replied with a thumbs up.

"Let's go" Gracie's answer came. Thomas raised his hand to the scientist.

"Start the countdown!" he called out. The woman looked from him to the controls and pressed the switches and buttons needed. The machine started up with a roar.

CHAPTER 13

Back inside the cave once more, Thomas clicked on his torch and made his way over to the gap. Gracie followed and Summers gestured for Jon to go next. The agent wasn't going to take any chances; he wanted to watch Jon closely.

A warm sun shine gently touched Thomas' face as he made his way out of the cave and into the daylight.

"What a beautiful day" Gracie said to him as she followed him out. Thomas looked out over the valley. "It certainly is" he replied with a smile.

Jon appeared next, followed closely by Summers. All four of them carefully made their way down the rocky pathway to the green grass below. As they reached the bottom, Gracie noticed someone kneeling by the large decorated, standing stone. She took a step closer and saw that it was Lagertha, Ragnar's wife. Gracie waved, and Lagertha looked up. As Gracie got nearer, she checked that the translator was switched on.

"Hello Lagertha" Gracie said as she reached the stone. The Dark Ages woman got to her feet. "Hello, I'm so glad you are back" she replied. She seemed upset.

"Are you all right?" said Gracie. Lagertha looked down and a tear fell from her eye.

"My father died last night" she answered quietly. Gracie moved over to her and placed her hand on the woman's shoulder.

"I'm so sorry Lagertha" Gracie replied softly.

"He will be sent to Asgard this afternoon" Lagertha replied with sadness.

"Everything OK?" Thomas asked Gracie.

"Her father has passed away" Gracie answered. Thomas switched on his translator. "Lagertha, I am sorry for your loss" he said.

She managed a smile. "Thank you" she replied. She turned round to face the village just over the hill. "Please, come back with me, the women are preparing his body to enter the next world, and Ragnar is going hunting. I'm sure he would love you to go along."

"OK, thank you" Thomas replied and gestured for her to lead the way. Jon followed a short distance behind, Summers just in front of him, turning every now and again to check on him.

As they walked into the village, the people smiled at them, but did not speak. The place seemed withdrawn and in deep mourning for the loss of an elder. They made their way towards Ragnar's and Lagertha's house, past the small well in the centre of the village. Lagertha suddenly stopped.

"I will stay here" she said, gesturing to the house on her right. "This is my father's house. The women are making his body ready, I will help." She gestured for the team to go up to her house. "Please, continue" she said as she disappeared through the door of her late father's home.

"Come on" Thomas said quietly and they walked up the small bank towards the massive longhouse at the top. As they reached the door, it suddenly opened. Gunnar was standing there. He looked surprised to see them.

"Ragnar!" he called out. "You have guests." The big Dane came out from the back of the building. When he saw Thomas and the others standing there a huge smile spread across his face.

"Ah, my friends!" he called out and made his way over to them. He gripped Thomas' hand and almost shook it off.

"Thank you" Thomas replied. "Your wife showed us here. As we appeared she was praying at the stone on the hill."

"Ah, yes, her poor father left this world last night" Ragnar replied. "We are giving him his send-off later this day."

"You all have our sympathies" Gracie said, moving forward and touching the big man's hand.

"Thank you" he replied with a smile. "We would be honoured if you were there at his funeral."

"We would be honoured too, Ragnar" Thomas replied.

"That's settled then" he answered and then looked

over at his friend, who was standing at the door holding a spear. "Gunnar and I are heading out hunting now, we have had word that some boar have been seen in the woods. Would you like to join us?" Ragnar asked Thomas, who was almost speechless.

"I would love to, Ragnar" Thomas replied. Ragnar grinned from ear to ear.

"Excellent!" he shouted out. He put a hand across Thomas' back and led him over towards the back of the house, to the area where the huge Viking kept his weapons. He picked up a long spear that was leaning against the wall and handed it to Thomas. "Here, you'll need this for boar" he said with a smile. Thomas took the spear from him. It was heavy, but well balanced.

"I see you have the scramasax I gave you, good" Ragnar said, looking at the long knife Thomas had pushed into his belt before they came. "Give me one moment, I need something." He walked off, going into a small room to the left of them.

Gracie came rushing over to Thomas. "Be careful Thomas!" she said, concern on her face.

"I'll be fine" Thomas replied. "And I'll be able to speak to him about us not being gods while we're out."

"I know, that's what I'm worried about" she said, holding his arms.

"Come now my friend" Ragnar said as he reappeared from the room. He now had over his shoulders a thick cloak of fur and leather, despite the warm weather. "Are you ready?" he asked.

"Yes yes" Thomas replied eagerly and lifted up his spear. He followed Ragnar over to the doorway where his friend was waiting for them. "Well, please, make yourselves at home, go where you please, do as you wish. My home is your home" the big man said. They all walked out of the house and into the sunlight.

"Be careful" Gracie called out as the three men walked down the bank and past the well. Thomas gave a glance back at her, a big smile on his face.

"Do you think he'll be all right?" Summers asked.

"I hope so" she replied quietly, still staring out, watching them leave the village.

"It is a massive building, isn't it?" Summers said, turning round and looking up at the high-beamed ceiling, trying to distract Gracie from her worry. But she didn't move. She was straining her eyes to watch the three hunters walk up the hill, past the standing stones and into the woods over to the right.

"He'll be fine, he knows what he's doing" Jon said, walking over to her. She glanced at him and smiled.

"I know he will. I have every faith in him" she replied. She walked out of the house and into the village, Summers following, as she went down into the centre, amongst the market stalls. She wanted to look at the wares displayed on the wooden tables.

Meanwhile, Thomas, Ragnar and Gunnar made their way quietly through the woods, it seemed dark as a canopy of leaves blocked the sunlight. Just the odd ray of light managed to pierce through, lighting up certain spots as they made their way.

Gunnar suddenly stopped and bent down, looking at the ground. He lifted up a piece of dirt and smelt it.

"This way, a boar came through here, not long ago either" he whispered.

Ragnar got down next to him and looked at the faint tracks on the ground. "Not long my friend" he said, looking up at Thomas, who was standing there holding his spear. They carried on a bit further, making their way slowly through the untamed woodland.

"Here!" Gunnar whispered. He was pointing at a branch that had recently been broken.

"Gunnar, make your way round to the right, our friend and I will go straight. We'll flank the animal" Ragnar said as he gestured to where he wanted his friend to go. Gunnar quickly made his way away from them, moving through the trees as if he were a part of the wood.

"Come!" Ragnar said and Thomas followed behind him, trying desperately not to make a sound.

"Ragnar!" Thomas whispered and pointed over to the right. The two men stopped dead. In the distance, standing in a clearing, was the biggest wild boar Thomas had ever seen. Its tusks were huge, curving round next to the creature's face. Ragnar looked over at where Gunnar was hiding and signalled to his friend, who started to creep slowly forward.

"Wait here until I call you" Ragnar whispered to Thomas as he too made his way closer to the boar. Thomas ducked down, still gripping his spear. Ragnar knelt, getting as low as possible. He glanced over at Gunnar and then nodded. With that, Gunnar ran forward, spear aimed straight at the huge animal. The boar let out a terrifying bellow and ran at Gunnar, its massive tusks lowered. Gunnar dropped and rolled to the side as the animal went past. Ragnar, seeing his friend fall, ran out, his spear high above his head. Then he drew back his arm and threw the blade straight at the boar. It hit the animal, the long spear protruding from its side, but the boar did not fall. It simply grunted and ran at Ragnar. The massive beast was upon him in seconds. Ragnar grabbed the boar's tusks just as the animal hit him and pushed him against a tree.

Thomas got to his feet, spear in hand, and ran forward, surprising the boar. He lifted up the spear and rammed it deep into the beast's neck. Blood spurted from the wound as the boar screamed. Gunnar came running over and stuck his spear into the still fighting animal. The boar staggered away from them and dropped, three long spears sticking out from its body.

"Are you all right?" Thomas asked, bending down to Ragnar, who was now leaning against the tree. He looked up at Thomas and slowly smiled.

"Yes, just winded" Ragnar replied.

"Well done" Gunnar said and slapped Thomas on the back. Ragnar slowly got to his feet, leaning on the tree for support. Thomas held his arm, lifting him up.

"Thank you, you did well" Ragnar said as Gunnar went over to the dead boar to remove the weapons.

"Come my friend, help me" Gunnar said, gesturing to Thomas to go over. "We need to carry the beast back home. I'll need to gut it, then we need to tie its legs to two of the spears. That way we can carry it back home across our shoulders."

He unsheathed his long knife from his belt and thrust it into the boar's stomach. Thomas looked away as Gunnar started the gory process of taking out the animal's insides.

"Come, we'll rest for a moment while Gunnar does this" Ragnar said and put his hand on Thomas' shoulder, leading him over to a fallen tree. They both sat down on the log, Ragnar still holding his chest.

"Are you sure you're all right?" Thomas asked.

The big man just smiled. "I've had worse than this" he replied.

"I'm sure" Thomas said with a smile. But he was worried. It was high time he explained to Ragnar that he wasn't a god. How would the huge Viking take it? Would he be fine with it, or would he be angry? Either way, he had to tell him. They had agreed. He looked into Ragnar's face.

"Ragnar, there is something that I need to tell you" Thomas began.

The big man stared down at him. "Yes?"

Thomas took a deep breath. "You think of us as gods, and with good reason" he began. "Our ways, our technology to you would make us seem that way." Ragnar gazed at him intently. Again, Thomas took in a deep breath. "Ragnar, we are not gods but humans, just like you."

He paused for a moment, waiting for Ragnar's reaction. The big Dane simply stared at Thomas with his piercing blue eyes.

Thomas carried on. "We are not from another world, mortal or godly. We are humans from another time, a time far in the future."

Still Ragnar stared at him. For a second Thomas just looked back. Maybe Ragnar didn't understand what he was saying, or maybe the translator had broken, but then the Viking suddenly burst into roars of laughter. Thomas looked at him in shock. Ragnar leaned towards him and slapped Thomas on the back.

"My friend, do you think me stupid, or simple?" Ragnar shouted out. Thomas didn't know what to do. "We know well you are not gods!" He started to laugh once more. Gunnar looked up, blood all over his hands. He looked over and also began to laugh.

"Our gods would have to be bigger. Much bigger!" Gunnar roared, looking down at Thomas.

"My friend, what you are is indeed special, and a gift from our gods, if not gods yourselves. This is the reason for us loving and worshipping you as gods" Ragnar said, still with a big grin on his face.

"Yes, you are a gift from the gods" Gunnar called over. Thomas looked at them both in turn.

"I didn't want to lie to you" Thomas said. Ragnar leaned close to him, putting his hand on Thomas' shoulder.

"I really do appreciate that, my friend" he said. "You have earned my trust. Now tell me what we should call you?"

"I am Thomas" said Thomas. "The girl is called Gracie, Michael is the man you gave the spear to, and the other is Jon" Thomas said. Ragnar stood up and put his hand out. Thomas shook it solemnly.

"I am honoured, Thomas" Ragnar said.

"All done" Gunnar called across, wiping the blood from his hands.

"Good, let's go" Ragnar replied, and walked over to help his friend. He bent down and picked up the spear that was now tied to the boar's legs. But as he straightened up, he dropped the boar and fell to his knees, gripping his chest.

"Are you all right?" Thomas said. The big man nodded.

"Broken rib I think" Ragnar replied. "I'll be fine though." Thomas picked up the front ends of the spears supporting the massive beast. Gunnar grabbed the two opposite ends and they lifted up the animal, resting the spears on their shoulders.

"I'll take the load then, you lead us home" Thomas said, looking at Ragnar. He looked back and gave Thomas a smile, nodding his head. The three of them made their way back through the woodland just as a light summer rain had started to fall.

Meanwhile back at the village, Gracie, Jon and

Summers were now taking shelter from the rain inside Ragnar's house. Lagertha was now there, after preparing her father's body. She had her disabled son in her arms; he was awake and recovering well from the infection. His eyes were open and he stared at the strange people in their black suits. Gracie came over and sat next to Lagertha.

"Hello" Gracie said, leaning over and touching the toddler's face. The little boy gave a giggle and gripped her hand, tightly.

"He has his father's strength, no?" Lagertha said with a smile.

"He does, he really does" Gracie replied, wanting to tell Lagertha that her little disabled son would one day be a great leader of the Vikings.

"The men should be home soon" Lagertha said, and straight away Gracie became worried once more. What if Thomas had been killed by the Vikings for telling them the truth? Or what if the hunting trip had gone wrong and a boar had harmed Thomas? She tried to put these thoughts out of her mind. After all, this was the man who had caught Jack the Ripper, won gunfights with Nazi soldiers, fought pirates on the high seas. Her brave Thomas could deal with anything. He would be fine.

As she was thinking, there came a knock at the door and a man came running in, a smile on his face.

"They have returned!" he shouted, and disappeared back through the doorway.

"Come" Lagertha said. She got to her feet, running

over to the door with her son, still gripping her tightly. Gracie followed with Summers and Jon not far behind. They stepped out into the drizzle to see Ragnar walking down the hill and Thomas and Gunnar following behind carrying the huge boar. The villagers cheered and called out to them as they entered the village.

"What a gift!" Lagertha said as she looked at the massive beast tied to the spears. Ragnar bent down and kissed his woman, but he winced as he got back straight again. "What is it?" his wife asked.

"Nothing woman, just a broken rib. Thomas here saved me from this damn boar sticking me with his tusks" Ragnar said, facing Thomas. Gracie went past them and grabbed Thomas, holding him close to her.

"I'm fine" Thomas said. She looked up at him.

"Did you tell him?" Gracie whispered, Thomas smiled, thinking of Ragnar's reaction to the truth. The loud laughter was still ringing in Thomas' ears.

"Yes, I told him" he replied, still with a big grin.

"And?" Gracie said, intrigued

"They knew anyway that we're not gods" Thomas answered. "It was quite embarrassing actually."

"Come now, this beast needs to be cleaned and prepared so it can be stored in the meat house" Ragnar said. Two men came running over and took the boar, carrying it over to a small wooden building. "Come now" Ragnar called out, and started walking up the small bank towards his home, Lagertha and their son by his side. Thomas and Gracie followed, their arms around each others' waists. Summers wasn't far behind them, while Jon was behind him.

Jon was furious that Thomas had told the Vikings they were not gods. These people should worship us, he thought, they should be taught a lesson. But not yet, the time wasn't right.

Summers turned round and looked at Jon standing in the rain. "You coming?" he called out to him. Jon just raised his hand to him, and made his way up.

Lagertha placed her son back inside his bed, came over to the long table and sat down opposite her husband. He was talking to Thomas as she sat. They were laughing and the mood seemed jovial.

"What's this?" she asked. Ragnar looked at her, a big grin on his face.

"Thomas here thought we believed they were actually gods" he replied, Lagertha quickly looked over at Thomas, who was sitting next to Gracie. She smiled at Thomas' embarrassed expression.

"Well, we did think you wouldn't be happy about it" Summers said as he took a sip of the mead which Lagertha had given to them all.

"Yes, we even thought you might have killed him!" Gracie said. Ragnar laughed out loud. "My dear, we wouldn't do that. We take care of our own" he said. He smiled. "And you have become one of us" he continued, looking at Thomas. Thomas glanced back at him with a warm feeling of joy, excitement and a feeling that this place, this time, was home.

"Thank you Ragnar" he said, and took a big gulp of his fermented honey and water. The drink was quite strong, but it tasted sweet.

"You like my mead?" Ragnar asked him. "Made it myself."

"It's delicious" Thomas replied and took another drink. Summers turned round from the table to see where Jon was. He glanced across the room to see the doctor sitting there with his arms folded, looking like a sulking child.

"What is wrong with your friend?" Lagertha asked.

"I'm not sure" Gracie replied quietly.

"I have a pretty good idea" Summers said, still staring at the angry Jon.

"Well, it is coming close to the time my dear" Ragnar said, getting to his feet and looking at his wife. She nodded her head and stood up. Ragnar put his huge arm around her shoulders, pulling her close to him. "We will give him a good send off" Ragnar said.

Thomas watched them for a few moments. Life and death were treated very differently here. Death was not the end but a transition from one world to the next. Lagertha kissed her husband gently on the lips and then moved away from him, walking to the sleeping area of the house. "You will still come?" Ragnar asked, looking over at Thomas and Gracie.

"Of course" Gracie replied, giving Ragnar one of her warm smiles.

"We would be honoured, Ragnar" Thomas said.

Lagertha returned, this time wearing a long red and green cloak with a huge golden buckle holding it in place. She bent down, picked her son up and wrapped a blanket around him. Then she handed the child over to a woman helper.

"I'm ready" she said. She picked up her sword from the table and fastened the sheath to her belt. At that moment, a knock came at the door.

"Enter" Ragnar called out. The door slowly opened and Gunnar came in.

"We are ready" he said, sadness in his voice. Ragnar gestured for his wife to go first; it was her father, she should have the honour of leading the way. She touched Ragnar's hand as she walked past him, and made her way over to the door. Gunnar went out and ran across to the cemetery. Lagertha stepped outside. The rain had now stopped, but the ground was muddy and wet.

"Just follow my lead" Ragnar whispered to Thomas. Then he walked out and stood next to his wife. "Come my dear" he said softly to her, and the couple made their way across the village towards the gathering of people at the cemetery. Thomas took Gracie's hand and they too started to walk, following the mourning couple. Summers walked just behind. He looked back to Jon.

"Are you joining us?" Summers asked. Jon nodded.

"Yes, of course" he replied, and he too started to make his way to the cemetery.

The body of Lagertha's father had been placed on top

of a huge pyre. He had been dressed in his finery, even with his shield and sword at his side, and his hand was gripping the hilt. The crowd of villagers had gathered around in a circle with Lagertha standing at the front. Ragnar leaned down and gave her a kiss, then stepped forward.

"We are here this day to say goodbye to my father in law, a great warrior, a great friend and above all else, a great father" Ragnar said. A tear rolled down Lagertha's cheek as she stared at the body on the pile of logs. "May he be reunited with his ancestors, may they welcome him home, to the halls of Valhalla, where the brave heroes will live forever." He took a burning torch from Gunnar, then stepped across and handed it to Lagertha. She stared at her father for a few short moments and then threw the flaming touch on to the pyre. The flames quickly spread.

They all stayed they for what seemed like ages, staring into the fire as Lagertha's father slowly burned to ashes. Thomas and Gracie stood at the back of the crowd, watching the ritual. Gracie looked over to the other side of the pyre to see Jon standing there, arms folded, no emotion on his face. She could see that something was not quite right with him. He had changed, and for the worse, she thought.

★ ★ ★ ★★

Some time later they all made their way back to a large

feasting hall where three long tables had been piled with food. They walked in, following Ragnar through the massive wooden door. A boar almost as big as the one they had killed that morning had been cooked on a spit and was now lying on the centre table. The hall was decorated with animal skins, and shields hung on the walls along with spears. A smaller table was set up at the end of the long hall. Ragnar walked slowly over to the end table and sat down in the middle. Lagertha sat next to him, and he gestured for Thomas and Gracie to sit the other side. A woman came over and placed a huge platter of meat and fruit in front of them, and Ragnar tucked in.

Thomas looked at the food, it did appear to be cooked well, but he wasn't sure. The last thing he wanted was food poisoning. Gracie smiled at him and leaned over. She took some of the food from the metal plate, placed it on her smaller one and started eating.

The evening went by fast, and now the night sky was lit up with a bright full moon and thousands of stars. Summers was sitting amongst the villagers. He raised his large metal goblet up to Thomas and caught Thomas' eye. Thomas laughed out and lifted his own cup.

"The food and drink is wonderful!" a rather drunken Gracie called across to Ragnar. He smiled under his bushy beard.

"I'm glad you like it" he called back.

"We do. Thank you Ragnar" Thomas said, and the big man put his arm around Thomas and squeezed him tight. Summers came over and pulled up a chair opposite Thomas and Gracie, then placed his cup down on the table and sat down.

"Have you seen Jon anywhere?" Thomas asked. Summers glanced quickly at Gracie. He had seen the way she had looked at Jon earlier at the funeral, and knew she had become suspicious of him.

"I saw him go outside about fifteen minutes ago" Summers replied as he looked back at Thomas.

"I'll go check" Thomas said and he stood up. Staggering a little from the strong mead, he made his way around the table.

"Be careful" Gracie called out as he walked through the hall. He turned round and waved at her, and then carried on through the door.

"He has changed, hasn't he?" Summers said, turning back to Gracie. She looked at him for a few seconds.

"You mean Jon, don't you" she replied. Summers placed his goblet back down.

"You know I do" he answered. She looked past him, through the crowd of drunken people towards the door, waiting for Thomas to return.

"Gracie" Summers said, getting her attention again. Her eyes moved back to him.

"There is something not quite right about him now" she replied. Summers leaned forward. "We will have to tell Thomas" he whispered. "He's becoming unpredictable. Too dangerous to come on the jumps now."

"I'll tell him when we get home" she said.

★　★　★　★★

Thomas looked around as he stepped outside. Jon was leaning against the well, staring up at the stars. Thomas walked down the few wooden steps towards him.

"You OK Jon?" he said. Jon didn't look at him, but continued to gaze at the night sky.

"I'm fine Tom" he replied quietly.

Thomas moved over, standing next to him. "Beautiful, isn't it" he said. "No pollution, no damage. It's perfect here."

"Shame about the people though" Jon replied.

"What do you mean, they have done nothing but welcome us!" Thomas replied.

"They're fools, simpletons, they know nothing" Jon said.

"Take that back!" Thomas said. Jon moved away from the well, giving Thomas an aggressive look. "What's got into you Jon? I thought you were all right now" Thomas said as Jon began to walk away. "Jon!" He ran after him and touched him on the shoulder, Jon immediately spun round, raised his fist and punched Thomas on the jaw. Thomas fell back into the mud.

"I didn't want to do that Tom, but it's ruined, you've ruined it all. They were meant to worship us. We were meant to rule them!" Jon shouted. Thomas sat up and looked up at Jon, his jaw throbbing. Jon walked away, heading out of the village and into the darkness.

"Jon!" Thomas called, getting to his feet. "Jon, come back!" But no reply came. Thomas rubbed his aching jaw as he walked back inside the feasting hall. Gracie got to her feet as Thomas made his way back over to her. She could see something was wrong.

"What's happened?" she said moving round the table to stand in front of him.

"Jon hit me" Thomas said, still shocked at what just happened.

"What? Why?" Gracie asked, checking his wound.

"I don't really know. Something's wrong with him."

"Well, you won't have to tell him now, will you?" Summers said, looking over at Gracie.

"What do you mean?" Thomas asked, looking at them both in turn.

"We could tell that Jon was acting strange, we were going to tell you when we got back home" Gracie replied.

"Thomas, Jon can't come on any more jumps" Summers said.

"You're telling me" Thomas replied, still rubbing his jaw.

"He's probably jumped back already. We'll catch up with him later" Summers said.

"Yes, but I think we should leave soon" Gracie advised.

"We'll go now, this very second. I'm not letting him get away with this" Thomas said, and he made his way over to Ragnar, who was unaware of what had happened and was still drinking and eating.

"I may have to place Jon under arrest" Summers whispered to Gracie. She looked over at Thomas. How could his best friend do this? Why had he changed so much? Clearly, some people can't handle power, she thought to herself.

"I know Michael, and that may be for the best anyway" she replied as Thomas returned to them, Ragnar just behind him.

"I'm so sorry you have to leave now" the huge Viking said as he approached. "Thomas told me about your friend."

"Yes, we will be back soon though" Gracie said as Ragnar led them across the hall.

"Ragnar, you and your people have shown us great kindness and welcomed us. Thank you" Thomas said. Ragnar put his arm around Thomas and hugged him tight.

"You are one of us now my friend, you are always welcome" Ragnar replied.

Gracie and Summers, followed shortly by Thomas, made their way out of the village and up the hill. The whole area was well lit by the bright moon, and the large standing stones seemed to glow a blueish grey.

"OK, activate the recall switches" Thomas said, and they all pressed their buttons.

★ ★ ★ ★★

"Where is he?" Thomas yelled as he stepped off the

platform. The scientists seemed shocked. They were looking around at each other, not sure what exactly Thomas was talking about.

"Where is Jon?" Thomas said to the woman standing at the control station. She glanced up at Gracie and Summers, and then back to Thomas.

"Sir, Dr Walker hasn't come back" she replied, timidly. Thomas looked at her for a second.

"What do you mean?" he said. She glanced back at Gracie, who had walked down from the platform.

"He hasn't jumped back, Dr Long" the woman replied again, still unaware of what was going on.

"Shit!" Thomas said and he made his way back to the platform. "I'm going back" he called out as he walked up the metal steps.

"But doctor" the scientist called back to him. "The machine needs to be cooled and reset first."

"Thomas, we need to rest first, we'll go back soon" Summers said, stepping up to Thomas on the platform. He took Thomas' arm, leading him off the platform and down to where Gracie stood waiting.

"Come on baby, let's get freshened up and get some rest" she said, taking Thomas' hand and walking him over to the equipment room.

"You need to inform me as soon as Dr Walker jumps back, understand?" Summers said, turning to the scientist.

"Yes, of course Agent Summers" she replied and he walked away, heading over to the equipment room.

★　★　★　★　★

Back in the dorm, Thomas was staring out of the window.

"You OK?" Gracie said as she returned to him. He looked up at her, giving her a smile and touching her hand.

"I'm fine" he replied quietly.

"I don't know why Jon is doing this. But we'll bring him back" she said, taking a seat next to him and gripping his hand tight. Thomas looked back out of the window, across the facility.

"He's my friend Grace, I've known him for years, since uni. And it feels like he's a stranger now."

"I know" Gracie replied. "Come on, we need to get some rest." She helped Thomas to his feet, leading him over to the bed. He lay down, still wearing his jogging bottoms and vest top and curled up, bringing his knees to his chest. He looked like a child, Gracie thought to herself, watching Thomas lying there. He was clearly very upset by Jon's betrayal. They needed to get Jon back, to explain himself.

SIX MONTHS LATER

Over the weeks and months following Jon's disappearance, Thomas, Gracie and Summers made many jumps back to the late 790s. They had become firm friends with the people in that time, exploring the region with Ragnar and Gunnar, fishing and hunting. Much was to be learned from this, on both sides. Summers and Gracie had seemed to give up on finding Jon, and did not even mention his name any more. But Jon was always on Thomas' mind. He was still alive, according to the heart monitors back at the facility control. But where?

Thomas sat next to the hearth, writing in his notebook, lost in his thoughts. Ragnar came in from the cold, snow sprinkled over his fur cloak.

"Ah, Thomas. It is cold today, no?" Ragnar said, walking over to him to warm his hands by the fire.

"Yes, it is" Thomas replied looking up at him.

"There is much on your mind, I can tell" Ragnar said, taking a seat next to him. Thomas just looked into the dancing flames. "It is your old friend on your mind, yes?" Ragnar said. He leaned over, touching Thomas on the shoulder. The coldness of his hands could be felt though Thomas' suit.

"Yes" Thomas replied, almost in a whisper.

"I wouldn't worry, he'll turn up. They always do" Ragnar said as he looked into the fire. "And Michael and Gracie are still here. You still have them" he continued, trying to lighten the mood.

"I know" Thomas replied with a smile.

"Where are they today anyway?" Ragnar asked him. Thomas had arrived alone that morning.

"They have work to do in our time" Thomas

answered him, and he turned round and placed his tattered notebook back inside his bag.

"Ah, very well" Ragnar said. He got to his feet, towering over Thomas. "Another time maybe?"

Thomas smiled at him. "Yes my friend, I'm sure they'll come back soon" he replied, getting to his feet.

"Well, my ship is ready to leave, I have some business to attend to" Ragnar said, hitting Thomas on the arm.

"Where?" Thomas asked, eagerly.

"Not far, just to the north of here, I'll be back in a few days" Ragnar replied as he picked up his broadsword and fastened it to his belt. "Lagertha is coming too, so, two of the women from the village will look after Ivar for us."

They walked over to the door. The air was freezing cold, snow lay everywhere and the sky was a dull grey colour.

"Well my friend, good luck, and I'll see you soon" Thomas said as he walked away, heading towards the frozen well. Ragnar walked with him and then turned off, heading to the dock.

"Thank you Thomas" he replied. "And I don't need luck!" He made his way down the slope towards the river. Thomas smiled as he returned through the snow-covered village towards the standing stones and the cave. He stood next to the snowy rocks and then turned round, looking out over the area. Back in his own time it was just as cold here during the winter months, he thought to himself. But, it didn't seem as beautiful as it did in this time. He was starting to feel more at home here with every jump he made.

★ ★ ★ ★ ★

As Thomas stepped off the red-hot platform, he saw Gracie talking to a group of scientists. She looked over and smiled and waved to him. Thomas made his way over to her, his suit still smoking.

"Hey" he said as he approached. She greeted him with a kiss.

"Hi, how was it?" Gracie replied.

"Yeah, not bad. Cold though" Thomas answered, as they both walked over to the equipment room.

"Yeah, I'm sure. Midwinter there now isn't it?" Gracie said as she swiped her keycard across the scanner. The door slid open and they walked in.

"That's right, bloody freezing" Thomas replied as he started to unfasten the conduit suit and remove the equipment.

"I can't wait to go back" Gracie said, sitting on one of the seats, near the lockers. Thomas glanced over at her.

"Grace" he said, still looking at her, she glanced back at him with a smile.

"Yes?" she replied, waiting for him to speak. He paused for a moment, and then smiled back.

"Nothing, it can wait" he said, not really knowing

how to say to her that he felt confused. The 790s now felt like his home, while it was his own time that had come to seem like a dream.

"Michael will be back soon, he's gone to the Pentagon again, a meeting of some sort" Gracie said.

"I managed to take some more notes this time" Thomas said as they made their way towards the mess hall.

"That's great" Gracie replied. "When we get back to the lab we can start our work on the finds again. And now we know who the skeleton is, that changes everything. We can work on how Ragnar died, and how old he was."

"Yeah" Thomas simply said, thinking to himself that really, he didn't want to go back at all. He was happier knowing Ragnar as he was, alive and well, not as a dusty, fragile skeleton.

"Coffee?" Gracie said as they got to the counter.

"Yes, please" Thomas replied and went over to find a table. A few minutes later Gracie returned with the two cups of coffee. She placed them down on the table and sat down opposite Thomas.

"Now what is it?" she asked him, he glanced up at her.

"What do you mean?"

"I know you too well Thomas, I can tell when something's wrong."

"You like it there, don't you?" Thomas asked her.

"Where?" she asked.

"In the Dark Ages, the 790s."

"Of course I do" Gracie answered. "Why?"

"Gracie…" Thomas began. He looked right into her eyes, there was love there, he could see that. "I want to stay there" he continued.

She put her cup down on the table.

"What do you mean?" she replied.

"I think you know what I mean" he said, still looking into those beautiful blue eyes. She stood up quickly, knocking her cup over and spilling the coffee.

"I cannot conceive of such an idea. It's ridiculous" she said and walked out, the door slamming behind her.

Well, that could have gone better, Thomas thought to himself.

★ ★ ★ ★ ★

That evening, after a long day doing his research in the main machine room, Thomas was ready for bed. He felt tired from the time jump earlier, combined with all the work at home. He packed up his book and tablet into his bag and started making his way over to the elevator.

"Thomas?"

He looked round. It was Summers.

"Hi, Michael. Good meeting?" Thomas asked as the agent approached him.

"Just fine. I've been informed that the rest of the hit men Mackenzie had hired have been caught" Summers replied with a smile.

"That's great news" Thomas said.

"It is" replied the agent. "Anyway, you look tired, I'll let you go. Good jump by the way?"

"Yes, good" Thomas called out as the metal doors closed. He made his way down the corridor and stopped at his dorm door. Here we go, he thought and swiped his card. The door clicked open and he pushed it, stepping in.

"Hi" he said, on seeing Gracie. She did not reply. "Grace, I'm sorry" Thomas said, walking over to her. She glanced over at him.

"Did you mean it?" she asked, Thomas placed his bag down on the bed and got closer to her.

"Yeah, I guess" he replied.

"No Thomas, you can't just guess at this" she said. "You either want to stay there, or you don't."

"Yes then, yes I want to stay there" said Thomas flatly. She stopped for a second, a tear in her eye.

"But I can't" she whispered softly, her voice breaking.

"Grace" Thomas said and went to hold her.

"No" she replied and pushed him back. "I'm sorry Thomas." She walked over to the door, opened it and walked out, the door slowly closing behind her. Thomas sat down and looked out of the window. Was he being selfish? It was a big ask. She had been loyal for years now. She had even moved to America with him, but this - this was too much. Another country was one thing, but another time was something else.

He made his way across to the bed and lay down. For a few moments he just stared at the ceiling, and then he looked across to the empty space where Gracie usually lay. He turned over, facing her side. The pillow still had her scent on it and he closed his eyes just as a tear formed.

★ ★ ★ ★ ★

The next morning Thomas made his way down to the machine room, his bag over his shoulder.

"Morning" Summers said as the elevator door opened. Thomas ignored him and carried on to the equipment room. "Thomas?" Summers called after him. He followed Thomas through he door. "What's wrong?" Summers said.

"I think I've lost Gracie" Thomas said quietly.

"Well, Gracie is ready for the jump today, she's already suited and waiting over by the control station" Summers said.

Thomas looked at him. "I thought she had left the facility?" He started to put the suit on as quick as he could.

"Well, speak to her before we go" Summers said and walked out of the room.

A few minutes later Thomas came out, his conduit suit on and ready. He looked over and saw Gracie by the machine. She glanced over at him, and he noticed a smile. He quickly made his way to her, and she met him half way.

"Grace, I thought you had gone" Thomas said as she neared him.

"No" she replied, a smile on her face. "I stayed in my old dorm."

"Are you OK?"

"I'm fine" she answered. Thomas took a step closer and held her hands.

"I was thinking last night, I couldn't sleep" he began to say. "About what's important to me in life. I love it there Grace, I really do." She stared up at him sad-eyed. "But I love you more" he said, and the smile returned. "I will always chose you."

Her smile turned to a grin. She grabbed him close and hugged him tightly.

"Glad that's sorted" Summers said to one of the engineers. "Come on, we have things to do."

Thomas turned again to Gracie. "I love you" he said. "Come on, let's go."

★ ★ ★ ★ ★

On arrival they switched on their torches to help them find their way through the darkness of the cave. "I love you too" Gracie whispered to Thomas, and he leaned down, kissing her. "Well, it's warm enough in here" said Summers with a smile.

They threaded their way one by one through the gap in the cave wall into the freezing Danish air. "Good god" Summers said as he stepped down into the snow.

Thomas helped Gracie down from the snowy rock. For a few moments they looked out over the beauty of the snow-covered valley. Gracie gripped Thomas' hand.

"I can see why you like it here so much" she whispered to him. He glanced down at her with a smile. "Come on" he said, and they started to walk down the hill and towards the village.

As they drew closer, Thomas could see that something was not quite right. The place seemed oddly quiet. He stopped and stared towards the houses.

"What's wrong?" Gracie said. Thomas' eyes moved frantically from building to building. Then he saw something; a person, lying on the ground.

"Wait here" he said and slowly made his way over. As he got closer, he could see bright red blood. He knelt over the lifeless body.

"My god, look!" he said. The dead man was someone he knew from the village. His body had a huge wound across the torso. A large blade had done this, he thought.

"What's happened?" Gracie called as she came running over to him. Thomas stood up and looked on down the row of houses. Other bodies lay scattered around. One man lay against the well, an arrow protruding from his chest. Summers drew his gun from its holster and clicked off the safety switch.

"Come on, stay close" Thomas said as he got to his feet, drawing his own pistol. They made there way, slowly across the village, past the empty buildings, making their way towards Ragnar's home.

Then Summers stopped in his tracks. Another body had caught his eye. The dead man was lying on the ground, the blood spreading out over the white snow.

"What is it?" Thomas said, looking back. Summers didn't reply, but moved closer to the body and bent down for a closer look. "Look" Summers said. He took hold of the man's leather cloak and moved it to one side. They could see a small circular wound.

"It's a bullet hole" Gracie said quietly. Summers looked up at them both.

"I think Dr Walker has made a return" the agent said.

"We don't know it's Jon" Thomas said.

"Well, apart from us, he's the only one with a gun around here" Gracie said to him.

"She's right Thomas" Summers said. Thomas glanced at them both.

"The weapon could have been taken from him" Thomas said, still trying to defend his old friend.

"I think you know the truth Thomas" Summers replied. He walked on, examining the other bodies as he went. There were several more with bullet wounds in them.

"Come on" Thomas said and he quickly made his way up the small slope to Ragnar's house, Gracie close behind him, her gun drawn ready. Thomas looked over at Summers standing on the other side of the doorway. Summers nodded and then Thomas pushed open the heavy wooden door. It creaked open slowly. Thomas walked in, his gun pointing forward, Gracie moved in after him, while Summers remained by the door as a lookout.

"Anything?" Summers whispered to them, Gracie turned round and raised her hand for silence.

Suddenly there came a shout and a scream and a woman came running out, sword in her hand.

"Wait, wait!" Thomas yelled. "It's me, Thomas!" The woman stopped dead. The sword dropped to the floor and she started to cry. She ran forward and grabbed Thomas, holding him tightly, her tears running down his black suit. He looked at Gracie as he held the woman close to him and she came forward and placed her arm around the woman.

"What's happened?" Thomas said. For a moment, she did not answer, her crying too much for her to speak. "Nothing can harm you now, I won't allow it" Thomas said, softly, trying to calm the woman.

"Vali, he came. Alrik Vali" she said. Thomas moved with her over to the table and sat her down.

"Where is the child, Ivar?" Gracie asked her, bending down. The woman pointed over to the corner of the house where there lay a pile of blankets and cloaks. Gracie looked at Thomas, fearing the worst. She made her way over. She bent down and slowly began removing the blankets until there, looking up at her with his big blue eyes, was the little disabled boy.

"He's fine" Gracie said. She brought him back over to the table and sat down next to the woman, cuddling the boy close to her.

CHAPTER 1

"Was anyone else with Vali?" Summers asked as he moved over to them.

"Not now" Thomas said looking up at him. He knew in his heart that Jon was to blame for this atrocity.

The woman looked up at Summers. "You mean your friend?" she said. Summers nodded. "Yes, he was here" the woman replied quietly.

"Was he with your enemy, Vali?" Summers asked her. Thomas desperately wanted her to say that Jon had come to help the villagers, that the people shot outside were actually Vali's men.

"Your friend" she began. Thomas waited. "He led Vali's men, with Vali himself."

Thomas closed his eyes. How could Jon do this? Why would he? He was a scientist, a physicist, not a killer. The thoughts came rushing into his brain. Summers glanced at Thomas. he could see that this news had hit him hard. The agent got to his feet and moved over to him.

"Are you all right?" Summers asked, placing his hand on Thomas' shoulder. Thomas looked up at him.

"I've just found out that my friend has committed genocide. What do you think?" Thomas snapped back. He looked back at the woman, giving her a smile and touching her shoulder. "You're safe now" Thomas said and got to his feet.

"We have to find him now" Summers said.

"I know" said Thomas. He got up, heading for the door.

"Thomas, don't go far" Gracie called after him. He looked back at her. "I'm just here. Need some air" he replied.

Gracie turned back to the woman. "We'll stay until Ragnar gets back" she said. The woman smiled and took the young boy from Gracie.

"Thank you, I must go and feed him now" she said and walked out towards the back of the house, into another room.

"I think she must be in shock" Summers said, taking a seat next to Gracie.

"Yes, who can blame her. We must keep an eye on her" Gracie replied.

At that, Thomas came running in. "Vali's men have returned!" he shouted. Summers unclipped his gun again and made his way over to the doorway and looked out. Six or seven men were running down the hill from the woods. "Gracie, stay with the woman and child" Thomas called to her. She nodded and ran into the other room.

"We'll let them come to us" Summers said as the men reached the village entrance. They were shouting insults and raising their weapons high above their heads. "Get ready" Summers said and clicked off the safety on his pistol. Thomas glanced at him and did the same, loading his weapon.

One of the warriors had a bow. He pulled back the string and released an arrow. "Watch it!" Thomas said as the arrow flew towards them. Summers stepped to the side as the arrow hit a post behind him.

"That was close" Summers said. He looked back at the men, who were now at the well. Thomas could see the blades on their weapons glistening. Summers aimed his gun at the man with the bow. He fired and the man dropped to the ground, a bullet hole in his chest and another in his neck. Thomas aimed his weapon, and another man fell. The firing continued, and the third and fourth men dropped.

"Come on!" Thomas yelled out to the remaining three men, who had wisely had taken cover behind the stone well. Thomas fired again and the bullet pinged off the wall, stone and ice flying across the ground.

"Save your ammunition!" Summers called over to him. One of the men suddenly appeared, running towards Thomas and Summers with sword raised. Summers aimed his pistol and another bullet found its target.

"Two left" Thomas called to the agent. Another scream and another man came running out

"They're certainly brave" Summers said and fired again. The man fell in the snow.

"One more" Thomas called. But the man did not run towards them with a war cry; instead, he chose to run the other way and save himself. Thomas aimed his gun at the man's legs. He fell in a heap, groaning in pain.

"I meant to do that" Thomas said as Summers looked at him.

"Question him?" Summers asked. Thomas nodded and Summers jumped down and headed over to the wounded man, Thomas just behind him. The man looked petrified as he lay there, gripping his bloody leg, looking up at the two strange men and their magic weapons

"Please, don't kill me!" the man cried out. Thomas bent down next to the wounded man.

"You have seen a weapon like this before haven't you?" Thomas said.

The man nodded. "Yes, the magic man. He has come to lead us to greatness" he replied, fear and pain in his voice.

"Where is he?" Thomas asked and raised his pistol, pointing it at the man's head.

"At our camp, down the coast to the east" the man answered and closed his eyes, waiting to join his ancestors.

"Thank you" Thomas said and stood up.

"I'll bind his hands, Ragnar can deal with him" Summers said. He took a piece of cloth from one of the dead warriors' shirts and wrapped it around the man's hands.

"We should bind his wound too, or he'll bleed to death" Thomas said. Summers looked down and nodded. Taking another piece of cloth, he wrapped the man's bleeding leg tightly.

"Help me" Summers said, taking the man's arm. Thomas took hold of the other side and both men dragged him over towards the large house.

"Leave him here" Thomas said as they reached the

doorway. The man cried out in pain as they dropped him down and Thomas and Summers walked back inside.

"Gracie?" Thomas called out. The door to the other room slowly opened and she stepped out, gun in her hand. "Is it safe?" she asked.

Thomas gave her a smile. "Yes, for now at least" he replied. Gracie came out, the woman and child following.

"I wonder how long Ragnar will be?" Gracie asked sitting next to Thomas.

"Not long, he should return this day" the woman said as she sat opposite them. Summers stayed by the door, looking out across the village, keeping watch for any more unwanted guests. He slid the empty ammunition clip out of the handle of his pistol and clicked a full one in.

"Well, I hope so" he said. "Don't know if we'll have enough bullets to keep them all away."

"We'll manage" Thomas replied. Gracie nudged him and he looked round. "What?" he whispered. She gestured to Summers, still keeping guard.

"Don't be so harsh with him. It's not his fault" Gracie said.

Thomas looked back to the hearth. "If this is anyone's fault, it's Jon's" she continued. Thomas looked at her once more, sadness in his eyes.

"I know Grace" he replied. He got up and looked at Summers. "Michael, I've been off with you, and I really am sorry about that."

"Don't worry. I understand" Summers answered and then looked back out to the snowy village.

"Jon's changed, and I didn't want him to. I took it out on you. I'm sorry" Thomas said. He patted Summers' back and walked back to Gracie and the woman.

"I don't know if there is any food left, I can check for you?" the woman said, still holding little Ivar.

"No, it's fine, don't worry" Gracie said. "Tell me, what's your name?"

"Asta" the woman answered.

"We'll take care of this Asta, you have our word" said Gracie.

The woman smiled and stood up. "I'll go put him to sleep, he's so tired" she said. She moved over to a straw bed made up on the other side of the room. She threw a blanket over it and laid him down.

"Someone's coming" Summers called over to Thomas. He drew his gun. "Down there." Thomas peered down the bank towards the river. The evening was closing in and it was getting dark. A row of burning torches was bobbing up the frozen pathway. Thomas stepped outside into the cold to get a better look. The torches got closer.

"It's Ragnar" Thomas said and he ran down the bank towards the Vikings. Ragnar had stopped, staring in horror at the scene of carnage. "Thomas, what has happened?" he asked desperately.

"It was Alrik Vali" Thomas said. "He attacked just

before we came. More came, but we took care of them."

Ragnar began to examine the corpses one by one. "My people!" he thundered. Now Gunnar had reached him, his huge axe in his hand.

"Ragnar!" his wife called to him from the bank. "What's happened?"

"Vali!" Ragnar shouted with anger.

"Ivar?" Lagertha said and looked at the house.

"He is fine, the woman Asta was there, she protected him" Thomas said.

"Thank the gods" Lagertha said. She ran up towards the house.

"Ragnar, if we had come sooner, we could have stopped this. I'm sorry" Thomas said. Ragnar looked at him, a tear in his eye.

"This is not your doing, Thomas. Not your fault. This is Vali. And he will pay."

"Our old friend Jon was with them" said Thomas. The big Viking looked at him.

"He used his weapon to kill your people" Thomas said, expecting the worst to happen.

"Then he too will pay for this" Ragnar replied as he looked down at the bloodied bodies.

"You are not angry with us?" Thomas said.

Ragnar looked straight at him, his hand on the hilt of his sword. "Thomas, you have shown us kindness and loyalty, this is not your doing" he replied.

"I knew something wasn't quite right about that man as soon as he came here" Gunnar put in.

"It is getting late. We'll put these souls to rest tomorrow, send them to Valhalla" Ragnar said. "Come, tonight we rest." He started to walk up the bank towards his home, Thomas and Gunnar following and the rest of his warriors shortly behind. As they got nearer the house, Thomas pointed to the bound man lying on the ground.

"We caught this man, he's one of Vali's warriors" Thomas said.

Ragnar walked over to him, and his hand gripped the sword hilt tightly. "We questioned him. He told us that Vali and Jon are camped to the east of the river."

"Good, well done Thomas" the Viking replied. He looked at Gunnar. "Kill him" he said and walked into his house. Gunnar raised his axe up above the crying man. Thomas looked away as it came down, but he could not avoid hearing the crunching noise of the blade's impact. Gunnar walked past him, his axe dripping in blood. Thomas did not look; he continued into the house. Ragnar's warriors followed him through.

Ragnar made his way past the hearth and straight over to Asta and embraced her.

"Thank you for protecting my son" he said, holding her tight.

"it was my duty, my lord" she replied as he released her. Ragnar walked over and stood over little Ivar, still sleeping soundly in his straw bed.

"I'm going to gut Vali personally" Lagertha said. Ragnar looked at her with a smile. "You'll have to beat me to it then" he replied.

Thomas had walked over to Gracie and Summers, who were sitting at the table.

"I have told Ragnar about Jon's betrayal" Thomas said, sitting down in between them.

"We'll have to see what happens now then" Gracie replied.

"I can imagine what Ragnar will do to him" Summers put in, staring at the hearth.

"It shouldn't have come to this" Thomas said, glancing at the agent. "He was my friend."

Summers put his arm around Thomas' shoulder. "I know Thomas, I know" he said.

★　★　★　★★

The next morning, after a restless night's sleep, Thomas was up and helping the Vikings move their dead brothers. Each of the victims had his own funeral pyre built for him at the cemetery, sixteen in all, arranged in a circle. Thomas and Gunnar carried the first of the dead men up the small bank and on to the holy ground.

"Ready?" Gunnar asked as they stood next to one of the pyres. Thomas nodded.

"Go!" Gunnar said and they both heaved the body on top of the wood.

"Thank you Thomas" Gunnar said, slightly out of breath.

"Yes, thank you" came Ragnar's voice. Thomas turned around. Ragnar was walking up the slope towards them carrying some weapons. He held them out.

"These were his weapons" Ragnar said. "He will be burnt with them, to take them with him to Valhalla." Thomas nodded. "Would you?" Ragnar said, handing the weapons to him.

"Yes, of course" Thomas replied, taking the sword and spear. He turned round and placed the spear next to the body, on the left. Then he placed the sword's hilt in the man's right hand and laid it across his chest.

"Thank you" Ragnar said and walked away as Thomas stepped back from the pyre.

"We will have our revenge!" Gunnar said, staring at the body.

"And I will help you" Thomas replied, looking at the Viking warrior. Gunnar turned his head, looking straight at Thomas.

"You are brave, you really are one of us" Gunnar said. He walked back down the slope.

Thomas turned and looked over the village. The warriors were preparing themselves, sharpening their weapons and cleaning their armour. The women were moving around, getting food ready, making sure the children were cared for, except for Lagertha, who was sitting near the men, a sword in her hand. Gracie was there, helping to tidy up the village after the attack yesterday, and Summers was sitting near the well, gun in hand.

"Thomas, we attack at dusk" Ragnar said,

approaching him. Thomas nodded. Gracie saw this and came running over.

"Wait, Thomas. You're not going, are you?" she said with deep concern. He reached up and moved her hair from her face.

"I have to, Grace. If Jon is there, Ragnar's men won't stand a chance" Thomas replied softly.

"But Thomas!" she said, almost pleading with him. He put his hand up, touching her lips.

"It'll be fine baby" he answered her, and leaned down, kissing her softly on her lips.

"Come, now, we send our dead home!" Ragnar called, and he led his remaining men up the slope towards the cemetery, Lagertha by his side. Thomas, Gracie and Summers followed behind them.

Ragnar took a flaming torch from one of the women and moved round the circle of pyres, lighting them as he went. He then stood in the centre and raised his arms.

"Welcome my brave warriors to the halls of Valhalla. Reunite them with their ancestors. Let them tell their tales of their brave exploits!" he shouted out. "I will be with you soon my brothers." He stepped away, Lagertha took his hand and they watched as their warriors began the journey to the afterlife.

★ ★ ★ ★ ★

Later that evening, just as the sky was changing to a dull

grey and the stars began to appear, Ragnar came into the main feasting hall where the others had gathered.

"Are we ready, my brothers?" he called out. All the Viking warriors shouted out and cheered loudly. Thomas was sitting with Gracie next to a small brazier. She gripped his hand tightly.

"I don't want you to go" she said softly. He put his arm around her, pulling her close to him.

"Gracie, I do love you" he said.

"Be careful" she whispered.

"I'll be there too" Summers said as he approached them, clipping his pistol into its holster. Thomas stood up next to him, took his gun out and checked the ammunition clip. Then he clicked it back inside the handle.

"I'm ready" Thomas said.

"Don't be long" said Gracie. He leaned down and kissed her. Then he moved away to follow the warriors out. He looked back to take one final glance at her, a smile on his face. She gave him a wave as he walked out into the freezing weather, Summers just in front of him.

They walked over to the well and gathered around Ragnar. Gunnar was standing next to him, his axe in his hand, a short sword at his side.

"Tonight we will have our revenge for our lost brothers!" Ragnar shouted out. He unsheathed his sword and raised it high above his head, and his men cheered. Slowly they made their way out of the village and up the hill towards the woods, Thomas and Summers just behind them.

★ ★ ★ ★ ★

Gracie sat staring into the fire of the brazier. A hand touched her shoulder. She looked round; it was Asta. Gracie gave her a smile.

"You get used to it" the woman said, taking a seat next to Gracie.

"Used to what?" Gracie asked her, the woman leaned forward and prodded the flames with a stick.

"The men, going off to war" Asta replied. "You never know who will come back and who we will be sending to the gods."

Gracie's heart sank. The woman meant well, but it was the last thing Gracie wanted to hear.

"But your Thomas has his weapon, his power. He'll be fine" Asta said, looking at Gracie.

"I hope so" Gracie replied quietly. After that, there was silence, both women staring into the flames, waiting.

CHAPTER 14

The warriors made their way slowly through the snowy woods, the moon their only light source.

"We could light torches" One warrior whispered to another.

Ragnar turned round quickly. "Don't be fools, we would be seen" he snarled. The two men kept silent the rest of the way.

As they drew closer, Thomas could smell the river. "We must be close" he whispered to Summers, who turned and nodded. Ragnar raised his hand and the warriors halted. He looked over at Gunnar and gestured for him to go ahead as a scout. Gunnar nodded and ran silently towards the edge of the woods. Ragnar turned to the other men and made a gesture with his hand for everybody to get down.

A few minutes went by, and then Gunnar came running back.

"They are there" he said quietly.

"And Jon?" Thomas whispered over to him. Gunnar nodded.

"OK, Gunnar, you take half the men, move round to the right, flank them" Ragnar whispered. He looked at Summers. "You go with him, and have that magic weapon of yours ready." Summers nodded and drew his gun, clicking off the safety. "Thomas, you're with me" Ragnar said and he got to his feet, unsheathing his broadsword. "Gunnar, go now."

Gunnar gestured for half of the men to follow him, Summers included. They made their way through the trees towards a rocky pathway leading down to the beach. Summers glanced back at Thomas and raised his hand. Thomas gave him a smile and nodded.

"Come now Thomas, let's go" Ragnar said and they moved forward, edging their way closer to the treeline. Ragnar halted his men with a gesture and they peered down, looking over at the men below. Alrik Vali and his men could clearly be seen, some sitting around a camp fire, others keeping guard at the edge of the camp.

Then Jon stepped out from behind a massive rock. He was still wearing his conduit suit, but around his shoulders he also wore a long fur cloak. He stood over the other men, including Alrik Vali himself. Jon was clearly in charge.

Ragnar stood up tall. He lifted his sword high above his head and screamed out a warcry. His men also got up and started shouting.

Vali's men below looked up at the terrible sound. One of Ragnar's men fired an arrow. It flew down, swift and straight and found its target, hitting a man in his chest.

"Come on!" Ragnar shouted out, and he ran down the bank, towards the shocked men below, who were scrambling to find their weapons. Thomas looked over and saw Gunnar and his men, including Summers, coming down from the right, shouting and yelling war cries. Then he heard shots ring out. Jon was standing there, his gun out. He had shot and killed three of Ragnar's men as they ran towards him. More shots, and another two went down. Thomas couldn't believe his eyes. Was this really his friend doing this, killing these men at will?

"Thomas!" Ragnar shouted. He looked down, still in shock at what was happening. As Ragnar ran forward, a warrior ran towards him, sword raised. Ragnar moved to the side and sliced the man across his stomach with his broadsword, spilling the man's guts. Another came at him and Ragnar's sword came straight down on the man's head, the heavy blade cutting through the man's helmet and into his skull.

"Come Ragnar!" It was Alrik Vali, standing there with sword ready. Ragnar bellowed and ran towards him. Thomas couldn't move. He watched as Gunnar and his men joined the battle. Summers was shooting any man who came near him, but Thomas' eyes kept moving to Jon. His old friend didn't move from his spot. He just kept firing at Ragnar's men, dropping them. Thomas gritted his teeth.

"That's enough" Thomas said to himself. He took out his gun and ran down the hill, and a man came towards him, spear raised. Thomas fired and the man fell. Thomas kept going, running straight for his old friend.

Ragnar ducked and Vali's sword went over his head. Ragnar lunged forward, hitting the enemy chieftain hard in the stomach with his fist. Vali moved back, winded from the power of the big man. Ragnar lifted his sword and swung it straight at Vali's chest, but Vali was younger and faster. He dodged the blade and it swept past an inch from his body.

"You are no match for me!" Vali said, taunting Ragnar. Ragnar snarled and leapt forward, and Vali moved and swung his sword, just catching Ragnar's arm. Blood spouted from the deep wound and Ragnar staggered to one side. Vali laughed out loud and looked around. He wanted the other warriors to see Ragnar defeated.

That gave Ragnar his chance. He leapt towards him, too late for Vali to react, and drove his sword blade straight through Vali's stomach. The younger warrior stood there for a second, a dribble of blood coming from his mouth. Ragnar snarled and withdrew the blade from Vali's flesh, blood seeping now from the massive wound. Vale dropped to his knees and fell forward, dead.

"Now you."

Ragnar looked around; it was Jon who had spoken. He had his gun aimed at Ragnar. "Now you die" Jon said. Ragnar dropped his sword, helpless in the face of the weapon from the future.

"Jon, no!" Thomas called out as he got to them, but it was too late. Jon slowly squeezed the trigger. The gun went off.

As the smoke cleared, Jon saw, standing in front of him, his old friend Thomas. He dropped his gun. Blood was coming from Thomas' mouth, and there was a smoking hole in his chest.

"Jon…" Thomas muttered as he fell forward. Jon caught him. Ragnar picked his sword back up and moved over to them, and Summers came running over.

"No!" he shouted, and pushed Ragnar back. "My god, Jon! What have you done?" Jon didn't reply. His eyes were still on Thomas.

Thomas looked up at him.

Jon knelt down next to his old friend. Blood had now started to seep from the wound in Thomas' chest, running down his black suit.

"Jon" Thomas said, raising his hand, touching Jon's face.

"I'm sorry Tom" Jon said. A smile came to Thomas' face.

"It's… It's all right" Thomas murmured. "Michael… tell Gracie I do really love her. Tell her… I'm sorry" he said glancing up at Summers.

"Of course I will, Thomas" he replied. Thomas moved his head back to face Jon.

"Jon" he said, quietly. Jon looked down at him, his face expressionless.

"Yes Tom?" he replied.

"I never lost faith in you" he said. His eyes fixed on Jon's face, his breath stopped, his mouth still open.

"He's gone" Jon said quietly, as he looked down at

his friend. A single tear fell from Jon's eye's, mingling with Thomas' blood. Summers stood up and looked down at Jon.

"Jon" he said, but Jon continued to look down at Thomas' face. "Jon, you have to come with me now" Summers said again. Jon brought his head up, glanced at Summers and nodded. He looked back at his old friend and reached up, placing his fingers on Thomas' eyes and closing them. Ragnar came over and stood next to Summers.

"We will carry him back" the Viking said. Summers nodded. "He would have liked that" he replied as he looked back at the body of Thomas, the man who had become his friend. His thoughts turned to Gracie. She would be devastated.

★ ★ ★ ★ ★

The journey back to the village was a silent one. Ragnar, Gunnar and two other warriors had placed the body of Thomas on a wooden stretcher and were carrying him through the snowy woodland. Summers had Jon handcuffed and was walking slowly behind. Jon stared at Thomas the whole way there, but Summers did not look up once. He just stared at the icy ground as they walked.

About an hour later they had reached the outskirts of the village. Lagertha came running out, along with two other women. She ran up the hill, to meet Ragnar and the warriors, and looked down at the stretcher.

"No, not him!" she said, Ragnar nodded to her.

"They are back" A woman called through the door of the feasting hall. Gracie stood up, a nervous smile on her face. She put down her metal cup and ran to the open door. As she got outside, she stopped dead. Summers was standing there grim faced.

"Where is Thomas?" she asked. Then she looked past him to see Ragnar standing there, along with the other Vikings bearing the stretcher. Summers held her arms, pulling her back in front of him. She looked up at his face, a tear formed in his eye.

"Gracie, listen" he said. She started to shake her head. Her smile turned to a frown and tears started to fall from her blue eyes.

"No, no, no!" she started to cry and Summers held her close to him as she wept.

"His last thoughts were of you Gracie, he wanted me to tell you that" Summers whispered to her. She gripped him tightly, tears streaming from her eyes. She looked up at him.

"How?" she said. Then she noticed someone standing at the back of the crowd. It was Jon. "It was you, wasn't it?" she shouted out.

Jon dropped his head. "You!" she shouted again. She pushed Summers out of the way and ran over to Jon. Then she raised her fist and punched him in the face.

"I'm sorry, I'm so sorry!" he cried out and dropped to his knees, his lip bleeding, his hands still cuffed.

"You were his friend!" she screamed at him.

Summers came over and tried to hold her arms, but she pushed him back. Then she stepped over to Thomas' body, crying as she went.

"My Thomas" she said. She put her hand on his cold face. "My Thomas" she said again, and placed her head on his bloody chest, her arms over his shoulders. "I love you. I love you!" she cried. Summers glanced away. Ragnar came over to him.

"We can take him inside?" the Viking asked. Summers nodded. "Gracie" he whispered, bending down. "We'll take him inside. You can stay with him for as long as you wish, on your own" he continued, and she raised her head and nodded. Ragnar, Gunnar and the two other men and picked up the stretcher and carried it over to the feasting hall, Gracie close behind.

A few moments later and Ragnar came out, followed by Gunnar and the two men. He walked over to Summers and placed his hand on his shoulder.

"I am sorry my friend" the Viking said. He then looked down at Jon, still sitting in the snow, staring towards the feasting hall.

"All this pain, all this heartache, all this misery, is down to you" Summers said. Jon looked up at him. He knew that what Summers said was the truth.

"Kill me" Jon muttered.

Summers frowned. "What?" he replied.

"Kill me" Jon said again, softly. Summers bent down, kneeling next to him.

"Do you think that I'm going to give you the easy

way out?" Summers replied, Jon just stared at him. "No, Dr Walker. You're going to prison."

An hour went by before Gracie stepped out of the feasting hall, wiping her eyes. Summers got to his feet and walked over to meet her. She looked drained of energy, her face red, her eyes bloodshot.

"Can we go home soon?" she muttered. Summers leaned down and put his arm around her.

"Yes, of course" he replied, pulling her close to him. "We'll take Thomas back too, or, I can return for him later."

She lifted her head up and looked at his face. "No" she said. "Thomas loved it here, he considered this time his home. He'll stay here."

Summers nodded. Gracie walked over to where Ragnar and Lagertha was sitting. "Ragnar" she said. He bowed his head.

"Gracie, I am sorry about your loss" Ragnar said. "I should never have let him come with us."

"It was what he wanted to do" she said. "Ragnar, I have something to ask of you."

"Anything" Ragnar replied, eager to help in anyway he could.

"You considered Thomas as one of you" Gracie started to say. Ragnar nodded.

"We did. We do" he replied, still holding her hands.

"Then bury him here, with your people. It's what he would have wanted" Gracie said.

Ragnar looked at her. "It would be our honour" he

answered. She gave him a smile and walked back over to Summers. He gestured over to Jon, sitting down and leaning against the well.

"What shall we do with him?" Summers asked. Gracie stared at him, at the man who had taken Thomas from her. She felt a strange sense of pity for him.

"He can come to the funeral" she said, still looking at him. "Now, I have to prepare Thomas' body." She began to walk away, back to the hall.

"Are you sure?" Summers called after her. She turned round and nodded, then carried on into the hall.

★ ★ ★ ★ ★

Later that evening, Lagertha came out and approached Summers. She was wearing her long red and green cloak again, with the big gold buckle.

"Michael, it is time" she said, and they both looked over towards the hall. Gracie came out, wearing a long white dress given to her by Asta. She wore around her head a simple circle of flowers. She stepped down, on to the snow, and then Ragnar and the other warriors came out carrying Thomas' body. His conduit suit had been removed, and he was now wrapped in a single piece of white cloth from head to foot. They all walked across the village, through the centre, past the well, where Summers took Jon's arm and joined the procession. Now they all slowly made their way up the slope towards the cemetery. No pyre had been built for

Thomas as he was not a Viking by birth, so a burial ritual would take place instead.

Lagertha moved forward and placed her hand on Gracie's arm. Ragnar moved across with his men and lowered Thomas into his final resting place. Lagertha handed Gracie some flower petals, and Gracie looked down at Thomas' wrapped body. She could still see the shape of his face through the white linen. A tear rolled down her cheek as she scattered the little pink petals on top of him. Lagertha stepped forward and gently placed a bright beaded necklace down on top of him. Then Ragnar knelt down next to the grave and placed by Thomas' side a small hunting knife.

"Goodbye my friend" he muttered, and then got to his feet. The big man moved back slightly, and coughed, to clear his throat. "Thomas, was... not born to us, but, he was one of us. He sacrificed his own life to save mine, so he is my brother. One day we will be reunited, in our great hall of Valhalla. We will speak together once more my friend." Lagertha moved close to Gracie and put her arm around her.

"Come, he is resting now" she said quietly, and then she led the grief-stricken Gracie away, back down the slope to the village. Summers remained at the cemetery, to help fill the grave with the other men of the village; his own way of saying goodbye to a man who had become his friend. He knew what Ragnar had meant when he said Thomas had saved his life, for he had done the same for Summers once, on their jump to the

1940s, when they had been under fire from Nazi soldiers. A tear came to his eye as he shovelled the earth into the grave.

★ ★ ★ ★ ★

Gracie stepped out of the room, back in her conduit suit once more. She gave Asta the white dress back with a smile.

"Thank you" Gracie said, as the woman took the dress from her and bowed her head.

"You will leave now?" Lagertha asked Gracie, sadly. Gracie gave a forced smile.

"Yes" she replied and Lagertha embraced her, holding her close.

"You will always be welcome here" she said, releasing Gracie once more.

"Thank you, all of you, for everything" Gracie said, looking at them all in turn.

The door slowly opened; it was Ragnar. "Michael is waiting" he said.

Gracie took one final glance around the longhouse, with its burning hearth and its high wooden beams. She knew now why Thomas loved it here so much. Everything was so much simpler. She walked over to Ragnar and looked into his face. A tear fell from his eye, dripping off his beard.

"You were his friend, Ragnar" she said. "He thought the world of you. Thank you."

Ragnar placed his hand on her shoulder. "Thomas will always be my friend" he replied. "And you have my word, I will tend his grave every day."

"Goodbye Ragnar" she said and walked out of the house, back into the cold air. Summers was standing by the village entrance, Jon still handcuffed next to him. "Ready?" Summers said, and she looked back, staring through the wooden buildings of the village and to the cemetery.

"Goodbye Thomas" she murmured.

"Come" Summers said and put his hand on her shoulder, leading her away up the hill and towards the standing stones. Once more she took a look back, over the snow-filled valley and the village. Then she looked down at Thomas' bag, which she was carrying across her shoulder. She touched the cold leather and glanced at Summers.

"I'm ready" she muttered. He nodded, and then looked at Jon. Summers gripped his arm tightly and reached down.

"OK, now" Summers said. Gracie pressed the recall button and Summers did the same, while holding on to Jon. The loud humming started and the snow around them began to melt and disappear.

★ ★ ★ ★ ★

When they stepped off the platform, the room seemed quiet. Gracie knew why; she could see that on the heart monitors, Thomas' trace was a long, red, flat line, going the length of the screen. She looked at it for a few moments.

"Come Gracie, you need rest" Summers said, leading her away past the silent workers and into the elevator. "I'll see you tomorrow" he said, still holding on to Jon. Gracie nodded her head and pressed the button, and the metal doors closed.

Summers looked at Jon. "Come on" Summers said and he walked the doctor out of the machine room, his old employees staring at him the whole time. Summers scanned a door with his card and it slid open. Three police officers were standing there, along with two CIA agents. Jon looked at Summers, a frightened look on his face.

"Dr Jonathan Walker, I'm arresting you for the murder of the late Dr Thomas Long" said Summers. Jon just stared at him. "You do not have to say anything, but anything you do say may be taken down and used as evidence" Summers continued. Still Jon did not reply; he just stared. "Do you understand?" Summers said, and Jon nodded. "Take him" Summers said, handing him over to the other officers.

As they walked Jon out of the facility, he kept looking back, watching Summers. "Goodbye Jon" Summers muttered to himself as the doors closed behind the officers and their prisoner.

Gracie approached the door to their dorm, took a deep breath and scanned the card across the lock. It clicked and she gently pushed open the door and stepped inside. She was half expecting Thomas to be there. The smell of his aftershave was still in the air and she closed her eyes as yet another tear fell. She walked in and placed his bag down on his desk. Then she lay down on the bed.

An hour went by, two hours, three. She kept staring at the empty space where Thomas used to lie, where Thomas should be lying. She reached up and gripped his pillow and brought it to her chest and held it tight. His scent was still fresh on the material. She gently fell asleep, holding it close.

★ ★ ★ ★ ★

The next morning she woke suddenly, as if from a bad dream. She looked around the room. It was no dream; Thomas was gone.

And then, she started thinking. She jumped out of bed, took off the conduit suit, which she had slept in all night, and threw on some jogging bottoms and a T-shirt. Then she ran out of the room and towards the elevator.

"Where's Agent Summers?" she asked one of the scientists.

"In Dr Walker's old office miss" he replied.

Gracie looked over at the machine. There were several engineers and scientists working on it, but she had no time to investigate. She ran back inside the elevator and pressed the button. The metal doors opened and she ran out, heading straight for the office.

"Michael, Michael!" she called as she opened the door. There were three agents in there, including Summers.

"Give us a moment please" Summers said to the others and the two men walked out, closing the door behind them. "You all right Gracie?" he asked her. She ran up to him and gripped the lapel of his grey suit.

"Summers, we can go back, back to before Thomas died, and stop him going. We can save him!" she shouted out with excitement. Summers shook his head.

"Gracie, Gracie, listen to me" he said. "The government is shutting the time project down."

She stared at him, shocked. "What do you mean?" she asked.

"We can't go back Gracie, not any more. The machine is being dismantled as we speak."

She let him go and started walking back. "Gracie!" he said, But she did not reply. She turned round and walked out, going back to the dorm.

An hour later there came a knock on her door. She opened it to find Summers standing there.

"Gracie, are you all right?" he said. She moved aside and let him in. He looked around the room. Her suitcase was on the bed, her clothes pilled into it. Her hand luggage was ready and waiting.

"Gracie?" Summers said. She went back over to the bed and carried on packing her case.

"I'm going home Michael" she said. "Back to England."

"OK" Summers replied. She turned round, her eyes glistening.

"I have to tell Thomas' father, he doesn't know yet."

"Yes, of course" Summers replied.

"If I can't save him, the least I can do is finish his work, back at the lab."

"That's what he would have wanted" Summers answered. She ran over to him and hugged him tight.

"Listen, I'll take you to the airport myself" Summers said. Gracie shook her head.

"I've arranged a cab to pick me up. You have work to do here" she said.

"Well, stay in touch, won't you" Summers said, looking forlorn.

"Of course."

"I'll leave you to finish then" Summers said and walked over to the open door. He took a look back. "Goodbye Miss Stevenson" he said.

She forced a smile. "Goodbye Agent Summers" she replied, and he was gone.

★ ★ ★ ★ ★

A short while later there came another knock on her door. She walked over and opened it. One of the workers stood there.

"Miss Stevenson, your cab has arrived" he said.

"Thank you" Gracie replied. She lifted her case off the bed and walked back over to the door.

"May I?" the man said. She smiled and handed him the case. She turned round and picked up her hand luggage and Thomas' bag, the one he had carried everywhere with him. She took one final glance inside, at the bed where she and Thomas had first made love, and at the desk where he had spent hours writing. She took a deep breath and closed the door.

★　★　★　★★

Back in the UK, the first thing Gracie had to do was to go straight to Oxford to see Thomas' father. He took the news remarkably well. At his invitation she stayed there for a couple of weeks, looking after him; he was now quite elderly. She said her goodbyes to him and promised to stay in touch, then made her way back to her own town, Worcester. She moved back into her apartment on the banks of the river Severn and took a job at the local university, as a lecturer in archaeology.

Months went by, three months, five months, eight. She was getting restless. One afternoon, after leaving work early, she returned home, made herself a cold drink and went to sit in the living room. She looked over at the cupboard against the back wall. She smiled and got to her feet, placing the glass down, then moved over and opened the small door.

Thomas' bag sat inside. She took it out and went back over to her seat, stroking the leather, her memories coming back to her of the two and a half years she had spent at the facility.

She undid the catch and opened the bag. She reached in and pulled out his old notebook, and a tear came to her eyes. She had thought she was doing well, getting over his death, but every now and again something would trigger more tears. She knew now that she would never be over it. He had, after all, been the love of her life.

She opened the book and read his words again. Now was the time.

* * * * *

Gracie packed a bag and made arrangements to leave for London, where Thomas' old lab was based. It was still in business and his employees were still there. She caught the next train.

"Miss Stevenson, it's so nice to see you again" Billy said as he came out to meet her.

"Hello Billy, how are you?" she asked him.

"Good, good" he replied, taking her bag. "I was so upset at what happened. We all were." He opened the door. As Gracie stepped inside, a shout of "Welcome back!" rang out. Party poppers went off, and there was a long banner reaching across the room which read 'WELCOME HOME GRACIE'. Gracie grinned as she looked around at the familiar faces.

"Thank you, thank you so much" she said.

"We've missed you, Gracie" A woman said, coming over and hugging her.

"Thank you" Gracie replied.

Billy came over and handed Gracie her name badge. "Here you are" he said, she laughed and took it from him and pinned it to her jumper.

"We still have all the finds we got from Denmark two years ago" the woman said, pointing to a room. Gracie walked over and peered through the glass. Inside lay some small trays which had been placed on tables, bearing their finds. Gracie smiled.

"Well, let's get started" she said, and the woman handed her a white coat. Gracie grinned and slipped it on. "Wow!" she said, walking in the room.

She looked into one of the trays. Reaching across, she grabbed a pair of latex gloves and put them on. She reached into the tray and picked up a fragile knife blade. The wooden handle had rotted away centuries ago, but the shape of the blade could clearly be seen.

"That was found inside the grave" Billy said, slipping on a pair of gloves himself.

"Yes, I remember" Gracie replied. Of course, the grave - Ragnar. A smile came to her face. "Dr Long and I managed to find out who the skeleton was while we were working away" she said, still looking at the little knife.

"Really?" Billy asked. "Who?"

"A Viking warrior called Ragnar Lodbrok" Gracie replied. She placed the knife gently back inside the tray. "Where are the bones?" she asked. Billy smiled and gestured over to a door.

"In there" he said. "They have to be kept at a certain temperature, helps stop the decaying process." He walked over to the door, punched in a key code and the door opened. He led her inside and she looked down at the ancient bones. *I knew this man*, she thought to herself.

"Has any work been done to them?" Gracie asked. Billy shook his head.

"No, Dr Long gave us instructions to leave them until his return" he replied.

Gracie smiled. "OK, we'll start with a CT scan then" she said. Billy nodded.

An hour later the bones had been placed on the sliding trolley at the entrance to the CT scanner. Gracie moved the fragile bones carefully, putting them in the right positions.

"Ready Miss Stevenson?" Billy called from the Tannoy system in the next room. Gracie turned and smiled at him through the thick glass, then made her way over to the door.

"OK, ready" she said, closing the lead-lined door behind her. Billy switched on the machine and the scanner started making a noise. Instantly, Gracie's mind went back to the time machine, the humming sound and the loud crackling.

"You OK Gracie?" Billy asked, looking up at her. She glanced at him, and then smiled.

"Yeah, I'm cool" she replied as the skeleton made its way slowly into the machine. A few short minutes later the computer in front of Billy started to bleep.

"What's that mean?" Gracie asked. Billy tapped on the buttons.

"Something's come up" he replied with a smile. "We've got something."

"Where?" she asked. He looked at the image on his screen.

"In the sternum" Billy answered.

"Is it safe?" Gracie asked, holding the door handle. Billy nodded and she made her way over to the trolley. She took from her pocket a small microscope and a pair of tweezers and bent down, looking closely at the bones of the Viking warrior.

"Got it" she muttered to herself. Right in the centre of the sternum was a small crack. She peered inside, then reached in with the tweezers.

"I've got it" Gracie called out, holding a small object up to the light. It appeared to be metal, but it was so corroded that she couldn't tell what it was. She straight away went back inside the other room and over to the electron microscope and placed the ancient object inside. Then she looked through the eyepieces.

"What is it, an arrowhead maybe?" Billy asked, still looking over the image of the bones on his screen. Gracie sat back in her seat, a look of bewilderment and shock on her face. Billy looked over at her.

"Miss Stevenson, what is it?" he said again. For a moment, she didn't answer. Then she replied.

"It's a bullet" she said.

Billy looked at her, confused.

"Can't be" he said. Gracie stared at the ancient, fragile bones displayed on the trolley. Then she ran to the door and opened it. She walked across to the skeleton and then stopped and looked down. She took off her glove, then slowly moved her hand down and touched the brow of the yellowed old skull. She stared down into its face. A tear fell from her eye and dripped on to the bone. She ran her finger gently across the top of the skull.

"Thomas" she whispered. "It's you."

ND - #0058 - 270225 - C0 - 203/127/24 - PB - 9781861510334 - Matt Lamination